Praise for the
of Lauren V

The Orchid A

"[A] supremely nerve-racking, sit-on-the-edge-of-your-seat, can't-sleep-until-everyone-is-safe read . . . successfully upholds the author's tradition of providing charming, three-dimensional characters, lively action, witty dialogue, and a continuous contemporary story line that enhances the events happening in the past."
                                                                        —*Library Journal*

"Willig's sparkling series continues to elevate the Regency romance genre."
                                                                        —*Kirkus Reviews*

"Willig combines the atmosphere of the tempestuous era with the perfect touches of historical detail to round out the love story."
                                                                        —*Romantic Times*

The Betrayal of the Blood Lily

"Newcomers and loyal fans alike will love brash, flirtatious Penelope's exotic adventure in Hyderabad, India, told [with] Lauren Willig's signature mix of historical richness and whimsical humor."   —*The Newark Star-Ledger*

"*The Betrayal of the Blood Lily* will delight readers with its vivid historical detail, deeply honorable characters fighting against truly wicked villains, and a plot filled with baffling mystery and heart-pounding danger."   —*BookPage*

"The latest sure-to-please installment to the popular Pink Carnation series transports the action to colonial India. . . . Willig hasn't lost her touch; this outing has all the charm of the previous books in the series."   —*Publishers Weekly*

"Willig brings colonial India to vibrant life through Penelope's eyes, and the sparks flying between Penelope and Alex generate plenty of heat. By taking the story to India, Willig injects a new energy in her already thriving, thrilling series, and presents the best entry to date."   —*Booklist*

"Reading the sixth book in Willig's Pink Carnation series . . . is like getting a plate of warm-from-the-oven chocolate chip cookies: it's hard not to eat them all at once, but you also want to savor every bite."   —*Library Journal*

The Temptation of the Night Jasmine

"Jane Austen for the modern girl . . . sheer fun!"
                                        —*New York Times* bestselling author Christina Dodd

continued . . .

"An engaging historical romance, delightfully funny and sweet . . . a thoroughly charming costume drama. . . . Romance's rosy glow tints even the spy adventure that unfolds . . . fine historical fiction . . . thrilling." —*The Newark Star-Ledger*

"Another sultry spy tale. . . . The author's conflation of historical fact, quirky observations, and nicely rendered romances result in an elegant and grandly entertaining book." —*Publishers Weekly*

"Honor and romance again take the lead in nineteenth-century England, as yet another flower-named spy continues this high-spirited and thoroughly enjoyable series." —*Kirkus Reviews*

The Seduction of the Crimson Rose

"Willig's series gets better with each addition, and her latest is filled with swashbuckling fun, romance, and intrigue." —*Booklist*

"Handily fulfills its promise of intrigue and romance." —*Publishers Weekly*

"There are few authors capable of matching Lauren Willig's ability to merge historical accuracy, heart-pounding romance, and biting wit . . . continues Willig's trend of making each installment even better than its spectacular predecessor." —*BookPage*

The Deception of the Emerald Ring

"History textbook meets Bridget Jones." —*Marie Claire*

"A fun and zany time warp full of history, digestible violence, and plenty of romance." —*New York Daily News*

"Heaving bodices, embellished history, and witty dialogue: What more could you ask for?" —*Kirkus Reviews*

"Willig's latest is riveting, providing a great diversion and lots of fun."—*Booklist*

"Smart . . . [a] fast-paced narrative with mistaken identities, double agents, and high-stakes espionage. . . . The historic action is taut and twisting. Fans of the series will clamor for more." —*Publishers Weekly*

The Masque of the Black Tulip

"Clever [and] playful. . . . What's most delicious about Willig's novels is that the damsels of 1803 bravely put it all on the line for love and country." —*Detroit Free Press*

"Studded with clever literary and historical nuggets, this charming historical/contemporary romance moves back and forth in time." —*USA Today*

"Willig has great fun with the conventions of the genre, throwing obstacles between her lovers at every opportunity . . . a great escape." —*The Boston Globe*

"Willig picks up where she left readers breathlessly hanging. . . . Many more will delight in this easy-to-read romp and line up for the next installment."
—*Publishers Weekly*

The Secret History of the Pink Carnation

"A deftly hilarious, sexy novel."
—Eloisa James, *New York Times* bestselling author of *A Kiss at Midnight*

"A merry romp with never a dull moment! A fun read."
—Mary Balogh, *New York Times* bestselling author of *A Secret Affair*

"This genre-bending read—a dash of chick lit with a historical twist—has it all: romance, mystery, and adventure. Pure fun!"
—Meg Cabot, *New York Times* bestselling author of *Insatiable*

"A historical novel with a modern twist. I loved the way Willig dips back and forth from Eloise's love affair and her swish parties to the Purple Gentian and of course the lovely, feisty Amy. The unmasking of the Pink Carnation is a real surprise." —Mina Ford, author of *My Fake Wedding*

"Swashbuckling. . . . Willig has an ear for quick wit and an eye for detail. Her fiction debut is chock-full of romance, sexual tension, espionage, adventure, and humor." —*Library Journal*

"A juicy mystery—chick lit never had it so good!" —*Complete Woman*

"Willig's imaginative debut . . . is a decidedly delightful romp." —*Booklist*

"Relentlessly effervescent prose . . . a sexy, smirking, determined-to-charm historical romance debut." —*Kirkus Reviews*

"An adventurous, witty blend of historical romance and chick lit . . . will delight readers who like their love stories with a bit of a twist." —*South Bay's Newspaper*

"A delightful debut." —Roundtable Reviews

Also by Lauren Willig

The Orchid Affair

A Pink Carnation Novel

LAUREN WILLIG

NEW AMERICAN LIBRARY

New American Library
Published by New American Library, a division of
Penguin Group (USA) Inc., 375 Hudson Street, New York, New York 10014, USA
Penguin Group (Canada), 90 Eglinton Avenue East, Suite 700, Toronto, Ontario M4P 2Y3, Canada
(a division of Pearson Penguin Canada Inc.); Penguin Books Ltd., 80 Strand, London WC2R 0RL,
England; Penguin Ireland, 25 St. Stephen's Green, Dublin 2, Ireland (a division of Penguin Books
Ltd.); Penguin Group (Australia), 250 Camberwell Road, Camberwell, Victoria 3124, Australia
(a division of Pearson Australia Group Pty. Ltd.); Penguin Books India Pvt. Ltd., 11 Community
Centre, Panchsheel Park, New Delhi - 110 017, India; Penguin Group (NZ), 67 Apollo Drive,
Rosedale, Auckland 0632, New Zealand (a division of Pearson New Zealand Ltd.); Penguin Books
(South Africa) (Pty.) Ltd., 24 Sturdee Avenue, Rosebank, Johannesburg 2196, South Africa

Penguin Books Ltd., Registered Offices:
80 Strand, London WC2R 0RL, England

Published by New American Library, a division of Penguin Group (USA) Inc.
Previously published in a Dutton edition.

First New American Library Printing, January 2012
10 9 8 7 6 5 4 3 2 1

REGISTERED TRADEMARK — MARCA REGISTRADA

New American Library Trade Paperback ISBN: 978-0-451-23555-8

THE LIBRARY OF CONGRESS HAS CATALOGED THE HARDCOVER EDITION OF THIS TITLE AS FOLLOWS:

Willig, Lauren.
The orchid affair/Lauren Willig.
p. cm—(Pink carnation series 8)
ISBN: 978-0-525-95199-5
1. Women spies—Fiction. 2. Governesses—Fiction. I. Title.
PS3623.I575O73 2011
813'.6—dc22   2010040588

Set in Granjon
Designed by Leonard Telesca

Printed in the United States of America

To my brother,
Spencer,
who wanted to be a privateer
but instead became a lawyer

The
Orchid Affair

Prologue

Paris, 2004

"That was a short flight," I said, peering out the window as the wheels of our plane touched tarmac at Charles de Gaulle. It was amazing how short a flight could be when one was in no particular hurry to arrive at one's destination.

"We can go back and do it again," Colin suggested. "Just to drag it out a bit."

I tilted my head so that my cheek briefly touched his shoulder. At least, that was what I'd intended to do. Instead I head-butted the side of his seat.

It's the thought that counts. "I knew we should have taken the Chunnel."

"Next time," he said, although both of us knew that there wasn't going to be a next time. At least, not for this particular trip. It was purely a one-off, and one on which neither of us had particularly wanted to go.

It sounds insane, doesn't it? Anyone would think I should have been delighted at the prospect of a long weekend in Paris with my still-new-enough-to-be-exciting boyfriend. We could stroll the Champs-Élysées, drink coffee in little cafés, smooch on the platform of the Eiffel Tower. Paris is for lovers. Everyone knows that.

Everyone had clearly never been summoned to Paris for a boyfriend's mother's birthday.

Some people had birthday parties. Colin's mother was having a birthday weekend. We're not talking your short, arrive-on-Saturday-morning, home-by-Sunday-evening type weekend either. The festivities kicked off Friday evening and carried on straight through Sunday night. Three whole days with Colin's charmingly dysfunctional family was not my idea of a romantic weekend. It was, however, my idea of an Agatha Christie novel. I kept checking over my shoulder for Hercule Poirot. I could just see him twirling his mustache, saying, "Ah, 'Astings, such a tragedy about zee leetle American girl. A pity she 'ad to be the first to die."

Meeting the parents is nerve-racking even under normal circumstances. Colin's family could not, by any stretch of the imagination, be called normal.

I couldn't really complain, given that I would never have met Colin if his ancestors had been, well, sane. As a fifth-year graduate student in pursuit of footnotes to eke out my dissertation, my reasons for being in London had been academic rather than amorous. Well, that isn't entirely true. When I came to London, I was in the throes of a doomed love affair with my dissertation topic. Some people are handed their dissertation topics by their advisors; others choose theirs for practical reasons, such as current trends on the academic job market or easy availability of sources. Not me. I had fallen madly in love with my topic: "Aristocratic Espionage during the Wars with France, 1792–1815." The Scarlet Pimpernel, the Purple Gentian, the Pink Carnation—what wasn't to love about dashing rogues in knee breeches racing back and forth across the Channel, outwitting the dastardly schemes of the French?

Ha. If my relationship with my dissertation was a love affair, we're talking one of those gloomy, nineteenth-century ones where everyone dies of consumption at the end and there's supposed to be a moral, but you can't quite figure out what it is, other than to make sure to insulate your garret and stay away from large bottles of laudanum. In short, it didn't love me back. The topic was dashing, it was glamorous, it was [insert your own adjective here], but like so many objects of affection, it had proved elusive.

Until Colin.

Colin's great-great-etcetera-grandfather had been one of those masked men. Under his chosen *fleur de guerre*, the Purple Gentian, Lord Richard Selwick had dashed around Europe in tights, rescuing aristocrats from the clutches of the guillotine. Colin liked to point out that at the time they had been called pantaloons, not tights, but a man in tights is a man in tights—call it what you will. Nothing says buckle and swash like a pair of skintight leg coverings.

Besides, a man who chooses to name himself after a flower can't be too picky about his pantaloons.

Whatever their choice in legwear, I was very extremely grateful to Colin's flowery ancestors. If they hadn't kept copious journals and letters, I wouldn't be where I was now: with Colin and the rudiments of a dissertation. I certainly wouldn't be in Paris.

"Where are we meant to find the shuttle?" asked Colin.

I consulted the instructions the woman from the hotel had given me. "She said it would be outside baggage claim."

"That must be it." Colin nudged me towards a van-like conveyance.

The driver pitched his cigarette out the window, wearily extracted himself from the front seat, and trudged around to open the back of the van so Colin could pitch our bags in, a quilted overnight bag for me, a big, complicated leather folding thing for him.

"Hôtel Minerve?" I said hopefully.

The driver grunted and set the car into gear. Okay. I'd take that as a yes. If he wanted to take us somewhere else, that was fine with me.

Just as long as it wasn't the Georges V.

Jeremy, Colin's stepfather, who liked to do people favors they didn't want, had booked us into the famous—and ridiculously expensive—hotel. We had canceled the reservation and booked ourselves into the much cheaper Hôtel Minerve, over on the West Bank. Neither of us was exactly flush with funds, I because I was living on a graduate student stipend, Colin because he was supporting a money-sucking estate. A grad student at the Georges V? So not happening.

Colin's stepfather hadn't been pleased by this decision.

Jeremy had an agenda for the weekend, and we were getting in the way of it. I wasn't entirely sure what that agenda was, although I suspected it was only partly about Colin's mother. Legitimation? Proving his place as head of the family? The latter was pretty ridiculous, given that Jeremy was only eight years older than Colin. Yes, Colin's stepfather was a fair chunk younger than Colin's mother.

I suppose this might be a good time to add that Colin's stepfather also happened to be his second cousin.

Jeremy was Colin's great-aunt's grandson, and he had run off with Colin's mother pretty much on Colin's father's deathbed. If you're having trouble following that, don't worry. It's not just you. As Colin had pointed out to me on a prior occasion, it was all very economical. By combining cousin and stepfather in one, he saved on the Christmas gifts. Kind of like two-in-one shampoo and conditioner, only with more years of therapy involved.

It was all more than a little reminiscent of the more improbable sort of soap-opera plot. I could only hope that I wasn't heading for kidnapping by the mafia or a three-episode-long bout of amnesia in which I would find myself embroiled with Colin's evil twin.

For the record, Colin has no evil twin. At least, none that I know of. Yet.

His sole sibling—the only one to whom he had confessed—is a sister named Serena. Serena had taken the whole cousin/stepfather thing a lot harder than Colin had. I had my own suspicions about Serena's relationship with Jeremy, but since that was going a little too soap opera, even for Colin's family, I'd kept them to myself. I could be wrong. I hoped I was wrong. And if I wasn't wrong, I didn't want to know.

We'd booked Serena into the Minerve with us. Not in the same room, of course. I'd been tempted to ask if they could put her on a different floor, not because I don't like Serena, but because there's something distinctly off-putting about knowing your boyfriend's sister is just one thin layer of plaster away. This might not exactly be a romantic dream weekend, but I still hoped to salvage some of it. It was Paris, after all.

I looked out the window at the stone houses with their iron balconies, at the striped awnings, brightly colored even in the gloom, at the narrow streets with their ineffectual metal posts, at the garbage truck backing up in front of us, blocking off traffic for a good three blocks down.

Yes, definitely Paris.

I leaned back into the crook of Colin's arm, resting my head against his shoulder. "Can you believe it?" I murmured. "We're in Paris."

"It would be strange if we were elsewhere," Colin pointed out. "Given the direction of our flight."

I dealt him a halfhearted swat. "You know what I mean."

For a moment, I felt his arm tighten around me. "Yes." Colin's lips fleetingly brushed my hair. Then he relaxed his grip, leaning back against the seat. "My mother doesn't want us until nine. What do you want to do before then?"

"I should get some research done." I wiggled my way upright, resting an elbow against the faux-leather backing. "I have a whole list of documents I want to look at in the archive of the Musée de la Préfecture de Police."

"So you really are planning to work?" It was part of the excuse we'd given Jeremy for changing hotels; the Prefecture and its archives were on the Left Bank, much closer to the Minerve.

"Yep. I want to look at the French operations of the League of the Pink Carnation. According to reports, the Pink Carnation was in operation in Paris from May of 1803 through the summer of 1804. What was she doing there?"

"Spying?" Colin suggested.

"Yes, but why, how, and on whom?"

"I suppose you have an idea?"

"Okay," I said, wiggling around on the seat to face Colin. "You know the Selwick spy school?"

"I am familiar with the concept," said Colin, straight-faced.

Of course, he was. It was his family. And the spy school had been run out of his home, albeit two hundred years before he got there. Colin's ancestor, the Purple Gentian, had founded the spy school when his marriage put him out of active service in early 1803.

"Well, anyway," I said, brushing that aside, "the Pink Carnation came back home for Christmas in 1803. Thanks to your archives, I have full documentation on that. While she was there, she solicited the services of a graduate of the Selwick spy school, a Miss Grey."

"A good name for an agent," commented Colin. He should know; not only was he descended from spies, he was writing a novel about them—although his novel, or so he claimed, was more of the James Bond variety, complete with extraneous gadgetry and hot and cold running women.

"They dubbed her the Silver Orchid. I suppose they couldn't

very well go around referring to her as Miss Grey in correspondence."

"Why not just 24601?"

"You don't think Victor Hugo would have objected?"

"He wasn't born yet," Colin pointed out.

"Details, details."

Colin raised a brow. "And you, a historian."

"Even historians go on"—the shuttle came to an abrupt halt, sending me lurching forward—"holiday," I finished breathlessly.

Okay, I got it; the shuttle driver wasn't a fan of academic history. Or of Hugo.

"Minerve!" he called back. With a long drag on his cigarette, he settled comfortably back into his seat, pausing only to exchange obscenities with a passing driver who had taken umbrage with his stopping in the middle of the street.

Colin went to check us in while I loafed around the inevitable leaflet rack. There were advertisements for various museums and attractions, some of which I had heard, others more obscure.

My attention was caught by one for a special exhibition at a museum I had never heard of. It was a single sheet, on glossy paper, with a diagonal band across the middle that read, in bold letters, *Artistes en 1789: Marguerite Gérard et Julie Beniet*. It was a little early for my time period, but close enough to pique my interest.

A large key dangled in front of my nose. "All set," said Colin. "Ready?"

"Ready." I shoved the leaflet into my pocket and took the key from him. As the one with a large shoulder bag, I automatically assumed the role of Keeper of Movable Objects, including, but not limited to, keys, tissues, cough drops, and airline tickets.

The elevator was a tiny thing, barely large enough for the two of us to squeeze in together, our luggage jammed in at our feet and my shoulder bag wedged between us like a modern chastity belt.

The wooden tag attached to the key, worn smooth with time and use, read 403. Room 403 turned out to be all the way in the corner. After two tries, during which I accidentally relocked the door while Colin tried to reach around me to help and managed to bang an elbow on the doorframe, the lock finally gave and we both all but fell into the room.

It was certainly cute. There was pink-striped paper on the walls, pink fleurs-de-lis ringing the green carpet, and a mural on the ceiling, featuring an idyllic image of fluffy white clouds, blue sky, and green foliage, with a few birds winging their way peacefully along. It was also about three feet square, the entire center of the room taken up by a double bed sporting a pink quilt and four suspiciously flat pillows. The ceiling sloped down at an acute angle behind the bed. On one wall, long windows opened out onto a view of an air shaft. On the other side, a narrow sofa covered in a pink and green print stretched across one wall. A desk had been jammed in the corner across from the door, with just enough space for the door to clear.

The room looked absurdly small—and absurdly pink—with Colin standing in the middle of it. His big leather folding bag took up the better part of the bed.

"It's cozy," I said, dumping my own overnight bag on the sofa. "Cute."

My bag was about an eighth the size of Colin's. Fortunately, cocktail dresses pack small. So does the aspirational lingerie that one buys in the hopes of things like romantic weekends in Paris, which then generally sits in the back of the drawer, gently yellowing.

That, I had to admit, had been a big part of the draw of this weekend's Paris jaunt, the chance to finally take out the That Weekend lingerie. I might not have the guts to wear it, but at least it was getting an outing.

Colin pointed at the painting on the ceiling. "Nice touch. Ouch." He'd banged his head on the slope.

Wincing in sympathy, I put a hand to his temple, sliding my fingers through his hair. It was beginning to get long on top, like the floppy-haired teen idols of my 1980s youth. "There?"

Colin angled his head for better access. "You can keep rubbing," he said hopefully. "A little to the left. . . ."

"I think you'll live." I patted him briskly on the shoulder and stepped back. "All right, BooBoo, let's go."

"BooBoo?" Colin looked at me quizzically as I jettisoned my in-flight reading from my bag. Because everyone needs three heavy research tomes and two novels for a forty-minute flight.

"You know. As in 'Sit, BooBoo, sit.'" Every now and then I forget that we're divided by a common language. I'd never felt quite so glaringly American until I started dating an Englishman. I decided to leave off the "good dog" bit. Even the most laid-back of boyfriends might take that the wrong way. "It was a commercial."

Colin decided to let it go. He twisted the door handle, conducting an elaborate shuffle in order to open the door without trapping himself behind it or impaling himself on the side of the desk. He managed it, but only just. "Shall we get a coffee before I lose you to the archives?"

"I'd love a coffee." I scooped up the key and gestured to him to move along so I could lock up. There wasn't room for both of us. "And maybe one of those marzipan pigs."

"Marzipan what?"

"Pigs." I hoisted my bag up on my shoulder and followed him back along the hall to the elevator, walking a little bit behind, since there wasn't room for us to go two abreast. "They were sort of a thing for me and—well, they were sort of a thing last time I was here."

I squeezed myself into the elevator next to him. No need to explain that the last time I had been in Paris had been with my ex, Grant. He'd been speaking at an academic conference and I had tagged along. A lot of Grant's time had been devoted to departmental schmoozing, which was only fair, considering that his department had been paying his tab, but I had managed to kidnap him for coffee and cake in between panels.

I had been delighted by the marzipan-coated pigs, Grant rather less so. He had been even less delighted when the pig attempted to carry on a conversation with him. Not that it was anything particularly deep. It had been more of the "Hello, Mr. Piven. Are you planning to eat me?" variety. Grant had been terrified that one of his colleagues would see him *in flagrante pigilicto*. Not very good for one's image as a mature and responsible member of the faculty of the Harvard gov department.

That was what he got, I'd teased him, for dating a grad student.

Not one of his grad students, he'd hastily specified. Dating one's own grad students was a no-no, punishable by expulsion. I was in another department; I was fair game.

So, apparently, were underage art historians.

But that had all been a long time ago. Two years ago, to be precise. It had been more than a year now since the breakup, two years since we had been in Paris together. This Paris would be a different city; my city with Colin, not with Grant.

The elevator decanted us into the lobby and we wiggled our way out, the strap of my bag snagging on Colin's coat.

"Marzipan pigs, eh?" said Colin, skeptical, but game, and I liked him even more for it, liked him so much that it made my chest hurt.

"You'll see." I threaded my arm through his. "The big question is, tail first or head first?"

"What do you usually do?" he asked.

"I generally start with the tail and work my way up."

"Prolonging the agony? Bloodthirsty woman." Colin sounded like he rather approved. He nodded towards the desk. "Shall we see if Serena's in yet?"

"We can get her a pig too," I said cheerfully. Serena needed fattening up. They say a camel can't fit through the eye of a needle, but Serena probably could. She was at the point of thin that crosses over from elegant to gaunt. And, no, that wasn't just sour grapes speaking.

I smiled ingratiatingly at the receptionist, who couldn't have cared less.

"*Est-ce que une Serena Selwick est ici?*" I asked in my very ungrammatical sixth-grade French. I can read the stuff; just don't ask me to speak it.

The receptionist was not impressed. She checked the book. "Selwick . . . 403?"

"Um, no," I said. "I mean, *non. Nous sommes dans 403.* Me and him. *Nous cherchons l'autre* Selwick. Serena?"

"*Oui.*" The woman seemed unfazed. She poked a manicured nail at the book. "Selwick. 403."

This was getting a little frustrating. "*Mais où est l'autre Selwick? Une autre Selwick?* There should be another reservation."

Now it was her turn to look confused. From the look on her face, she was thinking, *Americans. Why do I always get the Americans?*

Colin stepped in. "My sister is also staying here," he said in accented but perfectly grammatical French. "Which room is she in?"

"Room 403," repeated the woman in the same language, frowning at him, although not as she had frowned at me. This was confusion, not annoyance. "The entire party is in 403. It is a room for three."

"What?" I yelped. Like I said, I can't speak it, but I can understand it. "Room for three" came across loud and clear.

Turning to me, she switched to English. "How you say? A . . . three-person," she said helpfully.

Not if I had anything to do with it, it wasn't. "There's been a mistake," I said.

"No mistake," she said peacefully. "Selwick, 403." She tapped the ledger for emphasis.

I was getting pretty damn sick of that ledger.

"That may be so," I said, "but we reserved two rooms, one for two people, one for one." I looked to Colin for support. "Didn't we?"

"Um . . ." Colin didn't quite meet my eyes. Never a good sign.

I shifted so that we were facing away from the reception desk, our bodies angled away from the receptionist, who was watching us with a certain amount of I-told-you-so, or whatever that might be translated into French. "What did you do?" I whispered.

"I didn't *do* anything," said Colin with patent untruth.

"All right," I said, with the same tone of exaggerated patience he had used on me. I wasn't going to quibble over syntax. There were more important things to quibble over. Like who was going to be sleeping on the couch. "What did you *not* do?"

"I rang and asked them to add an extra."

"An extra room or an extra person?"

Colin jammed his fists in the pockets of his Barbour jacket, pulling it down taut around his shoulders. "I don't remember."

There went my moral high ground with the desk woman.

I bared my teeth in a fake smile, just for her benefit. "Try."

"Does it matter?" Colin raked a hand through his already disordered hair. "Look, we'll get it sorted, all right? It's not that big a deal."

Not that big a deal? If he wanted to share a bed with Serena, that was just fine with me. My lingerie and I would be elsewhere. Like back in London.

If I stayed any longer, I was going to say something I would regret later, and that wouldn't be good. For either of us. Discretion might not be the better part of valor, but it saves you a lot of apologizing later on.

"Here," I said, thrusting the key into his hand. "You got us into this; you get it sorted. I have research to do."

And with that, I fled out into the rain.

Chapter 1

Paris, 1804

"Around the back," said the gatekeeper.

Laura scrambled backwards as a moving wall of iron careened towards her face. From the distance, the gate was a grand thing, a towering edifice of black metal with heraldic symbols outlined in flaking gilt. From up close, it was decidedly less attractive. Especially when it was on a collision course with one's nose. Her nose might not be a thing of beauty, but she liked it where it was.

"But—" Laura grabbed at the bars with her gloved hands. The leather skidded against the bars, leaving long, rusty streaks across her palms. So much for her last pair of gloves.

Laura bit down on a sharp exclamation of frustration. She reminded herself of Rule #10 of the Guide to Better Governessing: Never Let Them See You Suffer. Weakness bred contempt. If there was one thing she had learned, it was that the meek never inherited anything—except maybe a gate to the nose.

"I am expected," Laura announced with all the dignity she could muster.

It was hard to be dignified with raindrops dripping off one's nose. She could feel wet strands of hair scraggling down her neck, under the back of her collar. Errant strands tickled her back, making her want to squirm. Oh, heavens, that itched.

She looked down her nose through the grille of ironwork. "Kindly let me in."

Ahead of her, just a stretch of courtyard away, across gardens grown unkempt with neglect, lay warmth and shelter. Or at least shelter. From the look of the unlit windows, there was precious little warmth. But even a roof looked good to her right now. Roofs served an important purpose. They kept off rain. Blasted rain. This was France, not England. What was it doing mizzling like this?

The gatekeeper shrugged, and started to turn away.

Laura resisted the urge to reach through the bars, grab him by the collar, and shake.

"The governess," she called after him, trying to keep any touch of desperation from her voice. She refused to believe her mission could end like this, this ignominiously, this early. This moistly. "I am the governess."

"Around the back," the gatekeeper repeated and spat for good measure.

Around the back? The house was a good mile around. Would it really have been so much bother to have let her in through the front? What had happened to *liberté, égalité,* and *fraternité*? Apparently, those sentiments didn't extend to governesses.

Laura took a step back, landing in a puddle that went clear up to her ankle. She could feel the icy water soaking through the worn kid leather of her sensible boot. At least, it would have been sensible, if it hadn't had a hole the size of Notre-Dame in the sole. Laura took a deep breath in and out through her nose. Right. If he wanted her around the back, around the back it was. There was no point in starting off on the wrong foot by fighting with the gatekeeper. Even if the man was a petty cretin who shouldn't be trusted with a latchkey.

Temper, she reminded herself. Temper. She had been a semi-servant for years enough now that one would think she was immune to such slights.

Gathering up the sodden folds of her pelisse (dark brown wool, sensible, warm, didn't show the dirt, largely because it had been designed to already look like dirt), Laura trudged the length of the street, skidding a bit as her sodden shoes slipped and slid on the rounded cobbles. The Hôtel de Bac was in the heart of the Marais, among a twisted welter of ancient streets, most without sidewalks. During her long years in England, Laura had never thought she would miss London, but she did miss the sidewalks. And the tea.

Mmm, tea. Hot, amber liquid with curls of steam rising from the top, the curved sides of the cup warm against one's palms on a cold day . . .

This had been her choice, she reminded herself. No one had placed a knife to her neck and demanded she go. She could very well have stayed in England and done exactly as she had done for the past sixteen years. She could have walked primly down the sidewalked streets, herding her charges in front of her, yanking them back from horses' hooves and mud puddles and bits of interesting masonry; she could have poured her tea from the nursery teapot, watching the steam curl from the cup and knowing that she was seeing in those endless curls a lifetime of the same streets, the same tea, the same high-pitched voices whining, "Miss Grey! Miss Grey!"

She didn't want to be Miss Grey anymore. Miss Grey might have warm hands and dry feet, but she wanted to be Laura again, before it was too late and the stony edifice that was Miss Grey closed entirely around her. It was time to get her feet wet.

Laura looked down at the soaking mess of her shoes. It was a pity Fate had to take her quite so literally.

The gatekeeper was waiting for her by the side entrance. He had an umbrella—which he held over his own head. Unlike the main gate, this one was designed for use rather than show, two thick slabs of dark wood leading onto a square stone courtyard. He opened the gate just wide enough for her to wiggle through, in an undignified sideways shuffle. That was, she was sure, quite intentional.

Rain oozed down the gray stone of the building, seeping through the cracks in the masonry, puddling in the crevices in the paving. Tucked away in a corner, a stone angel wept over the round mouth of a well, raindrops dripping down her face like tears. The long windows were the same unforgiving gray as the stone.

After the bright, modern town houses of Mayfair, the great bulk of the seventeenth-century mansion looked archaic and more than a little threatening.

From very long ago, a whisper of memory presented itself, of the fairy stories so in vogue in the fashionable salons of her youth, of castles under curses, their ruined halls echoing to the fearsome tread of the ogre as a captive princess shivered in her tower.

Laura didn't believe in fairy stories. Any ogres here would be of the human variety.

One ogre, to be precise. André Jaouen. Thirty-six years old. Formerly an *avocat* of Nantes. Now employed at the Préfecture de Paris under the ostensible supervision of Louis-Nicolas Dubois. Commonly known to be a protégé of Bonaparte's Chief of Police, Joseph Fouché, to whom he bore a distant relation. It was his department through which any word of suspicious personages in Paris would come. It was his job to hunt down and secure these threats to the Republic.

Which meant that it was Laura's job to get the information to the Pink Carnation before he could get to them.

They had dubbed her the Orchid—the Silver Orchid. The Carnation had chosen the name, with her usual perspicacity. It seemed appropriate, thought Laura, for the Carnation to have named her after a flower that drew its sustenance from others, dependent on more firmly rooted flora for its very existence.

Her mission was simple enough. She was to embed herself into the household of the assistant to the Prefect of Police. There, she was to keep an eye out for suspicious behavior and useful information, taking specific instructions from the Pink Carnation as directed.

Just a simple little task. Nothing to write home about. She had nothing to do but outwit a man whose very business was the outwitting of others, with no training but sixteen years of governessing and a six-month course at a spy school in Sussex executed in a way that could only be called cheerfully haphazard. The Selwicks had taught her to blacken her teeth with soot and gum (just in case she wanted to play a demented old hag); to ask the way to Rouen in a thick Norman accent; and to swing on a rope through a window without breaking the glass or herself. None of these skills seemed entirely applicable to her current situation.

Laura wasn't under any illusions as to her qualifications. The Pink Carnation would have been happier inserting a maid into Jaouen's household, or a groom—someone with more experience in the field, someone less conspicuous, someone with a proven record—but Jaouen hadn't needed a maid or a groom. He had needed a governess, and governess she was.

If there was one role she could play convincingly, it was the one she had lived for the past sixteen years. She just had to remember that.

Laura looked levelly at the gatekeeper, trying not to wince at the rain that blew below her bonnet rim, plastering wet strands of hair against her face.

"Hello," she said, as if she hadn't been forced to walk half a mile in the rain when there had been a perfectly good gate right there. "I am the governess. Your master is expecting me."

The gatekeeper jerked his head brusquely to the side. "This way."

There had been a formal entrance on the other side, equipped with a grand porte cochere designed to keep the rain off more privileged heads than hers. No such luxuries for a potential governess. Shivering, Laura picked her way along behind the gatekeeper across the uncovered courtyard, trying to avoid the slicks of mud where the stone had cracked and crumbled, ruinous with neglect. Whatever equality the Revolution had preached, it didn't extend to domestic staff.

Laura squelched her way down an uncarpeted corridor after the gatekeeper, her sodden shoes leaving damp prints on the floor. If possible, it felt even colder inside than out. Despite the frost on the windows, there were no fires in any of the grates. The Hôtel de Bac was as cold as the grave.

Pushing open a door, the gatekeeper managed to force two full syllables through his lips. "Wait here."

With that edifying communication, he stalked off the way he had come.

Shaking out her damp skirts, Laura turned in a slow circle. *Here* was a once-grand salon, entirely bare of furniture. Smoke had dulled the once-elegant silk hangings on the walls and filmed the ornate plasterwork of the ceiling. Darker patches on the wall revealed places where paintings had once hung, but did no longer. The gold leaf that had once picked out the frame of a painting set into the ceiling had flaked off in large chips, giving the whole a derelict air. The painting was still in its rightful place, but dirt and wear had given the king of the gods a decidedly down-at-the-mouth look.

Most of the decay was due to neglect, but not all. The coat of arms above the fireplace had been hacked into oblivion. Deep gashes scored the shield, obliterating both the symbols of rank and the ceremonial border around them. Beneath a now lopsided border of plumes, the gashes gaped like open wounds, oozing pure malice and mindless hate.

Laura felt a chill run down her spine that had nothing to do with the January cold. So much for the old family de Bac. She wondered what this new regime did to spies. That particular information had not been part of her training course, and probably for good reason.

Laura caught herself digging her nails into her palms and made herself stop. The gloves were her only pair; she couldn't afford to claw out the palms.

Stupid, Laura told herself. Stupid, stupid, not to have expected this. Stupid to have believed that the Paris to which she returned would be the Paris of her childhood. It had been seventeen years since she had last been in Paris. There had been a little event called a revolution in between. That was why she was here, after all.

During her training in Sussex, Laura had memorized the new Revolutionary calendar, with its odd ten-day weeks and renamed months. She had learned which place-names had been changed and which had changed back again. But what was a name, more or less? Nothing had prepared her for the scars the city bore; the bloodstains that never quite came out; the damaged buildings; the air of anxiety in the streets, where any man might be an agent of the Minister of Police, any soldier on his way to foment yet another coup, where the blood might run from the Place de la Révolution once again as it had before. The charming, urbane, decadent city of her youth had become anxious and gray.

Laura gave herself a good shake. Of course it felt gray. It was raining. She wasn't going to let herself throw away a heaven-sent opportunity all for the sake of a little fall of rain. This was her chance. Her chance to do something more, to be something more, to throw off the yoke of governessing forever, even if the only way to do it was to pretend to be the governess she had once been in truth. She had only to prove to the Pink Carnation that she could spy as well as she could teach.

Only, Laura mocked herself. As simple as that.

The door of the salon snapped open, the hinges giving way with a strident squawk that made Laura half trip over the hem of her own dress.

Through the doorway strode a man in a caped coat. Raindrops sparkled in his close-cropped brown hair and created dark patches on the wool of his coat. The fabric made a brisk swooshing sound as he walked, as if it were hurrying to get out of his way.

Laura couldn't blame it. Jaouen walked with the purposeful stride of a man who knew exactly where he was going and woe betide anything that stood in his way.

His clothes were simple, serviceable, of the sort of fabric that lasted for years and didn't show dirt. Whatever he was in this game for, it wasn't for the pecuniary payoff. There was nothing of the dandy about him. His black boots were flecked with fresh mud and old wear. His medium brown hair had been cut short in what might have been an approximation of the Roman style currently in vogue, but which Laura suspected was simply for convenience. Her new employer—her potential employer, she corrected herself—didn't seem the sort to waste unnecessary time preening in front of a mirror. He looked like what he had been, a lawyer from the provinces, still wearing the clothes he had worn then.

Laura was standing, as she always stood, in a corner of the room, her drab dress blending neatly into the shadows. She was an adept at that. It was the reason the Pink Carnation had recruited her, her ability to be neither seen nor heard, to be as gray in character as she was in name. But André Jaouen seemed to have no trouble finding her, even in the gloom of the room. Without wasting a moment, he made directly for her.

"Mademoiselle Griscogne." It was a statement, not a question.

He wore spectacles, small ones, rimmed in dark metal. His dossier had not specified that. Perhaps whoever had compiled it hadn't thought it important. Laura disagreed. The glint of the glass sharpened an already sharp gaze, sizing her up and filleting her into neat pieces all in the space of a moment's inspection.

"Monsieur." Laura forced herself not to flinch away.

Beneath the twin circles of glass, Jaouen's eyes were a bright, unexpected aquamarine. In contrast to his drab brown cloak and weather-browned skin, there was something almost frivolous about the color, as if it had been an oversight on the part of nature.

There was nothing frivolous about the way the Assistant Prefect of Police was looking her up and down.

There was nothing about her appearance to give her away, Laura reassured herself, fighting to keep the prickles of fear at bay. They had been very careful of that. Her attire was all French-made, from the scuffed half-boots on her feet to the hairpins driving into her scalp. Her real wardrobe, the wardrobe she had worn in her past life as Laura Grey, governess, as well as her small cache of books and personal keepsakes, had been left in Sussex, in a trunk in a box room in a house called Selwick Hall—sixteen years of her life boxed away and reduced to three square feet of storage space. There was no more Laura Grey, governess. Only Laure Griscogne.

Governess.

Ah, well.

Whatever André Jaouen saw passed muster. Well, it should, shouldn't it? French or English, she looked like the governess she was. "Apologies for keeping you waiting," he said. "I can only spare you a few moments."

As apologies went, it wasn't much of one. Still, the fact that he had offered one at all was something. Laura inclined her head in acknowledgment. Servility had come hard to her, but she'd had many years in which to learn it. "I am at your convenience, Monsieur Jaouen."

"Not mine," he said, with a sudden, unexpected glint of humor. Or perhaps it was only a trick of the watery light, reflected through rain-streaked windows. "My children's. The agency told me that you have been a governess for . . . How many years was it?"

She would have wagered her French-made hairpins that he knew exactly how many, but she supplied the number all the same. "Sixteen."

That much was true. Sixteen excruciating years. She had been sixteen herself when she began, stranded and friendless in a foreign country. She had lied with all the efficiency of desperation, convincing the woman at the agency that she was twenty. She had scraped back her hair to make herself look older and ruthlessly scowled down anyone who dared to question it. Mostly, they hadn't. Hunger and worry did their work quickly. By the end of that first, desperate month, she could easily have passed for older than she claimed. Her upbringing might have been unconventional, but it had left her unprepared for the shock of true poverty.

"Sixteen years," her prospective employer repeated. Through the spectacles, he submitted her to the sort of scrutiny he must have given dodgy witnesses in the courtroom, as though he could fright out lies by the force of his look alone. "Think again, Mademoiselle Griscogne."

Laura pinched her lips together. Sixteen years ago, she had learned that the expression made her look older, more reliable. People expected their governess to look like a prune who had just been sucking on a lemon.

By now it came naturally.

She had to succeed in this mission. Had to, had to. Anything rather than face being a governess forever, feeling her face freeze a little more every year into a caricature of herself until there was no Laura left beneath it.

For the next few months, she would be the very best governess she could be, if only it meant—please God—that she never had to be a governess again.

Laura squared her shoulders beneath her sodden pelisse, steeling herself against the urge to shiver. "I assure you, Monsieur Jaouen," she said frostily, "my experience as a governess is quite as extensive as the agency has claimed. I provide elementary instruction in composition, literature, Scripture, history, geography, botany, and arithmetic. I am proficient in Italian, German, English, and the classical languages. I teach music, drawing, and needlework."

André Jaouen's eyebrows lifted. "All that in the same day?"

Laura's brows drew together. Was he joking? It was hard to tell. Either way, it was always better to ignore such lapses in one's employers. If they weren't joking, they tended to take offense at the assumption of levity. If they were, it was dangerous to encourage them.

The reflection helped settle her nervous stomach. She felt on firmer ground here, putting a prospective employer in his place. She had played this game before.

"I tailor the curriculum to fit the specific needs and interests of the children in my care," she said loftily. "Not all subjects are appropriate in every situation."

André Jaouen made an impatient gesture. "No, of course not. I doubt my son would appreciate your tutelage on needlework. You are free to start immediately?" At her look of surprise, he said briskly, "I wish to have this business dealt with as quickly as possible. Your references were excellent."

Of course they had been. The Pink Carnation employed only the best forgers.

Was it just her nerves acting up again, or had that been too easy? Shouldn't he question her about her references? Ask her more about her teaching methods? Tell her about the children?

"Mademoiselle Griscogne?"

"Yes," she said hastily. "I can begin whenever you like."

André Jaouen motioned her forward, already in motion himself, making short work of the distance to the double doors through which Laura had entered. "I have two children, Gabrielle and Pierre-André. Gabrielle is nine. Pierre-André is almost five. Until now, they have been with their grandparents in Nantes. This is their first time in Paris." He spoke as he walked: direct, economical, no effort wasted.

"And their prior education?" Laura lengthened her stride to keep up, her wet skirts tangling in her legs as she followed him past a wide staircase, the marble balustrade gone a dull gray with grime. An empty pedestal stood on the landing, marking the place where a statue must once have stood. Tapestries still lined the walls, but they hung crookedly, and several bore poorly mended gashes.

"Their grandfather taught them at home."

Laura did her best to suppress a grimace. Fairy stories. Basic reading. Arithmetic. If she were lucky. She would have to start from the very beginning with them. The boy, Pierre-André, was nearly of

an age to be sent off to school. She would have to bring him up to the
level of other boys his age.

No, she wouldn't. The thought brought Laura up short. If she
did her job well, she wouldn't be around long enough for it to matter. She had been thinking like a governess again, falling back into
the old patterns.

Jaouen was still talking, words marshaling themselves into neat,
economical sentences. Behind the measured cadences, Laura could
detect just a hint of a Breton burr. There was no faux-aristocratic
ostentation there, no pretense. "Your wages will be paid quarterly.
Room and board will be provided to you. Ah, Jean." That last had
been directed to the gatekeeper. "Tell Jeannette to find Mademoiselle Griscogne a room. Something near the children."

Jean and Jeannette? His servants couldn't be named Jean and
Jeannette. It was too much like something out of the Commedia
dell'Arte. Did the still-unseen Jeannette run around in a parti-
colored costume smacking Jean over the head with a big stick, like
Pierrot and Pierrette? Perhaps they were spies too. If so, one would
have thought they could have come up with better aliases.

"Jeannette is the nursery maid," Jaouen said as an aside to her.
Without waiting for them to be handed to him, he scooped up his
own hat and cane off a marble-topped table by the door. "Jeannette will see you settled and make you known to Gabrielle and
Pierre-André. If you need anything, either Jean or Jeannette will
see to it."

With a nonchalant push, Jean the gatekeeper shoved open the
door, letting in a blast of damp air. The rain looked as though it were
contemplating turning to snow. The icy pellets stung Laura's cheeks as
she followed Jaouen to the door. She was still wearing her pelisse, and
her pelisse was still just as wet as it had been when she had entered; the
entire interview, such as it was, had taken all of ten minutes. Ten minutes to embark on the most dangerous gamble of her life.

A carriage was waiting in the courtyard, plain and black like the cloak draped over Jaouen's shoulders, the horses pawing impatiently at the cobbles.

She had clearly been dismissed. And hired. She had been hired, hadn't she?

Jean the gatekeeper gave her a disapproving look as she followed her new employer out under the porte cochere. Or perhaps that was just his normal expression. "I will need to fetch my things," Laura said desperately. "And settle my account at my current lodgings."

Reaching into his waistcoat pocket, André Jaouen took out a purse and shook several coins out into his palm. He thrust what looked to her untutored eyes like a substantial sum in her direction.

"An advance," he said impatiently, when Laura looked at him uncomprehending. "On your wages."

Laura's back stiffened. "My own funds are more than adequate to settle my current obligations."

He looked at her curiously, then shrugged, returning the coins to his pocket. "Will you bite my head off if I offer you the use of the carriage?"

He cocked an eyebrow, waiting for her reply. There it was again, that glimmer of what might be humor.

"There is no need, sir," Laura said coolly. "My lodgings are not far and I am more than accustomed to managing for myself."

Jaouen eyed her speculatively, his glasses glinting in the light of the carriage lamps. "I can see that." And then he ruined it by adding, "I wouldn't hire you if I thought it were otherwise. My occupation is a demanding one. I have no time for domestic squabbles."

That had put her in her place. Between fear and relief, she felt almost giddy. "Squelching squabbles is one of my particular specialties."

Jaouen forbore to comment. With the air of someone getting done with a bad job, he continued. "You may be troubled from time to time by my wife's cousin, who persists under the unfortunate delusion that my home is his own. Ignore him."

Ah, one of those, was he? Once, she might have claimed that she wasn't the sort of governess to inflame a young man's lusts. But she had learned the hard way that, after a certain degree of inebriation, all it took was being female, and sometimes not even that. She had also learned that employers seldom took kindly to their elder sons, nephews, or houseguests being hit over the head with a warming pan, candlestick, or chamber pot. Laura appreciated both the warning and the implicit authorization to do whatever she needed to do.

It was comforting to know that the intimidating M. Jaouen had an Achilles' heel, even if that Achilles' heel was only a cousin by marriage. It made him more human, somehow. And human meant fallible. Fallible was good, especially for her purposes.

"I will. Sir."

Jaouen nodded brusquely, her message received and accepted. Hat in one hand, cane in the other, he started for the carriage. At the last moment, just beyond the protective cover of the awning, Jaouen jerked his head back over his shoulder. Laura shot to attention.

"Why did you leave your last position?" he asked abruptly.

"My pupil married." If he had hoped to shock her into an admission, he would be disappointed. Her pupil had married in June, leaving her once more without a situation. The family had been kind; they had kept her on through the wedding, but there was a limit to the charity she was willing to accept. "She had no need for a governess anymore."

But the Pink Carnation had had need of an agent.

Rain pocked Jaouen's glasses as he treated her to another long, thoughtful look. He held his hat in one hand but didn't bother to put it on, despite the rivulets of rain that silvered his hair and dampened his coat. "An occupational hazard?"

Laura permitted herself a grim smile. "One of the most hazardous."

She had never thought much of matrimony herself—her parents had set no favorable example—but it had been distinctly unsettling to make a place for oneself only to be flung out into the world again. And again and again. Some of them, the sentimental ones, sent letters for a time, but those generally tailed off within the first year, as the daily demands of the domestic state outweighed sentimental recollections of the schoolroom.

"You shan't have to worry about that with Gabrielle. Yet."

She wouldn't be around long enough to worry about that.

"Indeed," she agreed. Noncommittal replies were always best in dealing with employers. Yes, sir; no, sir; indeed, sir. It came out by rote.

Jaouen clapped his hat onto his head. "Tomorrow morning," he said. "The children will be expecting you."

Jean the gatekeeper slammed the door shut behind Jaouen as he swung up into the carriage. The horses' nostrils flared, their breath steaming in the cold air as the coachman clucked to them, setting them into motion. Through the rapidly misting glass of the window, Jaouen was nothing more than a silhouette, a blurred image in tans and browns.

That was it. She had done it. She had really done it. Blood surged to Laura's cheeks and fingertips, sending a rush of warmth tingling through her despite the freezing wind gluing her soaking skirts to her legs. Whatever else came of it, the first step was accomplished; she was a member of Jaouen's household. She was in.

Between the rain and the sound of hooves against the cobbles, Laura could just barely hear her new employer call out his instructions to the coachman.

"To the Abbaye Prison. As fast as you can."

Laura swallowed hard, turning her face away from a sudden gust of wind that tore at her bonnet strings and snatched away the very breath from her throat.

Oh, she was in all right. Way over her head.

Chapter 2

The carriage rocked abruptly forward and then back as it came to a stop in front of the Prison de l'Abbaye. The stone bulk of the Abbaye squatted sullenly in front of the carriage, the towers set in each side jutting out like a pair of angry elbows. Torches illuminated the entrance, burning greasily against the early dark of a wet winter night.

"So kind of you to finally join us." A small man in unrelieved black stepped out from under the lee of the portal at the entrance of the Abbaye Prison.

"Us?" André said mildly, taking his time climbing down from the carriage. He'd be damned if he'd hurry for the likes of Gaston Delaroche. "I had no idea this was to be an ensemble event."

Delaroche positioned himself so that the guttering torches on either side of the entrance cast an eerie glow over the polished silver of his coat buttons, bathing him in an unnatural and unholy light.

Bloody stagy, if you asked André's opinion, which no one had.

Delaroche liked to claim he had once been the second-most-feared man in France. André would have put his position at fourth or fifth at best. Voicing that opinion had not endeared André to Delaroche.

"How very . . . unlike you to be tardy, Jaouen." Delaroche bared a set of unnaturally yellowed teeth. André suspected him of buffing them with tobacco and a side of tea leaves. "It is, I suppose, no surprise that you would be distracted—now that your children are come from Nantes."

There was no point in asking him how he knew. They were all in the business of knowledge. Any self-respecting senior official in the Ministry of Police employed his own private system of informers, above and apart from those sanctioned by the state. They spent as much time monitoring one another as they did the enemy.

André forced himself to shrug. "A nursery is a nursery, whether in Paris or Nantes. They provide no impediment to my duties."

Delaroche's eyes glinted red in the torchlight. "Paris is a far cry from Nantes, my friend. So much more . . . dangerous."

Rain ran beneath André's collar from the back of his hat, sending an icy sluice down his spine. André favored Delaroche with a hard stare. "Can any relation of Fouché, however young, be deemed to be in danger? They are not unprotected," he added pointedly.

Delaroche shrugged, a shrug that made André want to take him by the shoulders and shake him like the little rat that he was. "Even so," he said.

Even so? Even *so*? What in all the blazes was that supposed to mean?

André pictured his children, Gabrielle with her snub nose, her plump child's cheeks, her hair that was beginning to lose its baby curl and the eyes that looked so uncannily like his own; Pierre-André with Julie's open, smiling countenance and hair like the gilded angels' wings in a church fresco, trusting, open, laughing. He pictured them as he had seen them the night before, asleep in bed, their limbs so small beneath the blankets Jeannette had drawn up over them, their faces smooth and vulnerable in sleep. They were so small, his children, so vulnerable, such tempting hostages to fortune.

Why did Père Beniet have to die? And why did he have to die *now*?

André seethed with the same mingled grief and anger that had wrung through him since the news had arrived from Nantes. Grief at the loss of a man who had been more of a father than his own father had ever been: old M. Beniet, first his tutor, later his father-in-law. Anger at Père Beniet's leaving them, and leaving them at so inopportune a moment. Not that mortality left any man much room for choice. André knew his anger was illogical, but that didn't stop him from feeling it. How could his old tutor, who had always been so sage, have misjudged so radically at the last?

A chicken bone. Père Beniet had choked on a chicken bone. A great soul brought low by a fragment of fowl. There were times when the divinity had a positively mordant sense of humor. All his knowledge, all his experience, brought to nothing against a splinter of bone lurking between a dumpling and a cabbage leaf in an innocent-seeming bowl of stew.

If that chicken hadn't been dead already, André could have cheerfully wrung its neck. Gabrielle and Pierre-André had been safe in Nantes, safe and well cared for, well away from the tangled intrigues of Paris. Well away from men like Gaston Delaroche.

André glanced at Delaroche, at Delaroche who resented his ascent, who wanted Fouché's confidence for his own. There was no point in saying that Delaroche wouldn't. Delaroche would. When it came to his position, there was nothing Gaston Delaroche wouldn't do. Especially now.

"What are you doing here, Delaroche?" André asked flatly.

Delaroche smirked, displaying his yellowed teeth. "Fouché asked me to assist you in this interrogation."

Had Fouché sent Delaroche to spy on him?

No. André dismissed the idea as rapidly as he had considered it. Fouché knew that André was his man, not only by marriage but by the bonds of necessity. Any position or power that André possessed came solely through Fouché. Position and power were terms that Fouché understood, tools he employed to grapple men to him. Loyalty, love, ideals—all those were as grass compared to the powerful motivator of man's self-interest.

It was far more likely that Delaroche had invited himself along and Fouché had conceded, deeming it an easy way to keep Delaroche out of his own hair.

"Excellent," André said briskly, clamping his hat under his arm and striding forward ahead of Delaroche into the foyer. The guards stood aside at his approach, recognizing him by sight. "How very considerate of my cousin to provide me with an assistant."

"With assistance," Delaroche corrected, trotting along behind him. "Not an assistant."

"Forgive me," said André insincerely. "My mistake."

He deliberately picked up the pace. He could hear the clip-clop of Delaroche's bootheels as the other man hurried to catch up. He lengthened his stride, nodding to the guards on either side as he hastened up the worn stone stairs to the second floor.

"Interrogation," Delaroche oozed—or wheezed, although he made a valiant effort to turn the sound sinister, even while scurrying to keep up. "Interrogation is an art. One that takes years of study and dedication to perfect."

"Or just a small room and a prisoner," said André heartlessly. "I hope you left your thumbscrews at home."

Delaroche regarded André with disfavor.

The two men came to a halt before a thick wooden door, the panels relieved only by a small metal grille. In the cell, a man sat slumped on a cot, his bare head bowed. His hair had been carelessly clubbed back with a ribbon, but chunks stuck out at odd angles, as though it had been accomplished without the aid of a brush.

As the guard unlocked the door, the prisoner sprang up. Hope and fear chased across his haggard face, as though he didn't know whether to fear to hope or hope to fear. Execution or pardon? The lady or the tiger?

A deputy sidled through in front of them to take his place at a square, sturdy-legged table on which paper, ink, and pens—several of them—had already been arranged. Nothing had been left to chance. Fouché was determined that Querelle would talk and talk now. He had gone to great lengths to ensure that it would be so.

"Good evening, Monsieur Querelle." André positioned himself in front of Delaroche, effectively blocking the smaller man. He needed no assistance from Delaroche for this; he had played through this script before. He wanted nothing more than to get through it as quickly as possible. "I hear that it is the will of the people that you will not be with us much longer."

The night before, the prisoner had been hauled out of bed and dragged before a military court specifically convened for that purpose. Still fuddled with sleep, Querelle had been tried and condemned to execution, then shoved back into his cell to contemplate his own imminent demise.

"The will of the people?" Querelle made the mistake of allowing his scorn to show. "What people? That was no real court."

André couldn't help but agree. Any court convened at three in the morning and presided over by the First Consul's brother-in-law, a man more famed for his hair than his wit, could hardly be accounted much of an ornament to the French justice system. However, he didn't think his employers would thank him for sharing that opinion. The law as he had learned it had no place in the new regime.

"No?" André said quietly. "The consequences, I assure you, are very, very real."

Delaroche trod on André's foot in his eagerness to get to the prisoner. "Have you looked out the window? You will find something there that might interest you."

The window was little more than a rough square hewn in the wall, lined with closely set bars that did little to keep out the elements. Frigid night air whistled between the bars, and with it the sound of activity in the courtyard below.

There was a scaffold already built in the courtyard. A man in a ragged wool vest was spreading fresh sawdust across the boards.

André saw the muscles in Querelle's throat work as he swallowed. To hear that one was condemned to death and to see the instrument of it, oiled and ready for use, were two very different things.

The Ministry of Police was nothing if not efficient in its work.

"That is for me?" Querelle asked hoarsely. He had to clear his throat before the last word.

"Not just for you." Delaroche folded his arms across his chest, giving the prisoner a superior look. Not hard to look superior, thought André critically, when your opponent was in chains and hadn't been allowed fresh linen in nearly a month. "Did you think you were the only soul in Paris with more pride than sense? Some of your comrades made the same mistake . . . and will pay the same price."

The prisoner looked at Delaroche uncomprehendingly. A sort of dull trepidation could be seen in his expression, as though he had some inkling of what was to come but knew himself to be powerless to ward against it.

"'Price,'" Querelle repeated. "Price?"

"Picot and Le Bourgeois have also been condemned to death," said André, ending with brutal simplicity what otherwise would have been at least ten minutes of ominous innuendo.

The two men had been part of the same Royalist network as Querelle, but they had been less fortunate in their captors. Kept in close confinement in the Temple Prison, they had been put to the question in fine medieval fashion. They had begged for death and in the end been granted it, not out of any impulse of mercy, but because Fouché had found what he hoped would be a weaker link: Querelle.

"Condemned," confirmed Delaroche, rolling the word lovingly on his tongue. "Condemned to an end on the guillotine. They, too, refused to cooperate with the officers of the Republic. Last night, they were taken before a military commission, tried, and"—Delaroche allowed a brief pause, during which time his gaze went meaningfully to the window—"sentenced. To death."

Querelle licked his lips, as though they had gone dry. "So fast?"

"Justice is swift, Monsieur Querelle. Ah, and there we see it in action. Shall we?"

It was a command rather than an invitation. In the courtyard, the torches burned sullenly in their brackets against the wall. The rain and wind made the flames sizzle and crackle. The flames cast an eerie red glow over the proceedings, like a medieval painter's rendition of hell, the red light lapping at the raw wood of the scaffold and glinting off the blade that hung so ominously suspended above.

From the lee of the building, a man stumbled forward, his hands bound behind him just as Querelle's had been. His head, too, was bare to the elements. The rain slicked his shirt to his skin. From the second-story window, they could hear him shudder, although whether with cold or with fear was unclear. He swayed as the wind buffeted him, his head and shoulders hunched against the stinging rain.

There was to be no grand state execution, no glorious death for his cause. Any speech made at the scaffold would be lost in the howling rain, blunted against the bored indifference of the detail of soldiers who were his only audience. They were prepared to dispatch the man as any farmer might dispatch vermin caught poaching on his crops, without mercy or regret.

It wasn't Picot. Both Picot and Le Bourgeois had been killed the night before. Tried, sentenced, executed, all within the space of an hour. This man was someone else entirely. A thief, a murderer, a rapist. Expendable fodder from Paris's overflowing prisons.

Querelle, of course, was not to know that.

In the rain, in the dark, one bound and hunched man looked much like another. It was necessary, for the sake of the charade, that Querelle think it was one of his comrades, that he see in the arc of the ax the intimation of his own mortality. To be told, at a remove, in simple, whitewashed words that his comrades were dead would not have at all the same effect.

It all made André sick.

"Such brave defiance," purred Delaroche, his chin practically resting on the prisoner's shoulder. "Such unwavering insolence. But, as you shall see, Monsieur, Madame la Guillotine will not be defied, not for all the bravery in the world."

Despite the freezing air gusting through the window, sweat beaded Querelle's forehead.

André spoke, his calm voice unnaturally loud in the waiting hush. "There is, of course, still a chance for a pardon."

Outside, two soldiers helped the bound man to kneel. With rough efficiency, they settled his head in the hollowed trough designed for just that purpose.

"A pardon?" croaked Querelle, never taking his eyes from the figure of the man on the block.

"A pardon," repeated André quickly, as Delaroche opened his mouth to say something, undoubtedly taunting, pointless, and time-wasting. "I have a pardon with your name on it. All it lacks is the First Consul's signature."

Querelle's nails scraped against the stone of the sill as his hands

opened and closed, seeking some sort of purchase. He cast an ago-
nized glance out the window, at the man kneeling on the scaffold.
He looked back, uncertainly, at André.

"Should you choose to change your mind, Monsieur Fouché
himself would personally obtain the First Consul's signature on
your behalf."

Delaroche pushed his way forward. "A throat is made to be
used, Monsieur. And, if not, it must be . . . cut."

Querelle looked from André to Delaroche and back again.
"How do I know you won't kill me anyway?"

It was an excellent question.

"Do you doubt the word of the Minister of Police?" demanded
Delaroche.

Since that was precisely what the man was doing, there was no
easy answer to that. Insulting one's captor might make good theater, but it made very poor sense.

André looked quellingly at Delaroche. "Should you do nothing," he said sensibly, to Querelle, "you will most certainly take
your place on that scaffold at dawn. Should you change your
mind . . ." He held up the rolled piece of paper, tied with an official-
looking red ribbon, letting Querelle's eyes and mind rest on it and
the possibilities it implied.

The condemned man's eyes darted back and forth, to the
window and back again, like an animal in a snare. André could
see the wild thoughts going through his mind. The still man on
the scaffold, the knife that hadn't fallen, the offer of pardon . . .
What if it were all a sham: trial, condemnation, execution, all of
it? What if it were only a bluff? A gleam of cunning lit Querelle's bloodshot eyes, gone glassy with fear and a desperate
man's desperate hope. If they were bluffing, he could continue
to refuse. . . . He had held out this long against Fouché; why not
longer? They might be lying about Picot and Le Bourgeois. If
they killed him, they would never know what he had to tell.

They wouldn't kill him, not now—nor that unfortunate dupe of a decoy in the courtyard, all done up to look like a prisoner. It was a bluff, a sham; it had to be. . . .

André only wished it were.

"And what if I don't?" Querelle said belligerently, just as the low rumble of a drumroll sounded in the courtyard below, like a swell of thunder in the night.

"Ah," said Delaroche, his eyes lighting with a feral glow. He turned to the window, leading the others to follow suit. "If that is your choice . . ."

With a shrill whinny of sound, the blade swooped down, slicing through flesh and bone before landing, with a moist *thunk*, on the wooden block below.

Delaroche watched with unmistakable pleasure as the soldiers went about their grim business.

André could see fear and disbelief warring on Querelle's torch-lit countenance.

The soldiers on duty barely looked at the head as they picked it up by the hair and tossed it into a waiting basket. Another grabbed the dead man by the legs, making a crazy pattern through the matted sawdust as he dragged the headless torso from the block. There was no roar from the crowd; there was no crowd to roar. This was nothing more than routine.

In the cell above, the condemned man's complexion, tanned from years on shipboard, turned an unfortunate shade of green, like an unripe olive.

"There were five of us," Querelle blurted out, levering himself away from the window with both hands.

"Five what?" prompted Delaroche, leaning forward.

Querelle took a deep breath, his lungs laboring as though he had been running. "Five of us who landed in October. In the service of the king."

André nodded to the deputy at the table, signaling him to begin writing. There would be an official report of Querelle's testimony prepared later, one that left out such inconvenient little details as the means employed in obtaining it.

Pushing away from the window, Delaroche advanced on the prisoner. "I take it this means that you are, at last, prepared to talk to us?"

Through the bars could be heard the terrible sifting sound of sawdust being swept with a long-handled broom, clearing the scaffold to make it ready for its next occupant.

With great effort, like a man with the ague, Querelle lowered his head down and then lifted it up again.

"You appear cold, Monsieur Querelle," said Delaroche. He gestured to the guard. "You! Fetch our friend a blanket. It wouldn't do to have him catch a chill. Not now that he has agreed so generously to assist us."

Something in Delaroche's voice made the condemned man shudder harder than ever. Which was, of course, exactly what it had been meant to do.

Cutting in front of Delaroche, André plucked the blanket from the hands of the guard and handed it to the condemned man. Querelle's hands shook as he attempted to arrange the square of wool around his shoulders.

"I do hope you will justify our confidence in you, Monsieur Querelle," said André quietly. "I should hate to think that you were abusing the generosity of the First Consul."

"There was a plot," Querelle said slowly.

This was it, the point of no return. André could see Querelle's hesitation; it leached out of every line of his body. Venal the man might be, but these had been his comrades. He had endured four months of questioning without breaking. The interrogators at the Temple, where Querelle had been held until now, were seldom gentle in their methods.

Squick, squick, went the sound of wet sawdust being swept off the scaffold below. The sawdust was matted black with blood. The red ran down with the rain, staining the sides of the platform.

Querelle turned back to André. "There was a plot. A conspiracy," he elaborated.

"To kill the First Consul?" asked André, holding up a hand to silence Delaroche.

"Oh no! N-no!" It would, thought André, be rather cheeky to admit to attempting to kill the same man from whom one was currently seeking a pardon. "We were just going to, er, kidnap him."

"A likely story," sneered Delaroche. "Think about it. Think hard."

The prisoner gathered the tattered shreds of his courage. He had only one card to play, and he knew it. "I'll think better once that pardon is signed," he said.

Delaroche's lips tightened.

"This might be for the best," interjected André, turning so that he stood between Delaroche and the prisoner. In a low voice, he said, "I can stay and speak to him while you go to Fouché with the good news."

Delaroche's eyes narrowed. "The good news?"

André kept his face carefully bland. "That you were able to get Monsieur Querelle to talk. After four months of silence."

Delaroche smiled at André, one of those lifts of the lips that never quite reaches his eyes. "I couldn't have done it without your . . . assistance."

"Be sure to relay that to my cousin," said André dryly, and was rewarded by a tightening at the corners of Delaroche's mouth. The reminder of that relationship never ceased to annoy him, which was precisely why André never ceased to employ it.

Delaroche moved backwards towards the door. "Fouché will want details. Names, dates, places. Monsieur Querelle would be wise to leave nothing out. Otherwise . . . What is a pardon, after all, but a scrap of paper? Paper tears, it blots, it burns. Paper is a fragile thing." Delaroche's eyes bored into the prisoner's. "Much like a man's life."

"Or the passage of time," said André pointedly, jangling the links of his watch chain. The evil speeches did begin to wear on one after a while. "It wouldn't do to keep my cousin waiting."

Delaroche refused to allow himself to be rushed. "So many things are fragile, Monsieur," he said meditatively. "The things of innocence in this world wither too soon away. A man's loyalties . . . a child's laughter." He looked to André, the long lines of malice graven in his face all the more apparent in the uneven candlelight. "We would all do well to remember that."

André had the uneasy feeling that Delaroche was no longer talking about the prisoner.

Chapter 3

When Laura presented herself at the Hôtel de Bac the following morning, the only one who seemed the least bit pleased to see her was Pierre-André. Even his enthusiasm waned when he discovered she hadn't come bearing sweets.

"Never had a governess before," grumbled Jeannette, the white lappets of her cap bobbing. She remained pointedly in her chair before the fire, her elbows sticking out over her knitting. She was a tall, rawboned woman, the lace of her cap incongruous next to the masculine contours of her face. "Poor poppets. As if they haven't had enough to get used to."

Jean the gatekeeper spat on the floor to signal either his agreement or his antipathy for Jeannette. It was hard to tell, since his basic scowl never changed. Without a further word, he disappeared the way he had come.

Pity. Laura had almost got used to him.

Laura set her portmanteau down on the parquet floor and smiled determinedly at the inhabitants of the nursery. No one smiled back except Pierre-André, but his smile was directed more to Laura's pockets than her person. He had obviously been bribed by indulgent adults before.

The rooms appropriated for the nursery were on the second story, just above the grand reception rooms. In other days, they might have been the suite of the Marquise de Bac. The day nursery—now schoolroom, Laura corrected herself—had been paneled in pale pink, with delicate plasterwork designs of bouquets of flowers outlined in flaking green, gold, and red paint. In the sunlight, the air of dilapidation hanging over the Hôtel de Bac was even more apparent than it had been the night before. The plasterwork was dingy, the upholstery frayed, and the windows could have done with a wash. But the nursery, at least, was warm. Whatever allowance for coal the household was afforded had gone straight to the nursery grate. For the first time since coming to Paris, Laura felt the blue tinge leaving her skin.

Although that might also have been because she was still in her coat, neither Jean nor Jeannette having made any offer to take it from her.

Unlike the rest of the house, someone had made an effort to render the nursery habitable. The small chairs and table were cheap and modern but new. A large doll's house sat on a low table and there were already toy soldiers, a hobby horse, and a series of paper cutouts scattered across the floor. A rug covered the hard boards of the floor, protecting tender feet and knees from splinters; and curtains, stiff in their newness, hung in ruffles across the windows. A little boy with a mop of brown curls was engaged in coaxing a toy on a string on a bumpy journey across the hearth rug. His sister, oblivious, pulled up her knees beneath her skirt and went on with her reading.

It would have been a charming scene, the nurse knitting by the fire, the little boy tugging at his horse, the girl reading on the rug, but for the matching scowls on the faces of the women in the room.

"Good day," Laura said in clear, crisp tones. "My name is Mademoiselle Griscogne and I am to be your new governess."

Jeannette sniffed.

Abandoning his toy, the little boy launched himself at Laura's legs. "Do you have sweets?" he asked winningly. It was clearly a ploy that had worked for him before.

Laura detached him from her lower limbs before he could go prospecting for pockets. "Good day, Monsieur Jaouen. Shall I teach you how to properly greet a lady?"

Pierre-André's forehead creased. "I'm not Monsieur Jaouen," he said apologetically. "I'm Pierre-André."

There had evidently been some mistake and it fell to him to remedy it, even if it reduced the possibility of sweets.

"But someday," said Laura, "you will be Monsieur Jaouen. I am here to help you accomplish that."

Pierre-André looked uncertainly at his nurse. "I like being me."

"You will still be you," Laura assured him. "Just an older, wiser, grander you."

Pierre-André considered. "Grand as in big?"

"Very big," Laura promised gravely.

"Big as a house?"

Laura thought of Hamlet, banded in a nutshell, but king of infinite space. "Not in size, but certainly in spirit."

Jeannette sniffed.

Laura turned to the girl by the hearth, who hastily jerked her book up so that it covered the whole of her face, only her eyebrows visible above the red morocco binding.

"You must be Gabrielle," said Laura, a little bit to the eyebrows, but mostly to the book.

The book slid down just far enough to reveal a pair of scornful blue eyes.

"Don't you mean Mademoiselle Jaouen?" Gabrielle said, in

what would have been a fine show of defiance if she hadn't marred it by glancing for ratification at Jeannette.

Jeannette smirked her approval. Gabrielle's hunched shoulders straightened.

"No," said Laura pleasantly. "Because Mademoiselle Jaouen would have stood to greet a stranger in her schoolroom. A little girl who hides behind her book can only be Gabrielle."

Jeannette bristled. "It's the nursery, not a schoolroom."

"No," said Laura. She had the feeling she would be getting a lot of use out of that syllable. She addressed herself to the children. Gabrielle, book at half-mast, was regarding her with open hostility. Pierre-André was busy trying to be a house. "From now on, this will be your schoolroom. You obviously have much to learn."

Gabrielle's eyes narrowed.

Good, thought Laura. Plot revenge. Think of ways to get me back. Nothing served as a better spur to learning than a strong dose of competition.

"Schoolroom, indeed," muttered Jeannette. "That's no way for children to live, locked up in a schoolroom, no fresh air, no playmates. Disgraceful, I call it."

Laura spoke over the nursery maid's grumblings. Little had her parents realized that those acting classes in her youth, the elocution and projection, would be used not to awe the audiences at the Comédie-Française but to overawe provincial nursemaids and defiant children. In her mind's eye, stone angels wept.

"I will teach you everything you need to know to comport yourselves as an educated young lady and gentleman. Provided, that is, that you have the capacity to learn." Addressing herself to Gabrielle, she asked, "What schoolbooks do you have?"

Jeannette jumped in. "Monsieur Beniet taught them out of his own library. And very bright they were, too, he said. He was a wise man, Monsieur Beniet."

"But his library, I assume, is not here?"

Jeannette nodded reluctantly.

"Is there a library in the house?"

"If there was, it's not here anymore, is it?" said Jeannette belligerently, as though Laura had accused her of personally appropriating its contents. "Not so much as a lick of furniture, scarcely a pot in the kitchen, not a pint of fresh milk to be had. But what can one expect of Paris? It's no place for a Christian."

"I take it that's a no to the library, then," said Laura. "Since I do not make a habit of traveling with all my books on my back, new ones will have to be acquired before we can begin our lessons."

Gabrielle smirked.

Laura clapped her hands together. Like animals, children responded well to basic noises. "Come along, children. I believe we can begin our acquaintance with an outing to the bookshop."

The smirk disappeared from Gabrielle's face. Jeannette drew herself up in her chair, prepping herself for outrage. "An outing? In this weather?"

Laura looked pointedly at the window. Through the grimed panes, the sun was shining and a bird chirped determinedly on one of the bare trees in the courtyard. "Better than being 'locked up in a schoolroom,' don't you think?" Jeannette might be obstreperous, but she wasn't stupid. She knew exactly when she had been had. Laura smiled beatifically at her. "If you would be so very kind as to help the children into their outdoor things, Manette?"

"It's Jeannette." The nurse set her knitting aside with an audible click of needles.

"Of course." Laura's smile didn't waver. "Jeannette."

For a moment, the nurse seemed prepared to defy her. The children watched, expectantly, as Jeannette remained stolidly in place, her hands firmly planted on the arms of the chair. Laura kept on smiling.

Finally, with a creaking of joints and a rustle of fabric, Jeannette hauled herself up. She levered herself out of the chair with obvious reluctance, making a production of the simple act of standing.

"Catch their deaths of cold," she muttered, but the battle had already been lost. She stomped her way to the clothespress, busying herself among a pile of miniature woolens, all sturdily made and decidedly provincial in cut.

Gabrielle cast a stricken look at her nurse's retreating back, clearly feeling this treachery deeply. Squaring her shoulders, she fought on alone. "What if we don't want new books?"

"If you prefer to remain ignorant," said Laura pleasantly, "that is, of course, your choice. It would be unkind, however, to stand in the way of your brother's education."

Gabrielle folded her arms protectively across her chest. "I like the books we have."

"If you only read the same things over and over again, how do you expect to learn? A narrow library leads to a narrow mind." As aphorisms went, it wasn't one of her better ones, but it got the point across.

"Books, books, books," sang Pierre-André, ignoring Jeannette's attempts to stuff his arms into his coat. "Books, books, books. Can I wear my red mittens? The ones with the tassels on them?"

The mittens having been provided, Jeannette turned her attentions to Gabrielle, yanking the collar of her pelisse so high that only the little girl's nose stuck out.

Pawing it down, Gabrielle looked challengingly at Laura. "What happens when we run out of room to put them all?"

Taking Pierre-André's mittened hand in one of her own, Laura herded Gabrielle in front of her, through a whimsically shaped antechamber, that led, through a cunningly concealed plasterwork door, onto the second-story hall, where tapestries four times the height of a man hung in the space above the great marble staircase. "I don't think you're going to have that problem here, do you?"

Gabrielle glanced over her shoulder at the vast bulk of the

house and fell sullenly silent. Round one to the governess. It was hard to argue that one couldn't fit the odd book or two into an immense city palace that had lost most of its furnishings somewhere between the Revolution and its occupation by its current owner. From the way Gabrielle and Pierre-André tiptoed past the statuary and started at the echo of their own voices against the soaring ceilings, Laura felt safe in guessing that their home back in Nantes had been more of the three-bedroom-with-room-for-two-servants variety. One could hide an army in the Hôtel de Bac and still have room for an amateur theatrical troupe, a haberdashery, and a few aspiring sopranos.

What was Jaouen doing in a house like this? The faded grandeur of the Hôtel de Bac sorted ill with the man Laura had met the night before.

There was no sign of the master of the house as Laura hustled his children down the stairs, their shoes sending up strange echoes along the time-dulled marble. Laura wasn't sure whether to be disappointed or relieved. Relieved, she decided. It was no bad thing to have time to get the lay of the land before encountering those too-keen eyes.

"Is your father at home?" she asked.

"He's never at home," said Gabrielle. "And he certainly wouldn't be at home for you."

"He's at the Abbaye," volunteered Pierre-André. He tugged at Laura's hand. "Monks used to live there, but they don't anymore."

"Monks are a degenerate relic of the old regime," said Gabrielle loftily. Not quite under her breath, she added, "Like governesses."

"I'm not quite a degenerate relic yet," said Laura, "but give me a few weeks."

Gabrielle looked at her uncertainly, trying to tell whether she was joking. Catching Laura watching her, she hastily looked away again.

"Coats buttoned and mittens in place?" Laura asked as they

approached the front door. No circuitous side routes for her today. Pierre-André proudly displayed his mittens. Gabrielle shrugged farther into the neck of her pelisse like an irritable turtle.

There were no servants to open the door, so Laura did it herself, feeling rather as though she had fallen into a strange variant of Sleeping Beauty's castle. This was the sort of establishment that should command a score of servants at the very least, but the only staff she had seen were Jean and Jeannette. The flower beds that lined the walk from the porte cochere to the gate were as scraggly with neglect as the interior of the house. The hedges bristled with several years' unfettered growth, while dead vines draped like widows' weeds from the grand stone arch that ran across the center of the courtyard. There had once been a clock in the middle of the arch, but the hour hand had dropped off, leaving only the play of sun and shadows to mark the time.

Laura half expected Jean to stop them, but he emerged from his lair by the gate without a murmur, shoving the gate so that it yielded with the maximum squeak. Pierre-André squealed delightedly at the noise. Gabrielle looked pained.

Gabrielle scuffed her shoes against the cobbles. "Is it far?" she asked in a way that made "Is it far?" translate to "If I make enough of a fuss, will you let me go home?"

"Not very far," Laura lied. "The walk will do you good."

That last part, at least, was true. As if repenting of the gloomy drizzle of the previous day, it was one of those crisp, clear January days where the air is cold and thin and the sunshine edged with ice, bringing everything into a relief so sharp as to be almost painful. It pinched the children's cheeks and quickened their step and brightened their eyes as Laura herded them through the gate and down the street. The buildings of Paris, so quick to turn gray in the rain, shone in the sunlight, in the shades of taupe and beige so peculiar to Paris, so unfamiliar to Laura after her time in London.

The Hôtel de Bac stretched along for a full city block, nothing but continuous stone wall. There were other houses like it as they walked, great town palaces hidden behind the anonymity of beige stone, recognizable only from the gates that offered glimpses into hidden courtyards marked by intricately carved pilasters and fanciful stonework. But there were smaller houses too, as they walked along, and little shops whose proprietors, encouraged by the good weather, had piled goods on tables beneath colorful awnings.

Laura led the children down towards the river, navigating by memory and instinct. Gabrielle expressed her feelings by trudging along as though every step pained her, puffing out her cheeks and scowling at the tips of her boots. Pierre-André danced along ahead, singing a song of his own devising, which consisted solely of the word "books," repeated multiple times at varying pitch.

Laura made a note to herself to begin his musical education immediately, if only for the sake of her own ears.

It wasn't far from the Hôtel de Bac to the Seine, but the crooked nature of the streets in the Marais made the trip longer. The temperature had dropped as the rain had lifted, freezing the mud in the streets so that the brown slicks shone like exotic minerals quarried in a faraway land. Laura handily caught Pierre-André just as the heel of his shoe went skidding on a patch of petrified mud.

"Gently, now," she warned. "You don't want to go flying."

Pierre-André was favorably struck by the idea. "Don't I?"

"Not like that," said Gabrielle, daring Laura to contradict her. "She just meant falling. People can't fly."

Pierre-André's lower lip stuck out. "Butterflies can fly."

Gabrielle assumed all the superiority of her nine long years. "Butterflies have wings," she informed her brother.

Pierre-André's face set in an expression of pure stubbornness. "Then I'll have wings too," he announced. He tugged at Laura's hand. "Can I have wings? Can I?"

Gabrielle started to exchange a "Boys!" look with Laura.

Recalling that Laura was the enemy, she abruptly pulled her chin back into her collar.

"Come close by me," Laura said, pulling the little boy to her side as they started across the river. Below, the boatmen plied their trade, ferrying passengers along the Seine. The narrow crafts looked like water bugs as they darted along between the banks of the river. "Or you'll need fins instead of wings."

"I don't want fins."

"You will if you fall in the Seine." When Pierre-André looked intrigued, she added hastily, "I wouldn't advise it. That water is icy cold."

"How cold?"

"Too cold for a butterfly to survive—or a little boy." She reached a protective hand out to Gabrielle as a wagon trundled past them, but Gabrielle jerked away. She hunched her shoulders up beneath her coat and walked faster, doing everything she could to distance herself from the new governess and her brother. To their right, the buttresses of Notre-Dame soared in a feat of medieval engineering, commanding the skyline, while beyond it, one could just make out the long façade of the Louvre palace. In the sunshine, they glowed golden, the windows sparkling like diamonds. Laura saw Gabrielle's eyes widen at the sight, then carefully drop to her feet, determined not to show she was impressed.

Laura let Gabrielle have her little act of defiance. It was dreadful to be nine. It wasn't an age one would want to live over: too old to be cooed over, too young to be treated as an equal, stuck betwixt and between, and happy with no one.

Laura and Pierre-André followed behind Gabrielle, responding to the little boy's chatter by rote as he kept up a running commentary on the boats, the sky, the other inhabitants of the bridge, and what it might be like to be a butterfly with fins.

"There are butterfly fish," said Laura absently. "But I believe they live in the tropics, not here. We can find you a book with pictures of them when we get to the bookseller."

Gabrielle twisted around. "There are booksellers," she said, pointing at the stalls by the side of the river. "Why can't we buy books there?"

"Those aren't the right kind of books," replied Laura imperturbably. "We're going to a proper shop."

The Rue Serpente, they had told her. What could be more innocent than a trip to the bookshop? Governesses taught. Teaching required books. Even a nasty, suspicious, French Ministry of Police–trained mind couldn't find any fault with that.

Laura summoned Gabrielle closer as they crossed over into the Left Bank, home of students and stews. There was a sour reek of spilled wine about the streets as they set off down a winding alley towards the Rue Serpente, but the bookshop itself looked respectable enough, with narrow, dark windows piled high with books. Despite herself, Gabrielle's eyes brightened at the display.

Ha! thought Laura. Got you.

A little bell tinkled as Laura pushed open the door. The shop gave the impression of being even smaller and more cluttered than it actually was, with books piled on tables and racks and stacked in uneven towers propped against the walls. A small coal brazier burned in one corner of the shop, puffing out smoke and warmth. In summer, the windows would be open to the street, with books spilling out onto tables outside, but now the windows were shuttered tight against the January chill, making the room feel like a bibliophilic Ali Baba's cave, dark and crowded with treasure.

The smell of leather, binding glue, paper, and coal dust brought back powerful memories of other bookshops. Laura paused just inside the threshold, giving her eyes time to adjust to the dim interior. There had been one place her parents had patronized, a little shop on the Left Bank, with a leathery, smoky smell just such as this, where the proprietor kept coffee in the back for his favorite guests. There would be impromptu recitations and loud political arguments and above it all the smell of leather and book glue and her mother's musk perfume.

"Owwww!" protested Gabrielle. "You poked me!"

"Did not!" Pierre-André was the picture of outraged innocence. Until he poked her again.

Laura came hurtling back from 1784. She wasn't twelve years old anymore, trailing along in the wake of her parents from bookshop to atelier. She was a thirty-two-year-old governess and the proprietor was giving her the sort of look reserved for people who bring dangerous livestock onto the premises.

"Gentlemen," she said severely, relocating Pierre-André to her other side, "do not poke their sisters."

Pierre-André pouted. "But—"

"People who poke are little better than savages, and savages Do Not Get Books. Am I understood? Come on," Laura said, taking Pierre-André by the hand. "Let's see what we can find for you. Maybe the proprietor will have something to recommend."

"Look! Look!" Pierre-André tugged, yanking her towards a book propped open on a stand. A black-and-white illustration portrayed an enraged Hercules whopping away at the heads of the hydra. The hydra looked justifiably alarmed.

Behind them, cold air gusted into the shop as the door opened, admitting another customer.

"If you behave, you can have it," Laura bribed him shamelessly, propelling him towards the counter and the clerk, determined to get there first, before the new customer could beat her out.

Pierre-André seized his advantage. "Can I have sweets too?"

The newcomer wafted his way down the narrow aisle, his head tilted at an angle that implied that he was in the process of listening to divine voices that sang only to him. He came down to earth long enough to wave a languid hand at Pierre-André. "This shop purveys celestial sweets, dear boy. The sweets of . . . learning!"

He was garbed with that deliberate air of dishabille that proclaims the artist the world over. Despite the cold, he wore no jacket, only a waistcoat over his flowing white shirt, and a rough cravat knotted at the neck.

Pierre-André was looking perturbed again. "Are those like candied almonds?"

The poet—he could only be a poet—pressed two fine-boned hands to his chest. "Better than almonds, my lively lad. In these Elysian fields one can sup on the sugared nuggets of choicest poesy."

All but concealed behind a display of books, Gabrielle rolled her eyes. Laura heartily concurred.

Pierre-André ignored Elysian fields and went straight to the important bit. "I want nuggets of posy," he demanded. "Sugary ones."

Laura wanted a cup of tea. Brewed black, milk, no sugar.

"In a minute," she said, but it was already too late. The poet had ranged himself in front of the counter. He had, she realized indignantly, cut her out. She tried tapping her foot, but the poet was oblivious.

He was more likely smoking the sugary fields of Elysium than supping on them, thought Laura bitterly. The Left Bank hadn't changed much since her parents' day.

"What have you today for *me*"—the man paused dramatically, swishing his sleeves for emphasis—"in terms of poe*tree*?"

Laura contemplated a swift kick to the *knee*. Preferably times *three*.

The shopkeeper reached beneath the counter and drew out a slim book bound in cheap paper covers. "You might want to try this, Monsieur Whittlesby. It's the latest from Porcelier."

"That rubbish!" An exuberant gesture sent a full yard of white linen sleeve swooping over Pierre-André's head. Pierre-André ducked and giggled. "The man has no feeling for the rhythm of the language, for the tripping trot of enjambed feet as they prance down that pulchritudinous path of poesy over which only the muse may rule as mistress." The speech was made all the more impressive by the fact that the poet managed to utter it without once pausing for breath.

The shopkeeper eyed him dispassionately. "Shall I put it on your account as always, Monsieur Whittlesby?"

The poet tucked the book up beneath one flowing sleeve, where it disappeared among the folds. "Yes, do."

Laura waited impatiently for the poet to step away from the counter, as the shopkeeper embarked upon the seemingly endless process of recording the transaction in a dog-eared ledger. Muttering to himself in rhyme, the poet wandered to the side, his nose buried in the despised poems of Porcelier. Laura could hear the occasional "Ha!" emerge from between the red morocco covers.

Laura tugged Pierre-André out from under one of the poet's sleeves, with which he was amusing himself by playing a private game of hide and seek among the excess fabric.

"May I have my posy now?" he demanded.

Laura put a hand on his head to quiet him. "Do you have any books appropriate for a child of five?" she asked the shopkeeper.

With Pierre-André beside her, the question sounded entirely natural, not at all like a set piece she had been instructed to recite.

Clicking his tongue against his teeth, the clerk rummaged about in an untidy pile of books. It was, thought Laura, an excellent performance. If it was a performance, that was. What if this wasn't the right clerk?

Well, then, Laura told herself, keeping a grip on a squirming Pierre-André, the worst that would happen would be that they would have bought a book appropriate for a five-year-old.

The shopkeeper held up a book, squinted at it, clicked his

tongue a few times more, and returned it to the pile, repeating this process before emerging triumphant with a large, ornately bound volume.

"You might want to try this," he suggested.

No, no, no. Laura wanted to stamp in impatience. That wasn't the right phrase. If he were her contact, he was supposed to say, "I usually recommend this for a child of seven," or eight or nine, with the number representing the page on which she would find the key word that would then be used to decode the message.

"Oh?" said Laura. "What is it?"

Whatever it was, she hoped Pierre-André liked it, because it obviously wasn't going to serve any other purpose.

Placing the book flat on the counter, the shopkeeper spread it open to reveal a delicately tinted engraving of a flower.

It was an orchid.

Chapter 4

It wasn't silver. There was no such thing as a silver orchid. But it didn't need to be. Laura knew exactly what it meant.

A thrill of excitement buzzed through her, heady as the champagne she dimly remembered drinking back in her pre-governess days.

"It's perfect," she said, and meant it. There would be no need for a page indication this time. She knew what her key word would be. "Silver." In one fell swoop, the Carnation's contact had confirmed his status and given her the code for the next message. "Natural history, is it?"

"Many young gentlemen these days are taking up botanical pursuits," said the shopkeeper blandly.

"Young ladies too," Laura said, feeling positively arch.

"So I have been told," said the shopkeeper, with something that wasn't quite a smile. "Some may find it unconventional, but I hear that they take to it quite well."

Laura felt an unaccustomed urge to grin. It was all she could do not to grab the shopkeeper by the hand and shake it, babbling, *Haven't we done well? Aren't we clever?*

Instead, she nodded crisply, tapping a gloved finger against the open page of the book. "It will be good drawing practice for my pupils. We'll take it."

Without betraying any emotion, the shopkeeper closed the cover, concealing the orchid beneath a nondescript façade of blue leather. "Will there be anything more?"

"I will also need an introductory Latin text," said Laura. That wasn't part of the code, but, while she was teaching, she might as well teach. It would be hard to explain her continued presence in Jaouen's household otherwise. "Do you have the *Orbis Sensualium Pictus*?"

"The—?" The shopkeeper paused to allow her to fill in the title.

It was a book she had often used to teach Latin before, especially to younger children. Brightly colored pictures were paired with the corresponding Latin and English translation.

"The *Orbis Sensual*—" Laura ground to a halt as she realized her blunder.

The second language after the Latin in the *Orbis Sensualium* wasn't French. It was English.

She had used the *Orbis Sensualium Pictus* to teach English children in England. How could that not have occurred to her? That was certainly one way to get herself caught in a hurry; go about asking for English books in a French bookshop. She might as well emblazon "SPY" on her forehead. In capital letters. In English. With a Latin translation underneath.

Or she could just bang her head against the counter and wish she had never gotten out of bed that morning.

Laura glanced guiltily over her shoulder, but the only other person in the shop was the poet, who was, mercifully, too absorbed in poetic reflection to pay any attention to her faux pas.

"Never mind," she muttered, and affected a cough to cover her confusion. She would have to be wary of slips like that. After sixteen years, she had become far more English than she had realized. So much for doing so well. Pride goeth, and all those other gloomy adages. She would have to be more careful in the future. "Er, do you have any picture books with Latin translations for children?"

Why hadn't she just asked that in the first place? That was what she got for trying to show off.

"I can see about finding something like that for you," the bookseller offered dubiously, "but it might take some time. We did have a copy of *Aesop's Fables* in a Latin translation. I could have that for you next week."

"Do you think it would be appropriate for a child of nine?"

"It very well could be," agreed the shopkeeper. His slow nod of approval made Laura feel marginally less like an idiot. Whatever message the Carnation next wanted to convey would be found on page nine of *Aesop's Fables*, corresponding to the code word "silver."

"That would be very good of you," said Laura, just as the door opened again with a tinkle of chimes and a blast of cold air.

Three women breezed into the store. Two were obviously ladies of fashion; the third, older by several years, was dressed with puritanical severity except for the truly alarming purple plumes that sprouted from her bonnet like a molting tropical bird. Laura sincerely doubted that any bird, even in the tropics, had ever dared to show itself among the avian haut monde in plumage of that shade.

Laura saw Gabrielle taking in the details of the ladies' costumes with hungry eyes. With a twinge, Laura remembered what it was to be nine and plain, with that horrible awareness that one didn't, somehow, look quite right. The child's clothes were sturdy and well made, but they could not, under any circumstances, be termed anything other than provincial. Laura's problem hadn't been quite the same—she had, if anything, always been dressed in far too mature a style for her age—but she could well remember that anxious desire to look just like everyone else, and the squirming humiliation of knowing she didn't.

She would have to speak to Jaouen about a new dress for his daughter. If books wouldn't win Gabrielle over, perhaps pretty clothing might. And it would give her an excellent excuse to seek out her employer.

The poet's sleeves expanded to hitherto unimaginable width as he flung his arms high in the air. Gabrielle hastily retreated back against a stack of books.

"My muse!" he cried, gesturing grandly at one of the ladies, who was magnificently turned out in a tight-sleeved, high-waisted sky blue pelisse finished in fur trim. She wore a bonnet with a silk-lined brim that shadowed her face, although not enough to curtain her from the eyes of her admirer. "Well met by midday, fair Miss Wooliston!"

Laura had to juggle to keep her grip on her book. Fortunately, no one was looking at her. All attention was on the lady in sky blue, the poet's muse.

Or, as Laura knew her, the Pink Carnation.

Laura felt a tug on her arm. "What's a muse?" demanded Pierre-André, in a whisper like a foghorn.

"Ah, the muse!" mused the poet, striking a pose like Jove about to throw thunderbolt. "The muse, my dear poppet, is a thing of glory, a flame of fire, a blazing comet of divine inspiration! In short—*she*!" He wafted his sleeve in the direction of the Pink Carnation.

The pretty lady didn't appear to be on fire, but Pierre-André prudently backed up against Laura's side in case she should blaze into divine inspiration and catch them all up in the conflagration.

Undaunted, the poet was courting artistic immolation. "I have just, this very morning, finished my latest ode to your sublime, um—"

"Sublimity?" suggested the Pink Carnation.

Gabrielle's eyes were like saucers and Pierre-André was tugging at Laura's arm again, hissing, "What's sublimmy? And can I have a shirt like that? Can I? Can I?"

Turning back to the shopkeeper, Laura said hastily, "The Greek myths in the front. We would also like a copy of that. If you are a good boy," she added to Pierre-André, "I'll read you about Hercules and the snakes later. You'll like the snakes."

With a nod, the shopkeeper set off to the front to fetch the book.

Behind her, the poet was in full spate, fluttering his sleeves at Miss Wooliston in a bizarre sort of mating ritual. "Sublimity is too limiting a term to encompass the range of my regard for so rarefied a creature as thou. Which is why, instead of one word, I offer you five cantos."

From somewhere in the vicinity of his left sleeve, the poet made good his word by producing a very thick roll of paper, beautifully tied with a pink silk ribbon.

"The pink," he added helpfully, "represents love hopeful. I discuss that at some length in the fourth canto."

Miss Wooliston eyed the thick roll of paper with comic apprehension. "You flatter me. Again."

Her friend, a fair-haired woman whose claims to beauty were marred by the length of her nose, came to her rescue. "When will you immortalize me, Monsieur Whittlesby?"

The poet swept an elaborate bow that set all his ruffles fluttering. "You, Madame Bonaparte, have no need of my humble pen to make you immortal."

Bonaparte. He had said Bonaparte, hadn't he? If there had been anything in Laura's mouth, she would have choked on it.

This Mme. Bonaparte was too young to be the First Consul's wife, so it was presumably his stepdaughter, Hortense, made doubly a Bonaparte through her marriage to the First Consul's younger brother.

That was a lot of Bonaparte in a very small space.

Mme. Bonaparte's lips lifted in a rueful smile. "No. My stepfather's cannon have done so already."

"And a copy of *Caesar's Wars*," Laura said brusquely as the shopkeeper set down Hercules on top of the botanical treatise.

What was the Pink Carnation playing at? She had known Laura intended to come to the bookshop today; in fact, it was she who had advised her to do so. Why come bearing a Bonaparte? Laura didn't like surprises, especially not in Bonaparte form.

"Gallic or Civil?" asked the shopkeeper laconically.

"Civil—no, Gallic," Laura corrected herself.

What was the Pink Carnation doing going about with a Bonaparte on her arm?

Laura supposed it must be an equivalent of the old adage about keeping one's enemies closer. When it came down to it, it wasn't all that different from her notion of bringing the children along to provide an air of innocence. No one would ever suspect Miss Wooliston of delivering or receiving treasonous material with a daughter of the First Consul in tow.

Laura might have been teaching for what felt like an eon, but when it came to espionage, she still had a great deal to learn.

"No cannonade more powerful than the grapeshot of your eyes!" declaimed the poet. "No fusillade could match the artillery of your wit, no cavalry charge the pounding of the hearts which beat only for you!"

"We really must get you near a proper battlefield, Monsieur Whittlesby," said Bonaparte's stepdaughter with amusement. "Or at least buy you a book on tactics to bolster your metaphors."

"Ought you to be encouraging him?" Holding out a hand to

the poet, Miss Wooliston said, "Give me that ode of yours, Mr. Whittlesby, and from now on apply your pen to worthier subjects."

Whittlesby gazed up at her soulfully. "What topic could be worthier than love?"

"Digestion," snapped the older woman without a moment's reflection.

"Digestion?" Whittlesby clutched his poem protectively to his chest and looked askance at the woman in the purple plumes. "My words are meant to be savored with the eye, not the tongue, Mademoiselle Gwendolyn."

"I don't believe she was planning to eat them, Monsieur Whittlesby," said Hortense Bonaparte reassuringly, patting the poet's sleeve. "Nobody's teeth are that good."

Mademoiselle Gwendolyn, or, in plain English, Miss Gwen, bared a set of teeth that gave the lie to Hortense Bonaparte's supposition. "You can mock all you like, but that doesn't change facts. Just look at the chronicles of history here in this shop! The Roman Empire was lost by rich sauces, not by love."

There was an idea, thought Laura. If all else failed, they could simply feed Bonaparte into submission, one cream puff at a time.

Considering that she had proved her point, the Pink Carnation's chaperone directed a look of withering scorn at the poet. "Attend to your diet before you talk to me of poetry."

Whittlesby made a valiant effort to rally. "But poetry is food for the soul!"

"Hmph. If that's true, your poetry wants fiber. Your adjectives are flabby and your nouns lack substance."

Radiating offense, the poet made a show of extending the roll of paper past Miss Gwen, into the waiting hand of Miss Wooliston. "I shall let my muse be the judge of that," he said sniffily. "Good day."

"Good day, bad poetry!" Miss Gwen called triumphantly after him. The door closed with a decidedly unpoetic bang.

Hortense Bonaparte stifled a smile behind one gloved hand. "Must you torment him so, Mademoiselle Meadows?"

Miss Gwen was unrepentant. "Anyone who writes drivel such as that deserves to have the stuffing knocked out of him. An eye for an eye, I say."

"Or an insult for an ode?" Miss Wooliston unrolled roughly two inches of her ode. "Oh, dear. He's gone and compared me to a graceful gazelle gliding gallantly o'er a glassy glade again." Shaking her head, she rolled it tightly back up. "If he must show his admiration, it's a pity he can't just do it with flowers."

"Roses," suggested Hortense Bonaparte, whose mother had made an art of cultivating them.

Miss Wooliston tilted her head, as though considering. "I have always been rather partial to carnations."

"Cheap, showy things," Miss Gwen said with a sniff. "Rather like that Whittlesby's poetry."

"At least he hasn't published any of his odes to you in the newspapers yet," contributed Hortense Bonaparte, cheerfully oblivious to botanical subtext. She slid her arm companionably through the Pink Carnation's. "One dreadful little man did that to me while I was still at Madame Campan's school. The other girls called me *la Belle Hortense* for weeks. It was very trying." Glancing over a display of books as she spoke, she lifted a large volume bound in red morocco from the table, angling it towards Miss Wooliston. "Have you read this yet? I heard it was rather good."

The Pink Carnation shook her head, making a show of looking around the shop. "I was hoping to find a copy of *The Children of the Abbey*."

"Do you mean to tell me there is a horrid novel you haven't read?" Mme. Bonaparte feigned shock. "I thought you had them all."

It struck Laura that the Pink Carnation was on remarkably good terms with the First Consul's stepdaughter. Well, what had she expected? That the Pink Carnation would conduct her career by skulking in dark alleys in malodorous disguises? It was much more efficient to do one's reconnaissance in a drawing room, properly garbed.

Miss Wooliston accepted the teasing in good grace. "I seem to have missed this one, and I am most distraught about it. Who knows what might be hidden behind those abbey walls? I simply must find out."

An abbey or an Abbaye?

Taking Miss Wooliston's statement at face value, Mme. Bonaparte laughed good-naturedly. "I shouldn't imagine you'll find anything out of the ordinary. Aren't those novels all the same?"

Miss Gwen let out a loud and offended harrumph that set her plumes a-wagging. "Only to the uninformed. How many have you read recently, missy?"

Mme. Bonaparte held out her hands in a gesture of defeat. "I was once very fond of *La Nouvelle Héloïse*."

"Ha!" exclaimed Miss Gwen. "That drivel! That Rousseau wouldn't know a proper plot if it bit him."

Mme. Bonaparte bowed her head in contrition. "I shall eagerly await the publication of your romance, Mademoiselle Meadows."

"In the meantime," said Miss Wooliston, neatly bringing the conversation back around. "I must have my *Children of the Abbey*. I find I am become quite urgent in my curiosity."

She said it in such a droll way that Mme. Bonaparte laughed, but Laura sensed a deeper purpose. "What do you expect to find?"

Miss Wooliston waved a dismissive hand. "Oh, the usual horrors, as you said. Ghosts, ghouls, strange reversals of fortune, lost princes . . ."

Was it Laura's imagination, or had there been an additional emphasis on that last phrase?

"Strange things can happen in abbeys on dark and stormy

nights—much like last night." The Pink Carnation added prosaically, "That must have been what put me in the mood for it."

Last night. Last night, after their interview, she had heard M. Jaouen direct his coachman to the Abbaye Prison. Something must have happened at the Abbey last night, something the Pink Carnation most urgently wanted to know.

"You couldn't be satisfied by *Otranto?*" suggested Mme. Bonaparte with a smile.

"I find I grow weary of my old books." Miss Wooliston made a face. "I crave more mysterious mysteries and more villainous villains."

Mme. Bonaparte looked slyly at her friend from beneath her bonnet brim. "What about more heroic heroes?"

The Pink Carnation raised both eyebrows. "Do you know any?" she asked dryly, and Mme. Bonaparte laughed.

"Will that be all?" the shopkeeper asked. It took Laura a moment to realize that he was speaking to her.

Laura hastily reached for her reticule, grateful that the Selwicks had made her take a course on currency at their spy school. She had sorted and resorted *sous* and *louis* and *livres* until she could fumble them out in their correct denominations in her sleep.

"Yes, we'll have the myths, the Gallic Wars, the botanical treatise and— Did you find something, Gabrielle?" she asked, looking down at Gabrielle, who was standing next to her, with a book folded protectively to her chest.

Silently, Gabrielle extended the volume. It was discreetly bound in dark leather, but the title belied the demure exterior. Like the Pink Carnation, Laura's new charge appeared to have a taste for horrid novels.

Laura took the volume from her, a French translation of Mrs. Radcliffe's *The Romance of the Forest*. "Does your father let you read this?"

Gabrielle hunched her shoulders defensively. "Grandfather did."

Laura turned the volume over in her hands, giving Gabrielle time to squirm. "I see no problem with your wallowing in ghosts and ghouls so long as you apply yourself to your lessons first." Laura plunked Gabrielle's book down on top of Caesar. "We'll have that as well."

"You can return it, if it doesn't suit," said the shopkeeper. "Just make sure you include the reckoning."

"Shopkeep!" Miss Gwen pushed past Laura, waving her furled parasol in the air. "Sirrah!"

Pierre-André stared, fascinated, up at Miss Gwen's headdress. "I like your feathers."

Miss Gwen favored the small boy with an approving look, an expression that involved the most marginal relaxation in her habitual scowl. "It is reassuring to find that someone in this benighted city has a sense of fashion." She wagged a finger at the boy. "Never let them tell you otherwise."

The Pink Carnation managed to look their way without ever looking at Laura, as though Laura were no more an object to be remarked than the table used as a counter or the smoke leaching from the brazier. A servant. Invisible.

It seemed like a good time to take her leave.

"Come along, come along," murmured Laura, wedging the four fat books under one arm and shooing Pierre-André ahead of her. "Gabrielle! You don't want to keep these nice ladies from their shopping."

With a protective eye on her book, which was currently bundled with the others under Laura's arm, Gabrielle fell into step.

Laura pushed with her shoulder against the door, holding it for the children to precede her.

As the door slammed behind them, she heard the Pink Carnation earnestly asking the stepdaughter of Bonaparte, "What *did* you think of Madame de Staël's latest novel?"

"Can I have purple feathers?" Pierre-André's shrill voice drilled into Laura's ears.

"Maybe," said Laura, shifting to readjust the clumsy pile of books under her arm. "What would you use them for?"

"Flying," he said, as though it were perfectly obvious.

"May I have my book?" interrupted Gabrielle.

"When we get back to the house," Laura said. "I don't want to undo the package while we're walking." She wondered if there would be another note hidden among the pages of the botanical treatise. She doubted it. The Pink Carnation's message had been clear enough.

Gabrielle crunched loudly down on a thin patch of ice. "I don't see why we couldn't take the carriage," she muttered.

"Because walking is good for you," said Laura bracingly. And because she didn't want the coachman to have a record of where they had gone. While there was no reason for Jaouen to suspect anything amiss about the bookshop, there was also no reason to lead him straight to it.

The road was busier than it had been when they had left, with people making their way home from offices and shops. The early-winter dusk was already beginning to fall, tinting everything it touched with gray and lending a curious appearance of insubstantiality to the landscape as they passed, as though the stucco walls of the narrow houses were made of fog. The high walls cast strange shadows into the street, creating wells of darkness in which the shapes of passing people took on an ominous aspect. It might have been the twilight or the children's flagging energy, but the walk back along the alleys of St. Michel seemed far longer than the walk there.

It was with relief that Laura emerged onto the Seine, holding one of her charges by each hand. Gabrielle had protested the gesture, but Laura didn't want to risk losing her in the growing dark. The lights from the houses on the Île de la Cité reflected in the river, creating shimmering patterns in the water.

"Stay to the side," warned Laura, as carriages rumbled past. "You don't want to get squished."

"Don't want to walk anymore," whined Pierre-André, burying his face in Laura's waist. Laura had to execute a hasty double-step to keep from tripping over him. "Tired."

"Just a little bit longer," she promised. "We're almost home."

"That's not home." If she had been a few years younger, Gabrielle would have probably been burying her face in Laura's waist too. Instead, she tugged her hand free and folded her arms tightly across her chest. "It's just where we live."

Laura knew what that felt like.

When was the last time she'd had a place that felt like home? Not since she was sixteen. Her parents had never kept a traditional home; they had moved from place to place as her parents' whims and fortunes took them. Nonetheless, by some strange alchemy of affection, her parents—her excessive, flamboyant parents—had managed to make the series of borrowed rooms and lodging houses feel like home. Wherever they had been, that was where home was. And when they were gone . . . well, here she was.

"Home is where the people you love are," Laura said, surprising both herself and Gabrielle.

Gabrielle gave her a look. Laura couldn't blame her. At that age, she wouldn't have understood it either.

"Home was in Nantes," Gabrielle said. It was evident that she thought Laura very dim not to understand that.

"Will you carry me?" demanded Pierre-André. "My feet hurt."

Laura herded the children towards the railing as a carriage drew alongside them, a little out of the ordinary stream of traffic. Instead of progressing, it slowed to a stop, despite the angry cries of the wagon owner behind it.

A man leaned out of the window, ignoring the various speculations on his ancestry being offered by the man behind him. He wore a tall black hat with a broad brim. The material had a threadbare sheen to it in the light of the carriage lamps. "Mademoiselle!" the man in the carriage called.

Laura put a hand on each of the children's backs and hurried them forward.

"Mademoiselle Jaouen!"

Gabrielle stopped and turned, leaving Laura tugging futilely at the back of her coat. The carriage glided smoothly along beside them. It was a narrow, black conveyance, designed to hold only one passenger, or two at most. "It is Mademoiselle Jaouen, is it not?"

Laura took a tighter grip on the back of Gabrielle's coat. "The children are not permitted to speak to strangers. Good day, Monsieur."

"But I am no stranger. I am a colleague of their father's." The man leaned farther out the window, arranging his thin features into what he clearly believed to be an ingratiating smile. "And this young man must be Pierre-André."

Pierre-André slunk back against Laura's side and buried his face in her pelisse.

"The children are very tired," said Laura, by way of explanation and apology. "I must get them home."

The gentleman's smile broadened. It reminded Laura of nothing so much as wolves in fairy stories. It was not a pleasing effect. "Allow me to assist you. I have the carriage at my disposal."

Perhaps it was the teeth, but Laura found herself ill-inclined to take him up on the offer. "And very little room in it. We would not want to impose."

The man held out a hand. "No imposition. Not when the children of a colleague are concerned."

Something about the way he said "colleague" sent Laura's hackles up. She pushed the children ahead, forcing them to move. "No need, sir. The walk will do the children good."

Gabrielle sent her a decidedly baleful look.

"Feet hurt," whined Pierre-André.

The man settled back in his seat, contemplating the mutinous children with an appraising air that made Laura think of a chef sizing up a joint. Perhaps not for this meal, but later.

"As you will, Madame," he said. "But do be sure to give my regards to Monsieur Jaouen."

"Who shall I say sends them?"

The man bared his yellowing teeth in a facsimile of a smile. "Delaroche. Gaston Delaroche."

Chapter 5

It was with a heavy tread and weary heart that André returned to the Hôtel de Bac.

It was twilight again, twilight to twilight, one day bleeding into the next. A candle sat unlit on the table by the door. Blundering in the vast darkness of the hall, André found the flint and lit the candle, bringing the area around him into a semblance of visibility. In the grand, high-ceilinged chamber, the single flame seemed to emphasize the darkness rather than combat it.

He had the notes from Querelle's interrogation with him. There was still a full night's work ahead of him, turning fifty pages of disjointed testimony into reports of varying sizes and shapes: a discrete paragraph for the ledgers of the Prefecture, a one-page summary for the First Consul's bulletin, and a more comprehensive account for Fouché's private use, all to be delivered by the following morning. Memory presented him with Querelle's face, skull-like in the candlelight, the skin sagging over the bones as he uttered the words that would condemn his comrades to a like cell in a like prison, and all their hopes with it.

This wasn't what they had fought for, he and Julie.

André took the candle with him, using it to light his way to the room he had appropriated as a study.

There was a crayon drawing of Gabrielle and Pierre-André propped over the mantelpiece, the only item of personal significance that André had brought with him from Nantes to Paris all those years ago. In it, Gabrielle was a curly-haired five, Pierre-André a round-cheeked infant.

It was the last work Julie had done before she died.

Perhaps she was the lucky one, Julie, not to have seen how it all turned out, all their brave dreams of a world reborn. How joyously they had donned the Revolutionary cockade, seizing the chance for all their philosophies to be made flesh. Ancient injustice was to be banished, feudal dues abolished, the antiquated system that pitted noble against commoner erased. The Age of Reason had at last arrived, and they were its heralds.

André had attended the National Convention as one of the Nantes delegation, raising his voice against the entrenched evils of privilege and power, while Julie put her arguments into paint, creating bold historical scenes, mostly drawn from Ancient Rome, all depicting the triumph of Republican virtue over aristocratic sloth. Her *Mother of the Gracchi* had been all the rage, eclipsing even David's *Oath of the Horatii* in its depiction of the sacrifices for one's country incumbent upon a good citizen.

But not these sorts of sacrifices. Nor the ones that had been demanded by the guillotine in the name of public safety. That wasn't the sort of world he and Julie had so optimistically planned to bequeath to their children.

Oh, Julie. André was tired and lonely and his head hurt.

Draping his coat over the back of his chair, André carefully lowered the fifty-odd pages of notes he held under his arm onto his desk. He would just go say good night to Gabrielle and Pierre-André before he went back to work. It was probably nothing more than a fancy, but he hadn't been able to rid himself of the unease that Delaroche's words had aroused in him. He didn't want Delaroche anywhere near his children.

André could feel the warmth of the nursery through the door even before he entered. It seeped through his bones straight into his soul, the knowledge that while outside the world might be mad, within lay peace and serenity, his children warm and safe.

André pushed gently at the door, one of the flimsy half panels to which the last century's aristocratic set appeared to be prone. The door gave an appalling groan as it opened, but there was no answering noise from within the room, no scramble of little feet or cries of "Papa!" There was only the crackle of coal, the click of Jeannette's knitting needles, and the creak of her chair as she rocked back and forth beside the hearth.

Pierre-André's hobbyhorse lay abandoned on its side; Gabrielle's book sprawled discarded beside the hearth.

André spoke into the stillness. "Where are Gabrielle and Pierre-André?"

Jeannette didn't bother to look up from her knitting, although the needles moved with a fervor that suggested repressed emotion. "They're off with their governess."

She pronounced the word as though it were something foul.

"Outside the building?"

"That's generally where out is," Jeannette said snippily.

Jeannette had always considered him an unnecessary adjunct to her Miss Julie, to be tolerated on sufferance because he was the means of creating new babies. Otherwise, he was simply an annoyance. An annoyance who paid her salary, but that was beside the point. Jeannette didn't allow herself to be swayed by such crass motives as money.

"And didn't I tell her that it was too cold out for the little mites? But, no. It was 'Walking is good for them' and 'They need the exercise.' As though the Paris air could be good for anyone, nasty, smoky stuff."

Outside, the shadows had congealed into full darkness. Bare tree branches shifted ominously against the window, scratching at the glass. "Where did she take them?"

Jeannette lifted her needles in the air, at great peril to her knitting. "Why ask me? I'm just the nursemaid. Not that anyone bothers to tell me anything. Oh no, I'm just the one who sat by them when they were sick and nursed them through their fevers and mopped their little brows."

Brow-mopping was always a bad sign, but André had other things on his mind. The streets of Paris were dangerous and ungoverned at night, no place for two small children. "How long have they been out?"

Jeannette looked darkly at her knitting. "Long enough that their poor little fingers will be quite frozen through. Out without a carriage, in this weather! And what's to say that she'll even bring them back, I ask you?" She glowered fiercely at André. "This is what comes of taking on *strangers*."

André spoke harshly to cover his growing fear. "If you suspected something amiss, why didn't you stop them?"

"Me, interfere?" Jeannette rocked back and forth in her chair. *Click, click, click* went the needles. "She's the governess. I'm just their old nursery maid. Never mind that I'm the one what's been with them since they was born, the poor motherless mites. Oh no. They have a fancy Paris governess now. . . . Wait! Where are you going?"

André was already halfway out the nursery door. "To find Jean," he said tersely.

André's heels clicked eerily on the old parquet floors, echoing off the marble walls. The old courtiers in the mural above the stair seemed to be laughing at him behind their fans, taunting, mocking. The references had checked out—but how hard would they have been to forge? Any of the families might have been bribed.

He could hear Delaroche's voice, musing on the frailty of young flesh, like the low notes of the chorus in an opera just before the pit opened onto hell and damnation.

André's candle cast grotesque shadows along the wall, pursuing him down the stairs, whispering warnings. Was it usual for governesses to remove their charges from the premises, and on the first day? He wouldn't know; he had never had one. But it felt wrong. He and Jean could fan out, search the streets. The children were related by blood to Fouché; a man would have to be bold, mad, or a fool to harm them.

Unfortunately, that still left a large portion of the population of Paris.

André quickened his steps, racing to outpace the nightmare images that dogged him. He was almost to the bottom of the flight when the door to the courtyard creaked open, bringing with it a blast of cold air and a small boy in red mittens whose color even the semidarkness couldn't dim.

André's foot came down heavily on the marble floor. He was speechless with wonder and relief.

"Papa!" Pierre-André cried gladly, and rushed towards him as Gabrielle followed behind, too old and grand to run at him, and the governess last, tidily closing the door behind them.

"Good evening, Monsieur Jaouen," she said, as though she hadn't just given him the worst fifteen minutes of his life.

"Where in the blazes have you been?"

The expressions on everyone's faces turned from pleasure to alarm, except for the governess, whose entire range of expression seemed to be limited to stony and stonier. It was hard to tell which was which, but André thought she went to stonier.

Pierre-André flung his arms around his father's waist. "We bought books, Papa! And I saw purple feathers."

André touched his fingers lightly to his son's head, feeling the silky softness of his baby curls. So precious. So fragile. André scowled at the governess. "What were you doing, taking the children out after dark?"

The governess very carefully stripped off her gloves, finger by finger. "It was light when we left. Sir."

André raised a brow. "Surely one so well versed in the natural sciences would know that when the sun rises, it also sets." His booted foot began to tap an angry tattoo against the marble floor. "I returned home from the Abbaye to find the children gone, with no word as to their whereabouts. Not a good beginning, Mademoiselle. Not a good beginning at all."

The governess's eyes shifted to Jeannette, who had followed André down the stairs and was standing just behind. She looked smug.

"But I told—" Catching herself, the governess pressed her lips tightly together, her chest swelling as she breathed in deeply through her nose. It took her only a moment to compose herself. Studiously not looking at Jeannette, she said, "Forgive me, Monsieur Jaouen. I had meant to return before dark. Our outing took longer than I intended."

She wasn't a snitch, the governess; he would give her that much.

"What was this outing that was so vital that it had to be accomplished immediately?" He folded his arms across his chest and stared the governess down. Or, at least, made the attempt.

Gabrielle sidled up beside him, ranging herself by his side, against the new governess. It offended André's sense of fair play. They were three against one. Four if one counted Jeannette, which André didn't. Jeannette would never willingly join any team to which he belonged.

The governess met his gaze without fear. "I took Gabrielle and Pierre-André to a bookshop. They were badly in need of basic texts."

Books. He hadn't thought of books. Given that he had lived most of his life among books, it was an alarming oversight.

"Why didn't you ask me?" he asked gruffly.

The governess chose her words carefully. "I wasn't sure," she said, "when the opportunity would arise."

"You might have sent a message to the Prefecture."

"I didn't wish to disturb you." The governess bowed her dark head. It ought to have been a pose of humility. Instead, André felt that he was the one being shamed. "Sir."

"Next time," he said imperiously, "make out a list and send Jean. He can fetch whatever you need."

"Thank you. Sir."

All those "sirs" were beginning to get on André's nerves. "Why didn't you ask for the use of the carriage?" he asked. "It would have been made available to you."

The governess lifted her chin, looking particularly governessy. "I thought the exercise would do the children good. It isn't healthy to keep them in the house."

It wouldn't have annoyed him so much if he didn't agree. "I would prefer you keep them close to home as much as possible. There are dangerous people about."

André half expected the governess to argue. In fact, he rather hoped she would. A nice, acrimonious exchange might go some way towards relieving his harried feelings.

Instead, she paused, her lips pursed. She looked thoughtful. Too thoughtful. "It was, perhaps . . . imprudent. I will not make the same mistake again."

André hadn't spent the last five years interrogating people for nothing. There was something she wasn't telling him.

"Papa!" Pierre-André was tugging at the edge of his waistcoat.

The governess distracted him from his speculations by adding, "Naturally, had Monsieur made his wishes clear, I should, of course, have respected those instructions."

So much for the show of meekness.

André held her gaze. Her eyes were a particularly dark brown, so dark they were nearly black, fringed by lashes as thick and dark as her hair, lashes a courtesan would envy. "Consider them instructed," he said.

Pierre-André wriggled under his arm. "We bought books, Papa!"

The governess inclined her head in assent, but there was something too regal about the motion to be called obeisance. "I will be sure to check with you before I arrange any other outings in the future."

"See that you do," said André, but the words felt rather like an afterthought. He had already been dismissed. Quite impressive, all around. It was enough to make one believe her claim that she had been keeping small children in check for sixteen years.

Pierre-André yanked on his waistcoat so hard that André saw stars. "Look at my books, Papa!"

Wincing slightly, André yielded to the pressure. He, after all, had not had sixteen years' experience with children. "Your books?" he repeated, with an attempt at interest. He felt suddenly very, very tired and more than a little bit dim, all the fear and anger leaching away into fatigue. "Oh. Books."

Right. The papery things for which the governess had dragged his children out around Paris. He really should have thought of books. It had never occurred to him. Père Beniet's library had been like the magic cave in a fairy story; one needed only to wish on it for the right book to appear. The books had been boxed; the house in Nantes sold. It seemed impossible that it no longer existed.

"Look, look, look!" urged Pierre-André.

Blinking, Jaouen braced his hands on his son's shoulders and looked down at the book he was holding out to him. The book was so large that Pierre-André staggered with the effort of holding it open. André took the book from him, stooping to hold it at his level.

"Those look like flowers," André said.

"Natural history is part of the education of a gentleman," said the governess primly.

"Which I would know if I were one?"

The governess froze. "I would never presume—that is . . ."

André decided to put her out of her misery. "I studied natural philosophy too, as a boy," he said, directing his words to his son. He glanced up at the governess. "Including botany."

"I will be starting them on Latin as soon as an appropriate text arrives," said the governess quickly.

"Primarily, I ask that you keep them safe." Feeling that he had made his point, André put a hand on his daughter's shoulder. Gabrielle looked solemnly back at him, all big eyes and snub nose, like a puppy waiting to be petted. "I'll be up to see the rest of your books by and by," he promised.

Pierre-André pouted. He had heard "by and by" before. Gabrielle didn't say anything, but her face closed up, like clouds drawing together.

"Come along, children," said the governess. "Jeannette will get you out of your outdoor things and then you can have a story."

In a shot, Pierre-André was away, scrambling up the stairs. "Jeannette! Jeannette!"

"Gently!" the governess called after him, and, for a wonder, Pierre-André actually checked his vociferous progress. For about two seconds.

Gabrielle looked to her new governess. Without a word, the governess took a book off the pile in her arms and handed it to her. Quietly, Gabrielle followed her brother up the stairs.

"Sir," the governess said, and dipped a curtsy as she turned to go.

The obeisance didn't suit her. The pretence of humility sat uncomfortably with her, like a garland of flowers draped across steel. There was something akin to armor about the stern gray of her dress. It fit snugly against her back, emphasizing the resolute line of her spine.

It bothered him that she felt the need to curtsy. It needled him deep in his Republican entrails.

"If you would, Mademoiselle—" What was her name again? Worse and worse that she was a member of his household and he couldn't even remember her name, just her position, as though she were a piece of furniture, something fungible, designed for his service.

It had been something to do with gray. Gray like her dress and the confining stone of the Abbaye. *Gris*. Yes, Griscogne, that was it.

"Mademoiselle Griscogne?"

The governess paused on the second step. She turned back to him, her face carefully expressionless. André wondered what she was really thinking. Nothing complimentary, he suspected.

"Yes, sir?"

"Tell Jeannette to send down a coffee and a headache powder to my study. I know she has them," he said.

"I shall do my best to extract them from her, sir," Laura said.

The faint outlines of a smile altered the tired lines of her employer's face. "Without thumbscrews, if you please," he said, and turned to go.

Laura paused, one hand on the banister. She thought that was a joke. She hoped that was a joke. With one who worked for Fouché, one couldn't be quite sure. Thumbscrews might be a requisite part of the job description.

For a moment, there, she had thought he intended to use them on her.

That had either gone very well, or very badly. She wasn't quite sure, but she did know she could use a headache powder of her own. Her ears were ringing, either from the prolonged exposure to cold or to Jaouen; either one would have the same effect. She seemed to have forgotten to breathe for the duration of most of that interview.

But he hadn't sacked her. Whatever else had happened, he hadn't sacked her.

This was, however, shaping up to be the oddest relationship she had ever had with an employer, and that included the viscountess who believed she was the reincarnation of Cleopatra. Laura's employer had spent most of her time draped across a sphinx in the salon trailing diaphanous draperies, but she had left Laura to do what she would with the children, who were named, appropriately enough, Mark and Anthony.

Laura watched discreetly as Jaouen walked briskly through a door at the far end of the hall. Even as visibly tired as he was, his movements vibrated with purpose. His study must lie that way, and in it whatever papers he had brought back from the Abbaye. By tomorrow, those precious papers would already be back at the Prefecture, out of her reach. She needed those papers and she needed them now, before Jaouen took them away with him again.

Jaouen had just given her the perfect excuse.

Laura paused on the threshold of the schoolroom as the germ of an idea began to form.

Jeannette, misinterpreting Laura's hesitation, jerked her head to the left, to a door all but concealed in the paneling. "I put your bag in there."

"Thank you," said Laura, and went where the nursery maid had indicated.

It must have been a dressing room in a more affluent time, back before the two large chambers next to it had been requisitioned as nursery room and schoolroom respectively. A fanciful, if faded, scene of elaborate birdcages, brightly colored birds, and lush foliage covered the walls, attesting to the taste of the last Comtesse de Bac. The dressing table was still in place, its ornate, gilt-framed mirror propped over a table topped in delicately veined marble, as was a grand armoire with curving ornaments on top, but a narrow bed had been shoved into one corner of the room, made up with sheets, a blanket, and one very flat pillow.

Laura stood in front of her new bed in her new room and pondered her options. The idea was risky, but it might just work.

Opening the armoire, Laura reached for her carpetbag.

Yes, there it was, among a jumble of similar remedies: a small twist of white powder. It was always best to keep dangerous items out in the open, among similar objects, or at least so the Pink Carnation said. The sleeping draught had been designed to look like an innocent packet of headache powder, just as the powerful emetics next to it had been disguised as bottles of stomach tonic.

Dosing Jaouen with an emetic that would have him clutching his stomach and writhing would certainly part him from his papers, but just might cause some suspicion. Maiming one's employer was generally not a wise way to go, especially when one's employer had daily access to sophisticated instruments of torture. But there was nothing at all out of the ordinary about an already exhausted man succumbing to sleep within a reasonable interval after taking a headache powder. The powder, her tutors in Sussex had told her, generally took about half an hour to take effect. One packet should put a man to sleep for at least a few hours.

Laura hoped she wouldn't need that long.

With hands that were surprisingly steady, Laura tucked the packet away into her left sleeve. The fabric pressed it snugly against her wrist. There were benefits to unfashionable attire.

In the brightly lit schoolroom, Pierre-André was occupied building a castle out of blocks under the supervision of Jeannette, who was furiously knitting away.

"Pardon me," said Laura. "Do you have any headache powders?"

Jeannette's needles clacked together with manic speed. "One day with them and you're already calling for headache powders?" Her tone clearly expressed what she thought of effete Paris governesses who couldn't even handle two darling angel children for one day without taking to their beds.

"Not for me," said Laura. "For Monsieur Jaouen."

She almost added "your employer," but held her tongue. She needed Jeannette right now, even if Jeannette didn't know it, and it would be easier not to antagonize her.

Clack, clack, clack went the needles. Jeannette gave her a narrow-eyed look. "And why would you be bringing headache powders to the master?"

"Because," said Laura, "he appeared to have a headache."

This irrefutable logic was wasted on Jeannette. Adding one and one, Jeannette arrived at forty-two. Stabbing at the wool, she said warningly, "If you're thinking of wriggling your way into the master's affections . . ."

Laura laughed at the sheer absurdity of it. "Can you imagine me as the wriggling kind?" If seduction were what the mission called for, she would still be back in London, listening to talentless adolescents plunking out Italian airs on the pianoforte.

She conjured up Jaouen's unshaven, hard-featured face, his thoughts and feelings guarded by more than just a pair of glasses. One might as well attempt to seduce a block of granite. Even if she were the seducing kind, which she most decidedly was not.

"I assure you, I do not, er, wriggle."

"Where are you from?" demanded the nurse. Laura recognized the abrupt question for what it was, a grudging olive branch and, in its own way, an apology.

"I was raised mostly in Paris." Both policy and politeness demanded that she answer, but Laura could feel the paper with the drug scratching against her wrist, urging haste.

"But what about your people?" Jeannette prodded.

Laura twitched her sleeve down farther over her wrist. "My father was from the Auvergne."

Exactly what he had been was another story entirely. He liked to claim that he was the illegitimate offspring of a noble family of that region, but Laura suspected that was nothing but a fairy story, part of the legend he had built around himself until he himself believed it. From what Laura had managed to glean, her father was, in fact, the unromantic offspring of legally wed petit bourgeois with a small legal practice somewhere in the Auvergne.

"Southerners." The nurse's Breton accent thickened as she said it with the Northerner's contempt for those lazy, immoral souls down south.

Laura couldn't resist needling her just a bit. "My mother was Italian."

Her mother really had been the illegitimate offspring of a noble family, the daughter of a Venetian aristocrat and a professional courtesan. She had been everything Laura's father had wanted to be.

"That accounts for your looks, then."

Laura didn't bother to explain that her mother had been Northern Italian, fair-skinned and blue-eyed. Her dark looks were entirely the legacy of her French father. "Or lack of them?"

There was nothing like a bit of self-deprecation to soften up a crusty old servant. "Now, now," said Jeannette, her voice and joints cracking as she laid aside her knitting and heaved herself up by the arms of the chair. "I didn't say that. I'll get you your headache powder. It's a kind thought," she added grudgingly.

"The children will be happier if their father is happier," Laura said piously. No need to tell her that Jaouen had requested it.

"Paris is no place to be happy," said Jeannette darkly, motioning Laura to follow her as she creaked her way across the nursery. "He's not been happy since he came to Paris, and the children can sense it, poor lambs. He would have done better to stay with them at home and not come gadding about these fancy foreign places."

Hiring fancy governesses. "How long has he been in Paris now?"

Jeannette clicked her tongue against the back of her teeth. "On to four years now. Or was it five? Miss Julie died in 'ninety-nine, and he didn't stay long after."

From the choice of address, Laura assumed it was a fairly safe guess that Jeannette had been with Mme. Jaouen before her marriage—most likely Mme. Jaouen's own childhood nurse. The story made a compelling picture: the grieving widower fleeing the gravesite, traveling halfway across the country rather than be faced with the daily reminder of his loss.

Torturing Royalists probably did make for an excellent diversion from grief, Laura told herself caustically. She had no special sympathy for the old regime, but she did have rather an objection to the breaking and grinding of limbs.

Laura said what she was expected to say. "He must have loved her very much."

"Everyone loved Miss Julie," said Miss Julie's old nurse. "Here's your headache powder."

"Thank you." Laura took the small packet of white powder in a steady hand. She could feel the other packet, the hidden one, pressing against her left wrist. "I'll take it down to Monsieur Jaouen right away."

"You'll want to give it to him with coffee," Jeannette called after her. "He likes his coffee."

"Thank you," said Laura again, and, with a purposeful tread, went in search of the kitchens to fix some coffee.

Chapter 6

Laura balanced her tray on one hip as she knocked on the door of André Jaouen's study.

"Yes?" called an impatient voice from beyond the panel.

Not exactly "Come in," but Laura chose to take it as such. Grappling for the door handle, she managed to turn it without losing her perilous grip on her tray. The door lurched open four inches as the crockery clattered.

The study was as sparsely furnished as the rest of the house, boasting only a desk and a cheap set of bookshelves, crammed with a disorderly collection of volumes of varying height and girth, all with cracked spines and blurred bindings that testified to their having been read again and again. Whatever expensive art had once decked the walls was long gone. The only decorations in the room were a crayon drawing of two children and a framed broadside of *The Declaration of the Rights of Man*, browning and cracked beneath its protective glass.

Laura could hear the scratch of Jaouen's pen as she pushed her way into the room. He was writing busily, an untidy sheaf of papers fanned out to one side as he wrote industriously on another, his short-cropped head bowed. He had a cowlick in the back, like Pierre-André's.

He glanced up as she entered, pen poised. "What is it?"

"I brought your headache powder." She would have put a flower on the tray too, if she could have found one, but that might have been a bit much. She didn't want to do it too brown. "Jeannette did have it."

There was a discreet rattle of china as Laura set the tray with its cup, coffeepot, and twist of white powder down on the side of the desk, a discrete distance from the sheaf of papers fanned out in front of Jaouen. Lifting the coffeepot, she began to pour into the single cup.

Jaouen eyed the small twist of white powder. "Knowing Jeannette, I can only hope she didn't send me an emetic instead."

Laura only just managed to keep the coffee from spilling.

"Aren't those generally liquid?" she said, as if it were a matter of the most abstract interest. "It would be hard to disguise in a twist of paper."

She set the pot down again on the tray, handle and spout perfectly aligned. She made good coffee. It smelled lovely, thick and rich.

She could see Jaouen breathing in the steam with appreciation. "You would be surprised at what people can do."

"Not after years of small children," Laura told him.

In an unconscious gesture, Jaouen lifted his glasses to rub his hand across his eyes. One earpiece was slightly crooked.

To see Jaouen with his eyeglasses off was a bit like catching Hercules without his club, or Samson without his hair. His cheeks, speckled with a reddish growth of beard, seemed to have sunken into themselves, throwing into prominence the strong lines of nose and cheekbones.

"You need rest," Laura said without thinking, as though he were one of her charges.

Jaouen's lips curled. "I would never have thought of that myself."

Apparently, tired men weren't so very different from tired ten-year-olds. They all got cranky.

"Cream?" she asked, reaching for the dainty cream jug, the handle shaped like the wings of a bird.

"Yes. And three spoonfuls of sugar." Catching the look Laura gave him, he laughed a rough laugh that wasn't much of a laugh at all. "My wife always mocked me for it. She preferred to take it black."

His wife. The divine Miss Julie. Without a word, Laura stirred the requested sugar into the cup. She made sure they were generous spoonfuls. Among other things, the taste would mask any oddity in the powder.

She could feel Jaouen's eyes following her movements as she measured each well-rounded spoon of sugar into the cup.

Abruptly, he said, "I owe you an apology for snapping at you like that. It was uncalled for. I should have told you what my expectations were."

Laura took her time stirring the sugar, around and around, the cream making milky swirls on the dark surface of the coffee. "It is within sir's prerogative."

She could hear the creak as Jaouen shifted in his chair. "Just because one has a prerogative doesn't mean one should abuse it. We fought a revolution over that."

Watching him, his angular face shadowed with sleeplessness, Laura came to a decision. He was trying to deal fairly with her; she could at least make the pretense of dealing fairly with him.

As she set the coffee down before him, she said, "You were not without cause. Someone did stop us on the way back. He said he worked with you."

Jaouen's hand stilled on the handle of the coffee cup. "Did he give you his name?"

Laura held out the white twist of sleeping powder to him, feeling like Lady Macbeth about to murder sleep. Nonsense, of course. She wasn't baring his breast to the blade, just giving him a few hours of unencumbered slumber.

But in that sleep, who knew what dreams might come?

Oh, for heaven's sake. Now she was mixing her Shakespeare. He wasn't banded in a nutshell, and she wasn't king of infinite space. Enough was enough already.

Laura surrendered the sleeping powder to her employer. "He said his name was Delaroche. Gaston Delaroche."

Jaouen cursed so vigorously that Laura blinked at him in surprise. Heavens. Was that what they were doing in Nantes these days?

Jaouen grimaced. "Forgive me," he said. Ripping open the paper, he shook the white powder into his coffee. "I work all day in conditions that—let us say that they do not encourage delicacy."

Laura watched the white powder dissolving into the coffee. "There is no need for delicacy. I may spend my days in the schoolroom, but I am no schoolgirl."

"No. I can see that." Jaouen's attention fixed on Laura with a suddenness and intensity that felt like a stab to the stomach with Miss Gwen's parasol.

So that was the trick of it, thought Laura dizzily. A totality of concentration, fixed on one object at any given time. Whatever task André Jaouen had at hand, he gave it his entire and unbroken concentration. To be on the receiving end of that was, to say the least, jarring.

He shrugged, breaking the connection. "Even so. What did Delaroche say to you?"

Laura scrambled to recall herself. "He greeted the children by name."

Jaouen gave another of those quick, keen looks, like the flash of a bird's wing on a summer day. "He recognized them?"

Laura frowned, remembering. "He recognized Gabrielle. He called to her by name first."

Jaouen cursed again, but softly this time.

Laura held up a hand. "You needn't bother apologizing. Monsieur Delaroche said he was a colleague of yours. He offered us a ride in his carriage."

Jaouen pierced her with his gaze. "Which you did not accept."

"I did not know if you wished to encourage the association."

There had been something off about the man, something that made the hairs on the back of her neck prickle. She didn't mention that bit. Prickling hairs were hardly a guide for conduct. Next she would be consulting the entrails of birds, like the Ancient Romans.

Jaouen let out a quick, sharp exhalation. "Well-done." Seeming to realize that some explanation was called for, he said briefly, "I prefer not to mix my professional obligations with my familial ones."

That was his explanation? Laura had heard better from four-year-olds with jam still smeared across their faces and bits of broken tart in their laps.

Jaouen tapped his finger against the side of the coffee cup.

Drink, thought Laura. Drink, already.

He didn't.

"You did well to tell me of this."

"Is there anyone else I should know to avoid?" Laura asked quietly. "Or from whom the children should be kept?"

Jaouen grimaced. "Everyone?"

Laura suspected he wasn't entirely joking. "Shall I bring you anything else? Bread, cheese?" More sleeping powder? "Your coffee must be getting cold. I can bring you a fresh pot."

He didn't take the hint. The cup sat untouched, steam curling harmlessly into the air, cooling by the moment, the precious powder wasted, of use only to the bright-winged cockatoo drowned at the bottom of the cup. Laura hoped it, at least, was enjoying a good slumber.

"No need." Jaouen sketched a quick, impatient gesture. "I didn't hire you to play housemaid."

"Someone has to."

Jaouen rocked back in his chair. "Are you saying my staff is inadequate?"

"Woefully."

"Jeannette keeps the nursery clean and comfortable," he said, as though that were all that mattered.

"What about the rest of the house? What about you?"

Jaouen lifted both brows. "We good servants of the Revolution have no need for the baser creature comforts."

Laura drew a finger along the edge of the desk, collecting a little pile of dust as she went. "Brutus may have been a brave man, but dust still made him sneeze."

"Are you offering to ply the duster?"

"I'm offering to interview the maids."

"Unnecessary," said Jaouen. "I only entertain guests once a fortnight, and I have a hired staff who come specially. As for the rest"—with one precise flick of the finger, he made short work of Laura's dust pile—"if to dust we must go, I can scarcely object to a bit of it on my desk."

"One might as well say that since we are bound for the grave, we ought to take our rest in a coffin."

"Sophistry, Mademoiselle Griscogne." But she sensed that he was enjoying himself. He was sitting up straighter in his chair, a light in his eyes despite the purple bags beneath them. "Is that what you intend to teach my children?"

"Rhetoric, Monsieur Jaouen," Laura corrected. "And I shall, as soon as I have the proper texts at my disposal."

"Heaven help us." His hand hovered for a moment over the

coffee cup and went instead to the papers, which he shuffled in a way that signified the interview was over.

Why wouldn't he drink?

"Will there be anything else?" Laura asked in desperation. How could she time the action of the drug if she didn't see him imbibe it?

He looked up, abstractedly, a piece of paper half-lifted. Laura tried to read sideways, but all she could make out were the words "question," "asked," and something that looked a bit like "squirrel," but couldn't be unless the new administration was now after nuts.

"Tell the children I wish them a good night." He thought for a moment and came up with, "Wish them sweet dreams."

There was no way she could eke this out further. "Yes, sir." She curtsied.

"Mademoiselle?" Jaouen's voice rose behind her. "There is one last thing."

"Sir?"

"Don't curtsy," he said. "It doesn't suit you."

And he turned back to his papers.

Laura would have curtsied to cover her confusion, but apparently it didn't suit her. She lurched for the doorway, only to come up hard against something that wasn't doorlike at all, although it did have the effect of arresting her progress and knocking the breath out of her. Laura found herself blinking into an expanse of blue wool, adorned with very hard and very shiny silver buttons.

"Oh, I say!" exclaimed a male voice that was obviously not Jean the gatekeeper's, any more than that coat could belong to Jean the gatekeeper. It was a plummy, well-educated male voice. A large pair of hands reached out to catch her by the hips, although whether to steady her or assess her contours was unclear. Her contours must have passed muster, because the hands lingered. He gave a good squeeze. "I am sorry. Didn't expect to see anyone coming out of there."

The hands were well manicured, with smooth nails and a smattering of fair hair along the backs. They were attached to a large young man in a regimental uniform, light brown hair brushed to a sheen above a pair of ruddy cheeks in a fair-skinned face.

"No harm done," said Laura crisply, twisting away.

"I should hate to be the cause of a lady's distress." The young man smiled roguishly down at her in a way that suggested he was more accustomed to causing distress than relieving it.

"The *governess*," stressed Laura, "is unharmed and thanks you for your kind attentions."

"Ah." Instead of being deterred, the young man propped an arm up on the wall above her head. "So you're the new governess. I must say, you're a sight better looking than Jeannette."

Hard to feel flattered when that was the comparison. "Thank you. Sir."

"Philippe?"

Behind them, the chair scraped against the wooden floor. Jaouen stood with one hand braced on the desk, frowning at the new arrival. The young man's polished appearance served only to emphasize Jaouen's rumpled clothes and unshaven cheeks. The twin lines in his forehead grew deeper as he looked at his guest.

He did not seem pleased to see him.

"Hullo, Cousin André!" said the young man boisterously. "Aren't you glad to see me?"

If he couldn't tell the answer to that just from looking at Jaouen, there was no helping him.

Of course, thought Laura. This was the cousin Jaouen had mentioned during her abortive interview. She began to understand why Jaouen had warned her about him. The young man was certainly well favored, and carried with him an air of aristocratic insouciance that suggested that he was used to receiving whatever he desired—a category that included the female staff. This was one who would always choose ease over effort, convenience over conquest. It was hard to imagine anyone less like Jaouen. This man's uniform looked like it was more for parade than service and his hair was as buffed as his buttons.

"I thought you were rejoining your regiment," said Jaouen, and there was a warning note in his voice that even Laura couldn't miss.

"I didn't want to miss all the fun in Paris," said the young man cheerfully. "It's much more exciting here."

Jaouen was not amused. "It won't be so exciting when you're court-martialed for desertion. Did you think of that? How would your poor mother feel?"

"Gloomy, gloomy, Cousin André." The young man sauntered over to the desk. There were two bright red spots in his cheeks that might have been from the wind or wine or a bit of both. "I have more faith in my stars than that."

"The stars have been known to shine on others before this. There is no need to actively encourage them to do so."

"Not my stars." Seizing Jaouen's coffee cup, he hoisted it in an exuberant toast. "How go the plans for the fête?" Dark drops of drugged coffee sloshed over the sides and onto Jaouen's papers. Any moment now, and the desk would be snoring.

No, Laura thought. No, no, no.

Reaching up, Jaouen snagged the cup, placing it firmly back on its saucer. "The fête may need to be postponed."

"Postponed!" Philippe shot up with all the indignation of a young child denied a treat.

Jaouen pressed his eyes tightly closed for a moment before turning to Laura. "You may go, Mademoiselle Griscogne. I wouldn't want to keep you from the children."

"Oh, I say!" intervened the young man, flapping a hand. With a nod at the coffeepot, he said winningly, "Do you think we might . . ."

"No," said Jaouen.

"Shall I bring another cup?" asked Laura, beyond hope of salvaging the situation. When the stars chose to frown, they frowned indeed. Who knew that putting one tired man to sleep would be so much bother? Now she had two of them in the study, drugged coffee all over the desk, and none of it in Jaouen.

"Yes," said the young man, just as Jaouen said, "No."

"Then I shall return to the children." Laura started to curtsy, remembered herself, and nodded instead. "Good night, sir."

"How about a brandy, then?" Laura heard Jaouen's cousin say behind her.

"Later," said Jaouen. "You'd best come with me. I have something to show you."

A door closed, and over the tread of male feet, Laura heard Jaouen saying quietly, "Didn't you get the news? Both Tante Hélène and Cousin Héloïse are indisposed."

"Merde!" Philippe's voice carried, echoing along the marble. "The same complaint?"

"I don't think they will be receiving again for a very long time."

"Well, that won't do—," she could hear Philippe saying, and then another door closed and the sound was blotted out.

Laura paused, tucking herself into the corner between the door and the wall in one of the endless strings of reception rooms that marched along the ground floor. She listened, but she couldn't hear them anymore. They must have moved sufficiently far away towards the other side of the house.

Leaving Jaouen's study, with all his papers in it, untenanted.

Perhaps the stars weren't so very unfavorable after all. Laura cautiously made her way back along the way she had come, taking care not to creep. Only suspect persons crept; persons with nothing on their consciences walked normally. She had lost a handkerchief, or a button. She had forgot to ask whether the children liked warm milk. She had come to collect the coffee tray, to make him a fresh pot, since this one would have gone cold.

Oh yes, she liked that one. Very good, very eager, very plausible. That was she, a regular Good Samaritan. Back in her prior situations, she would never have stooped to so menial a chore. She had jealously guarded her prerogatives in the cutthroat world of the household hierarchy.

Like an echo, she could hear Jaouen's words of half an hour before. *Just because one has a prerogative doesn't mean one should abuse it.* A curious sentiment from an employer to an employee. It certainly wasn't one to which any of her previous employers had subscribed.

The study door had been closed, but not latched. At times like this, the understaffing of the Hôtel de Bac was a decided advantage. Jeannette was with the children, Jean in his cubbyhole by the gate. There was no one to see her as she turned the latch on the study door. The door squeaked as she pressed it forward, but there was no one to hear it.

Laura hoped that whatever it was that Jaouen had to show his cousin took a very long time indeed.

The study was just as it had been before, the crowded bookshelves, the almost empty walls, the papers scattered along the desk. Without Jaouen in it, it felt, perversely, smaller, as though his presence had lent the little room depth and dimension. Strange what force some personalities had, to shape the world around them. Her own was as a nullity, scarcely creating an eddy in the landscapes through which she passed.

That was, she reminded herself, a good thing, especially in situations such as these.

Tucking her skirts close to her legs to keep them from rustling, she slipped around to the far side of the desk, to the document Jaouen had been writing when she interrupted him. It appeared to be a bulletin of some sort, a report of the latest interrogation.

Laura quickly scanned Jaouen's summary. His writing was neat, precise, just what she would have expected from him, with no wasted flourishes or curlicues: At the Abbaye the night before, he had interrogated a Royalist agent named Querelle. Querelle confessed to a plot to kidnap the First Consul, replacing him with a member of the royal family who would claim the throne in the name of Louis XVIII. All fairly standard stuff, so far. This was to be accomplished by the work of five generals, four of whom he had named under interrogation. Arch-agitator Georges Cadoudal was known even now to be in Paris. Jaouen recommended an immediate watch be set for him. He would be known by his extreme girth and Royalist sentiments.

How did one identify Royalist sentiments? Were they emblazoned on one's hat like a Revolutionary cockade?

The plot struck Laura as distinctly far-fetched. Kidnapping the First Consul? Expecting five generals to all work together instead of jockeying for power and selling one another out? It was a plot so naïve only a man could have come up with it.

There was no mention of lost princes.

What had the Pink Carnation been talking about in the bookshop? Laura spared a thought for the lost Dauphin. If (and it was a very large if) this Cadoudal's cell had somehow found and secured the lost Dauphin, if the member of the royal family they intended to produce was indeed the lost Louis XVII—if, if, if—this far-fetched plot might not be so very far-fetched after all. The people of Paris wouldn't rally for five bickering generals, but they just might for the son of Louis XVI. There was a romance already to the legend of the lost Dauphin, and hardheaded though they otherwise might be, the people of Paris loved a good romance.

But there was no reference to the Dauphin—or, for that matter, any prince at all—in Jaouen's report.

With a feeling of deep resignation, Laura turned to the larger sheaf of papers. It was written in a different hand, not Jaouen's, clumsy and sprawling, marred with blots and cross-outs and bits of dripped wax. It had to be at least fifty pages long, in a sort of hectic shorthand, where essential verbs appeared to be left out in the interest of speed.

Laura skimmed as quickly as she could over the first section, sweat prickling under her arms as she read, one ear trained on the door, alert for any sign of movement. The ink was cheap, the paper bad, and the coffee drops didn't help. It was the same as what she had seen already in Jaouen's report, except more disjointed and at greater length. Only the answers had been set down, not the questions—nor the means used to acquire them.

This Querelle insisted that the plan was merely to kidnap the First Consul until he agreed to abdicate voluntarily. Laura snorted. If he believed that, he was more naïve than she. If the First Consul didn't agree to abdicate voluntarily—

Laura turned the page and came up short. A good five pages of the report had been ruined, soaked through with ink, as though someone's elbow had jarred against an ink pot. It must have been a full ink pot; the paper had been utterly saturated, washing out most of the writing beneath, except for some fragments around the edges and bottom that had missed the deluge. It looked, curiously, as though the spilled ink were darker in color than the ink in which it had been written, although that might have had more to do with quantity. It had all long since dried.

Hmph. Jaouen was going to have to write up this part of the report from memory. Laura frowned, wondering how she was going to access it. She held the top sheet to the light, squinting at it, but it was no use; the spilled ink had obliterated everything in its path. All that was left were disjointed fragments—not even full words most of the time.

Laura turned the page. The stain was lighter farther on. The bottom page wasn't legible, but one could at least make out the vague shapes of what must have been words—an "and" here, or a "Consul" there, and sometimes what looked like part of "general" or "troops" (unless, of course, the prisoner had simply said "oops," but Laura rather doubted they would bother to take that down).

She was amusing herself with that concept when something caught her attention that wasn't amusing at all. It was the remains of a word, only four letters of it clear, the rest covered under the pervasive ink stain. "—ince."

The blotted word was "prince."

Chapter 7

*L*aura dreamed of lost princes and woke up with a headache.

Fortunately, she still had the headache powder Jeannette had given her for Jaouen the night before. Laura stirred it into her tea and set about teaching. If she was to make so elementary a mistake as bungling a simple administration of sleeping powder, she might at least make sure her teaching was satisfactory.

It was going to be an interesting challenge, communicating with the Pink Carnation when she wasn't allowed to leave the house.

That afternoon, as Jeannette reclaimed the children for feeding, bathing, and general clucking, Laura drafted a brief note to the bookseller. On reflection, she wrote, she had decided to delay the children's introduction to botany until they were further along in their general studies. She would be along on her half day the following Sunday to collect the Latin texts she had requested. His with the greatest expressions of respect and esteem, etcetera, Laure Griscogne.

She stuck the note just within the front cover and entrusted the whole to Jean to deliver. Monsieur Jaouen had said she could, after all. And if he were to open the note, there would be nothing at all he could find there to excite his suspicion. She only hoped the bookseller caught her double meaning. Or that the note didn't fall out along the way. Or that Jean didn't just drop the book on the floor of his gatehouse lair, put his feet up, and spit in her general direction.

There was no reply that night. Laura sat by the fire and read aloud to the children from Mme. Le Prince de Beaumont's fairy tales. Jeannette rocked back and forth and pretended not to listen while Laura read and brooded, the old, familiar phrases rolling off her tongue with very little relation to her brain. As Beauty wandered into the Beast's castle, Laura wondered whether the bookseller had missed her meaning. By the time the Beast's favorite flower was dying, Laura was quite sure that Jean had resorted to a drop and a spit. Jean, she had learned, used spitting the way other, more evolved, creatures used speech: to convey a whole range of emotion. And wouldn't it be just like him to hold on to the book just to thwart her?

Of course, he couldn't realize just how much it would thwart her. If he did, she would really be in trouble.

"Read us another!" exclaimed Pierre-André.

"Tomorrow," said Laura, and closed the book.

That might be it! She could send to the shop for more fairy tales. Or . . . she could wait and see what happened. Prudence over impatience, she counseled herself. Even a governess could only patronize a bookshop so much before people started getting suspicious. And by people, she meant the Ministry of Police. All she needed was to draw their attention to the bookshop on the Rue Serpente and bring the whole edifice crashing down upon all their heads.

On the second day, she taught lessons in the morning and set the children passages from Racine to memorize in the evening, Pierre-André's significantly shorter than Gabrielle's. Pierre-André lost his place and giggled. Gabrielle slunk off with her *Romance of the Forest.* Jeannette knit. When Jean appeared to deliver the evening's load of coal, it was all Laura could do not to jump up and shake him.

But she didn't.

By the third day, Laura was feeling distinctly twitchy. She had never imagined that it would be possible to feel marooned in the midst of one of the major cities of Europe—utterly cut off from everyone and everything but the play of light in the nursery grate, Pierre-André's giggles, Gabrielle's sulks, and the *click, click, click* of Jeannette's needles as she carried on with her everlasting knitting. One more *click*, and Laura wasn't going to be accountable for the consequences.

"Who wants to go exploring?" Laura asked impulsively, flinging down the slate she had been using to demonstrate the principles of long division.

"Papa said we weren't to leave the house," said Gabrielle primly.

Laura eyed Gabrielle appraisingly. They had come to what Laura could only consider an armed truce; Gabrielle was tolerating her until such time as someone had the sense to throw her out. There were no frogs in the bed (the youngest Marchmont child), no ink down her back while she marked up compositions (Harry Littleton), and no midnight apparitions by ghosts in bedsheets (Laura had particularly enjoyed that one, especially when the littlest ghost had taken a header into the fender). Gabrielle wielded good behavior like a weapon, performing her lessons punctiliously and with a minimum of personal communication. Infinitely preferable to the frogs.

"But have you been exploring within the house?" Laura demanded.

"A house is a house is a house," contributed Jeannette, spinning her woolly web like a spider who had hijacked a sheep.

"Not this sort of house." Laura lowered her voice thrillingly. "Who knows what might be in the other wings."

"Toys?" asked Pierre-André brightly.

"Perhaps," said Laura noncommittally, but she was watching Gabrielle. No reader of Mrs. Radcliffe's could resist that sort of possibility. Skeletons in closets, secret passageways, moldering manuscripts . . . "The house is very large and very old. There's no telling what we might find."

Gabrielle grudgingly dragged herself out of her chair. "If we have to . . ."

Ha! Laura had her. She didn't know if they would find secret passageways, or a large manuscript entitled *How to Thwart Royalist Plots* by André Jaouen, but goodness knew what else might be there. At least she would be doing something instead of waiting, waiting, waiting. If she was to be marooned on an island, at least she might make full use of all the resources it offered.

They passed through room after empty room until Laura was dizzy with it, although it was easy enough to navigate by keeping one eye on the courtyard through the window. There were three of them—the larger garden court in front, two smaller courtyards in back—all perfectly symmetrical. Any internal symmetry, though, had been marred by the improvements of successive generations. There were strange crannies where the shapes of rooms had been altered to create fashionable ovals or octagons, leaving odd, triangular spaces behind; there were doors into narrow, windowless hallways running along behind the formal rooms, the openings cunningly disguised within the paneling.

Pierre-André made tracks in the dust, shuffling to watch his footsteps blur. The children hunted for lost jewels in the depths of old armoires, and danced to watch their own reflections twirl in the tarnished mirrors of the ballroom.

When the Parisians looted, they looted well. The only furniture remaining were those pieces too large to be easily tossed out a window or chopped up into firewood. Even bits of the wood paneling had suffered the latter fate, leaving gashes in the walls and empty hinges where doors must once have hung. After corridor after corridor, room after room of dusty emptiness, they all came to an abrupt stop at finding a third-floor room crammed full with bundles and boxes. They had climbed and wandered so much that Laura wasn't quite sure where they were, other than that it was somewhere towards the back of the house, overlooking the service courtyard.

The boxes were wooden crates, the lids sitting askew where the nails had been prized out. There were canvases and framed pictures propped facedown against the wall, rolled rugs piled in corners, even a large, padded chair sitting in state all by itself among the boxes, as though waiting for someone to sit in it.

"But these are ours," said Gabrielle, hanging over the side of a box. "These are our things from home."

"Grandfather's globe!" exclaimed Pierre-André, spotting something sticking out of one of the other boxes, and went to go pull at it.

"Don't!" said Gabrielle fiercely. "You'll break it."

There was a brief scuffling match, resolved only by Laura lifting the globe out of the box for them and setting it on its stand. It wasn't a particularly grand specimen. The paint had begun to crack in places and some of the boundaries were out of date, but it was obviously well used and much loved. Pierre-André gave it a well-practiced spin, turning the hard-won products of war and dynastic alliance into little more than a multicolored blur.

The box next to Laura was filled with books—books of all shapes and sizes, with dog-eared pages and broken spines. She leaned over the box, turning them over in her hands, one after another. Plato rubbed shoulders with Rousseau, Aristophanes with Molière, and Seneca with *The Sorrows of Young Werther*. Weighty treatises on law lounged cover by cover with thin volumes of poetry: Petrarch,

Scève, Ronsard, du Bellay. There was Greek and Latin, German and Italian, and even a very small smattering of English titles, although those seemed the least thumbed of the lot. Ah, well, who really wanted to read Blackstone's commentaries on the laws of England?

Laura sorted busily through the box, setting aside those that might be useful in the schoolroom—yes to Racine, no to Blackstone, yes to Plato, no to Ronsard—when something made her pause. She stood with her hands clamped on either side of the box, staring down into it, at a small red book with faded gilt lettering on the cover. The sound of the children's voices receded into the background, replaced by other, louder voices, dead now for so many years.

Reaching into the box, Laura let her fingers close around the book, lifting it with care. The red morocco cover was worn now, eaten away at the edges by time and use, the pages spotted with brown.

Venus' Feast by Chiara di Veneti.

Then, under it, in smaller lettering, *Chansons d'Amor*.

Her mother had never believed in the subtle approach.

Laura could remember it fresh and new, just this same edition. She could picture the book in her mother's hands, her fingers unnaturally white against the red cover, rings glittering in the candlelight, bracelets jangling on her wrists. Above it all shone the great mass of her golden hair, never powdered, always with long curls tumbling around her shoulders as though the bands of any headdress ever made could never hope to contain the vibrancy of it.

She would stand there, Laura's mother, in all her shining wonder, the little volume of poetry small and insignificant. Then, just as the laughing, chattering crowd had begun to grow restless, to shift and whisper in their seats, she would let the covers fall open and begin to read.

Everything else would be forgotten—the jewels, the hair, the artful dishabille of her dress. Friends, lovers, former lovers, the lovers of former lovers, no matter how petty or vicious, how inebriated or exhausted, would all fall silent, enchanted into immobility by those words, those wonderful, rolling, searing words. It was better than music, better than dance, thought and form in perfect harmony, painting images in words, addressing all the old, visceral emotions in a powerful combination of lyric and rhyme.

There wasn't a person who could resist Laura's mother when she read. She was a force of nature, pure, elemental.

To see those poems confined to printed words on a page was to leach them of half their power. Laura remembered her surprise, at first learning how to read, to find how small the print looked, how meek and faded in comparison to the ringing, rolling tones of her mother's voice. How could something so large possibly be contained within something so small?

Laura slid a finger between the pages, letting the book fall open at random. But it was all wrong. Instead of black print on paper, bordered in the majesty of broad white margins, the pages were covered with doodles.

Someone had scribbled all over her mother's book.

It wasn't her book, Laura reminded herself. It was one of thousands, thousands and thousands. Her mother had scattered volumes across Europe like handkerchiefs, and one wouldn't feel all sentimental about a used handkerchief, would one? She had no business feeling sentimental at all. It was all a very long time ago and nothing to do with who and where she was now. Laura swallowed hard, pushing back against the childish sense of betrayal. It was just a book, just paper and ink and leather and someone's silly sketches along the margins.

Only, they weren't silly.

Laura flipped slowly through, her attention caught despite herself. They were little more than pencil sketches, most of them, but they contained such a sense of energy and movement that they seemed much more. There were children dancing, acrobats balancing on a wire, fantastical bouquets of flowers, old wives hanging out the wash, and one particularly detailed rendition of lovers trysting within a glade—although the lady wore a rather wry expression as she glanced away, a whole world of expression in one twist of the pencil. Each poem had been dramatized in some way, Laura's mother's words turned flesh in a miracle of ink and suggestion, doing with line what Laura's mother had done with language.

Curious, Laura flipped backwards, to the title page.

To Julie, it read, in bold black letters, just below Laura's mother's name. *Who sees no use in poetry. Shall I make you change your mind? André.*

There was a sketch beneath, a pretty girl perched on a low wall, laughing down at the man seated at her feet, who read aloud to her from a book that was subtly but unmistakably the one in Laura's hands. His face was tilted up, hers down, in a way that left the viewer in no doubt as to her answer to his question.

Laura slammed down the cover, feeling as though she had been caught spying. She could feel the ghosts all around her: Julie in her light summer muslin; her mother, all paste jewelry and riotous curls, declaiming to a rapt audience in that throaty voice to which just a hint of an Italian accent still clung; this younger M. Jaouen, this André, with hair that curled down around his neck, sprawled on the ground reading from a book held aloft in one hand.

Something brushed past her and Laura jumped, her heart in her throat.

It wasn't a ghost but Gabrielle, her face like a thundercloud. She snatched at the volume, tugging it out of Laura's hands. "What are you doing? That was my mother's."

My mother's too, Laura almost said, but didn't. Chiaretta with her sparkling jewels and undulating gestures was far away, too far to follow.

Relinquishing the book to Gabrielle, Laura said only, "Your mother was very talented."

Gabrielle hugged the book close to her chest. "I know." She glowered at Laura over the top of the book, half-defiant, half-defensive, as though daring Laura to say more.

"We'll have to start you on drawing lessons," said Laura mildly.

Gabrielle stubbornly shook her head, her hair snarling around her face. "I don't have the talent."

"Talent is no prerequisite to proficiency." She of all people should know that. Not every talent was hereditary, much as one's parents might wish it so. "You don't need genius to learn to draw a clear line, just a steady hand and an attentive eye."

She could see Gabrielle starting to digest that, still hostile, but thinking.

Laura followed up on her advantage. "If we only did those things for which we had a talent, most people would never do anything at all. Yes?" Pierre-André was tugging at the corner of her skirt.

But what a Pierre-André! She was never going to hear the end of this from Jeannette. The little boy's disordered curls stuck up like devil's horns; his previously clean smock was liberally striped with dirt; and there were twin streaks of grime across his cheeks. What was more, he was half-smothered within an immense garment that dragged down from his tiny shoulders, so large that the sleeves trailed straight down to the ground. Laura, who had been forced to memorize the various uniforms of the French forces as part of her training in Sussex, recognized it as the coat of a lieutenant in the Consular Guard. On Pierre-André, the waist fell nearly to his feet and the tails fanned out behind like a train.

"Look at me! Look at me!" Pierre-André tried to twirl and got tangled up in his own dangling sleeves. The long tails of the coat trailed behind him, picking up a decorative trim of dust as they swished across the floor.

Laura lunged to catch him before he could go over.

"There are more!" he exclaimed in glee. "We can play sol-diers!"

"Not in here, you don't."

Laura looked up to see Jean standing in the doorway, looking like a hobgoblin in a fairy tale.

"The children aren't supposed to be in here." It was the longest sentence Laura had ever heard Jean say. "No one is supposed to be in here."

Two sentences! They were truly honored.

"Then someone should lock the door, shouldn't they?" said Laura tartly.

"An excellent suggestion, Mademoiselle Griscogne," said some-one from behind Jean, and another shadow fell across the crowded floor.

"Papa!" exclaimed Pierre-André, tripping over his tails in his excitement. "Look! I'm a soldier!"

"That will teach Cousin Philippe to leave his spare uniform here," murmured Jaouen. For Pierre-André's benefit, he said, "Very dashing, but why don't you take it off now. We'll have to find one for you closer to your size."

"Really?" Pierre-André began to shrug out of the jacket, get-ting hopelessly tangled in the too-long sleeves. "Can I have one? Can I? Can I?"

Laura would have gone to help him, but Jaouen beckoned to her. "If you will, Mademoiselle Griscogne."

She wondered what he would do if she said she wouldn't. Why ask if one would, when there was no won't? She would have pre-ferred an outright command, such as, "Come here. Now." Sit. Roll over. Play dead.

Laura followed Jaouen to the window embrasure. So much for their rapport of the previous night. She wondered if he would like to reconsider his policy on curtsying.

When he spoke, though, his voice was mild enough. "Why aren't the children in the nursery?"

The most dangerous animals weren't the ones who barked and bayed. They were the ones who took their time to bite and sank their teeth the most deeply. The cunning ones. The quiet ones.

The sun slanted through the window with all the desperate brightness of a winter sunset. Laura put up a hand to shield her eyes from the orange glare. "They finished their lessons for the day, so I took them exploring as a treat."

"I'd rather you hadn't."

Laura looked around, trying to figure out what was so objectionable. It was amazing how much havoc two children could wreak on a pile of boxes in a scant few minutes. Books littered the floor; a pile of canvases that had rested against the wall had toppled over; and the globe, detached from its stand, had rolled into a corner of the room. "If it's the mess . . ."

"It isn't the mess that concerns me." Jaouen's eyes were on Pierre-André, still figuring out how to get his arms out of the too-large jacket. He looked back at Laura. "It is unsettling for the children to be around their mother's things."

Pierre-André didn't look particularly unsettled to her. In fact, he seemed to be enjoying himself immensely. Gabrielle, on the other hand, still maintained her death grip on her mother's volume of poetry as she watched her father and the governess with a decidedly inimical expression.

Jaouen might have a point there, but Laura wasn't willing to acknowledge it. She went on the attack instead. "More unsettling for them to have that death's head following them around." She jerked her head in the direction of Jean. "He frightens them."

"He wouldn't, if they stayed in the nursery," said Jaouen pointedly.

What was the point of Laura having gained access to the household if she was confined to the schoolroom? At the end of the week, she would be able to provide the Pink Carnation with a stirring account of Gabrielle's Latin translations and Pierre-André's progress in sums. If she was ever allowed out of the house to deliver it.

"Forgive me, sir," Laura said with heavy sarcasm. "When you instructed me to keep the children indoors, I mistakenly believed that your directive referred to all the walls of the building, not merely those that confined the nursery. Shall I keep them in the schoolroom alone, or might their parole extend to the night nursery as well?"

Jaouen braced a hand against the windowsill, fixing her with that disconcertingly blue stare. Sunlight winked off the lenses of his glasses, dazzling Laura with sparks of silver and gold. "Have your other employers allowed you to speak to them like this?"

Laura took a gamble. "No," she said bluntly.

For an endless moment, Jaouen was silent. Resting his head against the window embrasure, he said, with amused resignation, "I suppose I am meant to be flattered that you reserve your special treatment for me?"

Laura seized her advantage. "You cannot expect me to confine the children to two rooms, Monsieur. There are animals who have wider cages."

Jaouen brightened with the zeal of the born debater. "We are each of us in a cage, Mademoiselle. Some more tangible than others."

" 'Man is born free, but everywhere is in chains,' " quoted Laura.

A spark of recognition lit in Jaouen's eyes at the familiar quotation from Rousseau. He raised a brow. "I wasn't suggesting you manacle them to the nursery rafters."

"How could I? The nursery doesn't have rafters."

"Surely someone so ingenious as you can find a way around such a minor obstacle."

"Not," said Laura demurely, "without securing prior permission from my employer. One would never want to overstep one's bounds."

She surprised him into laughter. He looked younger when he laughed. It filled out his cheeks and hid the dark circles beneath his eyes. For a moment, she could see him sprawled on the grass, a poetry book in hand.

"A point to you," he said. "Well played."

"What do I get if I win the match?"

"To keep your position."

Ouch. Laura felt as though she had been dealt a summary slap across the face. Foul, she wanted to cry. But she couldn't. He was, as he had just reminded her, her employer. Quite different from any employer she had ever had before, but still her employer.

Before she could muster her scattered wits to make an appropriate—and tactful—response, Jaouen made a noise of irritation and reached into his jacket. "I nearly forgot. This came for you."

As Laura looked at him in confusion, he held out a folded note, with her name written on the back of it. There was no wax on it; it must have been delivered unsealed.

Taking it from him, Laura began unfolding it, saying, "I can't imagine who would— Oh."

"Oh?" said Jaouen.

Laura displayed the letter to him. "I sent a query to a bookseller about a text I wanted for Gabrielle and Pierre-André. He doesn't have it, but he knows someone else who might."

She had no doubt Jaouen had already read the note. It was dated a good two days before. She sent a sideways glance at Jean, who was looking about as smug as a hobgoblin could look, which, considering that hobgoblins were seldom known for their modest and retiring natures, was very smug indeed. Jean must have received the note on her behalf and held on to it until he had the opportunity to show it to his employer.

No matter. There was nothing in it that even the most suspicious Ministry of Police official couldn't be allowed to see. The bookseller was desolated to inform her that he was unable to provide her the Latin fables she had requested, but he believed that a fellow bookseller on the Rue Saint-Honoré might have the item she desired. There had been two copies the last time he had inquired. He suggested she inquire after them at her earliest convenience.

Her earliest convenience was her half day, Sunday. As for the rest . . . Two copies. Two o'clock? That seemed the likeliest explanation. She had a rendezvous with an agent of the Pink Carnation next Sunday at two o'clock in the bookshop on the Rue Saint-Honoré.

Jaouen looked thoughtfully out over the piles of boxes in the center of the room. "You might find what you need among Père Beniet's books."

"Père Beniet?"

"The children's grandfather. My wife's father."

It was a strange way of phrasing it, but that wasn't what caught Laura's attention. *Beniet.* The name nagged at her memory. It might have been from the Pink Carnation's files on Jaouen. His wife's family's name would have been in there somewhere, along with all of the other pertinent details, especially since it was through his wife's family that he was connected to Fouché. But that wasn't it at all. Beniet. Julie Beniet. She could hear someone saying it, with the English inflection, not the French. Candlelight glinting off claret, crystal glasses above a polished table. She had been brought in as an extra to round off a table, seated all the way at the end by the vicar's brother-in-law. But at the top of the table, the talk was all of Julie Beniet.

Laura looked wide-eyed at Jaouen. "Your wife was Julie Beniet?"

The drawings in the poetry book, the canvases piled by the wall, that charcoal drawing of Pierre-André and Gabrielle in

Jaouen's study . . . She knew it was rude to stare, but she couldn't help it. André Jaouen and Julie Beniet! It was like finding that Fouché had been married to Élisabeth Vigée-Lebrun, or Leonardo da Vinci to Lucrezia Borgia.

"The very one." There was a tightness to his voice that ought to have signaled a warning, if Laura had been listening for it.

"I saw an exhibition of her paintings." Laura almost added, "in London," but caught herself in time. "They were . . ."

"Awe-inspiring? Groundbreaking? Life-changing?"

"All of that."

She might not have any artistic gifts herself, but she could appreciate them when she saw them. No wonder the sketches in the margins of her mother's poetry had seemed to leap and dance. Julie Beniet. She had been invited to paint the Royal Family and refused. Her work had caused a brief sensation in London, both for her painting and her politics.

It was said that Élisabeth Vigée-Lebrun had gone into a sulk that lasted for months.

"What—," Laura began, and then snapped her mouth closed. There were some questions one didn't ask, and especially not of one's employer.

"What happened to her? Not that." Jaouen obviously hadn't missed her brief, betraying glance at Pierre-André. In a clipped voice, he said, "It was a fever."

Laura had thought she was immune to embarrassment, but it had her in its grips now.

"I am sorry," she said. It sounded painfully inadequate.

Jaouen apparently felt the same way. He pushed away from the window. "So am I. Do you have any more personal questions you wish to ask?"

Laura's spine stiffened. "No."

"Good. The children have my permission to explore the house. But take care where you go."

Without another word, he turned and walked away, his boots clicking against the dusty floor.

"Papa!" Pierre-André scrambled after him, tripping over the long coattails of the uniform jacket.

Gabrielle, her arms wrapped around the book of poetry, gave Laura a dirty look.

So much for winning the love and trust of her charges and building a rapport with her employer.

Blast.

Proper governesses didn't curse, but Laura had been raised in a different school.

Blast, blast, blast.

Chapter 8

*B*last. In multiples.

So much for a romantic weekend in Paris with my boyfriend.

At least the rain had let up. It hadn't stopped entirely, but it was more of a mist than a drizzle. I furled my umbrella and dashed across the crosswalk, which seemed to operate less on lights and more on an honor system—i.e., if you moved fast enough, they wouldn't actively try to mow you down. Slow-moving pedestrians were fair game. I made it safely to the other side and paused, panting, considering my options.

Across the street, I could still see Colin through the window of the Minerve, sweet-talking the woman at the desk.

I knew that this weekend was more stressful for Colin than for me, that I should be kind and patient and all that politician's-wife jazz, but I still wanted to shake him. Wasn't this weekend stressful enough without sharing space with his sister? I set off grimly down the Rue des Écoles, in what I hoped was the direction of the Musée de la Préfecture de Police. I had a miniature Lonely Planet guide with an equally miniature map buried somewhere in the bowels of my bag, but it was very hard to stalk effectively while consulting a map. Right then, stalking took precedence.

On some level, I knew that I was being cranky because I was nervous. I didn't like Jeremy and I didn't like what I had heard of Colin's mother, but she was still his mother and I still had to meet her and I still wanted her to like me, because on some level her opinion still counted. At the same time, I was worried about Colin and what this weekend was going to do to him. I was also worried about Serena and how seeing her mother and stepfather was going to send her off the deep end. And of course, if Serena went off the deep end, there it would be, all dumped on Colin again, and I was worried about that too. It was all a great big mess.

I sloshed through the rutted streets, the Parisian puddles seeping through the untreated leather of my brown suede boots. They had been very snazzy at one point, but they had not been designed for utility. I could feel my stockings soaking up the icy water. It might be March, but it felt more like January.

I was looking for the Rue des Carmes, the home of the Musée de la Préfecture de Police. Not that I trusted myself to get much work done. I was one, big churning mass of undigested emotion: guilt, anger, trepidation, indignation. Should I go back and apologize? I stopped, wondering whether I ought to turn around and find Colin and make nice. It really hadn't been fair to walk out on him like that.

I reached into my pocket for my mobile. Something crinkled under my palm.

I pulled it out. It was the flyer for that special exhibit at the Musée Cognacq-Jay. *Artistes en 1789: Marguerite Gérard et Julie Beniet.*

The name Julie Beniet sounded familiar. AP art history, perhaps? On either side of the diagonal band announcing the title, the flyer showed a picture. The top was a family grouping: a woman with frizzed and powdered hair, wearing a natural-waisted dress in blue-and-white-striped silk, a filmy fichu at her throat, holding a young boy in the crook of one arm, a man seated at a desk next to her with another child. Marguerite Gérard, perhaps?

Below was an entirely different sort of woman. This one was dressed in the new fashion, in a high-waisted gown of white muslin. Her flyaway blond curls were held back by a white bandeau. She was portrayed alone, looking directly out at the viewer, a paintbrush held suspended over a palette. She seemed to be laughing—at herself or at the viewer.

10 Février 6 Avril 2004, it read on the bottom. *Musée Cognacq-Jay, 8 Rue Elzévir, 75003 Paris.*

The exhibition would be closing fairly soon. It would be gone by the time I came back to Paris in July for a final research wrap-up.

I flipped the flyer over to the back. It was closely printed with a paragraph about each artist, and under that, in even smaller print, *Informations Pratiques*, about fees and visitor hours.

Marguerite Gérard had been sister-in-law of Fragonard . . . all very exciting. I skipped down to Beniet. Trained in the studio of Antoine Daubier, big in Revolutionary circles, pals with the young David . . . married to André Jaouen.

Ah.

That was how I had heard of her. Julie Beniet had been the wife of the man in whose household the Pink Carnation had placed her spy known as the Silver Orchid.

I checked Julie Beniet's birth and death dates. She had died four years before the period in which I was interested. Well, that made sense. Based on the reports I had been reading back in the archives of Selwick Hall, it might have made for some marital discord had it been otherwise. The tension between the Silver Orchid and her employer struck me as more than a little sexually charged. Or maybe I had just seen *The Sound of Music* one too many times?

The museum turned out to be one of the many minor mansions

that dot the streets of Paris, smooth stone walls unremarkable from the street until you enter a courtyard and realize that you're in a private palace. The Cognacq-Jay wasn't quite a palace, but it was certainly a substantial gentleman's residence. I made my way through the small, stone courtyard to the entrance, presumably a servants' entrance back in the days of affluence. An attempt had been made at modernization. There was a very ugly desk at the front with a very functional cash register and a very grumpy concierge. The permanent collections were free; the special exhibits five euros, three euros fifty for students. A bargain! I flashed my student ID, handed over my *tarif réduit*, and was pointed down a narrow hallway to the special-exhibition rooms.

I showed my ticket to the guard and walked in, breathing in that museum smell of flaking paint and old fabrics. It was dark in these rooms, a stark contrast after the bright, white-walled modernity of the hallway, with its plastic racks of flyers and brochures. These rooms looked as they must have done in the mid- to late-nineteenth century—paneled in dark wood, the lights kept low to avoid fading the art.

The first room of the exhibit was devoted to early works by Gérard and Beniet—set side by side to emphasize the distinction between Marguerite, the more traditional; and Julie, the Revolutionary in art as in politics. These early compositions were mostly pictures of friends and family—men in periwigs and women in wide, sashed dresses.

Even there, Beniet's paintings had a different tone from Gérard's. Many of Beniet's were little more than charcoal sketches—vivid, living things that looked as though she had tossed them off in a moment, her hand racing impatiently across the page. There was a gaunt woman with hands on her hips, knitting sticking out from under her arm; an elderly man in spectacles, napping in his library; a baby sleeping in a basket in a garden. But it wasn't just her family she had portrayed; there were street hawkers, vagrants, old women doing the washing . . . anyone, it seemed, who came within range of her pen.

One portrait caught my eye. This one was part of a series done in crayon, shaded with color rather than black and white. It showed a man in buff breeches with white stockings. His shoes were plain black and slightly scuffed. No fancy buckles or other decoration. He wore a long, brown coat over a red waistcoat—not a flashy red, but a deep maroon color, quiet and serviceable. His hair was shoulder-length, unpowdered. He certainly wasn't a dandy. His appearance should have been unremarkable.

What you noticed about him was his gaze. He looked directly out at the viewer, interested, unapologetic. Beniet had caught the way the light limned the frames of his spectacles and the bright blue of the eyes beneath them.

I didn't need to check the card underneath to know who he was.

I looked at the card anyway and found that I had been right. The picture was of André Jaouen, husband of Beniet, the likeness taken during his time as a member of the Nantes delegation to the National Assembly. It was thought to be a study for a larger painting that was never completed. That might be accounted for, the card noted primly, by a shift in Beniet's career that had taken place shortly thereafter. Soon after arriving in Paris, Beniet had abandoned personal subjects for allegorical topics on a grand scale. Those paintings, considered her finest, could be seen in the next room.

The stillness of the room was suddenly broken by an obnoxious electronic sound blaring out a version of Mozart that would have made Mozart howl.

Oh, crap. That was me.

I snatched the phone up out of my bag and hit Receive, scooting crablike towards the exit while the other two patrons glared and the guard gave me one of those peeled-back-nostril looks that suggested that he smelled something very, very bad but wasn't going to lower himself so far as to acknowledge it. It's a look the French have down pat.

"Hey," I muttered, scuttling down the hallway towards the front desk. I leaned hard against the door into the courtyard, feeling the glare of the concierge burring into my back like an engraver's awl.

I had a feeling the museum authorities wouldn't be exactly thrilled with me for whipping out the modern technology, so I sidled off to the side, phone pressed to my ear. There was a bench. It was wet. I plopped down on it anyway.

"Where are you?" demanded Colin, without preamble. He sounded short of breath. He also sounded distinctly pissed, and I don't mean in the British sense of the word.

"At the Musée Cognacq-Jay. They're having an exhibit on women painters of the French Revolution."

There was a strangled sound on the other end. "Right," Colin said shortly. "Stay there. I'll be over as soon as I can."

"Wait," I said belatedly. "Where are you?"

"I," said Colin grimly, "am with the police."

"What?"

It was no use. I was speaking to a dead line.

I pressed Redial, but Colin must have turned it off. It went immediately to voice mail.

Turned it off . . . or had it taken from him?

All sorts of improbable possibilities began to unroll in my head. Jeremy had gone ballistic, murdered Colin's mother, and framed Colin. Serena had arrived early, gone ballistic, murdered Jeremy, and framed her mother. Jeremy was the head of a gang of international art thieves and had framed everyone.

I wondered uneasily if I was supposed to be sprinting to the Prefecture to rescue my boyfriend. Would Colin need bailing out? Did they even have bail in France? And if so, would they take traveler's checks?

On the other hand, Colin had told me to stay put. He had also said he would be over as soon as he could. That didn't sound like he was expecting to be incarcerated in the Château d'If. Not for a long stay, at any rate.

I didn't go back inside. Instead, I lurked around the courtyard, pretending to scroll through my saved text messages, but really scanning the street for signs of Colin.

When my phone buzzed, I pounced. "Hello?" I said eagerly, not bothering to check the caller ID. "Colin?"

"Aren't you supposed to be *with* Colin?" It was a woman's voice, with a unique mid-Atlantic drawl, neither quite American nor quite English.

Damn. Pammy. I've known Pammy since I was five, which is why she can begin a conversation without so much as a hello or how-are-you. And I love Pammy; really I do. She's a constant source of entertainment and advice. I appreciate the former and usually ignore the latter, especially when it has to do with guys, clothes, or guys and clothes. In contrast, her long-term investment advice is usually fairly sound. That's Pammy for you. Sounds like a ditz; business brain like a steel trap.

As I was saying, I love Pammy. But hers was not the voice I wanted to be hearing on the other end of my mobile at that precise moment.

"It's a long story," I said with a sigh. The damp from the bench was creeping through my underwear. It was a very depressing feeling.

"Well, never mind that." Pammy and I have been friends long enough that the social niceties get dropped. At least, Pammy drops them. I usually make a pretense. "Do you remember Melinda Horner?"

"What?" Pammy had a thing for non sequiturs, but even for her, this was taking it a bit far.

I could practically hear her snapping her fingers in the background, willing me to keep up. "You know, Melinda Horner. You've only known her forever. You can't have forgotten her."

I'd tried to forget. She had been one of the "popular" girls in our class at Chapin, the tiny all-girls' school Pammy and I had both attended from kindergarten on. You form some pretty strong friendships when you're in the same place for thirteen years. You also form some pretty firm enmities. Melinda fell somewhere towards the latter end of that spectrum. She wasn't my least favorite person from our class, but she was probably second or third.

I'd heard she'd started calling herself Melynda von Horner for a while—plain old Melinda Horner, apparently, not being quite glitzy enough for the purposes of Page Six—but switched back to received spelling when someone had confused her with a German porn star. For a few weeks, the Chapin alum phone lines had been buzzing with the delectable gossip that Melinda had become a porn queen, but it had all fizzled out fairly quickly. Among other things, no one could figure out how she had picked up sufficient German. She was not the brightest bulb in the fixture.

"What about her?" I asked.

"I saw her in London last night." Despite the fact that her mother had whisked her off to London when we were in tenth grade, Pammy kept in touch with more of our class than I did. Pammy's contacts list was a thing of wonder, akin to the begat chapters of the Bible in length and complexity. "She's PA to Micah Stone!"

I gathered I was meant to be impressed by this. "Who?"

"For heaven's sake, Ellie! Where have you been living? Under a rock?"

"The British Library?"

"Same difference."

"Mike Rock?"

Pammy let out a long-suffering sigh. "Micah Stone," she said, with exaggerated patience. "He is only the new Keanu Reeves."

I was tempted to say, "Who?" just to annoy Pammy, but controlled myself. Even I knew who Keanu Reeves was. Plus, I had just spotted Colin approaching the museum.

"Hey!" I gave a little wave in his general direction. "Pams, can I call you back?"

"Whatever. I just wanted you to know that Melinda's in Paris this weekend."

Colin spotted me and executed a brisk turn. He did not look precisely thrilled to see me.

"Um, thanks," I said into my mobile. I wasn't sure why she was telling me. Melinda and I don't exactly move in the same circles. Even her third-grade birthday parties were far cooler than mine. "I really have to go now."

"Ta," trilled Pammy. "Don't do anything I wouldn't do. Smooches!"

"Right back at you," I said, and hit End, just as Colin came through the gate.

I shot off the bench. There was a big wet spot on my behind, courtesy of said bench, but that was the least of my worries.

"Hey. I mean, hi." Colin did not return my energetic greeting. He seemed to be working on his glower. He did a very good line in glower. I shifted from one boot to the other. "So, um, what were you doing with the police?"

"I thought you were going to the police archives."

I felt guilty without even being quite sure why. "I was. But then I saw the flyer for an exhibit here and changed my mind."

"Brilliant," said Colin. He spoke very slowly and clearly. "Your police archives are in the sodding police station."

I thought through the ramifications of this.

"Oh," I said. Guiltily.

"Yes," agreed Colin. "Oh. When I asked them if they'd seen a redheaded American girl, they thought I was trying to file a missing-persons report. I kept waiting for them to ask what I'd done with you. I was afraid they were about to go off and dredge the Seine."

Can one dredge a river? I decided it was safer not to ask.

"Oh, dear." Trying not to laugh, I slipped an arm around Colin's waist and buried my face in his sweater. It was a particularly welcoming sweater—lambswool, nice and fuzzy. "I'm sorry?"

"You'd better be." But his arm came around my shoulders and I could feel his cheek briefly brush against my hair. After a moment, he said briskly, "The Serena situation is all sorted, by the way."

I removed my flushed face from his sweater. "Is it?"

I hoped by "sorted" he didn't mean "ensconced on the couch in our room."

"They've put her in the Famiglia next door. Their sister hotel," he clarified.

"Is she okay with that?" I asked. It seemed more tactful than turning cartwheels and letting out a big hip-hip-huzzah. Plus, I didn't think the Cognacq-Jay people would appreciate my turning cartwheels near the windows. Especially in heels.

Colin shrugged. "If she isn't, she'll have to take it up with them." Then he spoiled it by adding, "I told her we'd meet her for drinks before joining Mum."

Fair enough. I could be gracious in victory. We were all going to need a little Dutch courage before the evening's festivities. And by Dutch, I mean gin. Lots of it.

"Let's go," I said. "We're all going to need it."

Colin looked down at me. He was giving me one of his inscrutable looks. "You can't even begin to imagine," he said.

Why did that not precisely fill me with confidence?

Chapter 9

The bookshop on the Rue Saint-Honoré was a different creature from the one on the Rue Serpente.

Silver bells chimed dulcetly as Laura pushed open the door. Sunlight streamed through the wide plate-glass windows, illuminating tasteful displays of books on specially constructed racks. Framed prints hung on the red-papered walls, featuring copies of etchings by the great illustrators of the past five centuries.

At the far end of the room, a disheveled figure in a ruffled shirt, topped only by a waistcoat, held forth to a distressed-looking proprietor.

Oh Lord. Laura prevented herself from rolling her eyes to the ceiling. Just what she needed. That poet. Again. Did he plague all the bookshops in the city, or only the ones she intended to patronize?

Taking a firm grip on her reticule, Laura marched down the length of the shop. After waiting more than a week for this rendezvous, she certainly wasn't going to be deterred by a longhaired windbag with more sleeve than sense. Laura itched to have a proper conversation with the Carnation or the Carnation's agent.

This whole business of keeping one's eyes and ears open and seeing what turned up was maddening. If they would only tell her what they wanted to know, in plain English with no nonsense about lost princes and horrid novels, she might actually be able to *do* something about it.

Laura bore down on the poet and the proprietor. The bookseller cast Laura a hunted look over the poet's shoulder as the poet waved a small volume dramatically in the air.

The poet struck a tragic pose. "You call this an illustration!"

Laura called it more of a blur as it wafted past her nose.

"Perfidy! Base perfidy! This is nothing less than a betrayal of the muse herself, whose divine trail we all must strive to follow."

"If you don't like it," said the bookseller grimly, "you can take your custom elsewhere. Ah, Mademoiselle!" He seized on Laura's presence with gratitude. "If you will excuse me, sir, I believe this lady—"

"With these rank scribblings profaning the pure prowess of my poetry? I crave—nay! I require!—the counsel and guidance of one of those members of the gentler sex whose minds are more attuned to the lilting call of Beauty's song." The poet also seized on Laura. On her arm, to be precise. "Madame—oh, whatever your name is! Would you lend your invaluable aid to the incalculable cause of pure poesy?"

"Er—," began Laura, very ready to tell him just what he could do with his poesy and his wayward hand. For an effete poetic type, he had a surprisingly strong grip.

"Those blundering oafs in the backroom have made an unpardonable hash of it." The poet thrust his book at Laura's nose. Laura sneezed at the scent of ink and glue. "Don't you agree, Madame—oh, whatever?"

Laura's tart reply died on her lips. Pressed inside the book, just where she could see it, was a white card embossed with the image of a small, pink flower.

"Unpardonable," Laura agreed. "Achoo!"

"Come!" The poet towed Laura towards a curtain at the back of the room. "Tell those oafs what they can do to improve their performance. Perhaps the gentle voice of a lady may reach those hardened hearts that the humble plaint of a mere *poet* has failed to move." In a lower voice, utterly unlike his unusual singsong drawl, Whittlesby said, "Come with me. Quickly."

Laura went, stumbling over her skirt. When he said quickly, he meant it.

In the back room, a large machine was buzzing and clanking. The air was acrid with the scent of ink and glue. An apprentice bustled busily about, feeding long rolls of paper into the great machine. On a long table, open pots of glue sat beside a litter of pages and pieces of cardboard and leather. The print shop conducted a varied business. In addition to the pages waiting to be sewn together into books, there were also piles of printed broadsides, advertising the performance of a new troupe of comedians, the Commedia dell'Aruzzio, performing a repertoire drawn from Molière, the classical dramatists, and the Commedia dell'Arte. Laura suspected that translated to people dressing in parti-colored hose, chasing one another around the stage with sticks while quoting the odd line purloined from the better known of Molière's comedies.

"Is it meant to rattle like that?" Laura stepped prudently away from the printing press, keeping her skirt clear of the vats of ink and glue.

"You should be grateful it does. No one can hear us over the din. If anyone asks, we're consulting over a verse translation of Latin exercises for small children."

"Or the illustrations in your new volume of poetry," Laura reminded him. Whittlesby acknowledged the point with a slight bow. Laura looked around, bemused. "Is every bookshop in Paris in this network?"

Whittlesby raised both brows. "I have no idea what you mean. I only come here for the inspiration afforded by the birthplace of the books we hold so dear." Dropping the pose, he said, in a businesslike tone, "What have you heard?"

Oh no. They weren't playing it that way. Now that she had a proper human being at her disposal, even such a one as Whittlesby, she wasn't saying anything until she had heard what she needed to know. "What did you want me to find? Lost princes are a highly indirect instruction."

"But the Abbey bit was clear, I imagine," prompted Whittlesby, as if he were talking to a very small child.

If he'd had any experience with children at all, he would know that was never the way to get results.

"Very," said Laura, refusing to be prompted.

Whittlesby moved to stand beside her, holding the book open in front of her as though consulting over the set of an illustration. "There is a plot afoot—not our plot," he added pointedly, "to depose the First Consul and replace him with a prince of the blood."

"Surely an outcome to be desired?" Laura kept her head bent over the book. The illustrations really were quite poorly done. Julie Beniet's careless sketches in the margins of *Venus' Feast* had contained three times their power.

Whittlesby turned a page at random. "The idea is excellent; the execution is execrable. Fouché has already arrested several of the lesser conspirators. If they get Cadoudal, the whole jig is up."

"What did you want me to do?" Laura traced the flank of a satyr with her finger. A smudge of ink came off on her glove.

Whittlesby pursed his lips as though contemplating the picture. "There are rumors that the prince, whichever he may be, is already in place. It might be Artois, it might be his son, de Berry. Neither has been seen in his usual haunts. All we know is that a prince of the blood is to plunge into place and take up the crown once Bonaparte has been oh-so-conveniently whisked away. We have instructions"—Laura noticed that Whittlesby didn't say from whom—"to get this prince out of Paris before the whole plot blows sky-high."

"How do you know it will, er, blow?"

Whittlesby shook his head. Out of character, his movements were entirely different from those of his assumed persona—quick, direct, to the point. "If they were to do it, it were best it had been done quickly. By dawdling, they've killed their chance. Now that Fouché knows of the plot, he won't rest till he's found the whole. It's all over before it's begun. There's no more chance of good, but it can cause us a good deal of harm."

"Where do I come into this?"

"If the prince is found, Jaouen will be the first to know. We need to get there before Fouché. Any word, any hint of a rumor, we need to know first."

"Why can't you simply ask Cadoudal?"

Whittlesby pulled a face. "Cadoudal is running for his life right now. His entire existence relies on not being seen. Even if we could find him, he might not tell. There is"—Whittlesby paused, weighing his words carefully—"a difference of philosophy between our two organizations."

"I see," said Laura. As she had been told during her training in Sussex, the French Royalist groups and those sponsored by the English government didn't always see eye to eye. Their goals might overlap, but they weren't necessarily the same. They were constantly tripping over one another's toes. "And the others in his organization?"

"Don't know where the prince is," Whittlesby said grimly. "Only that he's here. In Paris."

"That was all that came out of the Abbaye," confirmed Laura. "A man named Querelle was put to the question."

Whittlesby nodded as though he knew what she was talking about. "Jean-Pierre Querelle. Go on."

"There's very little to go on with. Querelle confessed a plot to kidnap the First Consul and replace him with a member of the royal family. Five generals, one of whom was this Cadoudal, were to manage the military coup. Four of them were to be shipped in from England, one suborned here."

"Moreau," provided Whittlesby. Laura looked up at him quizzically. "It's no good. Fouché is already onto him. They're simply waiting to give him enough rope to hang himself. Anything more?"

"There was something about a prince, but ink had been spilled across those pages."

"Ink," Whittlesby repeated flatly.

"Lots of it." Laura's nose wrinkled at the stench of it. In quantity, ink could be a very noxious thing. "Someone had an accident with an inkwell. I was able to make out the word 'prince,' but little more."

"No names?"

"No names," Laura confirmed. "At least, none that survived the ink spill. If Jaouen knows of any, they're in his head, not on the page. I saw a copy of the official intelligence report. There was nothing there, either."

"Either they know and Fouché is reserving the information for his own purposes"—Whittlesby clasped his hands behind his back, pacing to and fro between machines—"or they don't know. My money is on the latter. Querelle was low on the chain. He wouldn't be told any more than he needed to know. But if they get Picot or Cadoudal . . ." He came to an abrupt halt in front of Laura. "Keep your eyes open. If you hear anything at all about any further arrests, notify us at once. Employ the usual channels. The code will be . . ."

He paused for a moment to consider.

"A request for Latin texts for Picot, Greek for Cadoudal, and a basic grammar book if the name is one I don't recognize," Laura supplied promptly. "If the information is such as to warrant an immediate rendezvous, I'll ask for a botanical treatise. That is, after all, where carnations are most likely to be found."

"Excellent!" said Whittlesby, with such approval that Laura found herself in danger of preening like a cat on a sunny window-sill. "I can be found most evenings at the Sign of the Scratching Cat in the Rue de la Huchette. If anything happens."

He didn't bother to specify what he meant. Discovery? Danger? *Anything* encompassed a broad range of possibility.

Laura pursed her lips and gave a very governessy sniff. "I trust I shan't need to use that information."

Whittlesby quirked a brow. "I, too. But it doesn't hurt to be prepared." He gestured towards the door. "You'd best leave before me. Be sure to look suitably harried and complain about mad poets."

"I shall do it most sincerely," said Laura, liking him despite herself. "Until we meet again, Monsieur."

"Mademoiselle!" Whittlesby's sleeve fluttered.

"Yes?"

Whittlesby grinned at her. It was a charmingly boyish smile, and Laura could see why the ladies of the First Consul's court cultivated him, despite his execrable poetry. "Here," he said, holding out a flat, brown paper–wrapped package. "I nearly forgot to give you this."

Laura regarded it with some trepidation. "Surely I don't merit my own copy of your latest volume of poetry?"

"I wouldn't be so cruel," said Whittlesby. "You'll find it contains *Aesop's Fables*. In Latin."

Laura took the parcel from him. "How fortunate I am that the shopkeeper happened to have just the book I was looking for."

Whittlesby smiled tiredly. "Fortunate, indeed," he agreed. "Now, if you'll excuse me, I have some poetry to compose."

Laura tucked her package neatly under her arm. "And I have children to teach."

They shared a long look of mutual understanding, two soldiers in the same regiment. It was, Laura thought, rather nice to have comrades-in-arms. It was an experience she hadn't even realized she had been missing until she had it.

Laura resisted the urge to salute as she left.

When she looked back, the poet was engaged in a vigorous and loud debate with the printer about the type set of his latest volume of poetry, *An Ode to the Pulchritudinous Princess of the Azure Toes (and other poems) by the Author of Hypocras' Feast, an Epic in Thirty-two Parts.*

"But I must have the illuminated capitals!" the poet was exclaiming. "How else can I properly demonstrate the celestial fairness of my glowing goddess of podiatric perfection?"

Did he ever worry that he might start to speak that way regularly?

Laura slipped out the shop door, wondering how one maintained that sort of pose so competently for so long. She was a fine one to talk, she realized. It was nothing more than she had done all these years in her role as governess. And yes, one did start to speak that way regularly.

If she were very good and completed this assignment successfully, perhaps the Pink Carnation would let her be something else next time around. But what? Laura's inner cynic jeered at her. She would make a very unconvincing courtesan.

Still, it would be rather nice to have the chance to try.

Laura contemplated the prospect as she wandered out into the sunlit street. There was a holiday atmosphere about the day, despite the cold. On a Sunday afternoon, the Rue Saint-Honoré was crowded with Parisians making the most of the clear weather before Monday called them again to their respective trades. Above the clatter and chatter, she could hear the faint peal of church bells, so familiar and yet so foreign. Only a few scant years before, those bells had been silent, the churches closed in favor of the deity Reason. With the First Consul setting the tone, the priests were beginning to come back, the churches to attract congregants again, but

Sundays were still days of leisure rather than worship: a day to shop, a day to promenade, a day to rest between labors. She was just one among many—another laborer using the day of rest to run errands, shop, and enjoy the sunshine. Everyone was dressed in Sunday finery, a veritable rainbow of bright colors and cheap trimmings, reflecting in a multicolored blur in the plate-glass windows of the shops and cafés that lined the street.

Laura looked in each with interest as she passed. Élisabeth Vigée-Lebrun had had her studio not far from here; she wasn't part of Laura's parents' set, but they had taken her there once or twice as a child. She remembered coming with her father and Antoine Daubier to the Café de la Régence to watch them play chess, the two of them finding it a great lark to sit her down at their seats and have her play, first for one, then the other, as the proprietor brought wine for them and macaroons for her.

Some things hadn't changed. The Café de la Régence was crowded with dedicated chess players. As Laura walked past, the crowd shifted and she caught sight of a man standing just outside, checking his pocket watch. He had left his hat off, and the sun glinted bronze off his short brown hair. He was turned slightly away from her. She could see the cowlick in back, so inappropriately boyish for a member of the Ministry of Police.

The crowd jostled Laura sideways, towards Jaouen. He looked up from his watch. Laura raised her hand in greeting.

"Monsieur Jaouen!" she called breathlessly.

She hadn't seen him since their run-in in the storage room. His comings and goings had been at odd hours, although she had more than once heard movements in the nursery at night. The first time, she had assumed it was an intruder. Taking up her poker, she had inched open her door and crept out into the schoolroom, only to find Jaouen, still cloaked and spurred, silhouetted in the open nursery door, watching his children sleep. Lowering her weapon,

Laura had slipped back into her room, easing the door shut behind her. Some moments weren't meant to be disturbed.

Jaouen turned at the sound of her voice, squinting into the sun. Already regretting the impulse, Laura did the only thing she could do. She raised her hand in greeting. "Good afternoon, sir— oooph!"

Her greeting turned to a grunt as the man behind her bumped into her, sending her careening forward. She rocketed into her employer, landing with a thump against his chest. Or perhaps that thump was the parcel hitting the ground. Laura didn't know, because she couldn't see. Her bonnet was knocked sideways over her eyes, the brim mashed somewhere between her face and Jaouen's shoulder.

Jaouen's arms closed around her, his body breaking her fall. The wool of his coat was rough beneath her cheek, warm from the sun and his skin.

Laura heard Jaouen's voice, somewhere just above her left ear, amused, if rather breathless. "A simple 'hello' would have sufficed."

She could feel the vibration in his chest as he spoke, pressed together as they were through all their layers of fabric. It was the sort of position in which no good governess allowed herself to be put, not even in the street, not even in the middle of the day. It was too intimate, too undignified, too . . . Too.

Laura wriggled. "You can let me go now," she said in muffled tones.

Jaouen released her to arm's length, his hands lingering for a moment on her upper arms, steadying her. "A unique way of saying good day, Mademoiselle Griscogne. What do you do for farewell?"

Laura could feel the press of his fingers, even after he let go. "I am so sorry. I didn't mean to . . . I'm afraid I lost my balance."

"One often does after being pushed." Jaouen moved to block her from the bustle of the street, using his only body as a shield. "Think nothing of it. I'm simply glad you fell onto me instead of the window. The patrons of the café might not have been amused to find you as an additional pawn."

Laura's bonnet brim stuck up at an odd angle, knocked askew by Jaouen's shoulder. She tugged at it ineffectually. "It was my own fault for stopping in the middle of the street. I should have known better than to . . . Oh, bother. My parcel!"

"You mean the large, heavy thing that assaulted my foot?" Jaouen leaned over to retrieve the package. It had been wrapped in brown paper, but none too carefully. The string had snapped when the parcel had fallen. "More books, Mademoiselle Griscogne?"

"It would be very difficult to teach without them," she said quickly, reaching for the volume.

Jaouen held on to it. "Buying volumes for the children on your half day, Mademoiselle Griscogne? I should have thought you would have been set on frivolity."

"Oh, certainly. I might dip deep into dissipation with a walk around the park, or even a daring visit to a public concert." Laura made one last attempt to wrench the brim of her bonnet into place. It stubbornly refused to bend. "Since I cannot take the children with me to the bookshop, I must go without them. On my half day."

"Touché." Jaouen tipped his hat to her. "A hit."

Jostled by someone in the crowd, Laura did a little half step to avoid stumbling into him again. "I would never think of sparring with my employer. It would be decidedly improper."

Jaouen raised an eyebrow at her. It was amazing how much sarcasm could be packed into one little arc of hair. "If this is your way of being peaceable, I would hate for us to be at war."

Little did he know. "Would I bite the hand that feeds me?"

"My guess? Yes." Something in the way he said it made Laura's cheeks heat. Jaouen cleared his throat, dropping his eyes to the book in his hands. "What's this, then? What tales are you telling my children?"

Laura resisted the urge to snatch it from his hands as her employer flipped at random through the pages. Each page contained a crude woodcut illustration, with verses in Latin and French beneath.

"These look familiar," said Jaouen, pausing at the image of a wolf flipping his tail at a cluster of grapes dangling tantalizingly just out of reach. "*Aesop's Fables?*"

"It makes an easier introduction to Latin than *Caesar's Wars*. The children learn faster when presented with something familiar."

Jaouen flipped another page. "I wish my Latin master had been half so accommodating."

Laura craned to see over the edge of the book. It was a crow this time, peering into the water. The Carnation wouldn't have left anything incriminating between the pages. She hoped. "The nature of the subject matter does not render the instruction any less rigorous, I assure you."

"I would never suspect you of being anything less than rigorous. I shouldn't want you to call me out for questioning your pedagogy."

"Are you afraid I would challenge you to Latin verses at ten paces?"

"It's the sums at dawn to which I object."

There was something oddly intimate about the image. Dawn. Disordered hair and tousled sheets, warm skin and dented pillows.

Laura pulled herself together. She was a governess, for heaven's sake. She wasn't supposed to think of such things. "The fables do provide excellent moral lessons."

Jaouen's fingers moved busily through the pages. "Do they? Here's one for you." Looking at the Latin below, Jaouen read aloud, "*Multi sub vestimentis ovium lupina faciunt opera.*"

He read it as easily as he read French. Whoever had taught him classics had taught him well. Laura thought she knew now to whom the Seneca, Virgil, and Plutarch had belonged.

Peering over his shoulder, Laura saw a woodcut of a wolf with a sheep's fleece draped half over his lupine shoulders. The wolf looked decidedly shifty.

"'Many do the work of wolves beneath the clothing of sheep,'" Laura translated for him.

Jaouen closed the book, none too gently. "A useful lesson. Especially here in Paris."

Laura accepted the book as he held it out to her. "Why Paris especially?" she asked. "Surely, no one city has the monopoly on deception."

"Have you traveled so widely, Mademoiselle Griscogne?"

"I have served in a great number of households," she said circumspectly. That much was true.

From down the thoroughfare, a rich voice bellowed, "Jaouen!"

Pedestrians gave way as a man approached, a massive figure in a coat of such garish crimson and gold that it hurt the eyes to look at it. His waistcoat, protruding below, was patterned in wide blue and white stripes, adorned with broad bronze buttons that served barely to contain his immense girth. A shock of silver hair framed his face like a lion's mane, sticking out from under the high-crowned hat jammed down on his head. He swung a bronze-tipped walking stick in greeting as he came towards them, deploying it like a bandleader's baton.

No. Oh no, no, no.

It couldn't be. The last time Laura had seen him, he had been slimmer. Not slim—he had never been slim—but he had been tall enough to carry the layer of fat well. His hair had still been its natural brown, streaked with the odd bit of gray, and usually held back by a bit of ribbon or string or whatever else he had happened to find in his studio. Even then, though, he had possessed a taste for garish colors, for waistcoats in all the shades he would never stoop to place on his palette.

Laura's mother used to laughingly accuse him of venting all his gaudiness on his person and reserving none for his paintings, which were meticulously detailed and rigorously controlled, in a palette that ranged from beige to brown. "With the odd bit of blue," he would say, and Laura's mother would smile and touch his cheek with the back of his hand. *"Caro, caro,"* she would say with a sigh, and Daubier would laugh his deep belly laugh while Laura's father propped his feet up on a stool, wine balanced on his flat stomach, lost in his own contemplations.

Sunlight flashed off the knob of his cane. Laura blinked, forcing her dazzled brain to clear. There was no point in denial or escape; he was ten paces away, five, moving fast. Painter, bon vivant, loving friend. He had given her piggyback rides, her hands tangled in his hair, dipping her to make her squeal.

He didn't see her at first. His goal was Jaouen. And why, thought Laura, with an ache she hadn't expected to feel, would he notice the drab thing in gray standing at Jaouen's side? Unlike Daubier, there was nothing to link her to the thing she once had been. She had changed out of all recognition.

Antoine Daubier fell on Laura's employer with an embrace as exuberant as his clothing, dealing Jaouen a smacking kiss on either cheek.

Jaouen untangled himself without injury. Daubier's welcomes, Laura remembered, took some getting used to. A lesser man might be smothered.

"You would think it had been weeks, instead of only last Sunday," Jaouen said dryly. "Are you that eager for our rematch?"

Daubier threw his arms wide. "Forgive me, my friend, for my tardiness! It wasn't trepidation that stayed my steps, but circumstance. I was waylaid by an unexpected guest. As, I see, were you,"

Daubier added, making a quick about-face as he noticed Laura. His waistcoat made ominous creaking noises as he swept a bow, forcing his tummy into directions it had not been designed by nature to go. "My dear Madame. I beg your pardon. I had not seen you."

Which was just the way Laura had wanted it.

"Sir." Laura bent her knees in a hint of a curtsy, head angled down.

Leaning to one side, Daubier peered shamelessly beneath her bonnet brim. "Do I know you? You look familiar."

Laura backed away. "I don't think—"

Jaouen stepped forward, settling the issue with his accustomed efficiency. "Let's not waste time on guessing games. Daubier, this is my children's governess, Mademoiselle Griscogne."

"Griscogne?" The old man's eyes lit.

What had made her think it would be a good idea taking her own old name? Because she hadn't thought she would meet anyone who knew her. They were supposed to be dead, gone, scattered.

Daubier rose up on the balls of his feet, like a griffon rearing on someone's escutcheon, crimson and gold against a field azure. "Did you say 'Griscogne'? Good God, it's been years since I heard that name!"

He stared shamelessly at Laura, with the license afforded by both his age and his profession. He took in her severely cut dress and her crooked bonnet, her sensible pelisse and her tightly drawn hair.

Laura felt an ache at the back of her throat as his expression of pleasure turned to one of puzzlement.

Incredulously, as if hoping it weren't the case, he exclaimed, "Not Michel de Griscogne's girl?"

Chapter 10

Who was Michel de Griscogne?

André saw Mlle. Griscogne press her eyes shut, then open them again. Looking resigned, she held out a hand. "Yes," she said simply. "How do you do, Monsieur Daubier? It has been rather a long time."

Daubier shook his head, his jowls wobbling. "Good Lord. Michel de Griscogne's little girl. I would never have thought . . ." Reaching out, he grasped her hand in his. It was the hand holding the book, but that didn't daunt him. He wrung the book with her hand. "Good Lord."

"You know each other?" André looked from his chess partner to the governess. From the expression on her face, the Lord had very little to do with it.

Daubier squeezed the governess's hand until André could practically hear the bones crunch. He sandwiched her hand and book between both of his, holding fast as though he feared she might run away. "Know each other? I've known your governess since she was in swaddling clothes!"

"Maybe not quite in swaddling clothes," Mlle. Griscogne hedged, looking embarrassed.

Daubier's buttons rumbled with laughter. "Ha! I even did the swaddling myself a time or two." Turning to André, Daubier explained joyously, "Mademoiselle de Griscogne's parents were among my dearest friends."

Mlle. Griscogne—Mlle. de Griscogne?—dipped her head in acknowledgment. "They had a gift for making themselves loved."

Was it only André who caught the edge to her comment? He looked at her sharply, but her face was turned away.

Daubier nodded heartily in agreement. "All of Paris mourned when the news came to us about your parents. Such a loss, such a loss."

"It was a very long time ago," Mlle. Griscogne said, making an effort to extract her hand.

"Too true, too true! Ah, those were the days. I didn't have this back then." Daubier dealt a resounding slap to his overflowing waistcoat. "And your mother . . . Your beautiful mother." Daubier shook his head hopelessly. "She was so full of life. So full of joy. To imagine her, dead and cold . . ."

"Daubier—," André cut in.

The artist ignored him. "I wept like a baby when I heard the news. They were missed, my dear, much missed."

"Thank you," said Mlle. Griscogne. "I really should be—"

Once started, there was no stopping Daubier. "Good God," he repeated. "Michel's little girl, all grown-up. Who would have thought it?"

"It is the usual consequence of the passage of years," said Mlle. Griscogne.

Daubier snorted. "Say that again when you've become as old as I have. I still have the portrait I painted of you as a girl."

For a moment she looked confused. Then a small gleam of recognition kindled in her eyes, spreading across her face, clearing the lines from her forehead, lifting the corners of her mouth in an echo of a smile.

"You painted me with a bird," she said, looking up at Daubier for confirmation. "A yellow one."

"A finch," supplied Daubier, enjoying himself hugely. His own compositions were his favorite topic.

"I remember now." Mlle. Griscogne cocked her head. As she looked up at the old artist, she looked softer, vulnerable. "He pecked me."

The old man's fleshy face creased into a smile. "And worse."

"And on my favorite dress, too," said the woman who had once been the girl with the finch.

"I painted it out," Daubier reassured her. "Before I exhibited you at the Royal Academy."

"Thank you," said Mlle. Griscogne seriously. "I should have hated to appear in public in a stained dress."

André felt left out. "I feel as though I'm missing something."

Daubier sighed heavily. "Twenty years, my boy, twenty years." Eyes narrowing, he squinted at André's governess. "No. More than that. How old were you when I painted you?"

A wrinkle creased Mlle. Griscogne's brow. "Nine, maybe? Ten?"

André tried to picture the woman in front of him at ten—a good foot shorter, hair in curls, features still unformed. It was a disorienting exercise. Governesses weren't meant to have had childhoods, or to be painted with finches. They popped into the world full-grown with a ruler in one hand and a primer in the other. "You would have been about Gabrielle's age."

"Yes," she agreed. "Just about. A long time ago, in any event."

She would have taken a step back, but Daubier took her chin in his hand, squinting at her this way and that. "You always did have such paintable features."

"You mean I was there to paint." She looked to André with a

rueful smile, the sort of smile he wouldn't have imagined could have existed on that controlled countenance. It was like being introduced to an entirely different person from the woman who had been dwelling under his roof for the past fortnight. Her face looked rounder, softer. "A spare child was nothing more but fodder for the artist's easel."

André knew what that was like. Julie had never seen any reason why Gabrielle shouldn't be plucked from her cradle, asleep or awake, to serve as a model when the inspiration moved her. An infant in the house was just another prop, and a far more interesting one than three apples, two oranges, and a pottery jug.

"I should be grateful my father never decided to cast me in clay," continued Mlle. Griscogne. "He might have forgotten to crack the mold."

Letting Mlle. Griscogne loose, Daubier waved that charge aside. "I should like to paint you again. If your employer can spare you," he added with a little bow to André.

André raised both hands in a gesture of defeat. "For art, what cannot be spared? But I would appreciate if you would come to the house to do it rather than remove my governess whenever the inspiration so moves you."

Daubier looked a little sheepish. "Fair enough. Call it an old man's whim, a contrast of now and then." He regarded André's governess thoughtfully. "I would resurrect the finch, but I don't think she would suit you anymore."

"Just hand me a bat," suggested Mlle. Griscogne. "Or perhaps a crow. Something suitably dark and sober."

As an attempt at a drollery, it fell flat. Daubier, good old soul that he was, looked troubled.

André felt obscurely guilty, without being quite sure why. Perhaps because he had, in his own mind, equated her with just that, bats and crows and other suitably dark and dismal creatures, designed to provide a necessary but uninspiring service. Yet, when he had caught her a few moments ago, that had been flesh beneath his fingers, warm and supple, rather than a compilation of old rulers and primers glued into the semblance of the female form. He had felt a moment of surprise that the limbs beneath his fingers were made of flesh and muscle, warm beneath their layers of wool and linen. Surprise, and something else entirely, something one had no business thinking of one's children's governess.

What had he expected, wrought iron? André asked himself irritably. Flesh was the usual matter of human composition, even in governesses.

Daubier dealt André a friendly whack on the back that nearly sent him staggering. "I don't know how you found her, but take good care of this one, Jaouen. Her father was one of the foremost sculptors of our generation."

Mlle. Griscogne's smile went sour around the edges, like milk curdling.

Why should she be valued only for her father's sake? Feeling like a very unlikely knight-errant, André heard himself saying, "That will hardly be necessary. Mlle. Griscogne informs me that she is accustomed to taking care of herself."

"And others, too," she said, lifting the package in illustration. "I should be getting back to Gabrielle and Pierre-André. I promised Pierre-André a story."

"On your half day?"

"What else am I to do with it?" She grimaced at André. "Curl my hair?"

Beneath the crooked brim of her bonnet, wisps had escaped their pins to curl around her face, surprisingly vibrant.

His governess, it seemed, was full of surprises.

André realized she was waiting for him to say something. "Shall you tell them about the wolf in sheep's clothing?"

"Or a sheep in wolf's clothing." Mlle. Griscogne turned to the old artist. "There's a theme for you, Monsieur Daubier, fables turned upside down."

"The world's been turned upside down, so why not the fables?" grumbled the old artist. "That I should live to see this day! Michel and Chiaretta de Griscogne's girl reduced to teaching someone else's brats."

"Since those are my brats you're talking about, I'll choose to ignore that," André said dryly. Turning to his governess, he said, "Chiaretta?"

Mlle. Griscogne shrugged. "My mother was Venetian."

"One of the great beauties of our age." Daubier's eyes had gone all misty again, so misty that André couldn't help but look at him sharply.

Julie's old teacher and Mlle. Griscogne's mother . . . ?

"And a great poetess too," Daubier added hastily, feeling André's gaze. "She was a beautiful person who wrote beautiful poetry."

"She would be pleased to hear you say that," said Mlle. Griscogne quietly.

The old man looked gratified.

André looked at his children's governess, searching for some sign of the Circe who had been her mother.

He could see what Daubier had meant about her being paintable; one didn't live with an artist for years without picking up a sense of what played well in oil and canvas. She had the sort of features that would have sent Julie running for her palette: high cheekbones; a long, thin-bridged nose; wide, well-defined lips.

She ought, he realized, to have been striking, but she had done everything conceivably possible to render herself otherwise. There was that infernal, ubiquitous gray that turned dark hair drab and olive skin sallow; there was the way she tucked her chin into her neck and pursed her lips to make them narrower.

Until she forgot. Until she let herself relax in a smile, a grimace, an unguarded motion. She was only plain because she made herself so.

"Do I have a spot on my face?" Mlle. Griscogne countered his gaze, and André knew, without a doubt, that she knew exactly what he had been doing.

Caught out, André went on the offensive, "Do you write poetry, Mademoiselle Griscogne?"

She hadn't expected that. "Only when I wish to torment my charges."

"Poetic justice?"

"In its purest form."

"If I'm late with your wages, shall I anticipate being bombarded with ballads?"

"I prefer to persecute with pasquinades. Much more economical."

Daubier shook his head. "No one ever doubted your technical proficiency, my dear. Not like listening to that poor Whittlesby creature. It was just the creative spark that was wanting."

Mlle. Griscogne's dark eyes slanted up at André. "Those who can't," she said, "teach."

"There, there, my dear." Daubier patted her comfortably on the arm. "The muse doesn't come to us all."

"Some of us," said André bluntly, "don't invite her. She's a demanding old jade. There's no telling what sort of havoc will be wrought when one lets the muse into the house."

The words came out sounding far more bitter than he had intended.

"The muse," asked Daubier, that shrewd old man, "or those possessed by her?"

"Does it make a difference?" said André dismissively.

But it did. To have one's own relationship with the muse, any muse, might be exhilarating. To have the muse as third party to one's marriage made for a crowded bed. There was a reason Daubier had never married, although the old man liked to volubly proclaim that it was because no woman would ever have him. André ascribed it to something else entirely. Daubier was already married—to his muse. Any other relationship would be bigamy.

He hadn't minded—he had told himself—when Julie would get out of bed in the middle of the night because an idea was too good not to commit to paper. He hadn't been hurt—he told himself—when she disappeared in the middle of their wedding reception. Hers was an amazing talent and he was privileged to be able to share that talent with her. He had his own work; how could he possibly begrudge her hers?

It was a moot point now, all long ago and far away. There was nothing left but a pile of unfinished canvases, linens packed in lavender, and, of course, Gabrielle and Pierre-André.

"My muse and I have come to an accommodation these days," said Daubier comfortably. "I leave her alone until after breakfast and she lets me sleep of nights. We're like an old married couple who know each other's ways. Did I tell you I've been invited to paint the First Consul?"

André's brows drew together at the seeming non sequitur. "No, you didn't."

"You can see how far I've fallen, my dear," said Daubier to Mlle. Griscogne. "I've turned society portraitist in my old age."

"Should I offer you congratulations or condolences?" said Mlle. Griscogne.

"Neither," said the old man. His eyes shifted to André. "Just wish me luck."

"When do you go for your first sitting?" André asked, but Daubier was given no time to answer.

A carriage clattered down the street, parting the pedestrians as they scrambled for cover on either side. André's heart sank. He knew that carriage, just as well as he knew its occupant. Someone rapped sharply inside the cab. The carriage came to an abrupt halt just beside Daubier.

The window shade rolled up, revealing the sallow visage of Gaston Delaroche.

"Good day, Gaston," said André. "Come to play chess, have you?"

Delaroche looked right past him, over his shoulder. His lips curved up in what passed in him for a smile.

With exaggerated surprise, he exclaimed, "Ah, Mademoiselle Griscogne. Such a pleasure to see you again."

Chapter 11

*L*aura looked at Delaroche in confusion. "You have the advantage of me, Monsieur."

This man, whom she had met only once, was smiling at her as though they were somehow complicit. She didn't recall telling him her name, although she imagined he could have found it easily enough. Although why bother? She was just a governess. Insignificant.

At least, she was supposed to be.

"A fine day, Mademoiselle Griscogne." There he went, lingering on her name again, pressing down on the syllables as though staking a claim to her person. "Is it not?"

"Out enjoying the weather, Gaston?" Jaouen stepped between her and Delaroche, although whether to shield her or block her, she wasn't sure. The briskness of his tone belied the seeming casualness of his words. "Or have you come to flirt with my governess?"

Delaroche continued to smile at Laura, although his words were directed to Jaouen. "I was told I would find you here. Playing . . . chess." He made the game sound like an aberration.

"As you see, you find me here, although the game has yet to begin." Laura got the feeling that chess wasn't the game Jaouen was speaking of. "What news?"

Delaroche took his time about answering. There was no mistaking the ring of triumph in his voice. "Cadoudal has been found."

Laura held herself very still, clamping carefully down on any reaction. Cadoudal. That was the man Whittlesby claimed was the sole link to their missing prince. If Cadoudal had been found . . .

"Found?" Jaouen stepped up to the window of the coach, all business. "Is he in custody?"

Was it too much to hope that Whittlesby was still at the print shop?

Delaroche's lips thinned. "The vole escaped the snare."

"In other words, no," said Jaouen dryly.

Laura resumed breathing. It was rather a relief to know that there was no immediate need to find Whittlesby, alert the Pink Carnation, free Cadoudal from police custody, and spirit an as-yet-unidentified prince of the blood out of Paris. The Pink Carnation would still have to be informed of this turn of events, but it wasn't as dire as it might have been.

"Cadoudal's manservant has been taken to the Prefecture. Fouché wants you"—Delaroche's lip curled—"to go through his lodgings."

"And you offered to play messenger? Terribly kind of you."

"Are you coming?" Delaroche demanded.

Instead of answering, Jaouen turned to Daubier. "Daubier, my friend, we shall have to postpone our match for another day. Will you see Mademoiselle Griscogne back to the Hôtel de Bac on my behalf?"

Escort? Or custody? Jaouen's face betrayed nothing more than polite regret.

"I should be honored." Daubier essayed a bow, but was thwarted by his own girth.

"Don't be honored; be swift. As I must be, it seems. Mademoiselle." Touching a hand to the brim of his hat, Jaouen put his hand to the latch of the carriage door.

Instead of shifting to make room for him on the bench, Delaroche remained precisely where he was, in the seat nearest the door, leaving Jaouen the choice of climbing over him or closing the door and circling behind the carriage to the other side.

Holding the door open, Jaouen looked patiently at Delaroche. "I can sit on you, or next to you," he said. "It is entirely your choice."

He would do it too, Laura had no doubt. Neither did the man in the carriage. Slowly, grudgingly, Delaroche shifted across the seat.

"Thank you," said Jaouen blandly, and swung into his vacated seat.

Delaroche gave Jaouen a look that could have dissolved rock. Even a yard away, Laura could feel the pure vitriol of it.

Colleagues they might be, but Laura felt very safe in guessing that they weren't friends.

"Shall we?" said Monsieur Daubier, startling her.

Laura pulled her attention away from the retreating carriage and squinted at her parents' old friend.

He had the sun behind him, turning his shock of white hair to silver so that he glowed like an unlikely angel—one of the larger, less kempt ones, too fond of his cloud and his comfort to have followed Lucifer on his expedition down to Hell.

"Come, my dear. The streets of Paris await us!" Daubier gestured expansively, opening his arms as though to embrace the entire street and everyone on it.

A matron in a flowery hat gave him an alarmed look and scurried over the planks to the other side of the street.

Laura shook her head at him. Her bonnet brim still skewed at an odd angle. Really, one would think the blasted thing could survive one collision. She gave it an irritated tug. "I am no fine lady to need escorting, Monsieur Daubier. Just a governess."

"Nonsense, my dear. As you can see, I need the exercise." Daubier dealt a resounding smack to his middle. He hadn't had quite that paunch when she was little, although the first signs of it had already begun to appear. He'd had only one chin then, rather than five, but otherwise it was the same Daubier, an expansive manner hiding a too-shrewd eye. "You would be doing me a service by taking me for a stroll on this fine day."

"It is fine, isn't it?"

"Not quite so fine as finding you after all these years. My little Laure, all grown-up." Daubier beamed down at her, but there was something hollow about it. The sentiments were correct, but his mind was elsewhere. "How did you come to be working for my old friend Jaouen?"

Daubier's cane tap-tap-tapped on the cobbles as they made their way towards the Hôtel de Bac.

Good heavens, did he really want the whole story? It was a very long story, starting with a storm off the coast of Cornwall and two people without the sense to stay indoors on dry land.

How could she even begin to explain to M. Daubier, whose world, from what she had seen, began and ended with the walls of his studio? What could she tell him of those sixteen years of scrabbling for positions, of the chance opportunity that had led her back to Paris?

Laura settled for the simple version. "Monsieur Jaouen needed a governess. I am one. It is simple enough."

Simple enough on the face of it, but Daubier didn't look reassured. "Was there no one who would take you in, when it happened?"

"When they died, you mean?"

Daubier looked a bit nonplussed by her frankness, but he soldiered boldly on. "Yes. There must have been someone, even abroad. Where were you when it happened?"

"Italy," Laura lied calmly. "They died in a sailing accident."

It had been England, but who was there to contradict her now? What did it matter whether it had been Cornwall or Lake Como?

"But surely," persisted Daubier, "one of their friends . . . Your parents had so many friends."

Laura couldn't argue with that. All across Europe, there was hardly a town where there hadn't been an open door, a spare room, an extra place laid at the table. Her parents had possessed the gift of making themselves loved, not deeply, but broadly. When they had died, they had left behind them a million acquaintances, but no family, no close friends, no one to whom she could reasonably turn for shelter.

To be fair, she hadn't tried. She hadn't wanted to be a charity case, Chiaretta and Michel's useless daughter, without the talent to be trained as an artist, too plain to be anyone's muse.

Over the years before their death, she had become something of a running project among her parents' friends. Her parents had sent her for drawing lessons to Daubier, for voice to Aurelia Fiorila, for drama, for dance, for anything at which she might conceivably be found to excel. Laura had become proficient at everything, but excelled at nothing. She had known, as children do without being told, that her parents would have preferred a few spectacular failures to her own particular brand of passionless mastery.

"You might," said Daubier tentatively, "have come to me."

He looked so uneasy at making the offer, as though still fearing that she might, after all these years, actually take him up on it, that Laura couldn't help but laugh.

"Nonsense, Monsieur Daubier," Laura said fondly. "You would have used me as a perch for your birds and I would have resented you horribly for it."

"Your parents—," he began again.

"Loved you dearly," said Laura firmly. "But you are too old to find yourself with child, and I am far too old to find myself with parent. Consider yourself absolved of all responsibility."

Daubier let out a little huff of breath. "I always told Chiaretta she ought to have named you Minerva rather than Laura."

"For my wisdom?"

"No," said Daubier, "for your domineering disposition."

Laura wasn't sure whether to be amused or offended. She had lived so long among strangers that she had forgotten what it was to be among old acquaintances, particularly old acquaintances who had known one since a little beyond birth and claimed all the outspokenness that was the privilege of age.

Perhaps it was true; she might have been accounted a bit assertive as an adolescent.

All right. She had been called domineering more than once. And officious. And occasionally headstrong. But someone had to make sure the bills were paid and the sculptures delivered on time and that her mother's many admirers didn't run into one another and cause scenes in the public rooms of inns. Her mother thrived on those scenes, but Laura didn't. High drama they might provide, but they invariably occasioned a search for new lodging. Hostelries with clean sheets and good soap were hard to find, especially when one had been banned from the bulk of them.

She had raged all these years about being abandoned, but the abandonment had suited her better than an adoption, especially an unwilling one.

Daubier broke into her recollections. "Let me find you another situation," he said abruptly.

Laura looked at him in confusion. "Another situation?"

"I can find you a post in another household. There are still plenty of affluent families in Paris. Many of them come to me for portraits. If you must earn your living, I can find you a nice family, a pleasant family."

Laura squinted against the sunshine, wishing she could see more clearly. "Are you saying that Monsieur Jaouen is not?" she asked, half joking.

Daubier's rumpled face was entirely serious. "I love André as a brother. Well, as a sort of nephew. Or maybe a first cousin once removed. But I should not want to see a daughter of mine in that house."

Daubier had never had daughters, partly because he had never been able to pull himself away from his canvases long enough to sire any.

"Why ever not?" demanded Laura. "Does Monsieur Jaouen turn into an ogre at the full moon? Hold wild orgies in the basement? Ought I to be on the lookout for headless wives bundled into a trunk?"

Daubier was not amused. "It isn't that," he said reluctantly. "André is a man of perfectly sound moral character and respectable habits. But . . ."

Laura's levity faded away as she watched the old artist poke at the cobbles with the tip of his cane. "You are serious, aren't you? Why?"

Daubier's eyes shifted from one side to the other. Lowering his voice, he said tersely, "It isn't safe to be so closely associated with Fouché's chosen successor. These are unsettled times."

"Are you referring to Monsieur Delaroche?"

Daubier glanced anxiously over his shoulder, as though expecting Delaroche to pop up behind them like a genie from a bottle. "Among others. You don't want to draw their attention to yourself, and you will if you remain with Jaouen."

"But you are associated with him yourself," Laura pointed out. "You play chess with him; you call him friend. Why should I be any more in danger than you?"

"I don't live under his roof."

"You are very kind, Monsieur Daubier, and I appreciate your concern, but—"

"I'm a meddling old man and you don't believe a word I say."

"I would never put it like that."

"Even if it is true," he finished for her.

They paused at the gate of the Hôtel de Bac. As always, Jean was nowhere to be seen.

"Tell me about Monsieur Jaouen," Laura demanded.

"What about him?" Daubier's eyebrows rose like caterpillars on a string.

Laura couldn't find a way to put it into words, so she settled for, "Anything you think I ought to know."

Daubier cleared his throat with a series of harrumphing noises. When the aural symphony died down, he said, "I was better acquainted with his wife. Julie."

Not surprising. Monsieur Daubier had always made it a practice to be better acquainted with the wives. Even as a ten-year-old, Laura had been aware of that. But then, growing up as she had, she had been an unusually precocious ten-year-old.

"Julie was a pupil of mine, you see," said Daubier, as if guessing what Laura was thinking.

Of course she was. Why hadn't Laura put two and two together? Naturally the most talented young lady of her generation would go to the most acclaimed artist of his.

"You remained friends with Monsieur Jaouen after Madame Jaouen's death?" Laura prompted.

Daubier assumed his most cherubic expression. "Jaouen plays a good game of chess. A competent chess partner is hard to find, even in Paris."

For all his practiced bonhomie, Daubier could be infuriatingly close-lipped when he wanted to be. Laura supposed he had to be, with all the secrets that came out over long portrait sittings, but she could hardly count it a virtue when she was the one questioning rather than concealing.

Daubier forestalled further questions by taking her hands into his, as he had long ago with the small child she had been when he had helped her up onto the plinth for her portrait. Even though she was a great deal older now, the gesture made Laura feel small again—small and cherished.

"If you change your mind, you know where to find me."

Laura smiled up at Daubier, feeling the sun glint against the tips of her eyelashes. Looking into his lined old face, as wrinkled and red as an apple, she felt a surge of affection for him, for all the memories she had all but forgotten and for his clumsy attempt at reparations now.

It was nice to have someone who might be just a little bit on one's side.

"You're not still in the old studio, are you?" There it was again, memory, coming back after all this time: sunlight slanting across a honey-colored floor, a green velvet drape cloth nubby to the touch, the prickle of tiny claws against her fingers.

"Yes, in the Place Royale. Having found a place I liked, I saw no reason to leave it."

Laura marveled at the wonderful sameness of it all. It was nice to know that some things remained the same, and that, come what may, through riot, revolution, and assorted new regimes, M. Antoine Daubier could still be found with brush in hand in the third-floor apartment in the southeast corner of the Place Royale.

Then Daubier ruined it all by saying, with a squeeze of her hands, "Do be careful, my dear. For your parents' sake." He reached up a hand to tap her cheek. "And for your own."

"Oy!" a surly Jean poked his nose through the bars of the gate, reluctantly executing his office as gatekeeper. "It's you, is it?"

Jean spat into the gravel. Laura recognized this as his *Hello, how are you?* spit.

"Good evening, Jean," she said, extracting her hands from Daubier's grasp. So much for emotional reunions. "Would you care to open the gate for me?"

The early dark of winter was beginning to fall, slanting across the building to cast a shadow across the court, so that while the street outside the gate was still in full sun, the courtyard brooded in shadow.

A bird perched above the porte cochere, rooting with its beak among its feathers. Its feathers were a deep, unrelieved black.

Naturally. It would be a raven.

Jean made a great production of hauling open the huge iron doors. "He coming in too?" he demanded, launching another wad of phlegm at Daubier. His supply seemed to be inexhaustible. Laura wondered that the First Consul didn't deploy him against the Austrians. That would be one way to damp their cannon.

"No, no." Daubier took a step back, lifting his hands in negation. The raven shifted restlessly on the roof, eyeing the shiny top of Daubier's cane.

"Will you be all right?" said Laura, thinking of the old man alone, on foot, in the dark. "Perhaps you should take the carriage?"

"No need," said Daubier. "These old legs can still bear me up. But . . ."

He broke off as Jean slammed the gate between them, metal hitting metal with an ominous clang. Daubier drew in a sharp breath through his nose. Coming straight up to the gate, he rested his hands on the ornate grille, his nose sticking through a particularly swirly curlicue. It ought to have looked comic, but the worry in his eyes killed any appearance of comedy.

"Take care," Daubier said somberly. "Take care. And remember. If you need me, you know where to find me."

Overhead, the raven cawed.

Chapter 12

"You should be more careful of the company you keep, Jaouen."

Despite the sunlight falling through the window, Delaroche managed to keep to the shadows in his side of the carriage. It was almost as though the dark recognized a kindred soul and knit itself around him.

André stretched his legs comfortably in front of him and managed a credible yawn. "Governesses, you mean?" he said. "Surely I could hardly do better than to follow your example."

Delaroche's eyes glinted like a rat's. "Sometimes even the teacher can be taught."

Not this teacher. André would have laughed if it hadn't been so important to keep Delaroche on a short string. He would have been more likely to suspect his governess of subversion had Delaroche not gone to such pains to make him do so. If the governess were really Delaroche's creature, the man would be a fool to draw attention to it. He was just trying to sow discord and dissension, as usual. It was what he did.

Delaroche was slipping, thought André critically. This really wasn't up to his usual standard.

Of course, it could all be a clever double fake—if Delaroche were that clever. But Delaroche wasn't that clever, and his governess wasn't that malleable. Judging from their prior interactions, André would have been willing to attest that Mlle. Griscogne was about as ripe for subversion as a balky mule.

Still, everyone had her price. It wasn't outside the realm of possibility that his governess was on Delaroche's payroll. Logic told André that it was perfectly likely. Gut instinct told him otherwise.

Over the years, André had learned to trust his gut.

Was he being foolish, allowing himself to be swayed by the fact that she had known Julie's old teacher, or that she had been, once, a very long time ago, the Girl with the Finch?

That painting had been one of Julie's favorites, although her own style had been grander, bolder, and more inclined towards vast allegorical topics than the narrow and domestic world of Daubier's portraiture. Against a plain background, the painting depicted a dark-haired little girl in a white dress with a bright orange sash and a finch perched on one raised hand so that she seemed in colloquy with the bird. The most striking thing about the portrait had been the girl's expression. Her dark eyes had been bright with curiosity as she contemplated the bird. The portrait had been hailed as a representation of the unbounded possibilities of the human intellect in a world of natural wonders, a popular theme in those bright days before the world had burst into smoke and blood.

André wondered if his governess knew that she had become a pre-Revolutionary icon, a symbol of the lost dreams of the Enlightenment. The girl with a finch, who had now become . . . what? The woman with a crow? A spy for the Ministry of Police?

Or simply what she claimed to be, a woman alone, orphaned, making her way as best she could in an inhospitable world, and doing a damned good job of it.

André forced himself to adopt a suitably bored tone. "Have you been essaying lessons, Gaston?"

Delaroche hated it when André called him by his first name, which was exactly why he did it. Baiting Delaroche involved a delicate balance; one had to goad him just enough to maintain the balance of power, but not enough to provoke him into overt retaliation. Even hobbled, Delaroche was a dangerous enemy to have.

Was there anyone who wasn't? thought André wearily. His world was a snake pit, in which even the smallest serpent's venom could prove deadly.

"I wasn't thinking of the governess," said Delaroche, licking his lips in a way that suggested he had an even better card to play. "I was speaking of artists. Painters, poets, actors. Like that friend of yours. The one in the flamboyant jacket."

"I don't know any actors, actually," André said, examining the seams of his gloves. "A lamentable oversight. As you know, Fouché has entrusted me with the monitoring of the artistic community. Such as it is."

How Julie would object if she knew that was her legacy, her connections with the artistic community used as a means of gathering intelligence for her least-favorite cousin. Once a month, André threw an open house in the grand and deserted salons of the Hôtel de Bac, inviting painters, poets, philosophers, and the ladies who patronized them. Sometimes they recited; sometimes they displayed their work; other times they just drank.

Fouché never attended. That would destroy the illusion that it was nothing more than a social occasion. A tattered illusion, but a useful one, nonetheless.

"I would be wary of spending too much time with them," Delaroche shot back. "Lest their habits rub off on you."

"What habits might those be?" André asked. "Good taste? Proper diction?"

Delaroche's eyes narrowed. "Improper allegiances, you mean.

There have been rumors about your friend, that Monsieur Daubier."

"Yes, I know," said André. "I've heard them too. A cause for congratulation, don't you agree, that he should be chosen by the First Consul to paint his portrait? It is not an honor extended to everyone."

"For good reason." Delaroche rested his palms on his knees as he leaned forward. "Someone allowed such intimate access to the First Consul might succumb to the temptation to treason."

"What are you saying, Delaroche?"

Delaroche smiled a nasty smile. "Exactly what it seems. Your friend has been known to accept commissions from unregenerate members of the Ancien Regime."

"All of whom are now accepted at the First Consul's court," André said acidly. Bonaparte and his wife had been assiduously courting the old aristocracy, seeking to add some luster to their increasingly pseudo-regal arrangements. "Daubier's paintings helped make the Revolution. You can't possibly mean to imply—"

"He wears very gaudy waistcoats," interrupted Delaroche.

André resisted the urge to shove the other man's hat straight down over his dour face. "Good God, man. If you arrested every man in Paris with the temerity to sport a gaudy waistcoat, there would be more people in the prisons than on the street. We'd have to declare a national emergency."

Delaroche glowered from under the brim of his highly unfashionable hat. "This is not a laughing matter, Jaouen."

Of course not. It didn't involve thumbscrews. The only diversions Delaroche found amusing were those that involved the crunching of cartilage.

"Naturally not," said André grimly. "Just think of the repercussions. The English would start shipping in waistcoats to our coastline, just to undermine our ordinances. The Austrians would probably contribute gold trim. You would find underground groups of waistcoat fanciers congregating in basements. And why? All because one elderly artist has a penchant for scarlet and gold."

Delaroche fanned out the tails of his own black coat, like a bird ruffling its feathers. "Scarlet and gold are royal colors. You can't deny that, Jaouen."

Neither would the First Consul, who had increasingly adopted those colors for his own use, along with the jewels, the throne, and several palaces. There was nothing like collecting all the accoutrements.

"All the more reason to appropriate those shades for our virtuous citizenry; wouldn't you agree? I doubt Daubier was making a political statement when he chose his waistcoat, any more than you were in wearing that hat."

"There is nothing wrong with my hat."

André leaned comfortably back against the seat. "I never said there was."

Delaroche had been devilishly touchy about his attire ever since being the recipient of a series of mocking notes on the topic from none other than Sir Percy Blakeney. He had claimed not to mind, but the mockery had obviously left its mark, if not any actual improvement in his appearance.

"You sound like that damned, elusive Pimpernel," snapped Delaroche.

André laughed. "Him? His accent is pure Versailles." He exaggerated his own Breton burr, knowing that it made his point for him better than any number of testimonials. His own Revolutionary credentials were impeccable and Delaroche knew it. "Besides, he's been out of the business for some time. You're behind the times, Gaston. Isn't there another flower making trouble these days?" He snapped his fingers as though trying to recall. "Something pink?"

"The Carnation," snapped Delaroche. "The Pink Carnation."

"Ah, yes. I forgot that you had personal experience of the creature."

Delaroche donned his most sinister expression, the one that made him look like someone had just pinched his nose. "I will find him."

"I'm sure you will," said André soothingly. "Eventually."

"Do you mock?" Delaroche demanded.

Always a dangerous question. If one had to ask, the answer was probably yes.

"No. I marvel," said André. "I don't see the point of fainting in terror at a pile of petals." André turned to the window as the ancient carriage lurched to a halt that threatened to detach the cab from the wheels. "Ah, look. We seem to have arrived."

Two guards stood outside a narrow structure. They were both, André noticed, employees of the Prefecture, rather than Fouché's personal staff. Fouché had a long-standing rivalry with Dubois, the Prefect of Paris. This, as a matter concerning Paris, would be technically in Dubois's purview. More important, he had gotten there first.

André looked back at Delaroche. Now he understood his colleague's eagerness to fetch him. As second in command at the Prefecture, André had automatic access. Delaroche, on the other hand, would not. At least, not without André.

Seeing André at the window, one of the guards hurried forward and yanked open the door for him, nearly capsizing the carriage in his eagerness to wrench open to the door.

"Monsieur Jaouen! Thank goodness you're here, sir."

"What happened?" asked André without preamble. He made for the house without looking to see if Delaroche followed.

"It was Cadoudal!" said the first guard excitably. "He had Louis Picot here with him posing as manservant. We recognized him from his picture in the *Bulletin*. We followed him back here."

The picture was becoming clear. "But Picot gave the alarm?"

"Picot gave the alarm," confirmed the second guard morosely. "He realized someone was behind him"—a dirty look at his comrade, who hung his head and looked at his feet—"and began bawling out the first verse of the 'Marseillaise.'"

"Their signal," guessed André.

The second guard nodded. "By the time we made it up here, Cadoudal was gone."

"Has anyone searched upstairs?"

The first guard shook his head. "We were instructed to wait for you."

André noticed them studiously not looking at Delaroche. So he had tried to get in, had he?

"Well-done," he told them, and watched the first guard preen like a puppy. "You've been very helpful. Where can I find the room?"

"Straight up," said the first guard. "The second floor, to the right."

The building was small but well maintained, the stairs swept clean, with cheap but fresh paper on the wall, no different from hundreds of similar boardinghouses across Paris. André took the stairs carefully, looking about him as he went. Contrary to popular opinion, a clever spy chose not a dark bolt-hole, but a tidy lodging house, a place where supper was served on time and the general population of low-level clerks was such as to not call the attention of the law. A man might hide indefinitely in such a situation.

Or almost indefinitely.

Cadoudal's lodging was innocuous enough in itself—one large room with a smaller beyond for the manservant, a washstand behind a screen, a camp bed in one corner with furniture arranged as a sitting area in the other. From the look of the room, Cadoudal had been prepared for early flight. On the table, a partly eaten meat pie and a hunk of cheese sat next to a half-empty glass and a carafe of *vin ordinaire* (where Cadoudal was, there was always food), and clothing had been scattered across the floor as though a portmanteau had broken in flight, but the room was curiously bare of either books or papers.

There would be a thorough examination made, ravaging the mattress, the walls, the floorboards, but André doubted anything more would be found; canny old campaigner that he was, Cadoudal must have kept his more sensitive documents packed in one place, ready to go at the first strains of "La Marseillaise."

André bent over the table. Some papers had fallen to the floor, wedged between the chair and the wall. One was a page from a *Bulletin*, the same bulletins that were delivered to him at the Prefecture, from which the master bulletin, the one that went officially to the First Consul and unofficially to Fouché, were prepared. There was only one problem. This *Bulletin* was dated as of the following week.

André held it wordlessly out to Delaroche.

Delaroche ignored it. He was rooting beneath the meat pie, like a particularly grubby sort of animal. A badger? André had always lived in towns. Natural philosophy might be part of a gentleman's education, but he was weak on wildlife.

"Ha!" said Delaroche, holding something aloft.

At first glance, the paper hardly merited his enthusiasm. Taking it by two fingers, André turned it gingerly, first this way, then that. It was a piece of a letter, one that had been deliberately been folded, ripped, and then folded and ripped again.

"... with the Prince in Paris ...," the fragment began.

"Prince," said André. "A code name?"

"Or no code at all," said Delaroche.

He sounded distinctly smug. Fouché had been warning the First Consul of a Royalist threat for months, a tune to which the First Consul had consistently turned a deaf ear. A Bourbon on the loose in Paris would make even Bonaparte sit up and take notice.

"You believe we have a prince of the blood on the loose in Paris."

Delaroche's lips twisted derisively. "So it would seem to say."

"Yes, seem," agreed André. All right, if they were going to play that game. "The Comte d'Artois would be the logical choice."

While it was the dead king's other brother, the Comte de Provence, who had been crowned Louis XVIII, the younger brother, Artois, had been the more active in fomenting schemes for the reinstatement of the Bourbon line.

"Ha!" said Delaroche. "The Comte d'Artois is too careful of his own skin to come gadding off to Paris. According to my sources, he is very happily ensconced on South Audley Street"—Delaroche pronounced the foreign name with distaste—"entertaining the heir to the English throne at games of whist."

"Likely," agreed André. "Highly likely. My sources also place the count in London. I doubt Provence would come himself. He's too precious for them to risk. Unless . . ."

"Unless?"

"Unless Artois wanted to make the way clear for himself by compromising Provence."

Despite the fact that it came from André, the idea of a double cross appealed to Delaroche. Reluctantly, he dismissed the idea. "No. They band together, these royal spawn. It must be someone else. Not Artois. Not Provence. But who?"

Why did André have a feeling he was going to tell him?

"The count has a son," pronounced Delaroche, as though he had just done Descartes one better.

"Two of them, in fact," supplied André. It wasn't exactly privileged information.

Delaroche paced back and forth, his boots leaving blots on the landlady's clean floor. "The Duc d'Angoulême has been seen in attendance on his uncle, the man they call Louis XVIII. No. I refer to the younger son, the Duc de Berry."

"The Duc de Berry?" André's lips quirked derisively. "The duke is a known womanizer and bon vivant, just like his father before him. Would he leave the comforts of London for a dubious expedition to Paris?"

"When a throne lies in the balance, there are few comforts a man is not willing to forgo."

"An excellent aphorism, but not exactly pertinent to the current situation." Lifting Cadoudal's wineglass, André tapped the base against the table. "It is de Berry's uncle's throne, not his own. His own situation would change little. And my sources still place him in London."

"Hmph," said Delaroche.

Lifting the glass, André examined the wine as if searching for lost pearls. "Did you happen to think that this proliferation of papers might not be a little too fortuitous?"

Admittedly, one fragment and one dropped bulletin was hardly a proliferation, but hyperbole was a recognized rhetorical technique. In other words, it generally worked.

André could tell Delaroche's attention was caught. The cold eyes fastened on him like a lizard sizing up a rat for its gastronomic potential. "Explain."

"These papers under the bed. Cadoudal is a crafty old devil. What if he seeks to shake us off his trail by sending us off in search of a will-o'-the-wisp? While we go hunting mythical princes through the back alleys of Paris, Cadoudal and his confederates have their way clear."

Delaroche's nose twitched as though he had sniffed something gone bad. "You believe this is a ruse."

"A clever one," clarified André. "A clever one, but a ruse nonetheless. Can you imagine the Duc de Berry scurrying around Paris on the off chance of mustering forces in his uncle's favor? He would be more of a liability than an asset. And Cadoudal must know it."

Delaroche's fingers drummed against the desk, once, then twice, like the drumroll summoning a man to the ax. "Berry is a prince of the blood."

"*Qu'un sang impur,*" murmured André, quoting the anthem that had spurred so many troops into battle against the royal forces, the same anthem that had been Cadoudal's cue to escape. "Be that as it may, it does seem telling that this is the first word we have had as to his presence. Querelle said nothing of the kind. He spoke only of Cadoudal and Pichegru and a traitor in our own military ranks. Nor has anything about a man answering de Berry's description come through the Prefecture. I would have known."

Delaroche acknowledged André's competence in that regard with an almost imperceptible flicker of his lids.

"It would be clever," Delaroche acknowledged grudgingly. "Cadoudal has shown himself cleverer than we had realized before. But the possibility of a prince of the blood in Paris cannot be ignored—will-o'-the-wisp though it might be. The gates of Paris will be closed and all vehicles searched. Fouché cannot do anything less." He perked up a bit at the prospect. There was nothing like a bit of prospective search and seizure to improve a man's day. At least, if that man was a mad megalomaniac.

"For how long will Parisians put up with that?" André asked quietly. The city was already restless, the quixotic population of Paris ever ready to shift their allegiances based on the grievance of the moment. Bonaparte had never been less popular. A lockdown of the city could be spark to tinder.

That, however, didn't concern Delaroche.

Delaroche smiled at him, revealing yellowing teeth. "For as long as it takes," he said complacently. "If either Cadoudal or our prince attempts to leave the city, they will be found."

Chapter 13

*H*aving satisfied themselves that the room contained no further items of interest, Delaroche and André went their separate ways, Delaroche to lay his own intricate plans, André to write up his report.

He would be wanted at the Prefecture, he knew. Not necessarily by the Prefect, but by Fouché, who would expect André to monitor the questioning of Cadoudal's manservant, not so much for the edification of the Ministry as for that of Fouché. André reported directly to Fouché; Dubois, the Prefect, didn't.

It was going to be another long night.

André directed the carriage to drop him at the Hôtel de Bac, instructing the coachman to be ready to depart again within the half hour. If he was to spend the night at the Prefecture, he could at least have a change of linen.

"Did Daubier leave any message for me?" he asked Jean as he came in.

Jean spit in negation.

Fair enough. He would see Daubier next Wednesday, for the

monthly meeting of the gathering of the artists. Daubier, who, it appeared, had once dandled André's governess upon his knee.

Now, there was an image.

Shaking his head, André found himself making his way not to his own rooms, but to the suite given over to the children. Terrifying to think that such an insubstantial thing, one life—his—stood between his children and desolation.

A fire crackled in the schoolroom hearth when he entered, but the children weren't there. He could hear their voices through the door in the far wall, the one that led to the nursery. From the sounds of it, Jeannette was scrubbing away the debris of the day, complaining bitterly about the durable nature of ink on skin.

In the schoolroom, there was only Mlle. Griscogne, her head bent over a book. Her hair was pulled back, revealing the nape of her neck as she leaned forward over her book.

It made her, thought André, seem surprisingly vulnerable, with the short wisps of hair dark against the paler skin beneath. Or maybe it only seemed so now that he had seen her without her usual armor, surprised into humanity.

That armor was off now. She was entirely absorbed in her reading, her hands braced on either side of the book, leaning forward as though intent on absorbing the words with her whole body rather than just her eyes.

Was it *Aesop's Fables*? Mlle. Griscogne's arm blocked his view, but he could see that this book was smaller and thinner. The cover was red rather than blue. It was older too, the leather worn off along the edges.

"What are you reading?" he asked.

"Sir!" Slamming the book shut, Mlle. Griscogne twisted around. Her cheeks were flushed, warm with either embarrassment or the wind.

"Is it a romance?" He had trouble picturing his professionally prim governess wallowing in gothic fantasies. On the other hand, it appeared that little about his governess was as it seemed. Michel de Griscogne's little girl, indeed.

"I leave those to Gabrielle." Mlle. Griscogne kept her hand pressed protectively to the cover of the book. "Were you looking for Gabrielle and Pierre-André? If you wanted them, the children are in the nursery."

That was just what he had wanted, but André paused for a moment. "Why didn't you tell me that you were the daughter of one of the foremost sculptors of our generation?"

"And a beautiful woman who made beautiful poetry," she reminded him.

"Daubier is nothing if not exuberant in his descriptions," André agreed. "But that doesn't answer the question."

She lifted her hands in the universal gesture of negation. "It didn't seem relevant to my employment. You were employing me, not my parents."

André's gaze dropped to the book on the desk, the gold curlicues outlining the name of the volume and the author. Good Lord, where had that come from? Memory stirred, of Julie, sitting in Père Beniet's garden, the apple tree in bloom above them and the sun slanting through the leaves, coffee and iced cakes on a small stone table, as he read aloud to her from the poems of Chiara di Veneti.

Chiara of Venice.

What had Daubier called his governess's mother? Chiaretta? *My mother was Venetian,* Mlle. Griscogne had said. Chiaretta of Venice.

Following his gaze, Mlle. Griscogne made an abortive grab for the book. "I didn't mean to pry," she said quickly. "Gabrielle brought the book down. I thought—"

André interrupted her. "Your mother was Chiara di Veneti?"

He still couldn't quite get his mind around it. Those lush, sensual verses of love had been written by Mlle. Griscogne's mother?

"It might be good for her to— What?"

"This. You." André tapped a finger against the cover of the book, the elaborate curls that framed the author's name. "You are Chiara di Veneti's daughter."

Mlle. Griscogne bit her lip. "You say it as though it were strange."

Strange? It was inconceivable. "You don't know how many times I read those poems. They were—"

"Awe-inspiring?" she provided. "Groundbreaking? Life-changing?"

The words sounded obscurely familiar, but André couldn't quite place why. "All of that. What in the devil are you doing as a governess?"

Mlle. Griscogne turned away from him, busying herself picking up Pierre-André's discarded toy soldiers. "They were my mother's poems, not mine. One can't eat a memory. I had to get my living somehow."

There was a wooden box open on the floor. Picking it up, André held it out to the governess. With a nod of thanks, she dropped the soldiers into it. "How old were you when they died?"

"Sixteen," she said crisply, closing the lid on the toy soldiers. "Old enough."

Considerably older than his children, but still. What would Gabrielle do in a similar situation? The very thought of it made the sweat start beneath André's arms, the prickling sweat of fear.

"Was there no one who would take you in?"

Mlle. Griscogne's lips lifted slightly at the corners. For a moment, he could see her as she had been in Daubier's painting all those years ago, the girl with the finch, wide-eyed and alive with possibility. "Monsieur Daubier just offered," she said.

"Now?"

She nodded.

"A bit late, isn't he?" said André, trying not to be annoyed.

Mlle. Griscogne scanned the rug for stray soldiers. "It was a kind impulse."

"Depriving me of my governess?"

His children's governess, technically. Despite the fact that she had lived under his roof for more than a month now, that was all he had known of her, that she was a governess, that she wore gray, that she came well recommended. He had never imagined that she might be the daughter of a poetess, or the girl with the finch— because he had never bothered to ask. But for that chance encounter with Daubier, he would never have known.

It was, as she had pointed out, not exactly relevant to her employment, but André couldn't help but feel that it was relevant all the same.

She seemed less formidable, somehow, and not just because their earlier encounter had knocked her hair loose. He remembered the feeling of warm flesh beneath his fingers, the curve of her back beneath his hand, not made of steel but of skin and bone.

On impulse, André asked, "Did you have a Christian name, in this past life of yours?"

Mlle. Griscogne bent down to pick up a cavalry horse, the mane missing. "A name, but not a very Christian one. They called me Laura."

"After Petrarch's muse?" It made sense for one poet to nod to another.

Mlle. Griscogne bedded the horse down among its fellows. "They were thinking more of the laurel crown," she said wryly. "The coronet of victors and the artist's reward. I think they hoped it would encourage me to garner laurels." She busied herself sorting soldiers. "They were disappointed."

"Julie gave Gabrielle a paintbrush before she could talk." André wasn't sure where the words had come from; they just came out.

"What happened?"

"She chewed it," said André dryly.

He surprised a laugh out of her, a proper laugh. André found himself laughing with her, although at the time it had been anything but comical. He wasn't quite sure what Julie had expected from a teething child, but she had taken it as a personal affront.

"Monsieur Daubier was always terribly kind about my daubs," Mlle. Griscogne said reminiscently. "But I could tell he was thinking, *Poor girl, her paintings will never hang in the Royal Academy.*"

André chuckled, as he was meant to, but he wondered about the little girl she had been. "Did you want them to?"

The question seemed to catch her off guard. "No," she said, after a moment. "Having grown up with two artists, I'm not sure I would want to be one. It isn't a very orderly life."

That was one way of putting it.

He looked around the schoolroom, all the books in their places, all the toys in order. The only thing out of place was the scarlet volume of poetry, a relic from another time and place: her childhood, his youth.

"Once a month, I hold a salon of sorts," André said abruptly. "It's nothing terribly formal, mostly artists of various sorts. Painters and poets and writers."

"How nice," she said politely.

André clasped his hands behind his back. "It all started when Ju—when my wife was alive. I've kept it up since, more out of habit than anything else."

Mlle. Griscogne was all that was professional. "Would you like the children to come down and recite? I've been teaching them excerpts from Racine and Corneille. Gabrielle does a lovely job with the Count's speech from *Le Cid*."

"No!" André said quickly. That was all he needed, to draw more attention to the presence of his children. "No. It wouldn't be appropriate. My guests are not always the most . . . circumspect of people."

"You mean they drink and curse," said Mlle. Griscogne calmly. Her matter-of-fact manner made an odd contrast with her demure façade. But then, she had grown up with Chiara di Veneti.

"They also recite love poetry." André nodded towards the red book on the table. "Instructive for the children, but not for a few more years, I think."

"If you want me to make sure they stay out of the way, that can be easily arranged," she said. "The house is certainly large enough to keep them well out of your way."

He was making a muddle of this. "No, no," he said abstractedly. "Jeannette can manage that."

Mlle. Griscogne looked at him quizzically. "Then . . . do you need assistance with the refreshments?"

André took a deep breath, feeling like a green boy asking a girl into a garden. Absurd, since there was no garden. And Mlle. Griscogne was certainly no girl. There was no need to make a to-do about a simple invitation.

"What I meant to ask was whether you would like to come. To attend. As a guest."

She looked genuinely confused. "You're inviting me? To attend?"

"That generally is what 'guest' means." André retreated towards the nursery, speaking rapidly. "The invitation is there, should you choose to accept it. It certainly isn't a requirement of your job. I thought Daubier might be glad of a chance to see you, that's all. And you might find other acquaintances of your parents there."

Stopping abruptly at the door of the nursery, André shrugged. "I leave it to you. It's your decision whether you want to attend or not."

He reached for the handle of the door. From the sputtering noises inside, Jeannette was rubbing down Pierre-André's face, cleaning off the day's accumulation of dust, jam, and anything else that might reasonably or unreasonably adhere to the face of an active five-year-old boy.

Mlle. Griscogne's voice arrested him just as he put his hand to the handle.

"It's very kind of you," she said. "But you needn't do this just because my father was the foremost sculptor of his generation."

André looked at her for a long moment, at the woman who used to be the girl with the finch.

"I'm not doing it for him," he said, and went to join his children.

Chapter 14

Before joining Serena for drinks, Colin and I went for a stroll along the Seine.

At some point over the course of the afternoon, the sky had cleared. As if repenting of its earlier behavior, it was treating us to a truly spectacular sunset. The spires of Notre-Dame floated in the water of the Seine against a backdrop of red and purple as fantastical as anything from an artist's absinthe-flavored imagination.

Strolling beside Colin, handsome in his dark blue sport coat and flannels, I felt like something out of an old Audrey Hepburn movie.

I winced as my inadequately shod foot landed in a puddle. All right, scrap the Hepburn bit. One could put on the black cocktail dress, but the whole grace and charm thing was harder. And a puddle was still a puddle. The rain might have cleared, but the ground hadn't. My open-toed heels kept slipping and sliding on the cracked and damp stone of the street.

We were meeting Serena at a café in the Place des Vosges, only a few yards from the gallery where Colin's mother's party was being held, but in the meantime we were both content just to walk, breathing in the cool, fresh air of a March evening after rain. Across the way, the long façade of the Louvre glowed golden in the setting sun, and next to it, the empty space where the Tuileries Palace had once been. Somewhere on the far bank, to the right of the palaces, set farther back from the river, was the house that had once been the Hôtel de Bac, where Laura Griscogne had played her dangerous game of infiltration. I wondered whether it was still there now, turned into a museum like the Cognacq-Jay or broken into flats and offices. Or, perhaps, like the Tuileries or the Abbey Prison, gone altogether now, leaving not even a blue plaque behind to mark its passing. Look on, ye mighty, and despair?

"Crap!" I'd lost the end of my pashmina again. So much for deep thoughts. I lurched for it, hoping to catch it before it trailed its way into a puddle.

Colin, more efficient than I, scooped up the errant end and tucked it up for me, anchoring it under his arm.

"Thanks," I said.

"All part of the service."

I looked over at my boyfriend, who was watching the boats go by on the water, and felt a deep surge of gratitude that we were where we were, with all the afternoon's accidents and alarums behind us. "I'm sorry to have been such a brat earlier."

"I wouldn't have said you were a brat."

Nice save, there. *Brat* was an Americanism. "Shrew, virago, harpy . . ."

"I should have checked the reservation." We were still in the warm and gooey make-up stage, where everyone is guiltier-than-thou and a bit of self-flagellation is par for the course. "It never occurred to me that they would put Serena in with us."

"And especially in that room!" I chimed in.

"I've grown rather fond of it," said Colin blandly, and my cheeks went pink. We'd had a very nice little make-up session there before changing for the party. Not to mention while changing for the party.

Not appropriate thoughts with just an hour to go before meeting his family.

"Well, anyway, I'm sorry for being cranky at you. I'm just a little"—I sketched a gesture in the air—"I don't know."

Colin's lips twisted in a wry expression. "So am I," he agreed. "Just a little."

"Are you . . ." I had no idea what I was trying to ask. "Nervous?"

When it came down to it, I didn't have much of an idea of how Colin felt about his mother and stepfather. We'd skirted around the topic, when circumstances had made it impossible to ignore, but Colin had deflected any attempt to extract anything resembling emotion. All I knew were the bare bones of the situation, not how Colin felt about it.

I got the impression that all wasn't exactly warm and cozy, but not because Colin had ever precisely said so. It was the little comments; the twist of the lips, the unguarded expression—all such ephemeral things, like the play of light on water, there one minute, gone the next. If I asked him about his family, Colin clammed up. It was only when I didn't ask that he volunteered.

It was like playing that child's game—red light, green light, one, two three—creeping and freezing, sent back to the starting line if you tried to move too fast.

This time, I could practically see the light flip to red. "These art dos always make me nervous," said Colin lightly. "I'm afraid I'll spill champagne on a Klimt. Look—have you seen the booksellers?"

Accepting the tacit change of topic, I let him draw me in his wake to the kiosks lined up along the side of the walkway, the green metal booths bolted into the stone walls. If he didn't want to talk about it, I wasn't going to force him.

If, however, after several drinks, he chose to make his feelings known, that was another matter entirely.

But what if, contrary to everything I'd been taught in every after-school special, talking about things didn't make them better? What if it only made them harder? There was something to be said for the stiff-upper-lip model. By discussing something, one made it real, gave it—in the words of Shakespeare—a local habitation and a name. There was no ignoring it after that. Maybe it was better for both of us to let Colin display to me the person he wanted to be, not the person circumstance forced upon him.

"May I 'elp you?" The stallholder eyed us suspiciously, as though suspecting us of having untoward designs on the merchandise.

I put down the book I was holding, though not before sneaking a quick glimpse at the price tag. Eek. This was an antiquarian bookseller, not a junk shop, and the extra zeros reflected that.

"Did you see this?" asked Colin, undaunted by the bookseller's glare or the price tags. He held up a small book with torn paisley paper covers. It was an edition of Ronsard's poems, a very old edition judging by the bindings.

"Mmm," I said, scanning the rows. Old books exert a strange fascination for me—their smell, their feel, their history; wondering who might have owned them, how they lived, what they felt. I spotted several early editions of Dumas and Hugo, as well as authors I had never heard of before. They were fairly bulky things, those nineteenth-century tomes, most in several-volume sets.

There were some smaller books among them. I reached for one at random, pulling it out. It was a slim volume, the red leather cover worn in places, the pages yellowed and spotted with age. The gold lettering on the cover had flaked away, making it impossible to read.

I flipped to the title page.

Venus' Feast. Chiara di Veneti. Chansons d'Amor.

A chill went down my spine. That was—well, too much of a coincidence. Chiara di Veneti had been, by modern academic standards, a minor poet of the eighteenth century. She had also been the mother of Laura Grey, the Silver Orchid.

I wouldn't have heard of her but for my research on the Selwick spy school, which led me to Miss Grey, aka Laure Griscogne. She wasn't the sort generally included in AP French exams, partly due to the extreme raciness of some of her subject matter. Admittedly, it had been a racy era, but di Veneti put the author of *Dangerous Liaisons* to shame.

It boggled my mind that she had been the mother of prim and proper Miss Grey, described by Lady Henrietta Selwick as "a forbidding, gray-toned thing who played the piano as though she were solving a mathematical equation, all logic and no passion."

I thought of Colin's mother and the pictures I had seen of her. A free spirit, Colin's great-aunt had called her, and not in a complimentary way. I looked at Colin, solid and dependable beside me, having assumed his parents' cares as well as his own. He kept an eye on his sister, looked after his aunt, made sure the family home wasn't run into the ground. At the same time, I certainly wouldn't call him all logic and no passion. The four walls of Room 403 could definitely attest to that.

I looked back down at the little red book in my hands. André Jaouen's wife had possessed a copy of *Venus' Feast*. Several contemporaries had mentioned it, and the droll illustrations with which she had decorated the margins. Moving very carefully, as if afraid to scare away the pictures, I slowly turned a page.

The pages were pristine, unmarked. Well, if by pristine you mean aside from the inevitable brown of mold and some tears around the edges where the old paper had ripped with time and turning.

I suppressed an entirely unreasonable sense of disappointment. Did I really think I was going to stumble on Julie Beniet's copy of

Venus' Feast at a secondhand stall on the Seine? All by sheer felicity? Felicity would really have to be working overtime there. The
Beniet copy was probably in a museum somewhere. Either that, or
long since scribbled in by small children, eaten by mice, or dropped
in someone's bath. It was coincidence enough finding any copy of
the poems. I wasn't sure it was the same edition—according to the
quick encyclopedia search I had done on Laura's mother, *Venus's
Feast* had been a runaway bestseller, rocketing through multiple
printings in the course of just a few years—but if it wasn't, it was
close.

"Excellent condition," said the bookseller in a thick accent.
"Very rare."

"Not so rare," I said. "Didn't Veneti go through multiple printings?"

"What did you find?" asked Colin, putting down his own book
to come up behind me.

"Oh, just some old poetry." I made as if to put it down. "Sentimental stuff of the late-eighteenth century. Nothing too exciting."

"Very good price," said the bookseller.

Colin consulted his watch, looking as bored as it was possible
for anyone to look. "We should be going. We're going to be late for
drinks."

We were early for drinks. I flashed the bookseller an apologetic
smile, flipped the corner of my pashmina back over my shoulder,
and started to turn.

"For you," said the bookseller, "forty euros."

The price on the sticker was fifty. Eighteenth-century poetry
must be selling particularly poorly this year.

Colin got him down to thirty. Before I could extract my wallet
from my impractical, beaded evening purse, he had paid the man
and tucked the book into my hand.

"Happy birthday," he said.

"My birthday was in November."

"Consider it a deposit on next year's birthday," he said, with that little crinkle at the corner of his eyes that still made my heart go flutter.

I liked the sound of "next year." Technically, I would be back at Harvard by next year . . . but I didn't want to think about that, not right now. It was enough that he was thinking ahead.

We had turned to cross one of the many bridges that span the Seine. Don't ask me which; I can never remember things like that. This one had little alcoves along the sides, with circular stone benches running along their circumference. We paused midway along the bridge, settling down on the still-damp stone of the bench.

Colin nodded at the book in my hands. "What is it?"

"It really is eighteenth-century love poetry. The woman I'm re-searching, one of the Pink Carnation's agents—her mother wrote it." I turned the small, red volume over in my hands. "Finding it seemed like a good omen."

"I won't turn up my nose at a good omen," said Colin somberly. It was another one of those moments, one of those red-light, green-light moments. It didn't take a crystal ball to divine that he was thinking of the evening to come. But should I press him on it? Or just let it go?

I went with the latter. "As methods of divination go, books are tidier than pigeon entrails. You know, like the ancient Romans."

"Have you eviscerated any pigeons recently?"

Even then, even after five months, his smile still had the power to make me go giddy. "Not for months. I've been relying on my Magic 8-Ball instead."

"Read me some poetry," Colin suggested.

"What a cliché," I scoffed, "love poetry on the Seine."

I opened the book anyway, flipping it open at random to a page somewhere in the middle. That was another superstition for you: the old medieval tradition of *sortes*—letting a book fall open at random to see what wisdom the page would bring. My finger landed on *like a fortress betrayed from within, my heart—*

Maybe I shouldn't be looking for omens, after all. *Sortes* was a very unreliable method of divining the future. Pigeon entrails might be more accurate, at that.

I closed the book over my finger. "Maybe later? I'd rather get a drink before the party."

"Fair enough," said Colin. "You can read me love poetry later."

I leaned over and pressed a quick kiss to his lips. "Don't expect any peeled grapes."

"What about the dancing girls?"

"They're against the fire code," I said serenely, discreetly shaking out my damp skirt. I giggled, remembering an old Cole Porter song. "They're too darn hot."

We amused ourselves the rest of the way to the Place des Vosges singing bits and pieces of the *Kiss Me, Kate* score.

We were so busy entertaining ourselves that at first I didn't notice the woman sitting at the table outside the Café Le Victor Hugo. She rose to meet us as we approached, the heat lamp striking orange glints off her smooth, dark hair.

The last time I had seen her, her hair had fallen past her shoulders; now it was cut short, in a modified flapper bob. The style made her seem even thinner and more fragile, her eyes wider and darker, like a fashion plate from the 1920s. She looked like a member of the Brideshead Generation, those lost souls trapped between World Wars I and II.

"You got a haircut!" I exclaimed. And then, belatedly, "Are we late?"

Serena dropped her cigarette and ground it under one heel before hugging me. "No, no," she said. "I'm early. I just wanted a little time to . . ."

Her thin hands floated through the air, white against the gathering darkness.

She had saved a table for us, at the far end of the outdoor seating area, a marble-topped thing surrounded by three deep wicker chairs. There was a champagne flute in front of her, three-quarters empty, with a sticky residue on the sides that suggested it had been a champagne cocktail of some kind rather than straight-up bubbly.

Colin nodded at the cigarette butt. "I thought you'd given it up."

Serena looked away. "Drinks?" she suggested, dropping down into a wicker chair. "We'll need them."

I wished they would stop saying that.

I made small talk with Serena while Colin dealt with the important matter of ordering the drinks—white wine for him, kir royale for me. When that was all set, I leaned my elbows on the table and looked from one sibling to the other. "Tell me more about the party tonight. What should I expect?"

All I knew was that it was being hosted by Colin's mother's Paris distributor—part birthday party, part private sale.

The combo seemed a little crass, but then, so did Colin's stepfather. Jeremy struck me as the sort of guy who would filch the fillings from your teeth and then sell them back to you at a markup. On the other hand, what did I know? Maybe it was Colin's mother's idea. All I knew of Caroline Selwick-Selwick-Alderly was what Colin's great-aunt had told me, and Mrs. Selwick-Alderly couldn't exactly be called an unbiased source.

"Lots of Eurotrash," said Colin. "And Americans. Art people."

Apparently, André Jaouen wasn't the only one to have gatherings of artists.

I grimaced at Serena, who worked in an art gallery. "Do you want to be offended or shall I?"

Serena mustered an unconvincing smile and took another drag on her cigarette. She was fidgeting. I had seen Serena sick; I had seen her flustered; but I had never seen her fidget.

I looked quizzically at Colin. "What is your mother like?"

There was an awkward silence. "She can be very charming," said Colin guardedly.

"When she wants to be," murmured Serena.

That was another first. I'd never heard Serena utter a nasty word about anyone, and she'd been given some provocation in the time I'd known her.

Serena took a long drag on her cigarette. "I shouldn't worry if I were you."

What was that supposed to mean?

"What she means," said Colin kindly, "is that Mum only notices people when she wants something from them. Usually men."

Serena ducked her head, her bird's wing hair falling gracefully over her brow. "I didn't say that." She twisted to look over her shoulder, her thin fingers toying with the stem of her glass. "Do you see the waiter? I think I'd like another."

The empty glass rocked and nearly went over, but she caught it just in time. I wondered if she'd eaten anything today. One drink on an empty stomach went a long way.

"Do you think we could get some snacks?" I said, too loudly. There was an uncomfortable quality to the silence, everyone trying to catch or avoid someone's eye, the mist from the earlier rain heavy in the air. "Do we have time for that? I'd love to get something to sop this up before I meet your mother. I don't want her thinking I'm a total lush."

Colin flagged down the waiter, ordering another round of drinks and some snacks high in carb and calorie content.

Serena drained the last three drops from the bottom of her glass, shaking it to make sure she got every last bit.

I tried to catch Colin's eye, but his attention was on his sister. "Are you all right?" he asked quietly.

"Fine. Perfectly." She slid another cigarette out of its crumpled paper case and jammed it against the tabletop. "Why shouldn't I be?"

"How are things at the gallery?" I asked quickly.

"I've been promoted."

I lurched across the table to hug her, nearly colliding with the waiter, who had appeared with Serena's glass of bubbly. "That's wonderful! Congratulations! I'm so happy for you!"

She suffered herself to be hugged and then twitched away. "It isn't anything to make a fuss about."

"Good on you," said Colin heartily. "When did you find out?"

Serena's eyes were fixed on the elaborate ballet of bubbles swirling and pirouetting in her glass. "I heard on Wednesday."

Colin looked genuinely confused. "Why didn't you say?"

Serena shrugged, the sharp lines of her shoulder blades showing through her shawl. "I didn't want to make a to-do about it."

"Does that mean that we get to make a to-do on your behalf?" I said, bouncing a bit in my chair for emphasis. I lifted my glass. "A toast! To—"

"No!" Serena hastily cut me off. She seemed, for whatever reason, genuinely distressed. "Don't. It's not official yet. I won't know for sure until Monday."

"Oh, right!" I said. That, I understood. "Okay, I won't jinx it by talking about it. Still, it's all very exciting."

Serena bit her lip. "Yes," she agreed. "Very."

"Speaking of excitement . . ." Colin nodded to the right, to the covered path that led along the side of the Place des Vosges. A woman was climbing out of a taxi on the Rue des Francs Bourgeois side of the Place des Vosges, taking her time about it, extending one long leg, then another, like a movie star in an old film. "There's Mum."

She didn't see us. She was too absorbed in her own toilette. She finished unfolding herself from the cab, twitching her scarf into place, adjusting the crystal earrings that cascaded like chandeliers from either ear. Her dress was shorter and tighter than either mine or Serena's, but there was nothing tarty about it. It didn't hurt that it screamed couture. There was a subtle pattern of diamond-shaped cutouts that stretched from one shoulder to the opposite hip.

I only hoped I looked that good at almost fifty.

A man followed her out of the cab, pausing first to pay the driver. This man I knew. I had met him once at a party in London, but I had seen numerous photos of him in the albums in Mrs. Selwick-Alderly's flat in London. It was Colin and Serena's second cousin Jeremy, their mother's husband.

Colin drained his glass. Pushing out his chair, he held out a hand to me. "I think this means it's time to get this party started. Coming?"

"I wouldn't miss it," I said.

Chapter 15

*L*aura wore her gray gown to the party.

She resisted the urge to tug at her cuffs as she made her way out of the darkened schoolroom on her way to the stairs. Jaouen had picked a fashionably late hour for his gathering of the artists. Jeannette had long since put Gabrielle and Pierre-André to bed, retreating to her own room to entertain herself with whatever pastimes she used to beguile her leisure hours, patently uninterested in the revelries planned below. As the schoolroom went silent, Laura had sat at the dressing table of a former Comtesse de Bac, among the voiceless birds and the scentless foliage, staring at her own face in the streaky glass of the mirror, resisting an entirely unaccountable urge to prink.

For what? And more important, with what? A governess's wardrobe didn't exactly lend itself to *grande tenue*. She was fresh out of silks and laces. And she didn't have the sort of natural beauty, so commonplace in heroines in fairy tales, that could be expected to stand out above humble raiment.

Still. She could do something with her hair. She might not be pretty, but her hair was well enough, thick and long and dark enough to pass for black. She could take it out of its accustomed knot, pile it up on top of her head, tie a simple white bandeau around it, pull out some little bits around her ears, imitate the artful disarray of the ladies in the fashion papers.

Yes, because that would go so well with her plain gray gown.

Why did she even care? It was only a gathering of artists, after all. Quickening her pace down the stairs, Laura could picture the scene—smoky air, red wine sloshing over the sides of a glass, careless disarray, and tawdry finery. She had seen it all from the fringes, all the carefree soirees of her parents' youth, assembled ad hoc, sometimes in a studio, sometimes in a tavern, deliberately free of ceremony.

Laura paused on the turn of the stair, one hand on the banister.

The entry hall of the Hôtel de Bac was all but unrecognizable. Below was revelry and laughter, bright jewels and expensive gowns, food piled in careless profusion on gleaming platters. From her position behind the bend of the balustrade, she could see the front door open and close, admitting a clutch of gaily garbed guests in a waft of cold air and expensive perfume.

The gentlemen wore stickpins that glittered even from a distance—diamond and ruby and sapphire—splashes of color against the snowy white of starched neck cloths. And the ladies— the ladies were something out of the fantastical pages of a fashion paper, clad in insubstantial wisps of muslin, shimmering with gold thread and precious stones, bracelets clattering on their wrists, decked out like a barbarian chieftain's burial hoard. What they lacked in fabric, they made up for in gems.

Just a little gathering of artists? Laura would have turned and fled back, but pride made her stay where she was, poised between floors in the shadow of the stair.

She wondered, with a pang, if Jaouen had known she would be out of place among his brilliant company. Had he meant it on purpose? Her mind skidded over their past conversations, over the invitation to this evening's entertainment. If this was his way of putting her in her place, of reminding her what it was to be the governess—well, it had worked.

One by one, Laura unclamped her fingers from the banister, forcing her uneven breath to calm. She was reading too much into it, being—heaven help her—oversensitive. Caring, when she had learned long ago that it was safer not to allow herself to care. The invitation had simply been what it was, a gesture of kindness, carelessly given on the impulse of the moment. He had meant to be kind.

Kind. The word grated against her tongue like sand. She wanted to rake it up and spit it out. She didn't need kindness. Not his, not anyone's. Hadn't she managed well enough these past sixteen years? She didn't need his pity or his charity.

She could go back. Back to her room, to her single candle, to the novel she had borrowed from Gabrielle. She could immerse herself in the tortured forests and gothic fantasies of Mrs. Radcliffe.

Laura breathed in deeply through her nose, stiffening her spine. She wouldn't be such a coward as that.

She was the daughter of one of the foremost sculptors of his generation. How many of them downstairs could boast as much?

"Darling!" she heard one bejeweled woman exclaim to another. The woman dropped her cloak carelessly in the arms of a silent servant, not the surly Jean, but someone white-wigged and liveried, standing at attention by the door as though he always had. "The cut! Exquisite! Madame Bertin?"

"Of course," said the other smugly, shaking out her skirts. The muslin was as thin and frail as gossamer, embroidered with gold thread as fine as a baby's hair. It looked as though it might blow away at a breath.

Laura's sarcenet skirts weighed on her like lead. She moved

silently through the chatting, laughing crowd. It might be February, but they were all dressed as though for high summer, arms bared, décolletages décolleté, bare toes showing beneath the delicate straps of fashionably Grecian sandals.

A troupe of elves had been at work in the dingy reception rooms of the Hôtel de Bac. The grime was still there, but hidden, behind delicate hangings of silver-tinted gauze that draped the walls and shaded the candle flames. Hothouse flowers blossomed in improbable places, burgeoning out of vast stone urns, festooned in garlands along the walls.

Jaouen hadn't lied. The artists were there, even if they were outnumbered by the fashionable. One room had been given over to a series of easels, each bearing a finished canvas. In another, the poet Augustus Whittlesby was in full spate, declaiming to an admiring audience of fashionable matrons who seemed to be ogling his pantaloons as much as his poetry.

To be fair, they were very becoming pantaloons.

"Do read again, Monsieur," one lady called, fanning herself vigorously with an insubstantial confection of pierced ivory and lacework. "Read us some love poetry. Something to warm a cold winter's night."

The woman's eyes telegraphed an unmistakable invitation.

Whittlesby shook out a long roll of paper, sending verse cascading into motion. "My poetry is all for my muse," he declared grandly, sweeping an arm in the direction of a group of ladies who had wisely arrayed themselves by the fireplace, warming themselves by means other than poetry. "For my princess of the pulchritudinous toes!"

The Pink Carnation detached herself from the group, putting her most pulchritudinous foot forward. "Are you starting at the bottom and working your way up? Or are my toes the sum total of my charms?"

What was she doing here? Didn't she realize she was in the lion's den?

Laura forced herself not to stare. To show any sign of recognition would be fatal to them both. There was no way a lowly governess would know one of the beauties of Bonaparte's court. Such a conjunction could cause nothing but suspicion.

She pretended interest in the poet, watching the group of ladies out of the corner of her eye. The Carnation was with Bonaparte's stepdaughter again, along with a third woman whom Laura didn't recognize—shorter and slighter than the other two, with straw-colored hair beneath an exuberant headdress of silver filigree and white feathers.

The Carnation's chaperone, Miss Gwen, was notably absent. Off on another mission? Or simply exploring the refreshment table?

"Really, Whittlesby," exclaimed the third woman. Her French was colloquial, but accented. American, determined Laura. "These interminable odes! Have you never thought of trying your hand at a sonnet or a sestina?"

The poet assumed an affronted expression. "Such short forms do not allow proper scope for my art," he declared grandly.

"Bother that," said the American. "Since when was poetic scope measured in the breadth of a pile of paper? It's content that matters, not size."

Behind her, the fashionably dressed matrons on the sofa snickered behind their hands.

The American shot them a repressive look. "*If* you would," she said. "We are discussing *poetry*."

"You may discuss it all you will, Madame Delagardie," said the poet, giving the American a look of what appeared to be genuine irritation, "but to discuss is not to create. It takes more than a moment's puffery to create the lilting syllables of that sovereign of all arts, that perfect marriage of meter and rhyme, that—"

"Poem?" The American cut him off mid-spate. Her feathers bounced as she raised herself on her tiptoes. "Is that a challenge, Monsieur Whittlesby?"

"A competition!" exclaimed Hortense Bonaparte. "A verse for a verse!"

"My muse does not work on demand," pronounced Whittlesby.

"Then sack it and get a new one," replied the American gaily. "It clearly isn't doing its job."

Whittlesby rapidly re-rolled his latest ode, shuffling it into a tight coil. "Maybe *my* muse has some discrimination."

"Or it's just lazy," suggested the American. "Lolling about on a cloud somewhere when it should be working." She looked pointedly at the thick roll in Whittlesby's hands. "It certainly hasn't been doing much editing."

The ladies on the sofa hissed their distress.

The American shrugged. "Well?" she demanded. "Have we a pact? Or has your muse gone on holiday?"

"I'll keep the wagers," volunteered the Pink Carnation, her voice rich with amusement. "Who wants to versify first?"

Whittlesby cast the Pink Carnation the sort of look that could melt stone. He smoldered quite nicely. "For *you*, loveliest of ladies," he said pointedly, "anything. The Augean stable would be but a trifle if you were to ask it of me."

The group on the sofa tittered and swished their fans.

"Am I meant to feel slighted?" inquired the American of the ceiling. "Heavens. How crushing."

Laura resumed her progress. If the Pink Carnation wanted to speak to her, the Carnation would let her know. It probably wasn't wise for her to be seen lingering around Whittlesby, either, not if he was to be her contact in future, as he seemed to have become.

He did put on a very good act. She might almost have believed that his adoration for Miss Wooliston was real.

Laura wandered through the long suite of reception rooms. Someone else was reading in an adjoining room, declaiming from a new work of fiction. It sounded very dull to Laura, but the audience seemed to like it well enough. By the refreshment table, a trio of artists was debating the best suppliers of canvas and pigments while piling their plates with free fare. She passed a music room, where a tenor practiced his trade; dimly lit rooms where couples sprang apart as she sailed through; and then, just as she was about to turn and go back, a couple of a different sort entirely.

Laura stopped in the doorway, recognizing them long before they saw her. They were too absorbed in their conversation to notice her.

Her host stood by the fire in the small anteroom with its green marble floor, one elbow propped on the mantelpiece, his attention fixed on Daubier as the artist spoke in a low, anxious tone.

Daubier's back was to her, but there was no mistaking the bright gold-patterned cerise of his coat, or the anxious tone of his voice.

"Keeps putting it off. Do you think he—"

"No," said Jaouen decisively, pushing away from the mantelpiece. "But Delaroche does. Time is running out."

Daubier moved as Jaouen moved, turning like the point of a compass towards the other man's magnetic North. "But what can I do? It's not as though I can—"

"Mademoiselle Griscogne!" Jaouen burst out, ruthlessly cutting Daubier off midsentence. He strode quickly towards her, blocking Daubier from her view. "How very, er, tidy you look."

"Thank you?" She made to move back through the door. "If I interrupt . . ."

Daubier hastily recovered his composure, beaming at her with an unconvincing facsimile of his usual bonhomie, like a painting executed in too-garish colors.

"A beautiful woman can never be an interruption!" He shook a finger at Jaouen in exaggerated disgust. "You'll have to do better than that if you want to play the gallant, André. No wonder your wee mites remain motherless."

"Without which I would never have acquired so charming a governess," interjected Jaouen gallantly.

Gallantry sat ill on him. Laura preferred him as he was, blunt and brisk.

Daubier pursed his lips. "Better, but still in want of work. Watch and learn, my boy, watch and learn. Your hand, if you please, my dear Laure."

"You will return it, won't you?" said Laura, holding out the requested appendage. "I do rather rely on it."

"A loan only," Daubier reassured her. "Now, André, watch how it's done."

Something in the way he said it made Laura suspect that he was talking about more than the rules of flirtation, but when she looked at Daubier, his rumpled face was as guileless as a child's.

"I am all ears," said Jaouen.

Daubier made a *tsk* noise before turning his attention back to Laura. With an elaborate flourish, he lowered his considerable bulk over Laura's hand. She could hear his corset strings creak with the effort.

"My dearest lady," he huffed, from somewhere in the vicinity of Laura's knuckles. "I am rendered speechless by your . . ."

"Tidiness?" suggested Laura, as he paused for a noun.

Straightening with visible difficulty, Daubier gave her a reproachful look. "Look how little material you give me to work with. I do wish you wouldn't dress like—"

"A governess?" Laura supplied. She meant it to come out lightly, but it sounded ungracious.

Jaouen broke the awkward silence. "Tonight you are not a governess."

She had been a governess for so long, she scarcely knew what else to be. "Then what am I?"

Jaouen never faltered. "My guest."

He meant it too. The simple decency of it staggered her. "Oh," she said. "Thank you."

Daubier, inattentive to byplay, was busy scrutinizing her dress. "It's not the cut that's the problem," he muttered, "but the color. A bright crimson, that's what you need. Something to bring out the tone of your skin and the luster in your hair. Something deep and rich. Silk velvet, not this drab stuff. Don't you agree, Jaouen?"

Jaouen took in every aspect of her appearance, every scrap of fabric, every hair loose. "Crimson, indeed. Tyrian purple in the fine Roman fashion."

"I hadn't realized this was a costume party," Laura babbled. "I could have come as something interesting. Like a tree."

Jaouen's lips turned up in a smile. "Botany, again, Mademoiselle Griscogne?"

"If I say I prefer nature to art, Monsieur Daubier will be offended."

"But doesn't art imitate nature?" Jaouen neatly turned the subject before she could retort. "Have you found the refreshment table yet?"

"I have," said Daubier complacently. "High art, indeed. Excellent pastries. You should let André fetch some for you, my dear."

Laura raised her brows. "The employer waiting on the employee?"

"Are you testing my egalitarian principles? Come along." Jaouen held out an arm to her. "I'll load a plate for you. Then perhaps you won't doubt me again."

Laura placed her fingers very tentatively on his arm. "Such drastic measures. Are you sure it's worth it?"

"These are dangerous times, *citoyenne*," he answered in kind, using the old Revolutionary address that had already all but fallen out of favor. "One can't be too careful. Would you prefer sweets or savories?"

"Savories," said Laura. "Sweets cloy."

Jaouen raised a brow at her. "One could never accuse you of that."

Behind them, Daubier beamed benevolently, a proud father sending his daughter off to her first ball. An illusion, Laura reminded herself, and a ridiculous one. Daubier had no daughters, and she made an unlikely debutante. She was thirty-two, not sixteen anymore. She was a working woman, not a girl from a fairy tale to be showered with belated blessings by a benevolent fairy godfather in a too-bright waistcoat.

On Jaouen's arm, the crowd that had first ignored her fell away for her, clearing a path, nodding and smiling. Such was the power of the favored successor of the Minister of Police.

He looked his role tonight. Gone was the usual rough uniform of old breeches and a brown coat. Instead, he wore black, tailored to a nicety, with a snowy white stock and a waistcoat in maroon and silver—all in excellent taste and richly made. His rough hair had been brushed smooth, but the cowlick still stood stubbornly up in the back. Other than that, he looked what he was—the master of this establishment, magically transformed for one night from dilapidation to elegance.

Laura wished, foolishly and futilely, that she had put her hair up after all. Just one curl, one frivolous gesture.

Oh, no. She wasn't meant to be thinking like this, and certainly not about her employer. It was only the fairy-tale trappings, she told herself—the ball, the candles, the prince.

Not a prince, she reminded herself. An employee of the Prefecture. The man on whom she was supposed to be spying.

Laura made to extract her arm from his, addressing him without any of the bantering tone. "I did mean it, what I said before. You needn't waste your time on me. You have other guests who want tending to, I'm sure."

Jaouen looked at her with amusement. "You don't accept anything graciously, do you?"

"What do you mean?"

"Invitations, carriage rides, advances on your salary . . ."

"Would you have?" Gratuitous gifts generally made her wonder why they were being given.

Jaouen understood without being told. "No good deed without an ulterior motive?"

Laura wondered what his ulterior motives might be. Especially regarding her. "Do you disagree?"

"Not at all," Jaouen agreed, tucking her hand more securely against his arm. "Most seeming acts of altruism tend to be motivated by something else. So much for the innate goodness of man."

His cynicism didn't ring true. She remembered the books in his study, the well-thumbed volumes of Rousseau and Sieyès. He had been a reformer once and, she suspected, an idealist.

"All right, then. If it's not altruism, why waste your time with me?"

"Because it pleases me to do so. And"—Jaouen added—"because I would rather speak with you than the rest of this lot." He eyed Augustus Whittlesby, garbed in the full splendor of flowing sleeves and artistically misbuttoned waistcoat, before adding prosaically, "I don't much care for poets. Or poetry."

Laura didn't mention the volume in the nursery with his name on it. To Julie, who saw no use in poetry. "Why fill your house with them, then?"

Jaouen shrugged. "Julie started it. I keep them on for her sake. Vol-au-vent?"

Laura waved the pastry aside. "Is it always the same group?"

"It varies. Daubier generally attends—but I'm sure you expected that."

"He never did like to miss a party," murmured Laura.

"You speak of him in the past tense. As if he were no longer with us." The candlelight danced along the rims of Jaouen's spectacles, turning base metal to gold. He was watching her too closely for comfort, picking her apart like the subject of one of his reports.

Laura shrugged uncomfortably. "That's what he was to me, part of my past. I haven't seen him for sixteen years. You would have used the past tense too."

He watched her, saying nothing, waiting for her to go on. An old technique, and an effective one.

Laura hastily changed the subject, gesturing out into the room at large. "Who are all these others? You don't expect me to believe that he's a poet." Laura indicated a prosperous-looking man with long gray sideburns. "Or she."

She pointed to the Pink Carnation, sitting with her hands folded in her lap, serenely accepting the accolades of a young man with wildly disordered hair. Another agent? Or a genuine admirer?

Apparently, it was the fashion to be in love with Miss Wooliston.

Jaouen's eyes passed over Miss Wooliston without interest. "He is a speculator in army contracts. A successful one. She, I believe, is the cousin of one of Bonaparte's courtiers."

His seeming casualness didn't fool her. She would be willing to wager he owned complete dossiers on each one. "Why invite them to your salons? They're hardly likely to paint the Sistine Chapel."

"Neither did Pope Sixtus. Where would artists be without patrons to pay them? All of the people in this room serve each other in some way. The beautiful young ladies play muse to their pet poets, and the elderly financiers pay for the pigments of the painters. They rely upon one another."

"So you bring them together." Laura raised a brow. "How very altruistic of you."

"Are you trying to catch me out, Mademoiselle Griscogne?"

For a moment, Laura sensed something beneath the bantering question, a hint of real wariness. But it was gone before she could catch it, hidden beneath the shimmering, shifting play of light on the glass that armed Jaouen's eyes.

"Well?" asked Laura daringly. "If there is no altruism, what is your motive for these gatherings?"

"Not the sonnets," Jaouen said dryly. Without discussion, they resumed their progress, walking arm in arm through the throng. Jaouen nodded in response to the greetings of a group of ladies but didn't stop. "Call it inertia rather than altruism. These gatherings were Daubier's idea originally, when Julie was first exhibiting. He held them in his studio."

"In the Place Royale," supplied Laura.

Jaouen glanced down at her. "Were you there? I should think I would have remembered."

"No. Those gatherings must have started after—well, after."

After England. She had come close to giving herself away there. She mustn't forget who he was, no matter how amiable he was making himself.

No matter how much she enjoyed his company.

Jaouen diverted the conversation into less dangerous waters. "Was Daubier's studio as much a mess then as it is now?"

Laura accepted the diversion gratefully. "I hadn't really thought of it for years. Not so much a mess . . . I thought of it as an Aladdin's cave. You never knew what you might stumble over. He kept all sorts of props scattered about—swords and shields and bits of pillars."

"And finches," said Jaouen. His eyes met hers in private communication, cutting out the world around them.

"Did he ever make you sit for him?" Laura asked quickly. "Daubier?"

"Me?" Jaouen's eyebrows rose over the rims of his glasses. "Never. Not all of us are innately paintable."

"You mean you didn't want to sit still." It was hard to imagine him as anything but in motion.

Jaouen's lips lifted at the corners. "That too."

"Did your wife never paint you?" As soon as Laura asked, she wished she hadn't. Jaouen had made it clear that his wife was a closed topic. "Never mind. I shouldn't have—"

"She did. The critics consider it one of her less successful works."

"Mmm," said Laura, for lack of anything better to say. "Well, she wasn't really known for realism, was she?"

"What makes you think I wasn't an allegory?"

Laura considered. "I can't really see you decked out in a bed-sheet, playing Peace and Plenty."

"Is it the concept you object to, or the bedsheet?" he inquired.

"Both," she said boldly.

"So did I." There was a pause, and then he smiled. "Especially to the bedsheet."

Somehow, the image was more unsettling without the sheet than with it.

"They are useful things in their way, bedsheets," said Laura at random. "But they leave something to be desired as an article of costume."

"Hmm," said Jaouen. His eyes narrowed on something over her shoulder, his attention directed elsewhere. "Will you excuse me, Mademoiselle Griscogne?"

Without waiting for her permission, Jaouen dropped her arm. Laura felt curiously marooned, like a promontory suddenly chopped into an island. "There is a matter that demands my immediate attention."

"Of course. Thank you. I shouldn't have kept you so long." Laura tucked her misplaced hand at her side, feeling for a pocket that wasn't there.

Jaouen nodded, but absently. He might have been gone already. "Mademoiselle."

And he was away, leaving Laura standing by herself in the center of the room.

Chapter 16

*H*ad she offended him with her comments about his wife? And bedsheets?

The elegantly gowned throng closed about Jaouen, half a dozen people clamoring for his attention.

Laura looked down at her own soot-colored skirts. Or was it simply that he had used up the time allotted for being kind to the governess? It had been too easy, for those few moments, to forget the nature of her position in his household.

Both her positions in his household.

She had overheard something in that green marble anteroom, something she hadn't been meant to hear, something that had made both Daubier and Jaouen visibly uncomfortable, each in his own way. She hadn't heard enough to decipher it, only the merest fragment of a phrase. She had been left only with an impression of something left undone.

If Jaouen's intention had been to distract her, he had succeeded admirably.

They had ended their tour of the rooms in a room lined with

easels, depicting various new works by emerging artists. Laura moved at random to the first easel, feigning interest.

Someone moved to stand beside her. Laura instinctively moved aside, making room.

There was a whisper of muslin as the lady followed, sidestepping as Laura sidestepped.

Laura moved again.

The lady moved with her.

Frowning, Laura glanced sideways, prepared to glare down the person intruding upon her space. She might be plainly garbed, but art was for everyone, and she didn't mean to be rushed.

She encountered an elegant, classical profile and one dangling blue enamel and seed pearl earring. The lady continued to gaze straight ahead, ostensibly examining the painting on the easel in front of them.

"An intriguing composition, is it not?" said the Pink Carnation.

Who in the blazes had invited Gaston Delaroche?

André twisted his way through the throng in the music room, hoping he was mistaken, but knowing he was not. Among the ladies' pale muslins and the flamboyant garb of the gentlemen, that rusty black coat was unmistakable. Delaroche stood out like a raven in a dovecote.

Delaroche was already setting the pigeons' feathers fluttering; André could hear the rustle of fabric and snapping of fans as people hastened to get out of his way. Everyone knew about Gaston Delaroche. He was as well-known as the Black Death and just about as popular.

"Gaston!" André hailed him from across the room. The former fourth-most-feared man in France hadn't bothered to remove his hat or cloak. Because they gave him extra height and bulk? Or for other reasons? André felt his blood quicken with apprehension, but he took pains not to show it. "How kind of you to patronize my humble gathering! I don't recall inviting you."

"The Ministry of Police needs no invitation." Delaroche's voice was pitched to carry.

A crash punctuated the statement. A lady had dropped her champagne glass.

André nodded to a waiter to clear it up. "I hadn't thought you cared for art, Gaston. Broadening your horizons?"

Delaroche frowned. "I have no time for fripperies. I am here on official business."

André couldn't quite bring himself to take the other man's arm, so he dealt him a comradely smack on the back instead. "Well, now that you're here, you might as well take advantage of the opportunity. I believe you know the First Consul's daughter, Madame Bonaparte?"

Hortense Bonaparte was nowhere to be seen, but André was counting on Delaroche's snobbery to override whatever mischief he had planned. For all his supposed egalitarian principles, the man was determined to regain his standing with the First Consul. André was gambling that he wouldn't make a scene in front of the First Consul's beloved stepdaughter.

The dice wobbled and fell off the table. Delaroche's thin lips twisted into a smile. "This concerns Madame Bonaparte, as it must all good citizens who have the welfare of the First Consul at heart."

Trepidation settled like a block of ice in André's chest. "As does everyone here," he said with forced bonhomie.

Delaroche's smile never wavered. A bad sign. A very bad sign. "Not quite everyone."

Right. Enough of the indirect approach. Taking the other man by the arm, André turned him to the side. "This is a private party, Delaroche. Whatever it is can wait until tomorrow."

Delaroche's expression was dangerously smug.

"No, Jaouen. I don't believe that it can."

❦

Laura concentrated on the painting in front of her, keeping her eyes squarely on the canvas.

Next to her, the Pink Carnation tilted her head, scrutinizing the painting on the easel. "A very bold use of color," she commented, as if to herself.

It was a historical allegory, commemorating some significant Roman moment or other. It was the sort of painting Julie Beniet had become famous for, but it had been executed without her skill. The painted figures' limbs looked stiff and unnatural, their togas like—well, like bedsheets.

"I find it overdone," said Laura stiffly. "There's no life to it."

Were they speaking in code? If so, Laura wasn't sure what the code was meant to be. She didn't know what to make of the fact that they were speaking at all.

The Pink Carnation nodded thoughtfully, setting her earrings swaying.

It would be very easy to hate her, thought Laura. Miss Jane Wooliston was the very image of the style currently in vogue—tall and slender, with a face that might have been modeled off an antique cameo. Her jewelry was muted, only a small gold locket on a blue silk ribbon and a pair of blue enamel earrings decorated with seed pearls, but it made the toilettes of the other women look overdone and gaudy. No wonder she was an ornament of Bonaparte's court. Nature had given her so much. Not only beauty, but the wit to employ it to good purpose.

It would have been easier to tolerate her if she had been beautiful but dim; or clever and plain. One could respect clever and plain. But to be beautiful and clever seemed like an oversight on the part of the gods.

She was young too, this Pink Carnation. So close, Laura could see the smoothness of her skin, none of the creases in her forehead or lines down the side of her mouth that Laura saw every time she looked in her own mirror.

How old was the Pink Carnation? Twenty-two? Twenty-three? A good decade younger than Laura in any event. It made Laura feel tired and more than a little depressed that this debutante, this marble creature in white muslin, should have achieved so much with so seeming little effort, while Laura, with all her struggle and strife, had managed so little.

The Pink Carnation tilted her head, examining the painting as if weighing Laura's opinion. "I agree," she said at last. "This one may be more in the current style, but I prefer that one."

She gestured to the next easel over, which held a much smaller painting in tones of green and brown, depicting a stretch of woods on a cloudy day.

Laura obediently moved to stand in front of it. "It's very . . . pastoral."

What in heaven's name was she trying to tell her?

The Pink Carnation gazed at the painting, her elegant profile serene. "Sometimes, among the bustle of town, it can be pleasant to lose yourself in a bit of greenery. It's so peaceful among the trees. So quiet." Without any change of inflection, she continued. "I often go walking in the Jardins du Luxembourg. I like to go in the morning, while the mist is still fresh on the ground. So refreshing, wouldn't you agree?"

Without waiting for an answer, she turned away, flapping a hand in the direction of the American woman.

"Emma!" The American looked around, caught in the middle

of haranguing Augustus Whittlesby. "Emma! Do come here and give me your opinion of this painting."

She had been dismissed, Laura realized, neatly and decisively. Anyone watching would have seen Miss Wooliston making the minimum of polite conversation with the awkward odd woman out, and then, as any of them would, calling for reinforcements.

The American complied, cheerfully enough. Whittlesby looked distinctly relieved.

"You know I'm hopeless at painting," the American said, squeezing her way in between Laura and the Pink Carnation.

Miss Wooliston rolled her eyes at her friend. "I'm not asking you to paint it, merely to critique it. Tell me if I'm about to waste my pin money."

The American eyed the first easel without favor. "Please tell me you're not planning to buy *Caesar's Last Stand*."

"No, not that one. The forest scene. It's like a walk in the woods at ten in the morning."

Emma examined it critically. "I would have said afternoon, but it's so overcast it's hard to tell. Wouldn't you prefer something a little . . . brighter?"

"Really?" The Pink Carnation slid an arm through her friend's, drawing her away, away from Laura. "I would have called it atmospheric, like something out of a novel by Mrs. Radcliffe."

"Hmm." The American was unimpressed. "Come see this one."

Laura drifted to an easel at the other side of the room, staring without seeing. She had a vague impression of color, but she couldn't have said with any authority exactly what it was she was looking at.

The Pink Carnation's message had been clear enough. The Jardins du Luxembourg, tomorrow morning at ten. There must be something important in hand, something very important if the Pink Carnation was concerned enough to break protocol and speak to Laura herself.

"Laura, my dear." She started as Daubier placed a fatherly hand on her shoulder and squeezed. There was reddish paint on his fingers, the marks that no amount of turpentine could scrub off. In Laura's uneasy frame of mind, it looked uncomfortably like blood. "Has André abandoned you already?"

"He was more than generous with his time." Laura forced herself into a lightness she didn't feel. "And with his vol-au-vent."

"I'll say that much for André," agreed Daubier. "He doesn't stint on the buffet. So, my girl, what do you think of this lot?"

He gestured expansively at the easels lining the room.

Laura's mouth settled into wry lines. With all the people asking her that this evening, she might as well hang out her shingle as an art critic. Everyone seemed so eager for her assessment.

She was spared answering by a disturbance at the doorway. Someone was forcing his way into the room, boots clomping against the time-dulled parquet floor. People scattered at his approach, like birds startled from their bread crumbs, hastily taking wing.

The crowd cleared, and Laura saw who it was. It was that man from the Ministry of Police, the one who had stopped them on the bridge. The one who had pretended to know her.

For an awful moment, she thought he was making for her, her subterfuge discovered, her death warrant signed. But his eyes passed right by her. He wasn't on the trail of the Pink Carnation. Laura could see one last swish of her skirt as she strolled easily through the far door, her arm twined through that of her American friend, seemingly oblivious to the commotion being created, as if she were merely the society lady she pretended to be.

Laura's relief turned to alarm as Delaroche stopped directly in front of Monsieur Daubier.

Everyone, including Laura, stepped back, giving the two men a wide berth. They stood alone in their circle of floor, people clustering around at a safe distance, like spectators at the Roman Coliseum.

"Antoine Daubier?"

"Yes?" Daubier's expression was politely quizzical, but there was something beneath it that made Laura's stomach twist.

She could hear his voice, from a very long way away, saying, *Do you think he—*

Whatever this was about, Daubier knew about it. He knew and he was bracing himself for the blow.

Delaroche seemed to grow taller. His sallow face blazed with triumph.

"Antoine Daubier, I arrest you in the name of the Ministry of Police."

Chapter 17

*A*ndré Jaouen pushed into the circle, breaking the spell.

"Not in my house," said Jaouen, his eyes never leaving Delaroche's. He spoke softly, but there was steel beneath. "Monsieur Daubier is a guest in my home. As are you. You overstep the bounds of hospitality, Monsieur Delaroche."

"Monsieur Daubier is an enemy of the Republic." It cut through the din of the room, slicing through conversations like the blade of the guillotine. "Do you deny it, Monsieur Daubier?"

Daubier tried for a jovial tone, but there was a gray tinge to his face. "My daubs are not so very unfortunate as that, Monsieur Delaroche. Surely the odd artistic failure is not to be accounted treason."

"It isn't your dabblings in oil which concern the Ministry of Police, Monsieur Daubier. As you well know."

To the other spectators, it might have seemed like something out of the Comédie-Française, all innuendo and allusion. But Laura felt apprehension grip her as Daubier shook his head, his face gray. This wasn't theater, not to him. "No, I'm afraid I don't."

Delaroche leaned forward. "You deny you have been conspiring against the First Consul?"

Daubier mustered an attempt at a smile. "I would be a fool not to deny it, even if such a thing were true. Which it isn't. The First Consul has commissioned a portrait from me. I would hardly go about conspiring against my own patron."

Daubier looked about, as if looking for support. None came. The people around him hastily averted their eyes, wary of contamination by association.

Jaouen finally stepped in. "There has been some mistake," he said flatly.

That was all? *There has been some mistake?* Laura regarded him with sudden wariness. Surely, for a man he called friend, he could muster some better defense than that.

Unless, of course, he didn't intend to. Unless he had never intended to.

It was his party, his guests. Was it also his arrest?

"There has been a mistake," agreed Delaroche. He turned to Monsieur Daubier, whose form looked oddly shrunken in his gaudy clothes, as if the bombast had been knocked out of him. "The mistake was yours, Monsieur Daubier, in underestimating the reach of the Republic."

"I—" Monsieur Daubier shook his shaggy head. "I do not understand."

Delaroche leaned forward. The crowd leaned in, straining to hear. "I think you do understand, Monsieur Daubier. I think you understand very well."

Jaouen looked at Delaroche and said, in bored tones, "Must this scene be performed to an audience, Gaston? If you will both come with me—"

"The only place Monsieur Daubier is going," said Delaroche, "is to the Temple."

The air grew chill.

"I was going to suggest my study," said Jaouen mildly. "It is nearer, and the refreshments are better. I am a little short on racks and thumbscrews at the moment, but I'm sure you can make do."

A nervous titter ran around the crowd.

"Do you mock my work?"

Jaouen raised his brows. "Far from it, Gaston. I admire your artistry. But we have many artists here tonight, all eager to show their works, and this . . . display is impeding their efforts. I suggest," he added, raising his voice so that it carried throughout the room, "that we all go back to enjoying the arts. Monsieur Whittlesby has a new poem for us, I believe?"

"In twenty-five cantos!" called out Whittlesby.

Someone groaned.

It had been the right thing to say. The nervous tension gripping the room broke. People turned to their neighbors; rustled in their reticules; drifted over to the refreshment tables. As far as they were concerned, the show was over.

Something dark and nasty passed across Delaroche's face, and Laura's stomach sank again. This wasn't over yet. The audience might have gone, but Delaroche was determined in his purpose, all the more determined now for having been publicly balked.

Jaouen turned to Delaroche. "My study?"

For a moment, Laura thought Delaroche meant to agree. Then Delaroche clapped his hands, once, sharply. From behind the thinning ranks of the spectators appeared two men in official costume. Like Delaroche, they were booted and spurred. There was no mistaking them for guests. They moved purposefully towards Daubier, who looked at them with dawning alarm.

Delaroche pointed a bony finger at Daubier. "Bind him."

"This," Jaouen said, "is a most marked breach of hospitality. Professional courtesy only goes so far, Gaston. Drop him," he said sharply to the guards.

The guards looked uncertainly from Jaouen to Delaroche and back again.

"The ropes," said Delaroche. "Now. This man is dangerous."

Even the guards looked askance at that. Daubier had never looked less dangerous. He looked like what he was. An overweight man well past the prime of his life with unkempt hair, a too-bright waistcoat, and paint on his fingers.

"I am willing," Daubier said with effort, "to do whatever I can to aid in unraveling this tangle, Monsieur. I will come with you peaceably—wherever you wish me to go. For the Republic."

It was a fine sentiment. It had no impact on Delaroche. "You will come as I wish you to come," he said sharply. "Like the traitor you are."

Jaouen let out a short, irritated breath. "One can't be too careful in dealing with the First Consul's chosen portraitist. Why don't we send to my cousin and see what he thinks of these proceedings?"

"Who do you think sent me?" Reaching into his coat, Delaroche withdrew a rectangular piece of paper. Shaking it free of its folds, he jiggled it in front of his host. "This is out of your jurisdiction, Jaouen."

Laura was too far away to make out any words. She could see only the imprint of a very official-looking seal. But whatever it was, it had the desired effect.

Jaouen stepped back. "My mistake." He shrugged. "I had thought this was merely your whim, Gaston. But in this case"—he extended an arm towards Daubier—"your prisoner, I believe."

How could he sound so completely indifferent? Everyone knew what happened to men in the Temple. Jaouen knew better than most.

Daubier gave him a sickly smile. "It is quite all right, André. An innocent man has nothing to fear."

They all knew that wasn't true.

Laura watched as Daubier meekly held out his hands to be bound. She had been away in England throughout the Terror, but she felt, for the first time, that she had an inkling of what she had escaped. The fear. The uncertainty. The helplessness.

But Daubier wasn't helpless. Laura caught at scraps. Daubier was said to be a favorite of the First Consul's wife; he was commissioned to paint a portrait of the First Consul himself. Surely they would intervene on his behalf.

Or not.

That hadn't saved Topino-Lebrun four years back. She had read about it even in England, the painter condemned for his supposed role in the Conspiracy of Daggers.

She looked at Jaouen, but the man with whom she had bantered about bedsheets, Daubier's chess partner, Gabrielle and Pierre-André's father, was gone. He was expressionless, emotionless, all indifference and cold intellect behind the icy lenses of his spectacles. He might never have joked with Daubier or called him friend.

Laura remembered that whispered conversation in the green marble antechamber. Had Jaouen conspired with him only to draw him on? Had it all been an elaborate trap? The exchange with Delaroche had lacked conviction, almost as though he were speaking lines set out long ago.

Had they concocted it between them, Delaroche and Jaouen? The supposed enmity, the chance meeting on the bridge . . . It might all be a blind.

But no. That made no sense. Why put on a show for her? She was only the governess. Jaouen hadn't known then that she had any connection to Daubier. She was thinking herself into circles, as tangled as the rope around Daubier's wrists.

Laura backed away, her gray skirts whispering against her legs, fading into the crowd. They would need some sort of proof, she imagined, even in this new regime. There would be at least the semblance of a trial, as there had been in the Topino case. They might torture a confession out of him, but they would have a much more difficult time of it if they couldn't find physical evidence— letters, instructions, autographed pictures of the Comte d'Artois.

Laura took a sharp left, into the servants' passageway that ran along the side of the house. They had been speaking of Daubier's studio earlier, she and Jaouen. Daubier's life was conducted out of that studio. If there were anything to incriminate him, it would be there.

Laura's steps quickened until she was all but running down the hallway. Whatever else happened, she was determined that Dela- roche's men would not find what they were looking for. That painting with the finch might have been a very long time ago, but she owed him something still, if only for offering to take her in when he no more wanted a daughter than she did a father.

The memory of that conversation almost made her stumble. He had tried to warn her against Jaouen. Had he suspected the other man of double-dealing with him? Or had it been on general principles only?

Jeannette had left her cloak by the back entrance, that same entrance to which Jean had directed Laura on that first rainy day a few millennia ago. It was a countrywoman's garment—a thick, solid piece of wool held by a tie at the neck, with a deep hood attached—a far cry from the fitted pelisse required by fashion. It also concealed far more.

Laura caught it up gratefully. With her plain dress and the heavy wool cloak, she looked like someone's maid. A superior sort of maid, perhaps, but not the sort of person anyone would ques- tion. Domestics came and went as they would.

The Place Royale was only four streets away, but it had never felt farther. The shops were long since closed, their shutters drawn, their awnings rolled up. The streets were deserted, illuminated only by the odd light from someone's windows. Laura forced herself to make her way with deliberation; she'd be no good to anyone if she slipped and fell in the ice-slick mud limning the un-paved streets. But every instinct urged haste.

Keeping close to the shadows beneath the loggia that lined the four sides of the Place Royale, Laura conjured the plan of Daubier's apartment in her memory. It had been simple enough, she recalled. There was a narrow entry hall followed by the studio, a large square room with windows on both sides. Beyond the studio lay his private apartments, all in a row: dining room, drawing room, study, and bedroom. Daubier had let her nap in his bed during some of those interminable parties of her youth. There had been a second stairway, leading out from the bedroom, presumably to a servants' entrance.

The concierge was napping at his post, his lantern half-shuttered beside him, the crumbs of his dinner in his lap. Laura slipped past him without a word.

She scurried up the broad, shallow stairs, past the first two flats. All was quiet. It must be near midnight now, late enough for the good inhabitants of the building to be asleep or engaged in other activities behind closed doors and drawn bed-curtains.

Daubier's flat was the third, four stories up. By the time she reached the landing, Laura was breathless with exertion and nerves. By now, Delaroche would have Daubier in a carriage. They might even now be entering the precincts of the Temple. How long before they sent someone to search Daubier's lodgings?

They might wait until morning.

She couldn't count on that sort of luck.

Laura tentatively twisted the knob. It turned smoothly, with-out sticking. Laura's face twisted into something that was half gri-mace, half smile. Daubier never remembered to lock his door. There was, he had liked to say, nothing worth stealing.

It was clever, Laura acknowledged. Clever to hide something treasonous in plain sight, someplace with no locks or bars. Who would think to look where everyone was invited to go?

The first room of the apartment was a narrow, rectangular entry hall. It was windowless, darker than night without a candle, but Laura could navigate it by touch. Nothing had changed. There was still the same long, narrow wooden table at the center, the same seventeenth-century bench by the far wall. As her eyes adjusted to the dark, she could make out the shadowy outlines of the paintings on the walls. Daubier had always used this space to exhibit the work of his pupils, a generous touch.

Did Julie Beniet's work hang here? No doubt. It was too dark to be sure.

The door to the studio was closed, but a fine line of light showed beneath it. That was like Daubier, too, to leave the candles burning against his return. He had always been careless with such things, burning money as quickly as he earned. He was lucky, Laura's mother used to say, that he hadn't burned the building down as well.

It was disconcerting, all these memories. People, words, conversations she hadn't thought about for years were flooding back, dogging her steps through the entryway.

Laura yanked at the door of the studio, tearing it open with a force that made the muscles in her shoulder cry out in protest. There were candles burning in all the sconces, dripping wax into the specially designed basins below. It looked almost exactly as she remembered it—props strewn about in careless profusion, a half-finished canvas on an easel, another propped against a wall. The platform at the far end of the room, cluttered with a dizzying selection of drapes and backdrops. Daubier's paints and brushes, the one exception to his glorious untidiness, lined with meticulous care on their respective stands. And from their perch in an elaborate filigree cage, Daubier's birds still sang.

It might have been the studio of Laura's youth but for one thing. There was a man on the platform, stretched out full-length on the chaise longue. In contrast to the elaborate brocade throw, he was wearing street clothes, an expensive but otherwise mundane jacket and breeches.

He scrambled to his feet as Laura entered, sending the pamphlet he had been reading skidding to the floor.

"Hullo," he said rapidly. "If you're looking for the artist, I'm afraid he's out— Oh." He broke off abruptly as Laura pushed back her hood. "I've met you, haven't I?"

He had. He had bumped into her in Jaouen's study, weeks ago.

What was Jaouen's cousin Philippe doing in Daubier's studio?

This night kept getting stranger and stranger. Laura scrambled to make sense of it. If Jaouen had drawn Daubier into a trap, the cousin might be in on it too, put there in the studio as security to make sure no one did exactly what she was doing now. But he didn't comport himself like a guard, and he wasn't treating her like a threat.

"I say, you're the governess, aren't you! I remember now." Philippe bounded down the two steps from the platform. "Did André send you? Do you have a message for me?"

"He knows you're here?" said Laura sharply.

Philippe blinked. "Here? Me? Oh, of course. Of course he knows. I was, er, just waiting for a sitting. Old Daubier's painting my portrait, don't you know. A surprise present for my mother."

"I see," said Laura. "A sitting."

"Well, you might call it a standing," said Philippe, with an overenergetic cheer that reminded Laura forcibly of Jaouen and Daubier earlier that evening. "He doesn't let me do much sitting. It's deuced tiring. I don't know how artists' models manage it."

Laura took a slow turn around the room, looking for anything out of the ordinary among the general debris. "An unusual time for a sitting."

"Yes, well, I'm an unusual person." Philippe grinned at her, piling on the charm like coals on a fire. "Why don't you come sit here near me and I'll tell you all about it?"

She had seen him before, and not just at Jaouen's. Laura stared at him, fighting to place the elusive memory.

Philippe patted the chaise next to him. "Mademoiselle?"

Apparently, he was used to being stared at by women; he seemed to be more amused than alarmed by her attention. Or simply used to being stared at.

With a final, fatal click, Laura remembered.

That was why he didn't look at all like Jaouen, or like his supposed cousins. There was no relation there, not unless one counted Adam and Eve. She had seen him once before, in England, riding by in an open carriage, surrounded by an admiring entourage.

The lost prince they were all searching for wasn't the Dauphin. It was the third man in line for the throne, the Duc de Berry.

And he was here, in front of her, in Antoine Daubier's studio.

Chapter 18

"Won't you sit down, Mademoiselle, er . . ."

The heir to the French throne patted the velvet seat of the chaise longue.

"Griscogne," Laura said numbly. "Mademoiselle Griscogne."

In this world turned upside down, even her name sounded curiously unreal, the syllables unfamiliar on her tongue. Here, in the disordered artist's studio of her youth, so remarkably unchanged over the years, one of the heirs to the French throne was urging her to a seat.

A mere fifteen years before, sitting in the presence of a prince of the blood would have been accounted a little sort of treason.

It was mad. Laura stared at the man on the pedestal, fighting to reconcile the evidence of her eyes with the outraged voice of practicality. Unutterably, irredeemably mad. But no matter how mad it was, her memory didn't lie. She knew him for who he was.

The Duc de Berry. Here. In Daubier's studio.

"Ah, yes," said the Duc de Berry, nodding. "Mademoiselle Griscogne. Of course."

But if he was the Duc de Berry, then Jaouen . . . Laura's mind fumbled after conclusions and fell short. Jaouen was the cousin of the Minister of Police, his most trusted confederate.

And he was harboring one of the heirs to the French throne.

Laura forced her dry throat to move. "But what am I to call you?"

"Well, you can't very well call me cousin as André does," said the Duc de Berry winningly. "Since we aren't. So I imagine it will have to be Monsieur Philippe."

Laura recklessly tossed the dice. "Or should I just say 'Your Highness'?"

His reaction was all the confirmation she needed. The Duc de Berry jumped as though she had just pinched him. "I say, I—What?"

"You know exactly what," said Laura, hearing her own voice as from a distance. Against it, she could hear the echoes of other conversations, Jaouen and Daubier in the antechamber that evening; de Berry's earlier visits to the Hôtel de Bac. "He's been hiding you, hasn't he? Daubier."

The Duc de Berry looked about as though looking for a place to bolt. "Don't know why you would think such a thing. Hiding! Ha. I'm simply on leave from my regiment. As my cousin André might have told you."

"He's no more your cousin than you are mine," said Laura brusquely. "Why did he agree to it? Jaouen? Is he helping you?"

De Berry backed away from the intensity in her voice. "I haven't the slightest idea what you're on about," he said, looking slightly hunted. "Are you sure you're feeling quite all right, Mademoiselle?"

No, she wasn't sure. But that wasn't the point.

Jaouen—a Royalist agent?

Laura felt as though she were clinging with one hand to the side of a cliff, watching the landscape sway beneath her, everything turned topsy-turvy.

She knew Jaouen's past as well as she knew her own. She had read every word of his dossier, committing it all to memory in the pleasant gardens of a manor house in Sussex. Avocat of Nantes, delegate to the Estates-General, committed republican, cousin by marriage to the all-powerful Fouché, Minister of Police. There was nothing in there to indicate any form of Royalist leanings, nothing. There was no time unaccounted for, no period when he hadn't been in the service of the Revolutionary regime for which he had so passionately advocated in the dying days of the old order.

And Daubier! Where was Daubier in all this? He was no more a Royalist than Jaouen, albeit for different reasons. He had never been political, not even when politics were all the fashion. King and country concerned Daubier only insofar as they provided him a place to hang his canvases. For those purposes, a Consul served him as well as a king.

Why?

And who was deceiving whom?

"Mademoiselle?" The Duc de Berry bent over her, too much a gentleman to toss her out the window. His mistake. If she were an agent of the government, such solicitude would sign his death warrant.

"I'm quite all right," said Laura sharply, brushing off de Berry's solicitous arm. "But you may not be. We have no time for these charades. Monsieur Daubier was arrested tonight."

De Berry looked at her in confusion. "Then are you—? Do you—? Jaouen didn't tell me that you were—"

"You don't imagine that he tells you everything, do you?" That might be more true than either of them knew. Laura wondered what Jaouen was telling. And to whom. "The agents of the Ministry might be here at any moment. Does Monsieur Daubier keep anything here that might condemn him? Other than you."

De Berry reacted without question to the note of authority in her voice. "His ledger. He has the code in his ledger."

"Where is it?" Laura asked. "Quickly!"

"He keeps it here, close by him," said de Berry, looking around helplessly. "As to where exactly . . ."

"It's a book?" said Laura. "A leather-bound one?"

De Berry nodded. "About yea high." He sketched it out with his hands. "Should be around—"

The door to the foyer burst open, spitting out Jaouen like a cork from a bottle. He was speaking as he moved, in a rapid-fire staccato that matched the brisk pace of his legs.

"Bad news. Dau—" Jaouen broke off, breathing hard. He came to an abrupt halt. His eyes locked with Laura's. "You. What are you doing here?"

Laura took a step towards him. "What are *you* doing here?"

"Shouldn't you be with the children?"

"Shouldn't you be at the Prefecture?"

They stared at each other, mirror images of mistrust, neither caring to let the other out of sight. Jaouen's breath was ragged from his hasty ascent of the stairs. Laura had no such excuse, but her breath came fast just the same, rasping against her throat.

"She's not with us?" said de Berry unnecessarily. "But I thought . . ." He blanched, as though realizing what he had so nearly given away.

"I know who he is," Laura said, addressing herself only to Jaouen. "There's no use pretending."

Jaouen didn't betray himself by so much as a flicker of the eye. "He?"

"Your supposed cousin. His royal highness, the Duc de Berry."

"I didn't tell her," de Berry said hastily, looking from one to the other. "She guessed. I thought she was one of us. She seemed to know. . . ."

Jaouen pressed his eyes together in a brief, telling moment of irritation. Laura couldn't blame him. The Duc de Berry must be a very trying coconspirator. He was rumored to be a man of courage on the battlefield and charm in the ballroom, but the world of subterfuge was not for one such as he.

Unlike Jaouen.

When Jaouen spoke, his voice was hard and flat. "Who are you working for?"

Laura spoke with a bravado she didn't feel. "The last time I looked, I was working for you. The question is, who are *you* working for?"

"We'll have to do something with her," said the Duc de Berry anxiously from somewhere behind her. "Tie her up or . . ."

"One word to the wrong person," said Jaouen, his eyes on Laura, "and you sign Daubier's death warrant."

"Are you here to save Daubier?" Laura demanded. "Or to hang him?"

"What is it to you?"

Laura met his gaze steadily. "More than you imagine."

There were noises from the stairs; Laura could hear the heavy tread of boots through the open door to the foyer.

"Too many damn flights of stairs," someone was saying. He didn't bother to keep his voice down.

The bubble encasing them shattered. Jaouen swung abruptly away, his head jerking towards the door.

Jaouen cursed, briefly and violently. "Delaroche's men. He wasted no time. *Merde.* Both of you, in the back room. Now."

De Berry danced from one foot to the other, spoiling for a fight. "How many of them are there? We could take them, you and I. There's a sword on the wall—"

"A pasteboard one," clipped Jaouen. "The last thing we need is a fight. What are you waiting for? Go!"

When a man said "go" like that, people went.

Grabbing de Berry's arm in both hands, Laura tugged. Caught

off balance, the prince staggered, stumbling after her through the door to the dining room. Jaouen followed after them, grabbing the handle of the door. His eyes for a moment lit on Laura's face, frankly mistrustful. She could see him frown.

"Your old friend's life," he said. "Remember."

Was that a warning? Or a threat?

Then he shoved the door shut, plunging the room into darkness.

He knew he should have paid his governess a higher salary.

André's eyes caught those of his governess as the door swung closed. She stared back, watchful, wary, giving nothing away. Damn. He wanted to shake her, to demand answers, to rattle her out of that impressive self-possession. Was she an agent of Delaroche? Or someone else? Or nothing more than what she said. A governess. A friend of Daubier.

He might not, thought André, with gallows humor, have to wait long to find out. If she wanted to hang them all, she could. All she had to do was cry out. It would be difficult explaining de Berry's presence in Daubier's studio. They might try to pass de Berry off as his cousin, but it was a threadbare deception at best. And even the taint of suspicion would be enough to damn them all.

He had told Cadoudal not to bring de Berry to France. Not yet. There were too many pieces still left to fall into place: key generals to be suborned, potential foes to be neutralized, an appointment at the palace to be procured. He had urged prudence, but hotter heads had prevailed, and now here they were, at the mercy of a governess who might or might not keep silent for the love of an old painter who had once been a friend to her parents.

Put that way, they hadn't a hope in hell.

The guards were almost upon him. "—hate these late-night assignments," one was saying companionably to the other. "The night was meant for sleep, not traipsing around the city after phantoms."

"A phantom? But I thought they said it was an artist," said the second man disingenuously. "Sir!"

Both men snapped to at the sight of Jaouen, who folded his arms across his chest and fixed them with a stern stare. He had learned more of theater these past few years than any actor in the Comédie-Française.

He recognized the men as the same who had been sent to Cadoudal's lodgings. The dim one was . . . Laclos. That was it. Laclos and Maugret. Neither was particularly bright, but dangerous, nonetheless. He would have to trust to the appearance of authority and the late hour to keep their suspicions at bay.

"You certainly took long enough." André kept his back to the door to the dining room. He knew better than anyone the danger of the betraying glance. "Where were you?"

"We came as fast as we heard," said Laclos quickly. "There was trouble on the bridge, an overturned cart—"

"Yes, yes," said André curtly, dismissing the man's excuses in a way that made clear just how much credence he gave it. André turned his attention to the other man. "What were your orders?"

Maugret's wandering eyes snapped back to André. He noticed too much, this one. He had been looking about with frank curiosity. "To guard the chambers of the traitor Daubier, sir. To make sure no one else entered."

"Well-done," said André, with a fine edge of sarcasm. "By now, half of Paris might have been in and out. Do you know how much time it takes to destroy evidence, Maugret?"

Maugret started to nod, then changed his mind and shook his head instead. "No, sir," he said sulkily.

"Less time than you would think." Almost as little time as it took to destroy a reputation. One false move, and it would be his head on the guillotine, Gabrielle and Pierre-André abandoned to the vagaries of an uncaring world. "You should have come more quickly."

Had that been a noise from the dining room?

Laclos hung his head. "That cart . . ."

His partner stepped in. "We weren't told you would be here, sir."

André stared him down, letting him know what he thought of that piece of impertinence. "Do you always expect to be apprised of your superiors' comings and goings?" Having made his point, he deliberately adopted a more matter-of-fact tone. "I only arrived here a few moments before you. The premises appear to be un-spoiled." André allowed his lip to curl. "Although, in these conditions, it is hard to tell."

Laclos obediently guffawed. His laugh turned into an embarrassed cough as he saw that André wasn't laughing and neither was his partner. Maugret cast him a disgusted look.

"We will have our work cut out for us, searching through this sty," said André, making a show of pacing the parameters of the far end of the room. "Monsieur Delaroche should have sent more people."

"He asked for them, sir," said Laclos eagerly, "but everyone else was on other assignments. Or at home," he added wistfully.

So it was Delaroche who had sent them. Had Delaroche reported to Fouché yet? Or to the Prefecture? Or was he biding his time, hoping for more sensational discoveries before he alerted his superiors?

A prince of the blood would be a coup indeed.

He had to get de Berry and the governess out of the way. If he could persuade Laclos and Maugret to remain out front, he could shoo the others down the back stairs. De Berry might not be a genius of subtlety, but he could be trusted to get Mlle. Griscogne back to the Hôtel de Bac and to keep watch on her while there. If she was an agent of Delaroche, they couldn't risk giving her the chance to get a message out.

234 Lauren Willig

André's mind shied away from the possibility. Why was it so hard for him to believe that she was Delaroche's creature? Because her mother wrote love poetry? Because he admired her nerve? Because she had seemed to him, for a moment, like a little girl lost in the woods, trying to keep the wolves at bay?

Sentiment had no place in espionage, at least not if one hoped to survive. All the evidence said she was danger. And danger meant Delaroche.

André surveyed the two constables. "The traitor Daubier undoubtedly has confederates," he said, thinking quickly. "As soon as they hear of his plight, they'll be here, eager to destroy the evidence. Maugret!"—he pointed to the more difficult of the two—"I want you to go to the square. Find someplace where you can see the front entrance. Take note of anyone who approaches. As for you, Laclos, station yourself hard by the door. Make sure you are well hidden. Be prepared to take into custody anyone who tries to enter."

Laclos nodded eagerly. "No one will get past."

André clapped him on the shoulder. "Good man. As for me, I will wait here. With the candles out," he added. "They won't come if they think someone is here."

And it would be easier to smuggle de Berry and Mlle. Griscogne out without the candlelight silhouetting them against the windows.

"If we lay our trap properly," André declared grandiloquently, "we will catch our mice."

It was a perfectly ridiculous statement, worthy of Delaroche at his best, but it appeared to make sense, even to the skeptical Maugret.

"Yes, sir," the man said.

André felt a weakening flush of relief. He had them convinced; he could tell. They weren't out of the woods yet, but they had a shot. If he could just get de Berry to move quickly and quietly . . .

If Mlle. Griscogne didn't give them away . . . André nodded brusquely to Laclos and Maugret, motioning them on their way, giving no sign of the turmoil of thought going on beneath his stern countenance.

A crash resonated from the other room. Porcelain, splintering.

André could feel it vibrating throughout his body, as though it were his own bones being dashed to pieces rather than one of Daubier's Chinese vases.

Maugret, the more acute of the two, jerked sharply towards the dining-room door. "What was that?"

"Something breaking?" volunteered Laclos.

Maugret cast Laclos a look of contempt. "It came from there, sir," he said to André, pointing to the door. "Shall I go in?"

Too bad that sword on the wall was pasteboard. It might come down to that fight that de Berry had so eagerly desired. André cursed, silently and violently. He cursed de Berry for foolishness; Cadoudal for overreaching; and himself for too many reasons to count, although the primary one involved a woman with a penchant for gray.

André flung up a hand, halting the constable's progress. "Maugret!" The other man stopped abruptly. André lowered his voice. "There is a back door, if I recall. Whoever it is might try to escape out back. I want you to—"

He never finished his order. The dining-room door swung open.

At first, all he saw was the candle, a small blaze of light against the darkness of the room beyond. It flickered off the contours of a female form, outlined the hollows of a collarbone, the curve of a shoulder.

There was a woman in the doorway, a red velvet wrap tossed carelessly over her bare shoulders. Her hair fell in long waves down her shoulders, tousled as though she had just come from bed. Her hair was dark and rough, swallowing the light rather than reflecting it. The fine white lawn of a chemise showed beneath the red velvet wrap. The fabric ended just below her calves, revealing a pair of decidedly shapely ankles.

Lifting a hand to shield her eyes from the light of her own candle, she took a step forward on slender, bare feet, blinking sleepily.

"Antoine?" she said.

Chapter 19

André stared, speechless, as Mlle. Griscogne undulated her way into the room.

He hadn't thought his governess had it in her to undulate. But there was really no other word for it. Her hips swayed as she sauntered into the room, setting the loose ends of the velvet wrap swinging rhythmically back and forth, back and forth as she moved, brushing against her hips with every motion—back and forth, back and forth.

André blinked hard, forcing himself to focus.

Making her leisurely progress into the room, she yawned and stretched, arching her back. "Do forgive, darling, I'm afraid I— Oh. Hello. Oh dear. I thought you were Antoine."

"Er, evening. Madame," said Laclos with difficulty.

André couldn't blame him. The old artist had been right. Crimson was Mlle. Griscogne's color. Her skin didn't look sallow against the velvet. Instead, it was the richest sort of cream—warm, inviting. The velvet wrap clung to her shoulders, faithfully following the curve of her breasts, leaving her throat bare, caressed by tendrils of wild, dark hair.

Who would have thought that she could have looked so . . . so . . . Well.

Mlle. Griscogne blinked, scrubbing a hand across the back of her eyes. The movement made the wrap slide along one shoulder, showing the hint of the white linen shift beneath. So she wasn't naked underneath it, then.

Just mostly naked.

"I'm so sorry," she said, looking up under her lashes, first at the constables, then at André. "I thought you were Monsieur Daubier. I fell asleep, you see."

She fluttered her lashes up at Laclos, encouraging him to join her in complicity at her own silliness.

From the way the constable blushed and shuffled his feet, you would have thought she had asked him to join her in her bed.

André frowned at his governess. What in the devil was she playing at? And why couldn't she do it with her clothes on?

"We didn't mean to wake you, Mademoiselle—er, Madame . . . ," Laclos said bashfully.

"Suzette," she said, smiling winningly at Laclos. "You can call me Suzette. Would you mind holding my candle?"

From the way he was looking at her, Laclos would be happy to hold anything she was willing to offer him. Bumbling forward, he willingly took the candle from her.

Clever, noted the one part of André's brain that still appeared to be in proper working order. That maneuver had neatly hobbled one of the constables. Laclos wouldn't be able to reach for his weapon without dropping the candle.

But that still left Maugret.

Whose side was she on? And what was she planning to do?

"Thank you." Suzette beamed her gratitude at Laclos, raising her hands to sweep the hair away from her face. Her hair was thick and dark and wild, a primitive image of wantonness.

Only André noticed how her hands shook.

"Sometimes I worry I might set myself on fire." The movement caused the velvet wrap to slide back, revealing a deep gap where her shift gaped open. "Don't you?"

"Er, uh, yes, Madame, er, Suzette. Ouch!" Laclos jumped as wax dripped on his wrist.

"Oh, dear." Suzette was all solicitude. "I hope you haven't hurt yourself?" Her long hair brushed Laclos's wrist as she leaned over to inspect the burn.

"N-not at all. All in the line of duty," Laclos managed to get out.

"How very brave you are." Her voice was like velvet—lush and inviting.

Right. He had let this go on long enough. "If I might recall you gentlemen to our purpose here?" rapped out André.

Blushing, Laclos retrieved his hand. He was still holding the candle, but at an angle that was creating a nice little wax slick on Daubier's floor.

"Purpose?" The governess still didn't meet his eye. Swishing her hair over one shoulder, she turned her attention to Maugret. "Are you here to see Antoine?"

"Antoine?" Maugret appeared to be having trouble focusing. Focusing on her face, that was. His question appeared to be addressed to her bust. It was, to be fair, a surprisingly impressive sight, and, from the look of it, owed nothing to padding, ruffles, or the other subterfuges to which young ladies resorted in eking out what nature had failed to provide. Those severely tailored gray dresses had been hiding a good deal.

What else was she hiding?

"Oh! Silly me!" Mlle. Griscogne placed a hand on Maugret's

sleeve as she rolled her eyes at her own folly. "I meant Monsieur Daubier."

Maugret gave a jerky nod, his eyes following the movement of her chest.

One would think they had never seen a woman before, thought André irritably. Of course, they probably hadn't. Not this much of one, at any rate, in these sorts of surroundings. The painted backdrops and outlandish accoutrements of Daubier's studio gave the whole an exotic air, a moment out of sensational fiction where anything might happen.

"Are you Monsieur Daubier's wife?" André asked, his voice deliberately insolent. "Madame . . . Suzette?"

"Suzette" flushed deep to the roots of her hair. Only part of it, André suspected, was an act. He didn't miss the quick movement of her fingers to the edge of her wrap, as though she were itching to hitch it up.

She recovered quickly, flinging herself back into the role. "Me? Oh no! I'm just his . . ." She hesitated delicately. "His model. For the paintings. He paints, you know."

Over her head, André exchanged a knowing look with Maugret. "His model," André repeated, a wealth of condemnation in the simple word. "And what are you doing here at this hour?"

"We were to have a session, you see," she said quickly, fussing with her velvet wrap in a way that did more to draw attention to its inadequacies than it did to fix them. "A painting session. Would you like to wait for him? I'm sure he'll be back soon."

"I wouldn't be so sure about that," muttered Maugret.

Looking at Mlle. Griscogne in a hangdog way, Laclos said, "Madame, er, Mademoiselle . . . I'm afraid we . . . That is . . ."

"Monsieur Daubier has been arrested," André said harshly.

"Arrested!" Mlle. Griscogne's hands flew to her bosom. "Antoine!" She swayed a little, as though contemplating the wisdom of a swoon.

Overdoing it there, thought André cynically.

Or maybe not. Laclos rushed in to support her. Mlle. Griscogne draped herself artistically over his arm, although André noticed she was careful not to lean too heavily on him. Even in character, she didn't like to put herself into anyone else's power.

A mistake. Never undertake a role one wasn't prepared to see through to the bitter end, come what may. He had learned that the hard way.

"Surely," she murmured, from the crook of the constable's arm, "there must be some mistake? Oh!" She pulled back, away from Laclos. "If this is about that carriage accident, he already explained about that! It was the other carriage, not his, that hit that cart. We just happened to be right behind them. And he paid for the apples."

"Er, um, no, I don't think it's the apples. . . ." Laclos was floundering.

Was it too much to hope that she had persuaded de Berry to sneak out the back way while the constables were otherwise occupied? He had been judging her as a potential enemy. But as a potential ally . . . she might be formidable.

Might be.

André frowned at Mlle. Griscogne. "Do you think the Ministry of Police concerns itself with apples, Mademoiselle Suzette?" he demanded in his best Delaroche imitation.

She furrowed her brow in exaggerated thought. "Well, someone ought to. Although these apples really weren't dearest Antoine's fault, not at all. And it was the purest bad luck that one knocked over that lady."

Clasping his hands behind his back, André paced back in forth in front of the artist's model, shooting questions at her in a curt, clipped tone. "Have you noticed any strange behavior recently in Monsieur Daubier, Mademoiselle? Any odd comings and goings?"

Mlle. Griscogne looked at him with wide eyes. "Strange?"

Twisting a lock of hair around one finger, Mlle. Griscogne looked up from under her lashes at first Laclos, then Maugret. "There's really nothing so terribly strange about Antoine. Unless one considers his waistcoats, but those aren't really so *very* bad once a girl gets used to them. Of course, there is his— Well, there's no need to talk about that." She hastily fluffed her hair.

"That?"

She looked bashful. "Every man has his little quirks. And he really is such a dear, and such a very good painter. At least so everyone tells me. Do you know he is to paint the First Consul?"

Not a point André wanted emphasized at this particular moment.

"An idiot," André said under his breath to Maugret, on his right. "Just our luck. I doubt we'll get much more out of her."

Maugret looked her up and down with hungry eyes. "Someone will."

"Not while you're on duty," André said repressively. Or after. Madame Suzette was going to be permanently out of commission as soon as this farce was done.

"Oh! Wait! I've thought of something!" Mlle. Griscogne turned to Laclos, having obviously marked him out as the softest mark of the lot. She put a hand on Laclos's sleeve. "Darling Antoine *has* been away a good deal recently."

"Away?" André prompted, wondering where she was going with this and whether he should let her.

"In the evenings. And after I'd made him such a nice supper— well, not made, exactly, but I did pick it up from the cookshop, so that does almost count, doesn't it?"

André gestured to Laclos and Maugret, indicating to them to pay attention. "Mademoiselle Suzette," he said, in a too-loud voice. "Do you know where he goes?"

She made a moue of distaste. "It's that warehouse of his."

André's chest expanded as he let out the breath he hadn't realized he had been holding. Daubier had no warehouse. In an instant, he saw her plan: to send the constables off chasing after a will-o'-the-wisp. He would have cheered if it wouldn't have given the game away.

"He says he has to check on his canvases—although why canvases should require hours and hours, I have no idea. He was never like that before."

"How long have you been, er, with him?" Laclos blurted out.

"Oh, a very long time!" she said enthusiastically. "Almost a month!"

"This warehouse," said André, giving Laclos a repressive look. He had to; if he didn't, he might start laughing, and that would be entirely inappropriate. "Do you know where it is?"

"Oh yes. But I've never been there, you understand. He wouldn't let me. Not even after I asked *so* prettily."

Her mouth stretched in an elongated O on the word "so."

For an innocent spinster, she managed to imbue that one syllable with a disturbing number of sexual overtones.

But she wasn't an innocent spinster tonight. She was Suzette, artist's model and supposed mistress of Antoine Daubier, painter.

André could practically hear the constables panting. Did Mlle. Griscogne have any idea what they were imagining?

An hour ago, he would have said no.

Now . . .

Who in the bloody hell was she? More to the point, *what* was she?

"Put your chin up, Laclos," André said curtly. "You're drooling." He turned back to Mlle. Griscogne. "Did he ever say anything to you about this warehouse?"

"He didn't like people to come there. Sometimes I wondered—" She shrugged, sending her chemise sliding down her shoulder. The movement drew the fabric taut over her breasts. "Well, never mind."

None of them did.

"I thought as much," said André loudly. "It is just as I suspected. Mademoiselle Suzette, do you know where this warehouse might be?"

"It was . . ." She dipped her chin, contemplating her own cleavage. "Wait, wait—I know I have it. . . ."

Between her breasts?

Laclos and Maugret inspected the area with equal attention. André resisted the urge to bang their heads together. She was doing brilliantly, far better than he was. He just wished she didn't have to do it quite so . . . bustily.

"Yes!" She gave an excited hop. The rest of her bounced with her. "That's it! Rue des Puces. I remember thinking that I shouldn't like to spend so much time on a street of fleas. It was number seventy-three. Or maybe seventy-four."

"Thank you, Mademoiselle Suzette," said André quietly. "That was most helpful, indeed."

His eye caught hers, and for a moment, just a moment, the mask dropped. There was nothing coquettish there now. She looked, for that moment, unsure, vulnerable, unclothed in a way that had nothing to do with physical dishabille.

André had an absurd desire to squeeze her hand and tell her it was going to be all right.

Nonsense, of course. He didn't know that it was going to be all right, or even whose side she was really on.

They were going to have to have a good, long talk once he had dispensed with their audience.

"Laclos, Maugret, a word." Taking his constables by the arm, he led them a little bit away, drawing them into a confidential huddle. Laclos's breath smelled of onions, Maugret's of cheap wine. "If Daubier's piece of fluff is telling us the truth—"

Maugret snickered. "That one? She's all tits, no wits. She wouldn't lie to us."

"Astutely observed, constable," said André dryly. "As I was saying, I doubt there is much more for us here. It would have been clever of Daubier to conduct his shadier affairs away from his official place of residence."

"But..." Laclos's rubicund face fell into concerned lines. "Monsieur Delaroche told us to stay at the studio."

"And I," said André pleasantly, "tell you to investigate the warehouse. Had he known of this further development, I am sure Monsieur Delaroche would agree. The trick to good police work," he added, in an avuncular tone, "is learning when to adapt one's plans to changing circumstances."

They absorbed the information solemnly, Maugret nodding thoughtfully. He was ambitious, that one. André thought he knew how to handle him.

"Laclos, I want you to watch the warehouse. See if anyone tries to enter. As for you . . ." André made a show of studying Maugret, making him wait. It couldn't hurt to let him sweat it out a bit. "Since your powers of observation are so keen, I entrust you with the task of examining the premises. Go carefully. This may yield information of value. Great value. You do understand what I am saying, don't you?"

Oh yes, he did. The prospect of patronage, promotion. They were in this together now, as far as Maugret was concerned. André had him.

"Yes, sir," was all Maugret said, but he sent a look of triumph at Laclos. It was wasted on Laclos, who was making moony eyes at Mlle. Griscogne across the room. She had draped herself artistically across the chaise longue, in the classic pose made popular by Mme. Récamier.

"As for myself," André said, in tones of weary resignation, "I will complete the search here. I doubt it will yield anything of interest, but it must be done."

"Nothing of interest?" Maugret leered at Mlle. Griscogne. "In that case, I hope we find nothing of interest in the warehouse!"

"Constable." André's voice was icy. "I recall you to your duty. I speak of those things of interest to the Republic. Or does your cock matter more to you than your country?"

It did the trick. Muttering apologies, Maugret took himself off with commendable rapidity, all but pushing his partner down the stairs.

André waited until the last heavy tread had faded away. Then he turned to Mlle. Griscogne. She was still lying on the divan, but she had propped herself up on one elbow, her pose anything but languorous. As André watched, she hastily swung her legs over the edge of the divan, pulling the fabric of her shift close about her calves. Her back was ramrod straight.

"Are they gone?"

"That was quite a performance." André raised an eyebrow. "They call her Suzette, the girl men can't forget."

Mlle. Griscogne hitched the velvet wrap up around her shoulders, not seductively this time, but with an awkward, jerky movement that was much more her own. He could see her shivering beneath the velvet.

"I hope they do," she said abruptly. "Forget. How long do we have before they come back?"

In the candlelight, her face looked too thin. The flickering light picked out the hollows beneath her cheekbones, the lines beside her eyes. She was no longer Suzette, artist's model, but a worried woman past the flush of her first youth.

André bit back the dozen questions that rose to his lips. There was no time. Daubier's life hung in the balance still. Daubier's life and all his plans, long years in the making.

"Not long enough," he said. Striding to the dining-room door, he yanked it open. "You can come out now."

"Are they gone?" The Duc de Berry's voice echoed down the corridor.

"For the moment." André looked back at Mlle. Griscogne,

clutching the red velvet throw around her shoulders. The chemise gaped open at the neck, revealing the deep gap between her breasts.

"Put some clothes on," André said harshly. "We're going back to the Hôtel de Bac."

"Here's your dress," said the Duc de Berry helpfully, pausing to pick something up off the dining-room floor as he sauntered across the threshold. He looked dubiously at the crumpled gray fabric. "A bit wrinkled now."

"Thank you." Mlle. Griscogne snatched the garment out of his hand, hastily shaking it out. Dropping the red velvet wrap, she shrugged her dress over her head, thrusting her arms into the sleeves. She twisted her arms behind her back, feverishly fumbling after her buttons. "Why are we going back to the Hôtel de Bac? What about Monsieur Daubier?"

She was struggling to reach the buttons, her hair getting in the way of her fingers. Without a word, André took her by the shoulders, turned her around, brushed her hair out of the way, and began doing up her buttons. She started at the brush of his fingers against her back, giving him a quick, wide-eyed look over her shoulder.

"Hold still, Suzette," he said dryly.

She frowned at him but complied, lowering her head so he could reach the buttons by her neck. André brushed the hair away from her nape, surprised to find his hand unsteady. It was the aftermath of a long evening, he told himself, the nervous tension of the confrontation with Delaroche, nothing to do with the long line of her neck, the curve of her spine, the intimate act of doing up a lady's buttons. The last time he had served this office had been for Julie.

André shoved the last button into its hole. "There," he said brusquely. "Let's go."

"Wait!" She yanked on his arm. "The ledger!"

André looked at the fingers on his arm and then at her face. "What do you know about the ledger?"

De Berry shrugged. "Sorry. I thought . . ."

"She was one of us," André finished flatly. "Right." The ledger was already burned, destroyed immediately following Picot's arrest, as soon as the net began to close. She might want it for one of two reasons, to save Daubier or to condemn him. "The ledger isn't here. You needn't worry about that."

"Good," she said, giving her tangled hair a quick twist. It promptly fell right back down. "I assume it's somewhere safe."

André raised his brows, but forbore to comment. "Come on," he said instead. "Time is wasting. They'll be back when they can't find that warehouse."

"Or they'll search the wrong one," she countered. She navigated the narrow hallway with the ease of familiarity. "A dispute with the owner will occupy them for a spell."

"You gave them a real address?" André almost ran into an ornamental urn.

Mlle. Griscogne's eyes met his. "It seemed the expedient thing to do."

Expedient? It was bloody brilliant. If there was a warehouse at the Rue des Puces, Laclos and Maugret could expect to be embroiled for some time with an indignant owner.

André yanked open the front door. "Who are you?"

Mlle. Griscogne slipped past him, through the open door, Jeannette's old cloak pulled tight around her shoulders. "Laure Griscogne. A governess." Two stairs down, she glanced back at him over her shoulder. "A friend to Monsieur Daubier."

André shoved the door at de Berry, catching up with her halfway down the flight. "You expect me to believe you would involve yourself in treason for him?"

"Is that what this is? Treason?"

She automatically started towards the square as they reached the base of the stairs. André grabbed her arm, yanking her into safety in the shadows, de Berry following behind. "Don't play games, Mademoiselle Griscogne," he said in an undertone, careful not to wake the sleeping concierge. "They don't suit you."

Mlle. Griscogne's voice was breathless from keeping pace with him. "Then deal with me honestly. Speak to me plainly."

André kept a tight hold on her arm. "You want plain speaking? Your old friend Daubier is bound for the guillotine unless we can get him out."

"There is no hope they will release him?"

"Intact? No."

"Can you get him out?" she asked urgently.

"I can try."

He could try, but he wasn't sure he could succeed. Years of building up his position, and yet his influence went only so far. One false move, and he condemned not only Daubier but himself.

Jean wasn't at the gate. André shoved it open himself, taking some solace in physical exertion, the simple act of pitting muscle against iron. If only it would be so easy to move the guards around Delaroche.

"In," he said brusquely. "You'll both stay here tonight. Cousin Philippe, make sure Mademoiselle Griscogne is well settled for the night."

He could hear the gravel crackle beneath Mlle. Griscogne's boots. "You mean you want him to guard me."

"In plain language, yes. Would you do otherwise in my position?" He pulled open the front door, holding it open for her with exaggerated gallantry. The guests had long since gone home, the remnants of the feast been cleared away, the gauze torn down from the walls. The Hôtel de Bac was as it had been before—an empty, ruined shell of a place. "We have a great deal of talking to do, you and I."

Mlle. Griscogne gave him a long look as she took up the candle that Jean had left on the front hall table. "I couldn't agree more."

A small voice piped up out of the shadows. "Mademoiselle?"

André saw a small figure huddled on the stairs.

"Pierre-André?" Pushing back her hood with her free hand, she moved quickly towards him. "What are you doing out of bed?"

Pierre-André stood on the first stair and wrapped his arms around her waist, burying his small head in her torso. "Nightmare," he mumbled.

André took a step forward into the hall, feeling strangely out of place with his own son, in his own family. Pierre-André hadn't seen him, he tried to reassure himself. Pierre-André would have come to him otherwise. Or would he? He had been little more than a stranger to his own children for the past four years.

And all for what? A plot that was fast unraveling, a cause to which his commitment was at best equivocal.

Mlle. Griscogne cupped Pierre-André's head with a practiced hand. "What kind of nightmare?"

Pierre-André burrowed against her stomach. "We were on the bridge and that man—the man in the carriage—"

Mlle. Griscogne's eyes met André's over his son's head. "Monsieur Delaroche."

"He pushed me into the water. Hard," Pierre-André added in injured tones. "I was drownding and drownding," he said dramatically.

"But you're not now," said Mlle. Griscogne, in matter-of-fact tones. "You're not in the Seine and you're not on the bridge. You're in your own house, all dry and safe."

"Mmmph," said Pierre-André.

She continued her rhythmic stroking of his hair. "It was only a dream, nothing more. It can't hurt you."

But Delaroche could. She knew it. André knew it. The worst nightmares were those that took place when one was awake.

Prizing Pierre-André's arms from around her waist, she leaned back just far enough to look André's little boy in the eye. "I'll put you back to bed, shall I?"

Pierre-André put up his arms and she hefted him up with surprising ease. André stood in the shadows, frozen, the full weight of what he might have done dragging at him like the waters of the Seine.

Pierre-André buried his downy head in the governess's shoulder. She looked back to André. "I'll be down directly."

"I'm off to the Prefecture. I may be some time." He added, with a flash of dry humor, "You needn't wait up."

Mlle. Griscogne's eyes met his over his son's tousled head. "But I will."

Chapter 20

*L*aura started awake as boots sounded against the wood of the floor.

She hadn't realized she'd fallen asleep. De Berry still snored peacefully away on his settee, one arm flung up along the back, but the candle had guttered into a puddle of wax and the pale light of dawn filtered through the windows. It was a particularly dispirited sort of dawn, as strained and gray as Jaouen's face as he strode into the room.

Laura rose clumsily from her chair, aware that the fire had burned down long since, that her fingers were stiff with cold and her toes numb in her boots.

"Well?" she croaked. Her voice was dry with disuse. Laura cleared her throat and tried again. "What news?"

"It was no use." Jaouen's customary vitality appeared to have deserted him. He peeled off his glasses to rub his eyes, that gesture so familiar, and yet, like everything else, so suspect. "Fouché's men have him under close watch."

Laura wiped her palms against the rumpled material of her

skirt. "I thought you were one of them," she said tiredly. "Fouché's men."

She still hadn't made sense of the fact that he wasn't. The entire world had turned upside down and spun on its head in the space of the evening.

"I was." Jaouen caught himself. "I am. For the moment."

Until Fouché found out the truth.

What was the truth? Laura was too tired to sort out plots and counterplots. To her tired eyes, Jaouen seemed sincere. But then, she had believed him before too, believed him to be whatever it was that he had claimed to be.

Laura sat back down, taking her time, using the motion as an excuse to study her so-called employer as she arranged her rumpled skirts with as much care as if they had been a princess's best ball gown, her brain swimming with crosses and double crosses, deceptions and counterdeceptions.

In the mist-laden silence, de Berry made a snuffling noise and rolled over.

What did royal dukes dream of? Laura wondered irrelevantly. Castles and coronets? Swift horses and beautiful women?

Jaouen spoke, so abruptly that it made her jump. "I can get Daubier out. But if I do so, the game is up, for all of us." Pressing his bloodshot eyes together, he breathed in deeply, shaking his head. "No. That's a lie. It's over already. It has been from the moment they arrested Picot. It's only a matter of time now until it all unravels. And not much time."

How did one tell the lies from the truths? She couldn't be sure whether he was lying to himself or to her. Or both. His words had the ring of sincerity, but she no longer trusted her own ability to discern fact from fiction. At least, not where Jaouen was concerned.

"What are you going to do?" Laura asked quietly.

Jaouen dropped heavily into the chair next to hers. She could hear the scrape of the legs against the uncarpeted floor. He let his head fall back against the wall, as though it had grown too heavy to carry. "I can get him out," he repeated. "I can go and present my cousin's seal and claim that I'm moving Daubier on Fouché's request. They'll believe me. It's been true often enough in the past. Once they discover the deception . . ." He let out his breath in a long, tired exhalation. "I'll have to arrange for the children first. There'll be preparations to be made."

He spoke as though he didn't expect to return. Laura twisted in her chair to face him. Her gray skirt brushed his leg. He was still wearing formal stockings and breeches, his garb from the party, but the white stockings were stained with mud, the shiny black shoes scuffed.

"And what about you?"

Jaouen rolled his head against the wall so he was facing her. His eyes were bloodshot and there was a night's growth of beard on his chin. He said nothing.

He didn't need to.

"You're not just going to give yourself up," Laura said disbelievingly. "Oh, for heaven's sake! You are, aren't you? Trading yourself in for Daubier? That's something straight out of—out of a bad chivalric romance!"

Unless, of course, he knew himself to be in no danger, the more cynical part of her mind whispered. That would be clever, to free the old artist—at seeming risk of his own life—only to follow Daubier to his confederates.

"Of course I'm not," said Jaouen irritably. "What do you take me for? Robin Hood?"

The paper of the wall was cool against Laura's temple. They were eye to eye, only inches apart. Without his glasses, his eyes were brilliantly blue. "I don't know what to take you for. Not anymore."

"Trust me," said Jaouen, "the feeling is mutual, *Suzette*."

Laura felt a sudden, absurd urge to tug up her bodice, even though she knew it to be quite firmly in place. "You're fortunate that Suzette appeared when she did. If those men had gone blundering off through Daubier's studio, we would be in worse case than we are."

"We?"

"Whose motives are the more in question?" she asked. "Mine? Or your own?"

"You don't flinch, do you?" he said admiringly.

"Not from what needs to be done."

Jaouen propped himself up on one elbow. His shadow fell across the wall behind her, blocking her in. "What needs to be done for whom? Delaroche? Or someone else?"

"I told you already. My interest is in saving Daubier. I will also," she said, in her driest, most governess-like tones, "admit to a certain interest in the future of your offspring. I have invested considerable effort in them. I would prefer not to see them fatherless."

It was as close as she could come to saying that she cared. On the children's behalf, of course. And Daubier's.

She shrugged. "You can believe me or not, as you choose."

"You needn't worry that I'm planning to hand myself over to the Ministry of Police on a platter. I'm going to do my damnedest to get out. I have no interest in martyrdom. Not in this cause or any other."

"Then why embroil yourself in it?"

Jaouen's face was as closed as the city gates. "Because it seemed like a good idea at the time."

All right, then. If he didn't want to talk about it, they didn't have to talk about it. "Didn't you have an escape plan?"

"We did." The use of the past tense was unmistakable. Whatever the escape plan had been, it was no longer viable. "I owe an obligation to Daubier," Jaouen said woodenly, with the dogged single-mindedness of exhaustion. "I intend to see it through."

Laura wiggled upright in her chair, girding for battle. "And what of your other obligations? Are you just going to abandon your children, abandon your cause, and let the Ministry do with you what they will? I call that poor spirited."

She had hit a nerve. Jaouen's lips curled back over his teeth. "I am *not* abandoning my children."

"Sending yourself off to be killed? And what will become of them? A return to Nantes with Jeannette? What would you call it?"

"Protecting them. Saving them from the consequences of my actions. They shouldn't be damned for my carelessness."

Carelessness. Like taking a boat out on the coast of Cornwall— the rocky coast of Cornwall—in the middle of a squall.

"Isn't it a bit late for that?" she said nastily.

Jaouen whitened as though she had slapped him.

"I—," he began, and stopped. She could see the words whirring through his brain—defense, denial, attempts at exoneration—all considered and discarded. He came out fighting. "Do you think you could do better?"

Well, since he asked. "Yes," said Laura.

Behind them, de Berry snored on.

"How?" Jaouen had his voice back under control, but there was a rough edge to it, half anger, half hope. She could see his knuckles white against the seat of the chair. "Pray, do enlighten me."

If he were what he claimed . . . She couldn't tell him about the Pink Carnation; it wasn't her secret to share. But if he were what he claimed, if he were the Duc de Berry's protector rather than his executioner, the Pink Carnation would want to know.

And, quite possibly, help.

The agents of the English government and those of the French royal family did not always work in accord. To smuggle the Duc de Berry out of Paris—when Artois's own organization had failed—would be an immense feather in the Pink Carnation's cap.

"I know someone—someone who might be able to help you. You could leave Paris with your children. With the duke. And Daubier."

"Grand promises, Mademoiselle Griscogne."

"I don't make any promises. But it is a chance."

"A chance." There was a bitter tinge to the word. Propping an elbow against the back of the chair, he asked, "Who is this someone?"

Laura shook her head. "I can't tell you that."

"And yet you expect me to trust you, with not only my own life, but those of my children?"

"Do you have any other choice?"

Jaouen pressed his bloodshot eyes shut. "There might," he said raggedly, "have been more politic ways of phrasing that."

"There might," she agreed. "But we are plainspoken people, you and I. Aren't we?"

Jaouen's elbow rested on the back of her chair. "Are you telling me you've never lied to me?"

Only about everything.

Nearly everything. What a cosmic joke it was that her deception had taken her from her assumed identity and put her back to what she was, Michel and Chiaretta de Griscogne's daughter. She had lied her way back to the truth.

"I don't make claims I can't keep," she countered. "Have I led you false yet?"

"Where do you find this friend of yours?"

"Alone," she said, and saw him wince. "You can't have expected I would have allowed you to come."

She saw his eyebrows lift on the word "allowed," but he forbore comment. The balance of power had shifted, and they both knew it.

"You do realize," he said slowly, "what a risk I take in allowing you to go alone. You might go straight to Delaroche."

"I might," she agreed levelly. "You might take de Berry and run as soon as I leave the house. We both act on faith."

"Faith," Jaouen murmured. "The last refuge of those with nothing else."

"You said it, Monsieur, not I."

"If you are to be our salvation, you might as well call me André." His lips creased in a weary smile. "You were never terribly convincing about the honorific."

"André," she said, testing the name. Perhaps there was a little bit of Suzette in her after all. She rolled the "r" on her tongue and watched his eyes follow her lips. "Are you sure you wish to allow me such liberties?"

"I think we are well past liberties, you and I."

There was a muffled crash behind them. Laura twisted, hastily, just in time to see the Duc de Berry hauling himself back up onto the settee, off of which he had fallen. "Not made for normal-size people," he muttered sleepily, before his bleary eyes focused on André. "I say! You're back. Is the painter—"

"Still in prison," said André bluntly. He turned back to Laura. "When can you see your . . . friend?"

"This morning. Wait for me before you do anything else. It would probably be best," she added, "if you go to the Prefecture as usual."

"Thank you," said Jaouen dryly, "for the advice. I would never have thought of that."

The Duc de Berry looked from one to the other. "Is . . . What?"

"Mademoiselle Griscogne," said Jaouen levelly, "has undertaken to help us remove from Paris."

"Remove?" The Duc de Berry woke up in a hurry. "But our plans—*the* plan—"

"Is over," said Jaouen brutally. "Without Daubier, we can't get into the palace. And there's more. All gates have been ordered closed and all carriages searched. We'll be lucky if we leave Paris with our lives."

Laura watched as the duke processed the information, all his grand ambitions scattering into dust around him. To his credit, he took it on the chin. He didn't protest or argue.

Instead, like the soldier he had been, he went straight to action. "How do we get out? If all the gates are being closed . . ."

"For that," said Jaouen, "we are forced to rely upon Mademoiselle Griscogne. And her friend."

The Duc de Berry's brow furrowed. He looked Laura up and down, from her trampled hem to her wildly tousled hair. "Then . . . she is one of ours?"

"That," said André Jaouen, his eyes on Laura, "is entirely up to her."

Chapter 21

Mist lay heavy over the graveled paths of the Jardins du Luxembourg. It wasn't so much raining as it was oozing; Laura's pelisse was already damp through, simply from walking in the moisture-rich air. Beads of liquid pearled the statues on their stone plinths. Inadequately garbed for the climate, Venus shivered on her pedestal, casting recriminatory glances at Mars in his boots and breastplate.

Would the Pink Carnation keep her appointment? The desolation of the gardens increased the risk of the meeting. If the gardens were bustling with activity, with nannies and their charges, young ladies sketching, clerks snatching a moment in the sunshine, it would be easy enough to contrive a chance meeting. Two women alone in the rain made a stranger spectacle.

Not, of course, as strange a spectacle as Suzette, the girl men couldn't forget.

Laura grimaced at the memory. To be honest, she had rather enjoyed herself. It had been nice, for a change, to shuck off restraint along with her dress and to play the sort of character she seemed destined never to be. For about ten minutes, she had felt beautiful. Desirable. She remembered the expression on Jaouen's face as she had made her grand entrance from the dining room, more courtesan than governess.

We are well past liberties, you and I.

If her mission succeeded, Jaouen would be gone within a matter of hours. Gone from Paris, gone from her life.

Onward and upward, she told herself bracingly. She wasn't meant to get attached, either as a governess or as an agent. In fact, one of her primary attractions for the Pink Carnation had been her detachment. She belonged to nothing and to no one.

When was the last time she had been invited to call anyone by his first name?

There was a young lady making her way down the path towards the ruins of the Medici fountain. She glanced anxiously at the sky as she walked, a sketchbook clutched beneath one arm. She held no umbrella, only a reticule that dangled from one wrist, swinging as she walked. As Laura watched, she frowned up at the sky, holding up a gloved hand as though to test the air. As if in response, a fat drop splashed down on Laura's nose. The clouds had gathered and the heavens were about to open.

The young lady appeared to have realized it also. She made an anxious survey of the gardens. Catching sight of the remains of the loggia that had once framed the fountain, she gathered up her skirts and dashed for shelter, holding on to her bonnet with one hand, her sketchbook and her skirts with the other.

Belatedly, Laura realized what she was meant to do. Grabbing hold of her own skirts, she followed suit, floundering as her hem dragged in the mud. She arrived, gasping, beneath the loggia.

"You don't mind?" she panted. "The rain—"

"No, no," said the Pink Carnation generously. "Do stand with me. Hopefully it will pass in a moment. So silly of me to come out without an umbrella!" She glanced ruefully at the sky. "When I decided to paint watercolors today, I hadn't thought nature meant to provide the water."

Laura looked at her sideways. "How very accommodating of it."

To her surprise, the Pink Carnation laughed, a genuine laugh. "I knew I hadn't made a mistake with you. I had hoped it would rain, but hadn't been sure I could count on it." Shaking out her damp bonnet, she regarded it complacently. "Anyone will see only two ladies marooned beneath an overhang, attempting to keep their dresses dry. There is no one within earshot. Miss Gwen will give the signal if anyone approaches."

Miss Gwen? Laura took a surreptitious glance around but saw no sign of the chaperone. Wherever she was, she was well hidden.

The Pink Carnation had called this meeting, presumably for reasons of her own, but Laura decided that the matter of the Duc de Berry took precedence.

"Thank goodness for the rain," Laura agreed. "Matters have taken a strange turn. I am much in need of your aid."

The Pink Carnation was instantly all alert. "Did Jaouen discover you?"

Laura could have laughed. Almost. "Say rather that I discovered him." She braced herself for disbelief. "Monsieur Jaouen claims to be working for the Comte d'Artois."

If she was surprised, the Pink Carnation didn't betray it. "Do you believe him?"

She only wished she knew. "If he is playing a double game, it's a very deep one."

A small line appeared between the Pink Carnation's perfectly shaped brows. "You haven't told him—"

"No!" Laura wasn't sure whether to be offended that the Pink Carnation had thought she might. "No. He thinks I've offered to help him out of affection for Monsieur Daubier."

"Daubier," said Miss Wooliston musingly. "The man who was arrested last night." She raised a brow at Laura. "Affection?"

Laura shook herself out of unprofitable reverie. "Monsieur Daubier was a friend of my parents. Monsieur Jaouen has been led to believe that I keep his secret on their account."

"How does Monsieur Daubier fit into all this?"

Laura examined her gloves, choosing her words carefully. "I gather—although I am not entirely sure—that Monsieur Daubier was to be their means of entry to the Tuileries. He had recently been commissioned to paint a portrait of the First Consul."

"A position of some intimacy," commented the Pink Carnation. "Providing exceptional access."

Laura nodded. "I saw uniforms in an unused room in the Hôtel de Bac. They were uniforms of the Consular Guard. Jaouen claimed they belonged to his cousin."

"I see." The Pink Carnation stared off into the rain, an impatient young lady eager to resume her sketching, bored with her current company. "If Daubier were to bring with him soldiers disguised as members of the Consul's own bodyguard . . ."

"I have no proof," said Laura hastily. "Well, not that sort of proof."

The Pink Carnation looked at her sharply. "What is it?"

There was no way to say it but to say it. "The Duc de Berry. Jaouen is hiding the Duc de Berry."

Miss Wooliston's eyes lit with excitement. "So that is where he is!"

"Not the whole time," said Laura honestly. "Jaouen has been passing him off as his cousin, but I gather he was hiding part of the time with Daubier and before that with someone they referred to only as Cousin Héloïse."

"Cadoudal," said Miss Wooliston. "Cadoudal would have wanted to keep him close until le Petit Picot's arrest. When the water got too hot and he realized he was himself in danger, he must have sent the prince off to Daubier." For Laura's benefit, she added, "We knew the prince was somewhere in France, but we didn't know where. Artois wouldn't say. This was not," she said primly, "an expedition we encouraged."

Laura wondered who the Pink Carnation meant by "we." The War Office? The English government? Either way, the general thrust was clear. Once again, the Royalist forces and the English ones were working out of concert.

"The duke will have to be got out of Paris," said the Pink Carnation determinedly. "It would be too embarrassing for everyone concerned if he were caught. I take it their plans have been aborted?"

"Jaouen seems to think that without Daubier, they have no hope of going forward."

The Pink Carnation nodded knowledgably. "Without Daubier to provide access and Cadoudal on the run, all they have is one Bourbon prince and a number of useless uniforms."

"Could we use the uniforms to get de Berry, Daubier, and Jaouen out of the city?" asked Laura.

"Members of the Consular Guard on a pleasure jaunt outside of Paris?" The Pink Carnation shook her head. "The governor of Paris has ordered the gates of the city closed and all vehicles searched. We'll have to be cleverer than that."

Laura felt an entirely unwarranted sense of relief at that word "we." "Monsieur Jaouen thinks that he can get Monsieur Daubier out of the Temple, but only at the expense of his position. He needs to leave Paris immediately—he, the children, Monsieur Daubier, and the Duc de Berry. Oh, and the nursery maid, Jeannette."

The Pink Carnation's expression was wry. "Would they like to add a few dancing bears and a small band?"

Lined up that way, it did sound rather ridiculous. But this was the Pink Carnation, who specialized in making the ridiculous possible. Who else would have left petals on Bonaparte's pillow? "Can it be done?"

"Possibly." Miss Wooliston's cool gray gaze settled on Laura. "You left yourself off that list."

"Me?"

The Pink Carnation's expression was thoughtful. "I would like you to go with them. I need someone trustworthy to ensure that the Duc de Berry doesn't come to grief between here and London."

"Why me?"

"You know Jaouen. He trusts you. Don't you think Jaouen would object to the inclusion of someone else at this late stage? You have the best opportunity of anyone to oversee de Berry's departure without causing additional suspicion."

Weeks on the road with Jaouen, working together rather than at cross-purposes, as equals rather than employer to employee.

"You're sure you have nothing more pressing for me in Paris?" said Laura.

"Remaining in Paris might not be . . . wise. Monsieur Delaroche has marked you out. When Jaouen disappears, you will be the first person for whom he'll search. Monsieur Delaroche's methods of interrogation are not pleasant."

The Pink Carnation wasn't trying to scare her. That wasn't Miss Wooliston's way. She spoke frankly, colleague to colleague. The reason the words sent such a chill down Laura's spine was that she knew them to be true.

That, and the fact that she was standing directly beneath a leak.

Laura hastily shifted sideways, out of the way of the cold drip. "I didn't imagine they would be. Do you think he . . ."

"Suspects you? No. But you were in Jaouen's employ and therefore can be presumed to have some notion of where he might have got to. Delaroche is of the sort who doesn't mind how many eggs he breaks in the acquisition of his omelet. In fact, I believe he rather enjoys it."

"Torture for torture's sake," said Laura. She knew she hadn't liked the man. "Lovely."

"No. Rather wasteful, really," said the Pink Carnation with the detachment of a professional. "But that is how Monsieur Delaroche operates—and will continue to do so unless Monsieur Fouché deems it worth his while to rein him in. I do not believe he will in this instance. Not in anything relating to Jaouen."

As Jaouen's cousin and patron, Fouché would be too closely implicated to make any exceptions to the rules. He wouldn't risk it. Not for a governess. She was, as the Pink Carnation had so delicately pointed out, expendable.

"It will," said the Pink Carnation, "be terribly embarrassing for Monsieur Fouché when this all breaks. His own position is currently less than secure."

"In other words," said Laura, her mouth unaccountably dry, "he will be inclined to interrogate anyone involved with more than unusual zeal. To prove that he himself is not implicated."

"That is about the shape of it," said Miss Wooliston matter-of-factly. They might have been discussing flower arrangements for a church fête.

"Should we break into smaller groups?" Laura asked. "I with the Duc de Berry and Daubier, Jaouen with his children?"

"I don't believe that will be necessary. Sometimes the easiest way to escape is in plain sight."

Something about the way the Pink Carnation said it made Laura very, very nervous. "What do you mean?" she asked.

Miss Wooliston countered her question with a question of her own. "How long will it take Jaouen to release Daubier?"

"Not long," said Laura cautiously. "At least, that was the sense I received. But he must be gone immediately after."

"If I gave you an address, could you make sure the entire party is there by dawn tomorrow?"

Laura thought of them all—de Berry and Daubier, the children, Jeannette. Jaouen.

"I believe so," she said.

The Pink Carnation's lips curved upwards in a decidedly cat-who-got-the-cream sort of smile.

"Excellent!" she said. "Here is what you need to do . . ."

❧

Rain dripped down from the brim of André's hat as he rapped smartly at the concierge's door at the Temple Prison.

André had taken the carriage to the Prefecture, then slipped down a side stair and out one of the Prefecture's many side doors. He had walked from there to the Temple, his coat held close and his hat pulled low over his head against the rain.

He had known for some time that his coachman was in the pay of Fouché, a fact that he now intended to use to good purpose. As far as the coachman was concerned, André was safely ensconced in his office in the Prefecture until evening; it would take hours before anyone realized he was missing.

It was a weak bluff, susceptible to all sorts of mischance, but every little bit helped.

The concierge had fallen asleep over his ledgers. He started awake as André rapped again, more forcefully.

"Monsieur Jaouen!" he exclaimed, rocking back in his chair. Papers sifted to the floor. There was a splotch of ink on the concierge's cheek and a corresponding blot in the requisition book. "I didn't expect you. No one told me—"

André waved aside his apologies. "No matter. I need the keys for"—he made a show of consulting the paper in his hand—"prisoner five hundred and fifty-two. Antoine Daubier."

"D-Daubier?" The concierge was still fuddled with sleep. He scrubbed absently at his cheek. The ink must itch. There was nothing like having a man at a disadvantage for getting results. The concierge looked with dismay at his papers. "But he was only just admitted."

André shared with him a look of man-to-man commiseration. "I like it no better than you. But the Minister of Police wishes him to be moved to the Prefecture. He believes Monsieur Daubier will find . . . better accommodation there." He raised a brow meaningfully.

"Ah." The attendant raised his chin and hastily lowered it again. In a loud whisper, much as one might speak of the devil, he ventured, "Bertrand?"

"Is in fine form," agreed André. Bertrand's interrogation techniques were legendary. Fouché had made use of them before.

"It is a pity," said the concierge timidly as he fumbled for his keys. "Monsieur Daubier seems like such a nice man."

"Even nice men have been known to stray, citizen. One cannot be too careful in these trying times."

"Indeed, indeed," the concierge agreed hastily. "Shall I come with you?"

"By all means," said André blandly. "You can see all the proper papers signed. We must do this by the book, mustn't we?"

"Papers," said the concierge with a sigh, letting himself out through the grille, skidding on a few of the despised papers on his way. He left a large footprint smack on top of the record of Daubier's admission. "Always papers. We have more papers than prisoners. Sometimes I have nightmares about it," he confided. "Piles and piles of papers, swallowing me whole."

"These are the trials of peace, I fear," said André, forcing himself to maintain an even pace. "There was no time for such niceties during the Revolution."

"It was easier, wasn't it?" agreed the concierge naively. "But bloodier too." Fishing out his keys, he inserted one in the lock of Daubier's cell. "Here's the prisoner, sir. Will you be needing a constable?"

"For one old artist?" André forced himself to laugh. "Unless he intends to tickle me with his paintbrush, I doubt I'm in much danger."

The concierge gave a nervous laugh. One did when powerful people cracked witticisms. "I doubt he'll be in much position to, after last night."

And with that, he pushed open the door.

It was a standard enough cell: a narrow cot by one wall, a single window barred by a grille, a chamber pot, a rickety table with a single candle. Daubier had been allowed no fire. Damp oozed off the walls.

He wasn't asleep. The old artist sat on the side of the cot, huddled into his clothes. His festive clothes of two nights before seemed incongruous against the bleak stone walls. Daubier himself appeared to have shrunk within them; his gold-trimmed coat hung loosely from his shoulders as he hunched over his knees, his white hair hanging limp about his face.

"Antoine Daubier?" André snapped. He didn't like himself for it, but it had to be done.

Daubier's lack of reaction was more alarming than any reaction would have been. He roused himself, but slowly, by increments, like a duck rustling its feathers. It took him a very long time to turn, even longer to lift his head.

Two days of stubble dotted his chin, giving him a derelict look. His linen stock hung untied around his neck, gray with dirt. But the worst of it was his eyes. They were empty. Dead.

What had they done to him?

"Antoine Daubier?" André repeated. He made a rough gesture. "Get up. You're coming with me."

Daubier shook his head. Even the simple movement seemed to cost him an effort. "Please," he said. "No. Just let me stay here."

He wasn't acting. He meant it. André narrowed his eyes at him. Daubier answered with a small shake of his head.

André made a snorting noise. "Pitiful," he said, for the concierge's benefit. "Come along. You can't evade your fate."

Daubier rose slowly to his feet, using his left hand to lever himself up off the cot. He still wore the breeches, stockings, and shoes he had been wearing when he was taken. They were all dirtied now, but otherwise he seemed to be intact. André's practiced eye conducted a quick inventory. There was no blood on Daubier's breeches, no signs of broken toes or shattered knees. He moved as though cramped by cold, but not in the way of one who had been beaten; André knew the signs.

And yet, somehow, they had broken him. Every line of Daubier's face spoke despair. It sat ill on his formerly jovial countenance. "It's not worth it," he said quietly, and André knew he thought of Gabrielle and Pierre-André and the risks André ran in freeing him.

Well, there were risks the other way too. Even the most determined man might talk in the end. André had seen what happened after a skilled master of the question had done his work.

Daubier raised his hand. His right hand. "Let me die here. There's no point to me anymore."

Daubier's hand was scarcely recognizable as such. Every single joint had been broken. The skin was a mottled mass of yellow, purple, and green. The fingers bent at odd angles, unsplinted, left to grow together again as they would.

The bastards. The bloody bastards.

André was filled with a cold rage, more determined than ever to get Daubier out. This was his doing too, at least in part.

If he had come sooner . . . if they had all been more careful . . .

What was the use of it? Practicalities came first. The important thing was to get them both out before Delaroche could wreak any more damage on Daubier.

"The Minister of Police disagrees," said André coldly. "He believes you still have many things to tell us."

"Please . . ." Daubier held up his broken hand, even that small movement causing him pain. Tears came to the old man's eyes. "Don't."

André forced his face to hardness. "Your caterwauling bores me, Monsieur. Will you come quietly, or shall I have you bound?"

Daubier gave him a look that spoke betrayal. What betrayal? He was risking his own life and that of his children to get the man out.

"Will you come?" André repeated.

Daubier nodded, slowly.

"Good," said André. He turned to the concierge. "I doubt he will be able to run in this state."

The concierge nodded, eager to be seen to be in agreement. "Oh no, sir. Not like that."

André nodded to a pile of fabric next to the cot. "Put his coat on him, will you? We don't want him freezing on us—not before he talks."

The attempt to pull the garment on over Daubier's wounded hand made the man scream with pain. André could feel his stomach twist with it. It was necessary, he told himself. Daubier would be grateful for it later. Daubier would need the cloak, wherever it was they were going.

It would have been nice to know where that was.

When Mlle. Griscogne had returned the previous afternoon, all she had told him was that everything was arranged. She wouldn't tell him what was arranged or how or where. Just an address and the instruction to be there, with Daubier, just past dawn the following morning. She would bring de Berry, the children, and Jeannette.

Hostages for his good behavior? It might, he knew, be a trap. If someone wanted a guarantee of his defection, strolling in with an escaped prisoner on his hands was sure proof. But as Mlle. Griscogne had so tactfully pointed out, he had no other choice.

They were a good half mile from the Temple before Daubier spoke. His voice was so low that André could hardly hear him. "You should have left me."

"You should know better than that," said André with an attempt at joviality that fell painfully flat. The mud sucked at his boots. "We were in this together; we'll get out of this together."

Daubier didn't answer. The rain had flattened his exuberant hair against his head. He wore no hat. He must not have had it to hand when he was arrested.

André cursed. But for him, Daubier would be still in his studio, his hand fully functional, badgering his apprentices and charming his models. "I should never have drawn you into it."

Daubier shook his head again. "I was already in it. You knew that. I'm not your charge."

"You're my friend," said André roughly. "That counts for as much."

"You should have left me there," said Daubier querulously. "You should have listened."

"If you keep saying that," said André, "I'll begin to agree with you."

Daubier scowled at the cobbles. "It's all done, André." His voice was unsteady with grief and anger. "Everything. There's no use to me anymore. You should have left me to die."

"Would you like to go back?" said André acidly. "It could be arranged."

Using his good hand, Daubier clutched his cloak closer around his shoulders and trudged ahead. Watching Daubier's bowed back, André felt pity and guilt and resentment all churn together in his gut, as noxious a brew as anything they served at the Temple.

It was unlikely Daubier would hold a brush in that hand again, at least not with his prior skill. But to count one's life lost for the loss of a skill? It was something André had never understood, even after all those years with Julie.

Someday, André assured himself, Daubier would thank him. Someday, when they were safely out of France and his hand had healed and—and what? He had settled down by a hearth somewhere, to slumber out the rest of his life to oblivion? It was impossible to imagine Daubier being anything but what he was—a painter. What was a painter who couldn't paint?

They walked the rest of the way in silence. Daubier seemed to scarcely know where he went. His feet moved as though they had no relation to the rest of him.

The address Mlle. Griscogne had given him led to a tavern. It was not a terribly prosperous one. It was a ramshackle place, with eaves missing from the roof and shutters hanging on luck and a prayer. But that wasn't what caught André's eye. The inn's yard was crowded with a series of gaudily painted wagons. They were scarcely in better condition than the inn. The red paint was peeling and the trim all but gone. But the legend on the side was still legible.

Commedia dell'Aruzzio.

Mlle. Griscogne stepped out from behind one of the wagons, Pierre-André clinging to her skirts.

"Good morning," she said with a lopsided smile. "Welcome to your new career in the theater."

Chapter 22

It was a comedy, all right. A dark comedy.

Colin's mother's party was being held in a gallery in the Place des Vosges, just two houses down from the building that would have once held Antoine Daubier's studio. The clear plate glass of the windows looked very incongruous between the heavy stone arches. Inside, the gallery space had been entirely gutted, the walls painted a glaring white against which the jewel tones of Colin's mother's paintings showed to even greater effect.

Colin led me up to his mother, Serena following quietly behind. Mrs. Selwick-Selwick-Alderly was talking to someone, a champagne glass already in one hand, but she turned as we approached, letting out a little cry of greeting as Colin approached.

Like Serena, she was thin, but her skin sat comfortably on her bones, making her slenderness a pleasant thing rather than a sickly one.

I hadn't realized, looking at old pictures, just how tall she was. In heels, she was nearly as tall as her son. He scarcely had to bend to brush her cheek with his lips.

"Mum," he said. "Happy birthday."

"My son, Colin," she said to the man standing next to her. "You've met Alan, Colin, haven't you? No?"

"You? A grown son?" The man had an American accent, vaguely Texan. "You're pulling my leg. I don't believe it."

When she beamed down at Alan, Mrs. Selwick-Selwick-Alderly's eyes crinkled at the corners just like Colin's. They were a different color, though, brown where Colin's were hazel. "I scarcely believe it myself."

"Not just a grown son, but a grown daughter too," said Jeremy, presenting Serena like a trophy. He had one hand on the small of her back, just where her shawl ended. From the expression on her face, you would have thought he was holding a gun in it. "Well, nearly grown."

Given that Jeremy was as near in age to Serena as he was to Caroline, I thought that was a bit rich. Colin's father had married late and Jeremy's father early, but they had been of the same generation—just as Jeremy was, technically, of the same generation as Colin and Serena. They were on the same line on the family tree, a line below Colin's mother.

Serena mustered a sickly smile. "Happy birthday."

Mrs. Selwick-Selwick made a face over the rim of her champagne glass. "I wish you would stop speaking of birthdays," she said plaintively. "You make me feel so frightfully old."

"You, Caro?" Another man slid an arm around Mrs. Selwick-Selwick's waist. "You can never grow old. If you're old, where would that leave the rest of us?"

"Positively doddering," she said definitively. She frowned at her daughter. "Darling, you need a glass. Jemmy, won't you go? And who is this? We haven't met, have we?"

She smiled politely at me, her eyes already drifting over my shoulder. She gave a fluttery little wave to someone who had just entered.

"This is Eloise, Mum," said Colin patiently.

His mother looked blank.

"Eloise," he repeated. "My girlfriend."

"Hi," I said quickly, before things could get awkward. "Thank you so much for having me to your party."

"Not at all," Mrs. Selwick-Selwick said vaguely. "Delighted to have you. Do enjoy yourself. Oh, Alan, be a love and snag Lydia for me. I've been longing to talk to her."

With a vague smile and a tap on the cheek for Colin, she drifted away, earrings tinkling gently.

I began to see what Serena had meant when she said I had nothing to worry about. This wasn't going to be your classic parental grilling. Watching her make the rounds, I could well believe that Colin could tell her he was joining an ashram in India, and her sole response would be "Darling! How lovely. Do enjoy."

"Champagne?" Colin asked me.

"Lovely," I said, and stepped aside to allow him room to maneuver past, towards the table that had been set up as a bar. There was a plate of tiny canapés set out on one side, but no one was eating them. The champagne, on the other hand, was going like gangbusters.

Given Serena's reaction to any mention of her mother, I had expected something straight out of *Mommie Dearest*, with snide comments and the odd sizzle of a cigarette burn. But it wasn't like that, at all. There were none of the digs about Serena's appearance that I'd expected, no unkind comments about her clothes or hair. But then, maybe one didn't have to be critical to be cruel. Maybe it was enough just not to care.

I watched as Colin's mother—"Caro," they all called her, fondly and familiarly—lit up among her friends. Despite her height, she had a way of tilting her head that made it seem as though she were looking up rather than down, an endearingly open way of laughing, and that crinkle-eyed smile that reminded me so viscerally of Colin.

Unlike the other women, Mrs. Selwick-Selwick's good looks were the product of fortunate genetics, not plastic surgery or expensive makeup. She made no effort to hide the wrinkles next to her eyes, or the brown spots from years of too much tanning. Her hair must have been assisted, but you would never have been able to tell; the dark blond, so like Colin's, looked completely natural, expensively cut but otherwise left free. The same was true of her manner. Her tones, unlike Jeremy's self-consciously estuary English, were the unapologetic cut glass of the English upper class, but she carried it naturally, just as she did her exaggerated earrings and too-short dress.

There was a childlike charm to Mrs. Selwick-Selwick. I'd almost call it an innocence.

It was all the more disconcerting given the nature of her friends. Colin hadn't been exaggerating when he referred to her cronies as Eurotrash. There was much dropping of names and discussion of private jets and ski resorts and this or that exclusive vacation spot. They were a type I recognized from New York—the genuine jetsetters, hard-eyed and hard-edged. Jeremy fit right in, a classic hanger-on on the scene. In contrast, Colin's mother was Alice in Wonderland, frolicking in perpetual wide-eyed wonderment through a psychedelic landscape.

The most incongruous part of the whole affair was that Caroline Selwick-Selwick, or whatever combination of hyphens she affected following her second marriage, was as good an artist as Jeremy had claimed. Whatever else might be an act, this much was true. Colin's mother was talented. Really, truly talented.

Leaving Colin to fight his way to the bar, I wandered along the side of the room, examining the paintings. Colin had one at Selwick Hall. From a distance, I had originally thought it was a Canaletto, until I noticed that the miniature people in the Italian piazza included a skateboarder and various folks on mopeds. Not all the paintings were street scenes; she had done still lifes as well, turning the traditional into the radical with a daring use of nearly neon color. One thing I did notice, though. Aside from the tiny figures in the Italian scenes, there were no portraits. Humans, as such, weren't of much interest to Mrs. Selwick-Selwick.

I tried to reconcile these meticulously constructed compositions with the aging socialite on the other side of the room, scattering "darlings" like diamonds, dashing from group to group and conversation to conversation. It was hard to imagine her capable of any kind of concerted attention, and yet, each of these compositions represented hours of painstaking work, away from the world, locked alone in a studio. They weren't the sort of things one could just dash off in a moment; if anything, they were the reverse of the rapid charcoal drawings of Julie Beniet, distinguished by precision rather than passion. Not at all what one would have expected.

I was turning away when someone bumped me from the other side. Champagne sloshed onto my toes.

"Sorry," I said automatically, even though I was the bumpee. And then, "Oh my goodness. Melinda?"

I couldn't say Pammy hadn't warned me. There she was in the flesh. A fair amount of flesh, since her dress draped on a diagonal from one shoulder and under the opposite arm, leaving a great deal of collarbone bare.

Age hadn't done much for Melinda. She had never been particularly pretty, but that hadn't mattered much when we were all in the same kilts and collared shirts, our hair crammed into scrunchy buns. Now her once-curly hair had been meticulously straightened and her naturally broad body dieted into angularity. She had tanned herself a color just short of orange. It didn't suit her. Not that it really mattered. What Melinda did, she did on connections, not looks—or, for that matter, brains.

I wondered if she was still spelling her name Melynda.

"Wow!" I exclaimed. "Small world. How are you?"

She blinked at me for a moment. Okay, we had only gone to school together for thirteen years. Neither of us had changed that much. I was pretty sure she knew who I was. On the other hand, this was the same woman who had gotten a six on her practice French Lit AP Exam.

That's six out of a hundred, in case you were wondering.

"Eloise. Oh. Hi."

The man next to her held out a hand. From their body language, I couldn't tell whether he and Melinda were together, or simply acquaintances of chance. He looked like he came from the art world side of things, a turtleneck under a sport coat. Judging purely on superficials, he was closer to Jeremy's age than ours. "I don't think we've met."

"Eloise Kelly," I said. "Melinda and I went to school together."

"It was a while ago," she said, with a rapidity that made me wonder just how old she was pretending to be these days. We were well past the point of doctoring our IDs to get into bars. Melinda had been a fixture at Dorrian's back in Upper School, twenty-one before she was sixteen.

"Pammy mentioned that she'd run into you," I said, determined to be nice. "What a great coincidence."

"Oh yes. I saw Pammy in London." She turned to the man next to her. "Pammy Harrington."

He nodded knowingly. Everyone knows Pammy. It's one of those laws of nature.

Melinda lifted a languid hand. "Nice to see you. Give my best to your parents."

"Likewise," I lied. Melinda's mother had been colloquially known as the Dragon Queen. Mrs. Horner had controlled the lists for all the junior cotillions. You've never seen pure, raw power until you've watched a society matron decreeing who shall be invited and who shall be denied.

"Eloise?" It was Colin, champagne glass in hand.

"Hi," Melinda said to Colin, tilting her head at a *Cosmo*-approved angle.

I will admit to a certain petty satisfaction as I slid my arm through Colin's and said quietly, "Colin, this is Melinda. Melinda, I don't believe you know my boyfriend, Colin Selwick."

"Selwick?" said Melinda.

"Caro's son," Colin added helpfully. "And you are?"

"Melinda went to Chapin with me," I said cheerfully. "She's assistant to—Mike Rock?"

"Micah Stone." Melinda drawled out the name as though she were used to the reaction it inspired, but her attention was all on Colin, her eyes narrowed as though she were trying to work something out and finding it rough going. I'd seen her look the same way during those Lower School math marathons called Mad Minutes. "You're Jeremy's stepson?"

Colin stiffened, ever so slightly. "The one and only," he said charmingly. "Are you friends with Jeremy, then?"

"I wouldn't say we were friends." Melinda was very careful about things like that. You wouldn't want to be caught being friends with the wrong people. "You mean, he hasn't told you?"

"Told me—"

Colin was cut off by the clink of a metal implement being wielded against glass. The stepfather in question was belaboring the side of a champagne flute with a cheese knife, calling everyone to attention.

"I've invited you here . . . ," I whispered in Colin's ear in a very bad fake British accent.

Colin grinned down at me. "To reveal the identity of the murderer?"

Jeremy upped the level of his clinking. "Everyone!"

That meant us.

Having successfully silenced the peanut gallery, Jeremy relinquished the cheese knife to a white-coated waiter but held on to the champagne glass. "I would like to extend my thanks to you all for joining us tonight to celebrate the birthday of my lovely wife, Caroline—my lovely and talented wife," he corrected himself.

Mrs. Selwick-Selwick crinkled her eyes at the assemblage and gave a shimmy of self-deprecation.

Jeremy turned back to his audience. "As you can see, we have a great deal to celebrate. There's Caro's new exhibition, which has been praised by—"

I have to admit, I tuned out a bit there. Jeremy went on for some time, listing various critics, whose names meant nothing to me—much as, I assume, the top historians in my field would have meant nothing to him. The overall message was clear, though. They all liked Mrs. Selwick-Selwick's paintings.

I clapped politely with the others and tried not to slosh my champagne, wondering if this meant that the party was almost over. Could we take our leave, or would we be expected to do family time after? I knew there was a birthday dinner planned for the following night—just Colin's mother, us, Jeremy, Serena, and ten of their closest friends—but I wasn't sure if that meant we were off the hook for tonight.

"—Micah Stone," announced Jeremy.

Jeremy said *Micah Stone* much the way Pammy had, as if it were just one step away from *God*.

Huh? I had missed something. When had we gone from Colin's mother to the new Keanu Reeves? I was very confused.

I poked Colin in the sleeve, and mouthed, *"What?"*

Colin raised his eyebrows and held out his hands in the universal gesture of "Search me."

"We have the great privilege of being among the first to know of Micah's new project." Jeremy held out a hand to my old classmate, who was sucking in her cheeks in an attempt to create cheekbones. "Would you like to tell them, Melinda?"

Not really. "It's a musical version of *Much Ado About Nothing*," she drawled. "It's Shakespeare. With music."

That was some enthusiasm. I had a feeling she might have mustered mildly more emotion for *Die Hard Five*. But Shakespeare? Nah.

That was okay. Jeremy was emoting enough for two. "There's more," he said, shifting his grip on his champagne glass.

More? What more could there possibly be than Don John doing a kick-line? Somewhere, Shakespeare was rolling. Hopefully with laughter.

I rolled my eyes at Colin, but Colin's attention was on his stepfather, who had abandoned all pretense of fêting his wife's birthday. He had stepped a little ahead of her, dominating the room, his jacket very dark against the white walls and white-coated waiters.

"After prolonged consultations and negotiations, Micah and his team have arrived at what I believe—and I do hope you'll agree with me—is the perfect location for the production. I'd like you to join me in raising your glasses"—Jeremy was practically sizzling with excitement, as effervescent as the bubbles in his glass—"to the new location of Micah Stone's latest and greatest film."

I looked around for Serena. She was standing all the way at the back, her knuckles very white against the raspberry and silver silk of her wrap. She didn't look bewildered. She looked sick.

Something was wrong. Something was very wrong.

I looked from Jeremy, smug; to Colin's mother, oblivious; to Colin, confused; to Melinda, bored.

Jeremy's lips spread in a grin that made me think of the Cheshire Cat, the one that lingers and lingers long after the cat himself has gone.

"To Micah Stone's new movie!" Jeremy hoisted his champagne glass high. "And to Selwick Hall!"

Chapter 23

"Welcome," said Mlle. Griscogne. "Welcome to the Commedia dell'Aruzzio."

André looked around the courtyard. There were five wagons in all, each painted a gaudy crimson with yellow trim, every one emblazoned with *Commedia dell'Aruzzio*.

Commedia. An acting troupe?

Mlle. Griscogne matched the wagons. She had shed her customary gray in favor of a white linen blouse and yellow skirt, full and belted at the waist, with a thick red shawl crisscrossed peasant-style over her shoulders. Her hair had been left down, pulled back at the sides and tied with a red ribbon.

Pierre-André abandoned her waist to fling himself at his father's instead. "We waited and waited and waited for you," Pierre-André said accusingly, as only a four-year-old could.

André absently patted his son's head. "The Commedia del what?"

"Aruzzio," provided Mlle. Griscogne helpfully. "Although I doubt any of them have been any nearer to Aruzzio than Bourgogne."

André looked about for the rest of his family. "Where are Gabrielle? And, er, Cousin Philippe?"

"In the tavern with Jeannette. They're having breakfast with the rest of the troupe. Both have already assumed their roles."

"What roles?" asked André warily.

"We're to be actors!" exclaimed Pierre-André. "And live in a house on wheels!"

His son evidently thought this was all a grand idea.

"Actors," repeated André.

"I'm sure you've heard of it," said Mlle. Griscogne. "People who pretend to be something other than what they are. Only in this instance, it involves a stage and a costume. I shouldn't think you should have too much trouble with that."

André took in the gaudy wagons. "Hardly inconspicuous."

"Call it escaping in plain sight." She looked anxiously about. "Where is Monsieur Daubier? Don't tell me you didn't bring him?"

"Monsieur Daubier—" André scanned the courtyard. He finally spotted the old artist, huddled on the steps of one of the wagons, hunched over as though his limbs had given out on him. "Monsieur Daubier is over there."

"What did they do to him?"

André took his son by the shoulders and turned him towards the tavern. "Go see if Jeannette has some bread and honey for you."

Pierre-André looked at him suspiciously. "Are you going away again?"

André shook his head. "Only with you. I'll be there in a moment. Tell Jeannette to order a coffee for me?"

Pierre-André nodded importantly and scampered off.

"Well?"

André took a deep breath. "They broke his hand."

"His hand."

"His right hand."

"His— Oh." Her face blanched as the full implications of it dawned on her.

"Finger by finger," said André grimly. "They cracked the knuckles and shattered the bone."

"Will he ever paint again?"

André shook his head. "Unlikely."

"Was there no way to stop them?"

It was what he had been asking himself. "If I had come a day earlier. Maybe."

She had asked for that day, that day's grace period, to make her arrangements, whatever those arrangements might be. André had used that day for purposes of his own, to tie up his own loose ends and cobble together a series of backup plans in the event his governess proved untrustworthy.

He had never thought that Delaroche would act so quickly. Usually, he preferred to begin with more mental methods, working slowly from mind to body, savoring the experience of playing with his prisoner. He had acted too fast this time. A sign of his own instability—and André's failure.

"If you had freed him right away," Mlle. Griscogne said unsteadily, "we might have hidden you while the hue and cry arose. We could have secreted you away somewhere."

"All of us?" said André. "A whole household? De Berry and Daubier and the children and Jeannette? Delaroche would have been on us like ants on honey." Red strands of wool snagged against the brown leather of his gloves as he grasped her by the shoulders, forcing her to face him. "We didn't know."

Mlle. Griscogne shrugged away, not meeting his eye. "I suppose you'll want to hear the plan," she said in a rough voice.

Fair enough. She didn't like to admit weakness any more than he.

"I have papers for everyone." She didn't say where she had acquired them. André didn't ask. "We are a theatrical family fallen on hard times. Monsieur Daubier is my father. Jeannette is your stepmother."

"Nicely cast," commented André. "She'll enjoy that."

Mlle. Griscogne's lip quirked a bit at that. "The—er, Philippe, is your younger brother. Gabrielle and Pierre-André are our children."

"Which makes us?"

"Husband and wife." She didn't meet his eyes. "For the duration of the journey."

"Hmm," said André.

"There wasn't any other way," she said defensively. She fussed with the edges of her shawl. "It would have looked very odd for us to be traveling in such a large group without . . ."

"Familial ties?" he provided.

"Precisely," she said gratefully. "It was simply a matter of expedience."

That certainly put him in his place. "So we are to be acting off-stage as well as on."

Including the bedchamber. He didn't know much about theatrical troupes, but he imagined they would be living in very close quarters. André looked over his shoulder at the wagons. All of them were far smaller than the smallest of the salons in the Hôtel de Bac.

Very close quarters, indeed.

"If you are to be my wife—for the duration of the journey—," he amended, before she could do it herself, "I should probably call you Laura, shouldn't I? Unless we are to be assuming other names."

She seized on his businesslike approach with relief. "The— My friend thought it best that we keep our own Christian names. They're common enough, and we're less likely to stumble on them. Our surname is Malcontre."

"Ill-met?" She had reason to consider it an ill day that she had fallen in with them. From governess to fugitive in one easy mis-step. "They might agree with that, once they've seen our acting. There might be a reason we've fallen on hard times."

"Cécile—their Columbine—is the only one who knows we aren't what we say. But that's all she knows. Just that we needed safe passage to the coast."

"Columbine. The maidservant?"

"You do know the Commedia dell'Arte, then."

"I was young once too." Like all young men, he had frequented the theaters, just as he had the debating societies and taverns. He had always preferred the formal stage to the exaggerated routines of the Commedia dell'Arte, but he was familiar with the form. A series of stock characters acted out various pre-plotted scenarios, mostly variations on the same themes. There were invariably young lovers, overbearing fathers, and saucy maidservants.

"With no scripts to memorize, it shouldn't be too difficult to pretend for the month it will take us to get to Dieppe," said Mlle. Griscogne earnestly. No, he reminded himself. Laura. "I have Gherland's book of scenarios in the wagon. As for the other troupe members, I've told them that Jeannette was our wardrobe mis-tress. And Monsieur Daubier—Monsieur Daubier was our set painter."

"If he's to be your father," said André, "you shouldn't go on calling him Monsieur Daubier."

"A fair point," admitted Laura. "We should begin as we mean to go on. The children have already been instructed to call him *grandpère*. They have," she added, "taken to this rather well."

Guilt caught at André's tongue, silencing him. It seemed to him the basest of ironies that actions taken in the grand name of his children's future should have come to this. He had meant to make the world safer for them. Instead, he had cast them into exile, with no set future before them. Even if they escaped, what then? He wasn't one of the Comte d'Artois's own. He had no faith in the gratitude—or the means—of the Duc de Berry. In the very best case, they would arrive in England as refugees, dependent on their wits for their bread, scrounging out a living as best they could.

It was a far cry from the Hôtel de Bac.

On the other hand, it was better than being guillotined. They owed a great deal to Mlle. Griscogne. Er, Laura. He looked assessingly at the former governess, her tired face at odds with her gaudy clothes. Droplets of rain sparkled on the red wool of her shawl, damping the white linen bodice beneath. She had gone to a great deal of trouble for them. Not just trouble, danger. There was every chance that she might have walked away from this all unscathed. Delaroche wouldn't waste that much time on a governess, especially one who had been in residence for fewer than three months.

By escaping with them, she placed her own neck in the noose. It was either an act of astounding generosity—for Daubier, he reminded himself; all for Daubier—or his former governess had unfathomable motives of her own.

Motives and connections.

"It was clever of you to think of this," he said abruptly.

Not only clever, but expeditious. To come up with a plan, acquire false papers, and engineer a new set of identities for six people within the course of twenty-four hours was no mean feat.

She hitched her shawl higher around her shoulders. "Don't say that until we're past the gates."

"And after we're free of the city?" André asked.

"The troupe's route takes them through Dieppe. If all goes well, a ship will be waiting for us there in one month's time."

"That long?" A great deal could go wrong in a month.

"It would cause talk if we barreled through without actually performing. The other actors would start to wonder. If we have to," she added, "we can always break away from the troupe and travel on our own."

"Hopefully it won't come to that." Better to transport Daubier in the relative comfort of a wagon rather than tramp across the fields by foot. Pierre-André and Gabrielle might find walking the fields and sleeping rough an adventure for a day or two, but it wouldn't take long for them to tire of it. It might be cold inside the wagons, but it would be colder outside of them. "How soon do we leave?"

"If all goes well, we should depart within the hour. Would you like to go inside and meet the troupe?"

"I probably ought . . . Laura."

She looked at him sharply.

"Begin as we mean to go on," he reminded her.

The ghost of a smile drifted across her face. "And we *are* past liberties. André."

For a moment, they faced each other, sizing each other up, coming to terms with their arrangement. She looked very different with her hair down, the shawl brightening her face. But the rest—the intelligence, the humor—that was all entirely hers, unchanged. Lucky for them.

"We were very fortunate to have you as our governess," André said slowly.

Mlle. Griscogne—Laura—shrugged, uncomfortable with praise. "I did tell you that my program was comprehensive." Without quite looking at him, she moved rapidly away. "I'll go fetch Monsieur . . . I mean, Papa."

He saw her squat down by Monsieur Daubier in the overhang of the wagon, speaking to the old artist in a low, earnest tone. One hand came out from under the enveloping wool of the shawl to cover Monsieur Daubier's. The left hand. There was something inexplicably tender about the gesture. She looked, he thought, like the daughter she claimed to be, Cordelia kneeling by Lear.

Hopefully, this drama would end more happily than that one had.

As André watched, Daubier allowed her to help him up, rising heavily to his feet. Antoine Daubier was a tall, heavyset man, but hunched over as he was, they looked nearly of a size. Laura braced an arm around the old man's back, supporting him. He leaned heavily on her, but she never faltered.

André moved quickly to the artist's other side, but the look Daubier gave him stopped him short. "I told her you should have left me."

"You know that's rot," said André.

Laura sent him a warning look.

"We need you," she said to Daubier. André was amazed by the calm of her voice. "Our story makes very little sense without you with us. I'm no actress." André could have disputed that, but kept silent. "Nor is Monsieur Ja—André. But you? You can design sets that will make them weep with gratitude."

"How can I, when I can no longer hold a brush?" Daubier's voice was hoarse, but there was a flicker of interest in his eye that hadn't been there before.

"You still have your left hand. If Milton could write blind, can't you paint left-handed? It might not be the same, but think what a broad canvas you have to practice upon. A set is a very different thing from an easel. Unless, of course," she said meditatively, "you think it's too much of a challenge for you. You've been painting portraits for so very long now. . . ."

"I cut my teeth on landscapes," protested Daubier. As if realizing he'd been tricked, he let his chin fall back into his chest. "I'll think about it," he mumbled.

"Cécile tells me our first play is to be set in Venice," said Laura. "In a great palazzo. Rather like that place where you visited us, in 'eighty-two."

"You mean when your mother . . ."

"Was having an affair with the nephew of the Doge?" said Laura calmly. "And Papa was commissioned to create a series of sculptures for his garden? Yes."

"It was a pretty little palace," said Daubier musingly, "right on the canal. When the sun set, the stones looked golden. It would be hard to reproduce just that shade. . . ."

"Would you mind getting the door?" said Laura demurely to André, casting him a look of triumph.

"With pleasure." He swung it open, inclining his head as she passed, giving credit as it was due. Daubier still looked like a nag put out in the knacker's yard, but he was standing a little straighter than he had before, his eyes a little more alert. He was abstracted, but it was a reverie of color and shade. They weren't out of the woods yet, but the immediate crisis had been averted.

"At last!" someone cried. A young woman came bustling over to them, her sprig muslin too light for the weather, her hair pulled back with a fashionable bandeau. There was an impish charm to her mobile face "Laura's André! We've been longing to meet you!"

Laura kept her arm through Daubier's. "Cécile, this is my father, Monsieur Désormais, and my husband, André."

Seen closer, Cécile wasn't so young as she had appeared. Beneath the youthful curls, her brown eyes were surprisingly shrewd. André saw her quick, concerned glance at Daubier. "Your father . . ."

"Was injured by the fall of a set. It was a most unfortunate accident," said Laura. "The troupe refused to let him stay on. That is why you find us as we are, looking again for work at this inhospitable time of year."

Cécile nodded approvingly. "I am sorry for your misfortune, but your loss is our gain. I don't know what we should have done without you." She held out a hand to André, taking his in a firm grasp. "Welcome, Monsieur, to our troupe. You see us in a sadly reduced state. It is very fortuitous that you should be out of work, just as two of our company were unexpectedly forced to take their leave of us. We have been half-distracted, trying to figure out how to divide the roles to maintain our engagements."

André raised both brows. "Forced?"

"By cruel circumstance." From the smug set of her mouth, André doubted there was anything the least bit circumstantial about it. "Our Capitano was taken ill last night. The doctors do not believe he should be moved for at least a month. Our Ruffiana has elected to stay with him, to nurse him back to health. So you find us two actors short. To make matters worse, Ruffiana also served as our wardrobe mistress. But now we have a new wardrobe mistress and your charming Laura to be our Ruffiana."

"The shrewish matron?" André looked quizzically at Laura.

"Don't cast stones until you hear your own part. Philippe is to understudy the heroic lead and help Mons—er, Papa, with the scenery. You shall take over the roles of the Captain and the Doctor."

The blowhard and the pompous ass. Point taken.

"I believe I can manage that," said André mildly. "Although I always fancied myself more of a Scaramouche."

Cécile cocked her head. "That might be arranged. Our current scenarios don't call for it, but if you wish to contrive another, you can submit it for the consideration of the troupe. We work on a democratic model, you see. Within reason."

"Meaning some of the demos are more important than others?"

Cécile put a finger to her lips. "Shhh. Don't tell them. We do like to maintain our illusions." Putting her hands on her lips, she turned and surveyed the company. She indicated an elderly man whose few wisps of hair were so white that they showed yellow against the pink of his pate. "That man at the trestle over there—the one in the pale blue satin—that's our Pantaloon. He's the head of the troupe. Others have come and gone but Pantaloon has been here since the beginning."

Pantaloon. The blustering father figure of the Commedia dell'Arte. This man looked like a good bluster would send him toppling right over. His skin was so pale it was practically translucent.

Cécile waved an insouciant hand. "You can just call him Pantaloon. We all do. He's been Pantaloon for so long, I doubt he remembers what his real name was. Next to him, in the green velvet, that's our Leandro. He plays all the young lovers. Balcony-climbing, sword fights, mooning about ladies' chambers, that's his job."

Like Pantaloon, Leandro didn't seem best suited for his role. He was a gawky youth, with arms and legs too long and thin for his frame. The long hair he wore loose about his face did little to disguise a bad case of adolescent spots. André only hoped that makeup and costume would compensate for what nature had failed to provide.

Mlle. Griscogne had never said the Commedia dell'Aruzzio was a *successful* theatrical troupe.

So much the better, thought André philosophically. Their own incompetence wouldn't show to such disadvantage.

Next to Leandro sat a short, ferret-faced man in a brocade jacket. "That's Harlequin. He rooms with Leandro and doubles as our cook when we're living rough. He may not look like much, but he cooks divinely." Cécile's mouth twisted. "And then there's Rose."

"Rose?" There didn't seem to be anyone else in the room.

Cécile nodded to the stairs leading up to the second story. "Ah. Pat on her cue, as always."

On the landing, a woman stood, her profile to the stairs. Blond curls tumbled down her back in artful disarray. She wore a gown more showy than stylish, flounced and frilled within an inch of its life. Long earrings, confections of enamel and seed pearl, bounced against her curls. She stood directly beneath the window so that what little light there was fell on her upraised face.

"That's our Rose," said Cécile acerbically. "Never misses an entrance."

"Your ingénue?" guessed André.

"The very one." It didn't take much to guess what Cécile thought of her colleague. "Inamorata. Both onstage and off."

Rose's carefully contrived pose wasn't intended for their benefit. As they watched, a man followed her onto the landing, drawn like a wooden horse on a string. His uniform coat was unbuttoned, his stock untied. It took very little imagination to guess what had been going on beyond the landing.

Rose held out both hands, her fingers all but hidden among lace ruffles. The man took them in both of his own.

And André took a step back, away from the stairs.

"What is it?" whispered Laura. "André?"

He slid an arm around her waist, drawing her into the crook of his arm, the pose of an old, married couple. She came stiffly into his embrace; he could feel the tension in every line of her body.

He set his lips by her ear. "Do you know who that is?"

She gave a short shake of her head. To an outsider, it might have looked like a nuzzle.

"Murat," he whispered. "Bonaparte's brother-in-law."

Not just Bonaparte's brother-in-law. The governor of Paris. The man who had ordered all the gates of the city closed and all carriages searched. It was Murat who had presided over the "trials" of Querelle, Picot, and the rest. Admittedly, the intelligence was not his own; he was only a figurehead.

But he knew André. Not well, but well enough to pick him out of a crowd, even among this group of ill-assorted theatricals.

Of all the ill luck. Of all the actresses in Paris, why did Murat have to be sleeping with this one?

Assuming, of course, that it was only ill luck.

Murat wouldn't know of Daubier's escape, not yet. But if he

saw André, or Daubier, with the troupe . . . The game would be up before it had begun.

"Silly, darling," said Laura, in a voice unlike her own. "Your cravat is crooked again."

She pushed him so that his back was to Murat, reaching up to fiddle with the bow at his neck. "Does he know you?" she murmured.

"Yes."

Laura swallowed hard.

Behind him, he could hear the sound of steps on the stairs, the click of Murat's boots, the gentle pat of Rose's slippers.

". . . just a short tour of the provinces," he could hear Rose saying. And ". . . miss me?"

André's chest was tight from holding his breath. He could hear the sounds of the coffee room with abnormal clarity: the click of Jeannette's knitting needles, Pierre-André's childish laughter, the slurping sound of Pantaloon drinking coffee from his saucer.

"Don't turn around, whatever you do," Laura muttered. "They're right behind you."

Breaking her own rule, she darted a quick glance over his shoulder. Whatever she saw must have decided her. Leaning forward, she placed a hand against André's cheek. She wasn't wearing gloves. Her hand was cold.

He lifted his own hand to cover it, both reassurance and warning.

"He can't be allowed to see your face," she murmured. He could feel her breath on his lips. Her eyes were very dark in her pale face, the pupil and the iris all but indistinguishable.

"Any ideas?" he whispered back.

For a moment, she hesitated. Then she tilted her head back, her dark hair tangling with the red wool of her shawl.

"This," she said, and pressed her lips to his.

Chapter 24

The last time Laura had kissed someone had been the summer of 1794.

She had been twenty-two; he had been the cousin of the family for whom she was working at the time, visiting for a house party. Generally, she knew better than to permit liberties. But it had been June and the garden had been in bloom. There had been a mist rising off the river and Chinese lanterns hanging from the trees. She had let him lead her by the hand, down the boxwood paths, to the place where the garden met the river, in the no-man's-land between dusk and dawn, knowing that it meant nothing more than what it was—a stolen bit of fleeting pleasure. He had departed the next morning and she had returned to her schoolroom. She couldn't remember his name, much less his face. There was only the shadowy recollection of a hand on her cheek, the brush of breath against her lips.

She had nearly forgotten what it was like, this pressure of lip to lip.

She would have said she was beyond such things, long since rendered immune to human desires. She intended the kiss entirely as an act of expedience. It was nothing more than a tableau, a set piece, two lovers frozen in embrace, their faces conveniently blotted from view.

That was the idea, at any rate.

André's hand slid up beneath the hair at the nape of her neck. She hadn't remembered this, the caress of bare fingers in her hair, disarranging her hair ribbon, making her skin tingle. His other hand slid around her waist, beneath the woolly mass of her shawl, holding her firm at the small of her back.

"Relax," he murmured against her lips. "You're as stiff as a board."

"Am n—," she began, but the word was lost as he bent her backwards and kissed her.

It was quite a thorough performance.

Laura clung to that thought, or tried to. Performance. Acting. Her arms went around his neck, holding tight. Holding to keep from falling, if she were being honest. She'd meant to monitor Murat's movements, but she found herself closing her eyes, clinging to André's neck, and, heaven help her, kissing him back. For the performance. All for the performance.

There were hoots and cheers from the company. Laura blinked, forcing her eyes to focus.

Murat was gone.

There were grins on the faces of many of their new colleagues. Jeannette was scowling at her knitting. Gabrielle was scowling at Laura.

Oh, dear. Perhaps they should tell the troupe that Pierre-André and Gabrielle were her stepchildren. That would explain the look of death on her so-called daughter's face.

"Well," Laura said. Her brain didn't seem to want to work properly. "That served its purpose."

"Purpose. Yes." André cleared his throat. "Good thinking, there. That was a, er, clever ploy."

Laura managed a crooked smile. "No one will doubt our relationship now." The words stuck in her throat, but she forced them out. "You're a very good actor."

"I had an excellent leading lady." He slid an arm around her shoulders and squeezed, in a counterfeit of affection. He was a very good actor, indeed. She needed to remember that. "Shall we meet the troupe?"

Laura nodded. "The sooner we're away from here, the better."

Jaouen's arm tightened around her shoulder. "I'll be a happier man once we're past the gates."

"Mmph," she agreed, clumsily matching her steps to his.

It felt odd, and more than odd, to be so intimately pressed against someone, with all the assumptions that went with it. When was the last time someone had held her so? Years.

A sham, she reminded herself. As flimsy as a scroll of scenery, rolled down for an audience one moment and the next rolled up again, reduced to nothing more than cloth and paint.

She would have to watch herself, to be wary of such intimacies. It wouldn't do to fall prey to her own deception. She knew what she was to him—a means of escape, nothing more.

"Well, well!" Harlequin was the first to rise to greet them, pounding André companionably on the shoulder. "I see you'll be usurping Leandro's roles next."

André dropped his arm from Laura's back, extending a hand to Harlequin. "André Malcontre. Your Inamorato is safe from me. I'm too old to play the lover."

Harlequin cast Laura a significant look. "You could have fooled me. Madame Malcontre, I take it?"

Laura made her curtsy. "The very one. But I hope we shan't be so formal. You can call me . . . Ruffiana."

Harlequin pursed his lips appreciatively. "Getting into role already! You'll put us all to shame. Except, of course, our Rose, who plays her love scenes both onstage and off."

Rose stuck her pretty nose in the air. "Simply because I won't play one with you . . ."

"Have you seen me serenading in the mud outside your wagon?" demanded Harlequin derisively.

The actress reddened. "I should have thought a wallow would have been just to your taste."

"Better my sty than yours."

"Just because some of us like *elevated* company . . ."

"Don't look too high, Rose," drawled Harlequin. "You just might fly too close to the sun."

"Too close to the sun?" The Duc de Berry stepped forward. "I should think the sun would hide its rays in shame. You eclipse it, lady, as the sun does the moon."

"That doesn't quite scan," murmured André to Laura.

Rose looked de Berry up and down, torn between a smirk and a snub. "And you are?"

"Philippe Malcontre," Laura put in hastily, before de Berry could speak. "My husband's younger brother. He is to understudy Leandro. He's also very good at carrying things. Sets, props."

"Oh. An actor."

"Like you," needled Harlequin.

Rose cast him a freezing glance. "Are we to stand here all day?" she demanded loftily.

Harlequin clapped his hands. "Hey, you!" he called. "Milady grows impatient. We can't have that, now, can we?"

De Berry stepped quickly forward. "You must allow me to help you to your chariot."

"You mean her wagon?" interjected Cécile.

"With you in it," de Berry said, never removing his eyes from Rose, "a farm cart would look like a phaeton."

"Poor, overused Icarus," muttered Harlequin, as they followed Rose and de Berry out. "That's twice in one conversation."

"You've studied the classics?" Laura asked politely. She

wouldn't have thought it. He had the wiry build and chipped teeth of the former guttersnipe.

Harlequin made a rueful face. "Used to be a schoolteacher. Then I got myself clapped up for debt. And now you find me here."

Laura nodded her understanding. "I was a governess once."

"Pounding Latin into the heads of the ungrateful young? Then you understand how it can drive one to drink. You have your own now, though." Harlequin nodded at Pierre-André and Gabrielle, being hustled along by Jeannette.

Laura leaned forward confidingly. "My stepchildren. André and I have only been married a year now."

"Ah," said Harlequin knowingly. He nodded at André as André fell into pace beside them. "Practically newlyweds."

Laura tilted her head up at André. "It feels like it. Doesn't it, darling?"

André threaded his arm through hers. From the outside, it looked like an affectionate gesture. Only Laura felt the warning pinch of his fingers. "As if every day were the first. May I borrow you for a moment, dear heart?"

"Why borrow what is yours to take?" said Laura extravagantly, but ruined it by skidding in the mud.

André hauled her upright again. *"Why borrow what is yours to take?"*

Laura snuggled against his side. "We've only been married a year. Look besotted."

André lowered his lips to her ear. "Was that wise? Telling him you were a governess? Rose may not be the only one with government connections."

"I hardly think it will damn us. I'm not the only former governess in Paris. The closer we stay to the truth, the less likely we are to make mistakes."

"Newlyweds?" said André.

"Aren't we?" countered Laura. "I certainly never contemplated marriage to you before yesterday."

"Fair point." André's tired face quirked into a smile. "You can't get much more newlywed than that."

His chin was stubbled with a day's growth of beard and there were dark circles beneath his eyes. But there was something about that smile that made it impossible not to respond. Laura felt her chest clench with something she couldn't quite identify.

"We'll make this work," she said softly. She hadn't intended to. It just came out. "You'll see."

He looked down at her, comrade to comrade, equal to equal. His lips softened. "I rather think you're right."

Little bits of icy rain pecked at Laura's cheeks. Why did she suddenly feel awkward? He was agreeing with her. Agreement was good.

Putting her nose in the air, Laura adopted her bossiest governess voice. "You ought to have realized by now, I'm always right."

"Always?" He sounded not just amused, but . . . fond.

He was, Laura reminded herself, an excellent actor.

"Well . . . frequently," she said hastily. "Oh, look, there's Cécile."

André gave her a funny look. "Yes, I could see that." He inclined his head to their de facto troupe leader, who had been bustling about, arbitrating disputes and supervising disposition of baggage. "Madame Cécile?"

"No need to stand on formality, Cécile will do well enough," said Cécile absently. "You have your baggage?"

"Yes," Laura said calmly.

Laura had braved Jaouen's lair, from which Jean had unceremoniously ceased guard, and bundled up linen, breeches, a brush, a shaving kit, a spare pair of spectacles. There had been precious little to choose between. His wardrobe was scanty and fairly repetitive. His room had revealed little in the way of secrets, other than a secret penchant for poetry. There had been a volume of

Ronsard's poems by his bed. She had been surprised to find that he read poetry still.

"We'll have to find a wagon for you and the others," Cécile was saying. "We've lost two, and there are eight of you. This may take some arranging."

"Philippe had best come in with us," said Harlequin, amiably enough, but there was a slightly malicious edge to his smile as he turned towards Leandro. "Leandro and I bunk together. We have grand times, don't we, Leandro?"

"It's well enough," Leandro mumbled. He was too busy watching de Berry flirting with Rose, who might not want to waste herself on an actor but certainly wasn't above accepting his skills as porter.

"Good," said Cécile definitively. "That solves that. Monsieur Désormais, you can share with Pantaloon. Il Capitano and Ruffiana had their own wagon; that will go to Monsieur and Madame Malcontre."

"And the children," put in Laura.

The idea of sharing a wagon with André didn't seem nearly as alarming with a wriggly Pierre-André in the middle, popping up and down half the night.

"Nonsense." Jeannette elbowed her way in. "The children will stay with me. Just as they always have. The precious lambs will have nightmares without me."

"The five of us, then!" said Laura. "One big, happy family."

Cécile made a face. "There's not really room, is there? Rose? Rose!" She snapped her fingers until Rose languidly turned her head, ribbons fluttering prettily. "If you give up your wagon to Jeannette and the children . . ."

"Me? Give up my wagon?" The threat to her privacy was enough to make Rose forget to put her best profile forward. "What about yours?"

"Either way," said Cécile firmly, "we'll have to share. Unless, of course, you'd rather take the children."

Rose wrinkled her nose. "Why can't they all go in with you?"

"Because," said Cécile, in the tones of one dealing with a substandard child, "two and three makes far more sense than four and one."

"That," said de Berry gallantly, casting Rose a smoldering glance, "depends on the one."

Leandro glowered.

Harlequin sighed.

Cécile rolled her eyes. "We're settled, then. Rose will share with me; Jeannette and the children will have Rose's wagon."

"I really don't mind having the children . . . ," Laura began, but Cécile cut her off with a shake of the head.

It was a fleeting gesture, intended for Laura's benefit only. Laura took the hint. Whatever her personal feelings about the woman, Cécile had her own reasons for wanting to keep Rose close. Given that Cécile was an associate of the Pink Carnation's and Rose an associate (of an entirely different kind) of the Governor of Paris, it wasn't, when she thought about it, altogether surprising.

Even if it did mean she had to share a wagon with André Jaouen.

Their wagon looked much the same as all the others—a rectangular structure hitched to two tired mules. There was a pallet on one side of the floor, a trunk that doubled as a makeshift table, and a haphazard miscellany of props and cookware jumbled into sacks. Whatever possessions the former Capitano and Ruffiana had owned had already been removed.

"Thank you for packing for me," murmured André as he hauled her carpetbag and his bundles into a spare bit of corner between a pile of spare blankets and three Roman breastplates.

"I couldn't let you traipse the countryside without a change of linen," said Laura tartly.

That was an exceedingly small pallet.

Admittedly, it was also a fairly small wagon, but surely one could eke out a little more bed room than that.

"And Ronsard?" André held up a small volume bound in paisley paper covers and waggled it in her general direction.

Laura shrugged. Throwing the book into the bundle had been a whim. They were taking so little, after all. And there had been something about that marked page . . . *Gather, gather, the rosebuds of today.*

"More verisimilitude," she lied. "I'd imagine that actors like poetry. It makes you seem more artistic."

"If a little behind the times," he agreed. He joined her in contemplating the pallet. "It is rather . . . small, isn't it?"

Laura shook her hair back behind her shoulders. It felt very odd to have it so, practically unbound. "Don't worry," she said flippantly. "We can always put a naked sword down the middle."

"That's not what I—"

"Laura? André?" Cécile's head appeared between the curtains at the back of the wagon. "We're ready to go. I assume you can drive a wagon."

André shook himself like a duck shaking off water and turned towards Cécile. "It's been a few years, but I think I can manage."

"Wait." Laura grabbed at his arm, her nails scraping against his sleeve. It was a terrible sound. Wincing, she drew her hand away. "Hadn't you better, um, take a nap? After your very late night of saying farewell to all your friends in Paris?"

"My very—ah." He drew back, comprehension settling over his face.

André looked, for a moment, as though he might have liked to demur. It couldn't, Laura imagined, be very pleasant to be smuggled out of Paris like a vat of wine, passively hiding inside a wagon while someone else did the driving. But there was no denying the validity of her concern. He had spent many years at the Prefecture. It wasn't beyond the realm of reason that he might be known to the guards at the gates.

"Yes," he said at last, although there was no mistaking the reluctance of it. "You might be right. I could use the rest."

"You know how to drive?" Cécile asked Laura.

"I can manage," she said, echoing André's own words.

She had driven a dog cart during her governess days, and the odd trap. The mules attached to their wagon didn't seem like terribly spirited beasts. It couldn't be that hard to point them down the center of the road and make them go. She had no aspirations of driving to an inch.

She looked from André to Cécile. "If Jeannette can spare them, it might be nice to have the children sit on the box with me. Just until we're outside of the city."

She didn't have to explain what she meant. There was nothing like children to lend an air of innocence to a scene.

"Naturally," said Cécile blandly. "You wouldn't want to be separated from your children." Her head disappeared again between the curtains.

"So that's what I've been reduced to," André said grimly. "Using my children as shields."

Laura paused in the act of following Cécile out of the wagon. "Don't you know they're glad to?" she said. "They love you, you fool."

Before he could answer, she bunched up her skirts and followed Cécile out through the curtains.

They might no longer be employer and employee, but it still felt like lèse-majesté, calling him a fool. Even when he was being one.

If she had a family . . . Well, she hadn't. Just a pretend one. She shouldn't let herself forget that.

Outside, the other wagons had been loaded, the mules hitched up. It wasn't an entirely inspiring sight. En masse, the general shabbiness was even more pronounced than it had been when the vehicles were scattered around the inn yard. Pantaloon sat on the box of one wagon, Harlequin another. Cécile climbed onto the box of the wagon she was to share with Rose, ably claiming the ribbons.

Pierre-André was snuggled next to Jeannette on the bench of the fourth, Gabrielle hunched beside them, cradling a book as another girl might have cuddled a doll.

Laura clapped her hands. "Gabrielle! Pierre-André! Won't you come up with me?"

Jeannette bristled.

Laura gave her what she hoped was a meaningful look, but probably succeeded only in making herself vaguely cross-eyed.

"Your father is sleeping," she called, "and I could use the company. If you like," she added cunningly, "I'll let you hold the reins."

Pierre-André wiggled in Jeannette's hold. With a look at Laura, Jeannette boosted him down off the wagon into Laura's arms.

"How long?" he demanded.

"That depends on how good a driver you are." Laura set him down on the ground, taking his hand in hers. The rain had lightened into mist, but his mittens were still damp.

Hot tea, Laura thought. Hot liquid of some kind. Once they were past the gates, she would send him into the wagon, where he would at least be dry, if not warm. The last thing they needed was the children getting an influenza.

Gabrielle wasn't as easily won as her brother. It took a whispered instruction from Jeannette to make her move, and even then only with the greatest of reluctance. She stalked past Laura, book under her arm, nose in the air, refusing Laura's offer of a hand to help her up onto the box of the wagon. So much for the hard-won entente of the past few weeks. That faux kiss in the coffee room seemed to have set them back to where they had been in the first week of January.

"This is for your father's sake," Laura murmured to Gabrielle as she settled herself down between the two children. "Just until we get him out of the city."

Gabrielle gave her a withering look. "How would you know what's good for my father?"

"Because I'm older than you," Laura replied, slapping the reins. "And because I said so."

Logic. It worked every time.

The wagons set off in painfully slow procession, mud churning beneath the wheels. It was a dreary sight, the bright paint dulled with wet, the sides of the wagons splattered with dirt. The drivers hunched down over the reins, intent on keeping the rain off their heads as much as possible. There was a reason most troupes traveled only in summer.

Laura checked beneath her shawl, making sure she still had the papers the Pink Carnation had forged for them. They crackled reassuringly in their greased paper wrappings, the seals thick and official-looking. Whatever forgers the Pink Carnation used, they were the very best of their kind. To Laura's eye, their papers, hastily made though they were, had seemed quite convincingly official.

Hopefully, the guards at the gates would feel the same way.

The cavalcade slowed to a halt as the first wagon paused at the gates. A guard, his cloak pulled up high around his neck, his hat pulled down low, came out to inspect Pantaloon's papers. Daubier sat beside him on the box, huddled into his coat, his mangled hand hidden within his sleeve.

For this, at least, Laura blessed the rain, which did more than any disguise to render men anonymous. There was nothing the least bit curious about a man pulling his hat down over his head or wrapping himself up in a cloak, not when the rain was dripping down and all honest men yearned for nothing more than to be inside and out of the wet.

The guard gave a perfunctory look at the papers and handed them back to Pantaloon. Thank God. She hadn't prayed in years, but Laura found herself breathing out thanks as the first wagon passed beyond the gates, the first step to safety. There was still a long way to go, but to be out of Paris meant that they had the whole of the countryside in which to hide, a million anonymous fields and unknown back roads.

Harlequin's wagon approached next, pausing for a moment as the actor exchanged quips with the guard. To Laura's eyes, de Berry's ruddy countenance was unmistakably Bourbon—but it had been more than eleven years since a Bourbon had been last seen in Paris. Likenesses on medals seldom approximated the reality.

De Berry was through, then Cécile, then Jeannette.

"Wardrobe mistress," Laura heard Jeannette say as she waved her knitting at the guard. Only Jeannette could contrive to knit and handle two mules at the same time. The guard eyed the yarn askance but let her through.

Laura edged her mules gently up to the gate. She was holding Pierre-André too tightly. He wiggled impatiently, making her fuddle one of the reins.

"Papers?" the guard said in a bored way.

Laura fished them out from beneath her shawl, fumbling with the wax-paper wrappings. "Here," she said, sounding more breathless than she would have liked. "For me and my family."

The guard shuffled through, looking once at Gabrielle, once at Pierre-André, matching names with faces.

"The children are yours?"

Laura put an arm around Pierre-André on one side and Gabrielle on the other. The little girl's shoulders were stiff beneath her arm. She prayed Gabrielle wouldn't choose this moment to act up. "Yes. My stepchildren."

Come on, come on, come on, thought Laura. The other wagons were well ahead, pulling away down the road. They had gone through one after another, with scarcely a pause.

She held out her hand for the papers, but the guard didn't seem in any hurry to hand them back over. He was frowning at the paper on the bottom.

"There are four passports here," he said abruptly. "But only three of you. Where is the fourth?"

Chapter 25

"Inside." Laura looked away. "I'm afraid he's—well, he celebrated our departure a bit vigorously last night. If you know what I mean."

The soldier weighed her words. "Sleeping it off, is he?"

"I could wake him if you like." Laura cast a nervous glance back at the wagon. "If you really need me to . . ."

Gabrielle wrenched away from her. "No!"

"No?" Laura echoed weakly. "Dearest, these are officers of the state. If they want . . ."

"No!" Gabrielle repeated in a fierce whisper. She glowered at Laura. "You know what he's like when he's been—when he's—"

"You know he doesn't mean it," Laura said pleadingly. "It's just that his head hurts so and you do make such noise." She turned back to the soldier. "It is, as you see, a very small wagon, Monsieur, and on rainy days, when the children are cooped inside . . ."

"Heavy with his hands, is he?" The soldier looked at Gabrielle, his expression grim. Gabrielle huddled into her seat, looking sullen. Laura couldn't tell whether it was part of her act or just reverting to form. "I have a little girl just about your age. What's your name?"

"Arielle," Gabrielle lied glibly.

Given that the name on her passport was still Gabrielle, the lie might not have been the most expedient tactic, but the guard didn't seem to take it amiss.

"Unusual name," commented the guard, winking at Laura.

Gabrielle straightened self-importantly. "Maman took it out of a play. It's the name of a sprite who flits from flower to flower."

"Never heard of that one. Here." Digging in his pocket, the soldier fished out a coin. He held it out to Gabrielle. "Buy yourself a sweet."

Gabrielle looked to Laura, who nodded her permission for her to take it.

"You are very kind, Monsieur," Laura said, and meant it. It was nice to remember, from time to time, that the servants of the Republic weren't all crazed maniacs on the order of Delaroche. Most of them were ordinary people, doing their jobs, trying to stay out of the rain, going home to their families at night.

"Do you have a little boy too?" Pierre-André asked hopefully.

"Pierre! Really." The tone of fond exasperation came out naturally, as if they were the family they pretended to be. Laura shook her head at him. "Your sister will share, won't you, Arielle? Now, I want you both to thank the nice man."

"Thank you, Monsieur," said Gabrielle in a singsong. "You are very kind."

Laura poked Pierre-André. "And what do you have to say?"

"Thank you," he muttered, hanging his head.

Gabrielle was acting; Pierre-André wasn't. The boy was a natural at being himself.

The guard chuckled, reaching out a hand to tousle Pierre-André's hair. It was the cowlick, Laura thought wildly. No one could resist that cowlick.

"Sorry to have disturbed you, Madame." He jerked a finger towards the wagon. "I hope he isn't too . . ."

Laura made a wry face, adult to adult. "So do I." On an impulse, she said, "Monsieur? Forgive my impertinence, but why did you stop us? We've never had trouble at the gates before. If it's that matter with the Comédie-Française . . . we didn't mean to use one of their plots. They did agree in the end that it was an accident."

The soldier grinned at her. "Stuffy bastards, aren't they? No, no, it's nothing to do with the theater. There's a dangerous man escaped from the Temple and another man with him."

"Dangerous?" asked Laura, gathering her children closer to her. Gabrielle gave an exaggerated shiver, her eyes wide.

"Not that kind of dangerous," the guard said kindly. "You don't have anything to fear. But they're having us search every carriage until we find them."

"Even theater troupes?" Laura grimaced comically.

"Even theater troupes." The soldier laughed with her at the absurdity of it. If Laura's laughter was a little strained, he didn't seem to notice. "Ah, well. Can't be too careful."

"It must be a bit tiresome," said Laura sympathetically.

"That's the word for it," the soldier agreed. "The traffic on the road isn't what it would be in summer, but it's still enough to keep us hopping. You'd be amazed how many carts go through this gate every day."

"At this point," said Laura honestly, "I doubt anything could amaze me."

Turning to the children, the soldier wagged a finger at them. "You be good and don't give your mother any trouble. Madame."

He handed her back their papers and waved them through.

Laura slapped the reins, setting the mules back into motion. Very slow motion. Theirs were not beasts that believed in bestirring themselves. It was probably for the best. A precipitate departure might have caused suspicion. She thought about André, in the back, listening and stewing. There was no noise from the body of the wagon. Either André had really gone to sleep or he was exerting extreme self-discipline.

It would take a great deal of self-discipline to perpetrate a deception such as he had for as long as he had.

How long had it been? In the rush of arranging their departure, there had been little time to speculate. She wondered just when Jaouen had made the switch from Revolutionary functionary to Royalist agent and whether it had had anything to do with his decision to leave his children behind in Nantes for so long.

Once they were out of earshot of the town walls, Laura turned to Gabrielle and said quietly, "That was beautifully done. Thank you."

Gabrielle scooted to the far side of the bench. Now that the immediate danger was done, their truce was over. "I wasn't going to let them hurt Papa."

Translation: Don't think I did this for *you*.

Still, Laura believed in credit where it was due. "Not everyone would have that sort of ingenuity. You saved us a great deal of bother."

And probably more than bother, but there was no point in scaring the girl by saying so. Gabrielle was a bright girl; she must have a fairly good idea by now of what they were up against.

Gabrielle eyed her suspiciously, searching for the catch.

Sighing, Laura twisted on the hard seat, looking down at Gabrielle. "I know you don't like this. I don't particularly like it either."

Gabrielle mumbled something.

Laura carried resolutely on. "We're saddled with each other, whether we like it or not. Your father needs both of us—"

That had been the wrong thing to say. Gabrielle's eyebrows were doing their best storm-cloud impersonation.

"Your father needs both of us to work together," Laura corrected herself hastily. "Your brother is too young to fully comprehend the dangers—"

"I'm not young! I'm four and three quarters!" piped up Pierre-André.

Laura raised her eyebrows at Gabrielle. "My point. But you're not. You understand the danger we're all in. It will take us a month to reach the coast. Once in England, you can be well rid of me. For that month, though, we need to pretend to be a family. A reasonably happy family."

Gabrielle considered.

Laura pressed her advantage. "I'm not your governess anymore. Whatever we tell the others, we both know that I'm not really your mother or even your stepmother. I have no claims on either your obedience or your affection. All I can ask is for your assistance. Not for my sake. For your family's."

Gabrielle toyed with the pages of her book. It was a nervous habit, Laura had noticed, as other girls might play with their hair or fiddle with a ring. She looked challengingly at Laura. "Why are *you* helping us?"

"Because I adore traveling through the countryside in the rain."

Gabrielle's face closed in on itself again. She shrugged down into her own wrap, her face sullen.

Laura could have kicked herself.

The girl was right; that hadn't been fair. If she expected Gabrielle to deal honestly with her, she had to deal honestly with Gabrielle. As honestly as she could, at any rate. She couldn't very well tell the girl that she was accompanying them because she had been ordered to do so by an English spy named after a particularly frivolous sort of flower.

"I owe you a duty," Laura said slowly. She could feel Gabrielle slowly looking at her, a bunched-up figure in the corner of the bench. Laura looked straight ahead, out over the road. "When I agreed to take on your education, I contracted an obligation to you. I don't believe in leaving tasks undone."

That much was true, at least.

"I thought you said you weren't our governess anymore." Gabrielle's voice was defiant, but there was a tinge of hesitation in it.

"Not officially," hedged Laura. Blast clever children. She decided to try another tactic. "To be honest, I mostly came for Monsieur Daubier. He was a friend of my parents' when I was your age."

Gabrielle cast her a quick, surprised glance.

"Yes, I did have parents once," said Laura dryly, and the little girl flushed and dropped her head. "Monsieur Daubier was always kind to me. It seemed only right to do something kind for him."

Not only was the sentiment mawkish, it was as riddled with potential inconsistencies as old cheese. Fortunately, Gabrielle's attention was elsewhere.

"What happened to your parents?" she asked awkwardly. Laura didn't miss the telling glance she sent over her shoulder, at the inside of the wagon.

"They went sailing in a storm," said Laura matter-of-factly. "The boat capsized."

"Oh," said Gabrielle. Laura could see her processing the information. She looked at Laura, almost belligerently. "My mother died of a fever."

"It doesn't matter how it happens, does it?" said Laura. "It hurts either way."

Gabrielle didn't answer, but her chin moved just the tiniest fraction of an inch. Laura took that as a yes.

Behind them, the curtains blocking off the body of the wagon rustled. André Jaouen's head appeared through the gaudy hangings. Beneath his spectacles, his eyes were the same bright blue-green as his daughter's. There was something else there too, a self-containment that they both shared.

"Feeling better, darling?" Laura asked flippantly.

André gave her a wry look. "Aside from the hangover I presume I'm meant to be suffering."

"That's what you get for being a dangerous, drunken beast."

"I take it we're clear?"

"Thanks to Gabrielle," said Laura, moving over to make room on the seat between herself and his daughter. "She very cunningly saved the day."

André clambered over onto the box, dropping into place next to Gabrielle. He placed his hand to his daughter's head in a fleeting gesture of affection. "I wouldn't have expected anything less."

He missed the look on Gabrielle's face, but Laura didn't. She was watching her father like a puppy left outside someone's back door, hoping to be petted but afraid to ask.

Oblivious, André turned to Laura and held out his other hand. "Give me a crack at those reins, will you? Let's see if I still remember how to drive."

❦

Taking the reins made André feel slightly less useless.

Slightly.

He had lain on the pallet in the back of the wagon, his hat tipped over his head, racked with the realization of his own incapacity. He wanted to be up there on the box, deflecting the guard, making everything right.

Instead, he was flat on his back, pretending to be in a drunken stupor while his nine-year-old daughter pulled his fat out of the fire. Oh, André knew it was the expedient course, but it rankled almost beyond bearing to know that the only way to ensure the safety of his family was to refrain from doing anything at all. Inaction was a great deal harder than action.

Some might say he had done enough already.

André looked at his son, half-asleep on the other side of his former governess. He was idly sucking his thumb, a habit André vaguely remembered from his babyhood. Julie had said it would spoil his mouth and put vinegar on his thumb.

On his other side, despite the jostling of the wagon, Gabrielle's head was bent over the open pages of a book. Every time the cart hit a rut, she clutched with one hand at the side of the wagon, never looking up. André put an arm around her shoulders, anchoring her. She shifted, uncomfortable, and he took his arm away again.

The wagons attracted a fair amount of attention as they traveled through the countryside, but none of the sort André had feared. Adults catcalled; children pointed and sometimes ran after them for a bit. But there was no pounding of hooves behind them, no shouting gendarmes, no cavalcade of soldiers.

The rain slowed their pace. The mud sucked at the mules' hooves and tugged at the wheels of the wagons. Jeannette drove hers with the same grim competence with which she plowed through her knitting. Pantaloon, deep in a daydream of his own devising, nearly ran his wagon into a ditch and had to be rescued by Harlequin, Leandro, and de Berry all tugging together. It was a sight for the history books, that one, a prince of the blood putting his back into extracting a battered theater wagon from a ditch on an unnamed road.

On the box next to him, Laura didn't fidget—she wasn't the fidgeting kind—but he caught her craning her neck, staring down the road behind them.

"Waiting for the cavalry?" asked André quietly.

Twitching her shawl, she twisted back into place. He could feel the brush of her skirts against his leg. Even when two of them were children, the bench was small for four. "I'll feel better once we're farther along."

Some of her hair had escaped its ribbon. Without thinking, André tucked it behind her ear for her. "You mean you'll feel better once we're across the Channel."

"That too." Re-tucking the hair he had just tucked, Laura pointed at the road ahead. "Oh, look. They've got Pantaloon unstuck. We might actually be able to move another three yards before dark."

They camped in the open that night. Cécile broached the decision as a money-saving measure—since some people, she added, with a pointed look at Rose, had been profligate with the group's funds during their last stay, cutting into the troupe's meager reserve.

The others had grumbled, but they had taken it as sense. Laura and André had exchanged a long look, silently giving thanks for Cécile's acuity. At an inn, there would be other patrons, an innkeeper, witnesses to relay information should Delaroche catch the scent of their trail. It might be cold and damp, but it would be safe.

The wagons were arranged in a rough circle, creating some small protection from the wind. André set about unhitching and provisioning their mules while Laura woke the sleeping Gabrielle and Pierre-André. Odd that after a day he already thought of them as their mules, just as the wagon was their wagon.

Freed from the wagon, Gabrielle had gravitated towards Jeannette, hovering awkwardly as Jeannette wrested control of the cook pot from Cécile. Cranky at being woken, Pierre-André was being clingy and whiny, clutching at Laura's neck. André could hear her speaking in a low, calming tone as she set him down, gently detaching his clutching fingers.

"... firewood," she was saying. "Leandro is relying on you to help him."

"Huh?" said Leandro, glowering at the Duc de Berry, who was helping Rose down from her wagon.

Even in the gloaming, André could see Laura roll her eyes. "You are relying on Pierre to help you gather firewood? Aren't you? Leandro!"

"Oh! Yes. Of course, I am. A big fellow like you, er—"

"Pierre," provided Laura. They had agreed it would be safer to drop the André. Pierre was common enough as a name, Pierre-André less so.

"Pierre, yes," said Leandro hastily. He clumsily patted Pierre-André on the head. "How do you feel about gathering twigs?"

Laura crouched down to Pierre-André's level "It's an important job, carrying firewood. Do you think you're up to it?"

They set out of the clearing together, the gangly Leandro nearly bent double as he held Pierre-André's hand, Pierre-André assuring his new friend that he planned to gather more twigs than anyone ever. André caught himself smiling as he fastened the feed bag. Modesty wasn't his son's strong suit. Next to him, Leandro seemed hardly older, very earnestly explaining the most effective twig-gleaning techniques. André could see his son's cowlick bobbing up and down in concentrated agreement.

Hauling the feed sack back into the wagon, André plunked it down next to the cookware, brushing his hands off against his breeches. Maybe, as counterintuitive as it seemed, this would be good for them. All of them together, in the same place, even if that place was a Commedia dell'Arte troupe. After the solitude of the Hôtel de Bac, a bit of companionship might not be a bad thing for Gabrielle and Pierre-André.

If only Delaroche didn't come after them.

Pierre-André returned proudly bearing a pile of sodden twigs, while Leandro staggered under the weight of logs that looked as though they had been cadged, on the sly, from someone's woodpile. André decided this wasn't the time to be a stickler about such matters as private property. The rain had stopped but the temperature had dropped with it, leaving everyone both clammy and chilled.

The fire smoked and hissed, but it was still better than no fire at all. The small crew clustered around, getting as close to the blaze as space allowed, sitting on blankets and cushions taken from the wagons. Judging by the stains on the cushions, they had been used this way before. Jeannette, having established her place as Empress of the Hearth, ladled stew into wooden bowls. Sated, Pierre-André stretched out full-length across André's and Laura's laps, his head in Laura's lap, his feet on André.

Low laughter came from the cushions on the other side of the fire, where de Berry was recounting a story for the delectation of the delectable Rose. A bawdy one, if the quality of her titters was anything to go by. Leandro moodily whittled a twig into a smaller twig. And next to him . . .

André poked Laura in the shoulder. "They look like they're going to come to blows."

Jeannette was standing over Daubier, hands on her hips. "—waste of perfectly good food."

"I'm not hungry."

"Nonsense," said Jeannette stridently. "You've been traveling all day. You need your strength."

Daubier's face seemed to have collapsed in on itself, all hanging skin where there had once been ruddy flesh. "What for?"

Jeannette snorted. "What for? I offered you stew, not philosophy. Now eat!"

"Next she's going to make him wash behind his ears," murmured André.

Laura twisted her head to look at him. Her hair hung loose down her back, gypsy-style. "You're enjoying this."

The heel of one of Pierre-André's boots was digging into one knee. The opposite thigh had gone to sleep under the weight of one compact four-year-old. The cushion under his backside was damp already, the wet seeping through the bottom of his breeches. André couldn't remember the last time he had felt this relaxed.

Clearly, a sign that the strain had driven him mad.

There was something bizarrely soothing about sitting there in the uncertain light of the campfire, listening to Pantaloon pick out a tune on an instrument that looked like the descendant of a lute, sharing the weight of his son with the woman next to him, his daughter a few feet away, listening with rapt attention as Harlequin entertained her with tales of the Commedia dell'Arte. Now that the worst had happened, the anxieties that had gnawed at him since the children had come from Nantes seemed to have drained away, leached out in fatigue and the rough wine the actors had shared with their supper.

It was a false comfort, he knew. Delaroche was still out there; Daubier's hand still needed tending; de Berry needed to be seen safely to the border. There were a thousand things that could still go wrong and a month in which they could do so.

But for now, for this moment in time, as Jeannette clucked over Daubier and Pierre-André permanently crippled his left knee and Laura Griscogne's shawl tangled on his sleeve, yes, he was content.

Not enjoying himself, per se, but content.

"Jeannette never liked me, either," he said blandly, deflecting the question. "It's nice to see her go after someone else for a change."

Gabrielle had elected to sit on her own cushion, her knees drawn up to her chest as she listened earnestly to Harlequin's tales of the misadventures of the Commedia dell'Aruzzio.

Catching André's eye over Gabrielle's head, Harlequin winked. "Surely, your father must have stories of his own," he said jovially, loud enough to be heard by the group. "We can't be the only ones to have fallen afoul of the muses."

André leaned back, resting his weight on the palms of his hands. "Which story do you want?"

Laura put a wifely hand on his arm. "Oh no. Once you get started . . . It's late and the children should be in bed."

Gabrielle gave Laura a look of death, not appreciating the reminder either of her youth or the lateness of the hour.

Struggling to his feet, Harlequin held out a hand to Gabrielle, sweeping her up. "Mademoiselle Malcontre," he said grandly. "I trust you shall favor me again with your company tomorrow."

His performance was such an obvious parody of de Berry's that the others were hard put to repress their smiles. Gabrielle, however, ducked her head and bobbed a curtsy, taking the compliment very much at face value.

It all made André very glad that she was nine rather than nineteen.

Like a bird of prey, Jeannette descended upon them to sweep up Pierre-André, bearing him triumphantly forth as though he were her own personal prize. One by one, the others rose too, Harlequin taking the precaution of extinguishing the fire. Lanterns burned on their hooks on the sides of the wagon, casting a dim illumination over the clearing, by which the actors found their way to their own lodgings.

And beds.

André and his supposed wife were the only ones left by the smoking remains of the fire.

Rising awkwardly to his feet, André extended a hand to Laura. "Shall we?"

Ignoring his hand, she made a show of gathering up the blanket, which might have been more effective if she hadn't still been sitting on it. André thought about pointing that out and decided it would only make a bad situation worse. She didn't like to show weakness, his governess.

Laura hitched herself off the blanket and straggled to her feet, dragging up the blanket with her. "It is rather late," she said, lurching down to grab the pillow. Her hair provided a screen for her face. "And we do have an early morning tomorrow."

"Very early," André agreed. "Dawn, most likely."

He appropriated the pillow from her, tucking it under one arm, although he knew better than to offer his arm again. He held aside the heavy curtains screening the back of the wagon, making room for her to precede him.

"We should probably get some sleep," she said, not looking at him.

The curtains dragged down behind him, shutting them into the narrow, dark chamber. The single lantern cast a dim light across the jumbled piles of cookware, the squat table, the pile of blankets. The bed.

"Yes," André agreed. "Sleep."

For a moment, neither of them said anything at all, both staring at the narrow pallet that was to be bed for both. One bed. One very narrow bed.

Then they both turned and started talking at once.

"Would you like—," he began.

"If we took some of the blankets—," she said.

Laura dropped the blanket she had been holding and pressed both her hands to her face. "This is ridiculous," she said indistinctly. "Ridiculous."

"But necessary," he reminded her. "It was your scheme to travel as husband and wife." He made sure to keep his voice pitched low. The walls might provide the illusion of privacy, but they weren't thick.

She took a step back from the bed—and from him—practically tripping her over her hem in her haste. "I didn't know we would be forced to interpret that quite so literally!"

Was the idea really that distasteful to her? André found himself mildly irked. "I wasn't planning to ravish you," he said irritably.

Laura bristled. "I didn't expect you were."

Perhaps that hadn't been the most politic thing to have said. André rubbed a hand over his eyes, doing his best to make amends. "I'm too tired to ravish anyone."

Laura plunked her hands on her hips. "Oh, is that supposed to make me feel better? I'm glad to know that it's only fatigue that preserves my slender hold on virtue."

André blinked. "Do you *want* me to ravish you?"

She sucked in air through her nose. "I *want* to go to sleep. Alone."

"I'm sorry not to be able to oblige."

She turned in a flurry of wool. "I don't see why not. There are certainly enough extra blankets. If I made them into a pallet . . ."

André held out a hand to stop her. She froze as his fingers touched her shoulder.

He said, more gently than he had originally intended, "Those are to use on top of us, not under us. It's going to get very cold overnight."

He could see Laura's throat work as she swallowed. She pressed her eyes briefly together, as though searching for composure. "I'm sorry," she said in a low voice. "This is just a very odd situation."

That was one way of putting it.

"I'm used to . . ." She struggled for words. "I'm used to my privacy." She tried, belatedly, to make a joke of it. "I don't share well."

"Think of it as being comrades in arms," André suggested. "Soldiers put their pallets together in the field for warmth. It's only sensible that we should do the same. That's all it is. Nothing more."

Nothing to be afraid of, he added silently. It wasn't, he sensed, so much the threat of ravishment that she feared, but the rest of it. The intimacy of it. As she had said, they were both used to their privacy.

Laura's shoulders were very stiff beneath the red wool shawl. She nodded without looking at him, her head slightly bent. "It makes sense. In this camp, one never knows who'll come barging in. It's better to keep up the pretense, I suppose."

André tried for levity. "Unless we have a fight and you boot me out of the wagon."

He was rewarded with a slight quirk of her lips, the distant cousin of a smile. "It might be a bit soon for that. But I'll bear it mind for later."

"Do you need help?" he asked. "With your laces or buttons or . . ." He gestured helplessly with his hands. It had been a long time since he'd had intimate acquaintance with the intricacies of feminine garments.

Aside, of course, from buttoning his governess back into her gray dress in the dark dining room of Daubier's studio. But that hardly counted.

"No, thank you." She backed away, clutching a rolled-up blanket to her chest like armor. "I thought I'd sleep in my clothes. For the warmth."

It wasn't an absurd notion. Most people did. There were whole parts of the French countryside where André suspected people hadn't changed their garments in years.

"That makes sense," he said mildly. He loosened the knot of his cravat, easing it out from around his neck, moving slowly and deliberately, like a gamekeeper trying not to startle the deer.

Laura began spreading extra blankets along the bed, arranging the edges with finicky care. "Do you think the children will be warm enough?"

There was something artificial about the very mundanity of the comment. André was reminded of children playing house, playing at being mother and father, with acorn caps for teacups and pinecones for children.

"Jeannette wouldn't have it otherwise. She's a tough old bird."

André began unbuttoning his coat. He'd sleep in his shirt and breeches, but the buttons on the coat itself would be uncomfortable. His hand bumped against something hard and heavy, shoved into an inner pocket. He fished it out, the edge catching on the lining.

He looked at it bemusedly. It looked very different, somehow, in the shadowy light of the small wagon than it had in his bedroom that morning. "Oh. I almost forgot."

"Forgot?" Laura glanced at him quickly, pausing in the act of plumping pillows that were already as plump as they could get.

André held out the book he had brought. He had taken it up on a whim that morning, before he left for the Temple. It had been by his bedside, along with the Ronsard, and he had stuffed it in his coat pocket, for reasons not entirely clear even to himself. "I brought this for you. I didn't know if you had your own copy."

Laura stood there, staring at the book in his hand. "I don't." She started to reach out for it, then abruptly dropped her hand. "But I can't take yours. Doesn't this . . . Isn't it? . . . Sorry. I don't know where my wits are."

"Back in Paris with mine?" he suggested. "Take it. I brought it for you."

"But it has your wife's drawings. I would have thought that"— she paused, as though looking for the right words—"that you would have wanted something of her."

"I have Gabrielle and Pierre-André." He winced at the sickly sweetness of the sentiment. It might be true, but it still sounded mawkish.

Laura didn't seem to notice. She was absorbed in reflections of her own, her attention focused on the book.

"I'll keep this in trust, then, for Gabrielle." She ran a finger over the faded gold lettering, lingering over it. "Thank you."

"You're welcome."

Silence fell between them as each looked at the other, waiting for a cue, the book still clutched in Laura's hand.

Well, there was no time like the present.

André gestured to the bed. "Would you prefer the right side or the left?"

Chapter 26

L aura couldn't figure out what to do with herself.

It was dark in the wagon—true dark, a world away from the diffused light of the city, with the embers of a fire still an orange-red in the hearth. Laura knew that André Jaouen was next to her, knew it from the regular rasp of his breath and the way the pallet dipped off to the side where his body pressed it down, but she couldn't see him.

Would it have made it better if she could?

It was a very strange thing, this having another person in bed beside her. Maids might have to share quarters, but a governess never did. Laura couldn't remember the last time she had shared a bedroom with someone, much less a bed, and a bed of proportions that would insult the average pygmy.

André Jaouen didn't seem to be bothered by it. It was safer to think of him by his full name, using the extra syllables as a wall to ward off the fact that there was no wall between them at all.

Her putative husband, on the other hand, had said his good-night, rolled himself in one of the blankets—they had separate blankets, at least; there was that much between them—snuffed the lantern, and gone to sleep. As simple as that. While she suddenly seemed to have too many limbs, all of which took up far too much space on the narrow pallet. Her elbows extruded, her knees stuck out, her forearms seemed to have expanded until they required an entire mattress unto themselves.

Laura tucked her knees into her chest, lying on her side with her back to the blanket-covered bundle that was André. Her left arm, scrunched up beneath her, was beginning to go numb. She cautiously wiggled her fingers, hoping her bedmate wouldn't feel the pull on the blankets. In and out, in and out went his breath, peaceful and even.

Laura scowled. How did he manage to sleep so easily? And why couldn't she?

It had been an exhausting few days. She should be exhausted. She was exhausted. So why wasn't she asleep? In peasant households, people piled six in a bed for warmth. In this very camp, Cécile was curled up beside Rose, de Berry stacked in with Leandro and Harlequin. She would be willing to wager they were all snoring peacefully away, dreaming their respective dreams, not a one of them lying awake monitoring the movements of the person on the pallet beside him.

Laura eased onto her back, wincing at the crinkle of straw. As pallets went, this one wasn't too terribly uncomfortable. The straw tick had been bolstered with enough blankets to keep scratchy bits of hay at bay. She had slept on worse over the course of her various employments. But alone. She had always slept alone.

One would think, in the dark, André Jaouen would be easy enough to ignore. It wasn't as though she could see him, other than as a shadowy blob of blanket. But she was ridiculously aware of his presence, of his breath, his smell, the warmth of his body through the blankets. He made the small space seem even smaller, the walls narrower, the roof lower—as though there weren't enough air for both of them to breathe.

Laura clamped her elbows against her ribs, making herself as narrow as her limbs would allow, neck stiff, legs straight down, arms at her sides. Breathe in . . . breathe out . . . breathe in. . . . If they made decent time on the road, they were to have their first rehearsal the next evening. Cécile had filled her in on the scenario, which was simple enough: Leandro was in love with the fair Inamorata, who was, in her turn, being courted by Il Capitano, whose suit was favored by her father, Pantaloon. In . . . Out . . .

Her neck hurt.

With a sigh, Laura rolled over again, trying to pummel the pillow into some semblance of comfort. The feathers had all but disintegrated with age. Whatever ducks had given their feathers for this pillow had died so long ago that their ponds had probably already silted over. The pillow felt like it was filled with grit. Maybe it was. Maybe she was just being difficult.

For heaven's sake, why couldn't she *sleep*?

"Laura?" The voice came from the next pillow over. It was little more than a murmur, but it sounded unnaturally loud in the small space.

Laura stiffened, instinctively playing dead. Was it too late to pretend to be asleep?

Punching the pillow had probably not been the brightest idea.

"Yes?" she said cautiously.

She could hear the rustle of blankets as he rolled over. Laura scooted even farther towards the end of the pallet.

"Is something wrong?" André's voice was heavy with sleep.

Was something wrong? They were on the run through the countryside with two small children, a royal duke, and an injured painter in their care, and he wanted to know what was wrong?

"I can't sleep," she said, and felt like a child. A cranky, petulant child. What was wrong with her? She hadn't been that sort of child when she was a child. "This bed is very . . . crunchy. And it's cold."

Better that than admitting the real reasons. And it was cold. She could feel the tip of her nose turning blue.

"What about you? Why aren't you asleep?"

"I was," André said pointedly. His jaws stretched in a long, uninhibited yawn. Hitching himself up a bit, he unfolded one arm, stretching it out along the top of the pallet. "Here."

Here what? Laura could see the shadowy outline of his sleeve, pale against the darker skin beneath. He had elected to sleep in his shirt, the strings untied at the throat, the cuffs open and folded back along his forearms.

She, on the other hand, was still entirely fully clothed, with the sole exception of her shawl. That was another problem. Her blouse itched.

When she didn't respond, André stretched out his fingers. "Come here."

Laura regarded his arm suspiciously. His arm couldn't possibly be less comfortable than the pillow. But . . . "Why?"

Although she couldn't see very well, she was fairly certain that he rolled his eyes. "For warmth," he said, "only for warmth. And because your fidgeting is keeping me awake."

Laura lowered herself cautiously into the crook of his arm, from sheer fatigue, she told herself, rather than anything else. They both needed their sleep. "All right. But I don't—"

His hand pressed against the back of her head, smushing her face against his chest.

"—fidget," she said into his shirt.

"Mmph," said André into her hair. It wasn't so much agreement or disagreement as a shorthand for *All right, that's all very well; can we go to sleep now?*

Shaking free of his hand, Laura turned her face so that she could breathe. Asphyxiation was seldom the route to a good night's sleep. She could feel the rub of much-washed linen beneath her cheek—like an old sheet, she told herself. It was best for all concerned if she thought of him simply as an extension of the mattress. A much warmer and firmer portion of the mattress. In fact, he made a much better mattress than the mattress. Mattresses, after all, seldom came with their own heating agents.

She scooted gingerly closer, finding a comfortable spot somewhere below his arm and above his ribs.

André moved obligingly to make room for her, adjusting the angle of his arm around her shoulders and tucking his chin against the top of her head.

His shirt smelled of soap and spilled coffee, thin enough that she could feel the faint prickle of the hair on his chest.

"Better now?" he asked sleepily.

"Certainly warmer," conceded Laura, and felt his chest rumble with something that might have been a chuckle.

"Good," he murmured. She could feel the dip of his chin against her hair. "Sleep."

To her own surprise, she did.

It wasn't a rooster that woke them, but Harlequin, shouting with appalling cheerfulness, "Wake up, lovebirds! It's morning!"

Laura blinked her gummy eyes open just in time to see his head disappearing back through the curtains. Doors. Doors were a good thing, she thought hazily. Much less permeable than curtains.

She yawned, feeling her eyes drift shut again, every fiber of her body resisting the imperative to wake up. She was heavenly warm and incredibly comfortable, curled up on her side, cradled in a nest of blankets. Laura stretched, and felt the blanket stir in response.

"Mmm?" said the blanket, and Laura came jarringly and fully awake.

That wasn't a blanket; that was a man. A man with one arm under her head and another around her waist. At some point in the night, they must have rolled over, because they were sleeping like two spoons in a drawer, the curve of his body mirroring hers, her back tucked up intimately against his front.

Very intimately.

It had been some time since Laura had had personal experience of the more masculine portions of the male anatomy, but she was fairly sure that wasn't his knee.

Laura bounded out of the bed, trailing half the blankets with her. Her blouse had come unmoored during the night, and she hastily yanked it back up over her shoulder.

"Good morning!" she babbled. "Time to wake up!"

André groaned, burying his head in the pillows, which all seemed to have bunched up on his side of the bed. Bizarre that there was already a "his" side and a "hers" side, but his side it was.

"Are you always this terrifyingly energetic in the mornings?" he inquired.

"No, it's just a special treat for our first night together," she snapped, then realized just what it sounded like. Deciding to quit while she was ahead, she said hastily, "Thank you. It was very kind of you to serve as pillow for me."

André propped himself up on one elbow. "It wasn't entirely selfless," he said. "Where did you put my portmanteau?"

"There." Laura pointed to the bundle she had packed for him. She did her best to sound nonchalant. "Not entirely selfless?"

André paused in the act of digging through the bag. He cocked a brow. "It stopped you thrashing about."

Laura plunked down on the small stool in front of their one table. "I wasn't *thrashing*. I was just . . . restless," she said with dignity. "It's been an unsettling few days."

"No argument there." André yanked his old shirt up over his head, revealing an expanse of chest lightly fuzzed with dark hair.

Laura swiveled around on the stool, reaching for her hairbrush. What with one thing and another, she had forgotten to braid her hair before going to bed, and it was a snarled mess. She attacked a chunk at random, wincing as the bristles hit knots. "Do you think Monsieur Delaroche is after us yet?"

André's head emerged through the top of the fresh shirt. He pulled the ties together. "I would be very surprised if he weren't. He'll be itching to get his hands on Daubier."

"And you," Laura pointed out.

"And me," André agreed.

"You seem surprisingly unconcerned."

"I slept well."

Laura made a face at him.

"I'm not unconcerned. Believe me," André said with feeling, "I couldn't be farther from unconcerned. But I did take some precautions before we left."

Despite herself, Laura was intrigued. She lowered the hairbrush. "What sort of precautions?"

"I planted a few false trails. Delaroche should be getting reports of a man answering my description heading with two small children in the direction of Austria."

"Austria?"

"In the fireplace of my study in the Hôtel de Bac are the charred remains of a series of letters with the Austrian foreign minister, bargaining for safe conduct. Such a pity the fire went out before it could burn down completely."

"Isn't that too obvious? Won't he suspect?"

"Trust me, it's very artful charring. He'll also receive conflicting reports about a fishing boat."

"Meaning," said Laura, "that he'll assume that the Austrian documents are a façade, but the fishing boat is worth following."

André looked smug. "Or the other way around. Delaroche's mind is just twisted enough to assume that the obvious falsehood must be real and the real-seeming option false. There should be enough there to keep him busy for some time. You, by the way, have accepted new employment in Provence and are on your way there even as we speak. It's a very old family. And very hard to find, given that they died out two generations ago."

"And Daubier?"

"Went to ground, presumably with Cadoudal. Someone is going to go to his studio to make it look as though he snuck back to get necessaries for himself."

"Someone?"

"I do still have some friends in Paris. The point is that it ought to look as though we're all in separate groups, with Daubier still somewhere in Paris. They won't be looking for us all together, and certainly not here."

"Unless Governor Murat saw," Laura countered.

"After your extraordinary efforts to prevent him doing so?"

André's voice was mild enough, but Laura felt a rush of warmth at the memory. After a night spent pressed together, body to body, it was absurd that the recollection of a bit of playacting could make her blush. That was all it had been—playacting.

Now, if only her body would remember that.

"There was nothing so extraordinary about it," Laura muttered. "Anyone would have done the same."

"Somehow," said André dryly, "I doubt Jeannette could have pulled that off in quite the same way."

"Well," said Laura. She tossed her brush aside and rose from the stool. "Let's hope my acting skills prove equally good on the stage."

"Nervous?" asked André.

"Nonsense," said Laura. "All one has to do is act out a scenario. What can possibly be so hard about that?"

❧

"Ruffiana? If you could, a little to the right?" called Pantaloon, for at least the third time in ten minutes. "You're blocking Harlequin."

Laura moved obediently to the right, knowing that it would be the left next time, or the middle the time after that. No matter where she was, it wasn't where she was supposed to be.

Apparently, dissembling and performing weren't quite the same skills after all. Leading a double life didn't seem to have prepared her for the exigencies of the stage. Lying one's way into someone's household didn't necessitate such skills as projecting one's lines or remembering to cheat out towards the audience. Upstage, downstage . . . Laura's head swam with it.

None of the others seemed to be having the same problem. André, it seemed, was a natural on the stage. She would have accused him of practicing on the sly but for the fact that he hadn't known about the acting troupe until after she had. It must be his background in debate, Laura decided. Like Commedia dell'Arte, being a public representative was an art form that demanded thinking on one's feet and speaking very, very loudly.

Being a governess didn't provide quite the same training.

Excuses, excuses. No matter how she attempted to parse it, the result was the same: She was an unmitigated disaster on the stage. Even de Berry had done better than she. He, at least, remembered to address his lines downstage.

"Shall we begin the scene again?" suggested Pantaloon wearily.

"What makes him think the tenth time will make any difference?" murmured Rose to Leandro.

Leandro blushed and scuffed his feet, torn between his innate good nature and the attentions of his goddess.

"Is it time for supper yet?" Laura asked hopefully.

Harlequin checked his watch. "It's four o'clock."

Blast.

Pantaloon sighed and rose from his perch on an overturned log. "Again, I think. We must have something to perform when we reach Beauvais."

Beauvais was to be their first stop, roughly a week hence. They were rehearsing in the open, in a clearing in a wooded copse. It had been deemed a good place to camp, largely due to the small pond nearby.

From Leandro, who did manage to string together complete sentences as long as Rose was out of eyeshot, Laura learned that they were taking something of a detour. Under normal circumstances, the troupe would have traveled by the major roads, stopping to give performances along the way, staying as many as three nights if the town were large enough and the take good. With so many new troupe members, Pantaloon had decreed it more prudent to take to the back roads, using the opportunity to put the new cast members through their paces. By avoiding the inns, they broke even. There was no revenue, but little in the way of cost.

It also meant they had no witnesses. There was no one to comment on the man with the strangely broken hand, the actor with the oddly aristocratic accent, or the two small children who just happened to have the same names as the small children of a wanted man.

According to Leandro, the decision had been Pantaloon's. Pantaloon was, after all, the nominal head of the troupe. Laura had a fairly good idea who had first broached the plan.

Laura wondered how much the Pink Carnation was paying Cécile. Whatever it was, she deserved double.

Laura thought back over the rehearsal. Make that triple.

"From the beginning, then," said Pantaloon. "Ruffiana, you have intercepted Harlequin, who is returning from a rendezvous with Columbine, who has given him a note from Inamorata to be delivered to Leandro. You want him to play go-between on your behalf with Il Capitano, but first you must feel him out to make sure he won't betray you to your husband. Understood?"

"Perfectly," said Laura. It wasn't the scenario she had trouble with. She could summarize it perfectly well. It was acting it that was the problem.

Apparently, one couldn't just walk up to Harlequin and say, "Hello, young messenger. Would you carry this letter for me?" No. One had to work around to it and make it sound natural. Preferably with sufficient double entendre to keep the audience amused, interspersed with a well-worn repertoire of physical gags.

André had been brilliantly comedic as Il Capitano, the blustering Spanish officer simultaneously attempting to seduce young Inamorata and repel the advances of her mother, Ruffiana. Even de Berry had been adequate as Leandro's two-faced best friend, who pretends to aid in the courtship of Inamorata while secretly wooing her for himself, although Laura did wonder how much of that was acting and how much the prelude to an actual seduction.

They began the scene again. Harlequin strolled "onstage," hands in his pockets, whistling a merry Mozart tune, only to be intercepted by Laura. She gave an exaggerated start of surprise. "You! You there!"

"I, Madame?" Harlequin waggled his eyebrows in a way that managed to be effortlessly comedic.

"Yes, you." Blast. What next? Molière this was not. Next time she escaped from Paris, it was going to be with a classical theater troupe, where one could simply memorize one's lines. Memorization, she could do. "You have the look of a lackey. Can you carry a letter for me?"

"For a beautiful woman"—Harlequin made the word "beautiful" a joke in itself, in complicity with the imaginary audience—"there's very little I can't carry."

"Er, good. Um. I have need of your skills. Your letter-carrying skills."

Pantaloon dropped his head into his hands.

"Where did you say you performed again?" said Harlequin jokingly, dropping out of character.

"I'm sorry," said Laura wretchedly. "I don't know where my mind is today. I must have offended one of the muses."

She meant to make a joke out of it, but it fell flat. The others exchanged significant looks.

"We're all tired," said André quickly. "After being based in

Paris for so many months, none of us are used to this much travel anymore. It saps the creative energy."

It hadn't seemed to hurt his creative energy.

Laura mustered an unconvincing yawn. "Please forgive me," she said. "I didn't sleep much last night."

"Didn't you?" murmured Harlequin. He winked at André. "You're a lucky man, Capitano."

She hadn't . . . Oops. Laura bit down on a quick negation. In any event, at least this furthered the pretense that they were married. She could cling to that small reassurance, at least.

It was a new and unsettling sentiment, feeling this incompetent. She didn't like it, not at all. She might not be particularly talented or inspired, but she had always at least risen to the level of competence.

"We'll have an early night tonight and resume again tomorrow," said Cécile briskly. "Everyone has a bad day now and again."

Laura trailed after her out of the clearing. One bad day, yes. But what happened when she failed again tomorrow?

How long before the other actors smelled a rat?

Chapter 27

"It shouldn't be this hard," Laura muttered. "It's simply a matter of knowing what to say and where to stand. How hard can that be?"

"Very," André said, propping himself up on one elbow.

He was sprawled comfortably across the pallet, waiting as his temporary wife prepared for bed. Since she didn't appear willing to remove much in the way of clothing, this consisted solely of yanking her hair back into a braid that looked as though it were intended as much for punishment as convenience. André winced in sympathy for her scalp as she crossed one section with another.

A brief squall of rain had driven the troupe from their campfire early tonight. As Pantaloon had commented, not unkindly, it was perhaps for the best. If they were to perform in Beauvais on Saturday, they would have a great many miles to travel the next day and an even greater deal of work to accomplish.

Seated next to Laura, André had felt her flinch at the words. She knew they were intended for her.

Laura gave the knot at the bottom of her braid a final, vicious yank. "But you manage well enough. Better than well enough. You were quite good."

André leaned back against the bunched-up pillows. "I've had more practice than you have. I participated in the odd amateur theatrical in my youth."

More than a few, in fact. There had been a large garden behind Père Beniet's house, with a terrace perfectly suited for balcony scenes.

They had been such innocent revels, those summer theatricals. They had all laughed a great deal—sometimes at Julie, who could never remember her lines; sometimes at Renaud, comrade in legal studies, who thought no play was complete without a duel and insisted on inserting them in the most unlikely places in the narrative.

Renaud had died long since, killed in the fighting in the Vendée during the war. He had never been meant to wield any weapon heavier than a law book.

The others, too, were gone, each in their own way. Julie, dead. Marie-Agnès, Julie's cousin, married with three children in Brest. Their entire enchanted summer circle, scattered and gone.

"Don't forget," he added wryly, "I've spent the past few years playing at a pretense. There's nothing like the threat of execution to improve one's acting skills. You wouldn't know that."

Something passed across her face, like a ripple beneath still waters.

Laura set her brush down very carefully on the table. "I had wondered," she said slowly. "You made such a convincing show."

"I had to," André pointed out. "I wouldn't be here otherwise."

"When did it start?" she asked. "And why?"

"Is it important?" He looked at her, perched on the three-legged stool, and thought how odd it was how unremarkable it felt to be here like this, sharing a room and a bed. She wore a loose blouse tucked into a high-waisted skirt—peasant clothing, convenient for travel. Her hair hung in a long braid over one shoulder. With her honey-colored skin and her dark hair, she might have been an Umbrian peasant in an old mural.

Abandoning the stool, she perched on the edge of the pallet, tucking her legs up beneath the wide folds of her skirt. "You don't have to tell me if you don't want to. It's your prerogative."

André remembered another conversation, another night. "I've always had mixed feelings about prerogatives."

"So you've told me."

It was folly, he knew, to confide in her. What did he know of her, after all, other than this? That she had been his governess; that she could teach Latin, literature, and the rudiments of nearly everything else; that her resourcefulness deserted her when it came to the stage; and that she curled an arm beneath one cheek as she slept. All of these things, he knew, but they told him nothing at all.

They did claim that sharing a bed brought out confidences, even though he suspected that this wasn't quite what they meant.

The urge to confide, after five years of silence, was surprisingly tempting, like water after thirst. He had kept his own counsel for so long. Père Beniet had known part of it, but not all. Jean had been Cadoudal's creature, just as the coachman had been Fouché's, both there to keep him in line. As for Daubier, he wasn't the sort of friend in whom one confided. Even if the stakes hadn't been what they were, Daubier was more interested in appearances than emotions; his attention tended to wander.

And then there had been Julie. He had tried to tell her, but she hadn't wanted to hear. She preferred the world as she transmuted it, translated into certitude by paint and canvas, no doubts or gray areas.

André looked at Laura, her dark eyes steady on his, waiting him out without saying a word. He thought of her as he had first seen her—a shadowy figure in gray, waiting, watching, listening. Whatever else she was, she knew how to keep her counsel. And she understood the shades of gray.

André peeled off his glasses, rubbing his eyes with one hand.

"It began four years ago. No," André corrected himself, frowning at the brown wool of the blanket. "If I'm being honest, it started before that. We were in Paris during the Terror, Julie and I." He looked up at the woman sitting on the bed next to him. "Were you there too?"

She shook her head wordlessly.

André rolled a bit of lint between his fingers. "Then I can't tell you what it was. It's the sort of thing that has to be experienced to be believed. I wish I hadn't experienced it. It all started off so well. We had a constitution, an assembly, all the things we had been demanding. Feudal privileges abolished, the common humanity of man exalted . . ." He broke off. "You have the idea."

It was hard, even now, to reassemble the rest. As a student of history, he could follow action A to consequence B, but at the time, event had followed event with incomprehensible rapidity.

"Julie wanted to stay in Paris, to paint. The Revolution opened opportunities for her, opportunities greater than any she had had before." Her friends had been more radical than his own. Through Jacques-Louis David, she had become close to both Marat and Robespierre. In the meantime, André's own party, the Girondins, were coming increasingly under attack.

Robespierre had commissioned her to craft a series of murals on the theme of Reason Exalted. Exalted? André had demanded. With their friends being arrested, carted off to one didn't want to imagine what? Julie had taken umbrage at that. For her, the ideals of the Revolution were still pure and whole. She didn't see the blood pouring down the Place de Grève or notice the gaps in their dinner parties. She had always had that facility, the facility of ignoring those things that didn't fit in her compositions. It was part of her charm. At least, it had been.

But there was one thing she hadn't been able to ignore, although she would have liked to have done. It was at the height of the Terror that she had become pregnant with Gabrielle.

"We moved back to Nantes when Julie was expecting Gabrielle. It seemed safer."

Laura's dark eyes followed him. "But it wasn't," she guessed.

"No," he said shortly. Even now, it was hard to bring himself to talk about it. "Have you heard of republican marriage?"

"Vows before a registry office?"

He gave a short, harsh laugh. "If only. The Republican Committee in Nantes came up with a new way of dispatching dissidents they oh-so-euphemistically termed a republican marriage."

"Yes?" Laura prompted.

André closed his eyes. Even now, he could see it—the winter-blasted bank of the Loire, the bare tree branches, the shivering bodies of the condemned. "They would take a man and a woman," he said in a monotone, "strip them, bind them together, and fling them into the river. It was January. Cold. They didn't stand a chance." His tongue felt dry at the memory. "Sometimes, they would run them through with a sword, from one straight through the other, one blade for both."

He might not have been on the Committee, but all those unwilling initiates into the "republican marriage" had been, in some part, his doing. All those heads lost on the guillotine. He had fought for the Revolution, lent his voice and his will to bring it about, and in the end, it had brought only death. He had helped unleash forces he had been powerless to control.

André felt Laura's hand on his arm—just a fleeting touch, a wordless gesture of sympathy. It was enough to bolster him to go on.

He drew a shuddering breath. "I spoke to Jean-Baptiste Carrier, the head of the Tribunal. He said it wasn't any of my concern. My day was over. What we had done in the Assembly was all well and good, but it wasn't enough. It was their turn now. And if I questioned too much, well, they might just start to doubt my loyalty as well. My loyalty and my family's." He looked at Laura, silent, attentive, her face still in the light of the single lamp. "They were burning books, Laura. Killing men for making the wrong friends. It was madness. He threatened Père Beniet—my father-in-law."

Laura nodded. "I know."

"I had intended to try to take up my legal practice and put together a normal life again. But there wasn't any such thing as normal. It seemed safer to try to work from within. At least, it made me and my family harder to denounce."

"I still don't understand how you came to be working for Artois," said Laura. "I wouldn't have pegged you as a monarchist."

André shook himself out of the past. "What was the alternative? None of the reforms we had dreamed of could exist in a world where coup followed coup and the army had the power to unseat the people's chosen representatives. Monarchy might not be the best of all possible systems, but at least it promised stability and, if done right, the rule of law."

"But what laws?" Laura asked sensibly. "I should think the value of the system would depend on the laws underlying it."

"To a point. There's something to be said for predictability. Even in a flawed system, at least one knows where one stands. Predictability is all."

"Not all. What if the laws decreed that ten people, chosen in a preordained way, were to be guillotined at ten in the morning every Sunday? It might be predictable, but it wouldn't be pleasant. Or just," Laura added, as an afterthought.

André propped himself up on one elbow. "That's to take the

argument to absurdity. It's as if to argue that because one cat scratched you, all cats should be declawed."

"No," said Laura, a glint in her black eyes. "That's your argument, not mine. You argue that all law is functionally the same. I argue for distinctions among them, between good law and bad law."

"What if it's neither good nor bad, but merely normative?" André argued back.

"What if I fling words about for the sake of saying them?"

"Isn't that what rhetoric is?"

"But is rhetoric conducive to law? Or to reason?"

André grinned up at her, feeling lighter-hearted than he had for some time. "You're too quick for me."

Laura's expression turned wry. "Only off the stage. On it, I can't seem to tell my right from my left."

On an impulse, André took her hand. He half expected her to object, but she didn't.

He rubbed his thumb along the side of it. "It will get easier; you'll see. You'll pick it up."

For a moment, her hand tightened on his. Then she pulled away, scooting off the edge of the pallet and yanking at the blanket.

"I hope so, or we're all in trouble," she said, the flippant tone of her voice at odds with the lines between her brows.

There was nothing he could say, so André did the only thing he could do. He stretched out an arm, making room for her in the bed.

Laura hesitated for a moment and then eased herself down next to him, resting her head in the crook of his arm.

André felt, absurdly, as though he had just won a difficult case in court.

"For warmth," he said, into her hair.

"For warmth," she agreed, and closed her eyes.

❧

Despite André's confident words, the next rehearsal wasn't any better, nor the one after that. By the time they arrived in Beauvais, Laura's nerves were as frazzled as her hair.

Despite everyone's efforts to coach her, she only seemed to get worse rather than better—more clumsy, more tongue-tied, more prone to tripping over props. Here they were in Beauvais, with only one night left before they performed for an actual audience. They were renting the town hall, three nights of use in exchange for ten percent of their take, whatever that take might be. If they had a take.

Laura just hoped the audience didn't ask for their money back.

Gabrielle was to be ticket collector; Pierre-André had been given the role of assistant prop-master (which, when translated, meant that he played backstage with the paper daggers until someone actually needed them). Jeannette had turned a pile of second-hand clothes into the last word in gaudy finery, embellished with enough frills, furbelows, and gold trim to keep even Rose happy. Everyone served a useful role.

Except Laura.

With one day to go until the performance, the troupe had dispersed to paper the town with playbills. At least, that was what they claimed to be doing. Based on the glint in de Berry's eye as he set off with Rose, Laura had her doubts.

"I had acting lessons when I was young," she fumed to André, slapping some paste on the back of a poster and slamming it with unnecessary force against the wall. "I was tutored by some of the best actresses at the Comédie-Française."

"What sort of lessons?" André asked practically, reaching over her to tug down a crooked corner. "Memorizing speeches from Corneille and Racine?"

"Yes." She had been rather good at those, actually. It had been easy enough to mimic the inflection of her teachers.

But that had been all it was—mimicry. She couldn't create Medea's madness on her own or Antigone's pain. Left to herself, she had all the creativity that God gave a duck.

"Well, that explains it," said André, in the sort of sensible tone designed to make someone want to claw his eyes out. And by someone, Laura meant her. "Those were set pieces. Memorization. It's an entirely different art form."

"Thank you so very much," said Laura acidly. "I would never have realized that."

For a man who had been married before, André was slow to pick up on the danger signs. "Classical theater is a highly ritualized form, while the Commedia dell'Arte is all about spontaneity and improvisation."

"You make me sound like an automaton." Laura knew there was no reason to take it so to heart, but she was tired and frazzled and her emotions felt dangerously raw. The self-control she had so assiduously cultivated over the past sixteen years was cracking around the edges, like a piece of pottery left too long in the kiln. "Wind her up and watch her go! But don't expect any original thought or any human feelings. She's not capable of those."

André looked at her in surprise. "I never said that."

"No, but it's true, isn't it?" Laura suddenly felt dangerously close to tears. She pressed down hard on a wrinkle in the poster. "Never mind. I'm just tired, that's all."

André's hands settled on her shoulders. "You've been pushing yourself too hard."

"It doesn't matter how I push myself. I'm not getting anywhere," she said bitterly.

André's hands slid down her shoulders, rubbing up and down over her arms.

Something about the gesture made the tears prickle at the back of her eyes again. Laura's legs were wobbly with the urge to sag back against André's chest and let him hold her up, his arms around her, his warmth comforting her. He was so familiar by now, the feel of his arms, the smell of his skin, the very contours of his body. It would be so easy.

If she were an entirely different woman.

"You're better than you were," he said reassuringly. "People train all their lives for this. You can't expect to pick it up in four days."

"Five," said Laura, to the playbill.

"Five, then." She could hear the smile in his voice, as he gave her shoulders a squeeze. "Because that extra day makes all the difference."

Shaking his hands off, Laura turned. Wedged between the wall and his body, she tilted her head up at him. "What if I ruin it for us all?" She couldn't keep the despair from her voice. "The others must suspect already. What if one of them guesses the whole?"

"They won't," said André confidently, his hands resting on her shoulders. She could hear the crackle of the poster behind her back. Behind his spectacles, his eyes searched her face. One of the earpieces was crooked. "I told Harlequin—in confidence, of course—that you had been wardrobe mistress in our last troupe, but that I had promised you a chance onstage. That's how we met, you know. You were measuring my tights."

"You bribed me into your bed with the promise of a glorious career?"

"Something like that."

"I'm flattered that you went to so much trouble to seduce me."

"Don't you think you're worth it?"

Laura turned her head away. "Right now, I feel like the scrapings off the bottom of a carriage wheel."

"That good?" André teased.

"The scrapings off the scrapings off the bottom of a carriage wheel." She ducked under his arm, taking her paste pot and heading for the next stretch of wall.

This was clearly a popular stretch of wall for notices. New ones had been pinned over the decaying remains of the old. Laura brushed aside the tattered fringes of an advertisement for Berowne and his amazing dancing bears. She was glad they wouldn't have to compete with that. Judging from the condition of the poster, the bears were probably hibernating by now. The placard next to it was of far more recent origin, the ink still bold and black, advising the good citizens of Beauvais that—

Laura groped for André, her fingers closing around his arm. "Look," she croaked, dragging him over. "Look at this."

"'Wanted,'" he read. "'André Jaouen, former assistant to the Prefect of Paris, for crimes against the state. Medium height, brown hair, spectacles. Likely traveling in the company of two children, a girl aged nine and a boy aged five.' They gave Pierre-André an extra year."

"That will make all the difference, I'm sure." Fear brought out Laura's sarcastic side.

André was studying the poster with more interest than alarm. "They don't mention Jeannette or Daubier. Or you."

"They didn't need to mention Daubier. Look." Pasted next to it was another poster. The Ministry of Police was also interested in any information as to the whereabouts of Antoine Daubier, painter. Elderly, obese, prone to brightly colored clothing, favoring his left hand.

That was one way to create an identifying characteristic: cripple a man before allowing him to escape.

Laura could feel sweat clammy under her arms.

"Well," said André calmly. "It's a good thing our posters are larger than theirs."

Appropriating the paste pot from Laura, he slathered a generous portion of paste onto the back of a playbill and slapped it right over the two government notices. Laura was fairly sure that to do so was illegal. On the other hand, they were already illegal, so what was a little more illegality?

An outlaw. They were all outlaws.

The Commedia dell'Aruzzio's advertisement completely covered the government notices, but Laura could still see the faint outline of print showing beneath the flimsy paper. One could attempt to paper over the past, but one could never eradicate it entirely.

"Those can't be the only ones." Laura's fingers tightened on André's sleeve. "You and the children. Someone might see these posters and recognize you."

"I'm not the only man of middle height with brown hair in France," said André sensibly. His eyes settled on her. "And the notice makes no mention of a wife."

"But we've already determined that I'm no actress. What if I ruin it for us all? What if my incompetence means we're caught?"

"Whether you like it or not," said André lightly, "you're part of the family now. We'd no more toss you out than we would Jeannette."

"You don't like Jeannette," she said accusingly.

"But I'm very accustomed to her."

"Don't protect me simply because I've become a bad habit. I'm used to fending for myself. If it becomes necessary for the general good, I'll go."

"Where?"

"Into the sunset and far away." There was no reason for the thought to be quite so depressing. They would have had to part ways once they got to England anyway. This fiction of being man and wife was just that, a fiction. She would do well to remember that. She was here only because the Pink Carnation had instructed her to see the Duc de Berry safely to England.

The recollection caught Laura up short. How long had it been since she had thought of the Pink Carnation? Or her obligation to the Duc de Berry? She had let herself get caught up in a fantasy, and this was the result of it.

"You're willing to give up this quickly?"

"I'm not giving up. I'm reassessing based on the situation. You might do better without me."

"Don't fool yourself. You're not the liability. I am. I'm the one Delaroche wants. None of us would be here if it weren't for my missteps. And then there's Daubier. But for me . . ."

The bitterness in André's voice made Laura blink. She had seen him, over the past few days, frowning in Daubier's direction, but she'd had no idea it had been weighing on him so.

She frowned up at him. "You're not responsible for his hand."

André's features looked as though they had been etched in acid. "If not I, who else? I promised to get him out. I failed."

"You did get him out," Laura pointed out. "Otherwise, he wouldn't be here. *Quod erat demonstrandum.*"

André didn't smile at the reference to *Candide*. "I may have removed him from the Temple, but not until he was rendered incapable of performing the one function that makes his life worth living. Trust me, he was very blunt about that." André's expression was bleak. "He told me to leave him."

"He didn't mean it."

"You didn't hear him."

Laura remembered that last night at the Hôtel de Bac, the anxious consultations, the preparations for the children, André's face gray with fatigue. "Did he realize what you were risking in going back for him? But for him, you might have stayed as you were. No one would have been any the wiser. I certainly wasn't."

Although she should have been. The clues had been there, if she had cared to piece them together.

André looked ruefully down at her. "Did you ever think of taking up work as an advocate? You would have been quite good at it."

Laura accepted the tacit change of topic. "Far better than I am as an actress."

André braced a hand on the wall behind her. "You had me quite convinced with your performance as Suzette. For a moment, I wondered if—"

"If?" There was no reason for Laura's blouse to feel so tight.

André shook his head, looking bemused. "If you were what you said you were. You play the seductress extremely well."

His eyes were the color of the remembered waters of her childhood, the shores of Italy on a sunny day. Laura couldn't seem to look away.

"It was all an act," she said, her voice unsteady. "Just an act."

André's hand was still braced on the wall above her head, but the space between them seemed to have contracted. "I thought you said you couldn't act."

Laura tilted her head up at him. An unnecessary gesture. They were nearly of a height to begin with. "I'm better offstage than on."

"Are you?" he said huskily, his lips so close that she felt the words as much as heard them, in the brush of his breath and the rise and fall of his chest.

If she closed her eyes, she didn't have to think about what she was doing or not doing. If she closed her eyes, she didn't have to see his hand rise to smooth the hair away from the side of her face, or his head tilt to match his lips to hers. If she closed her eyes, it was none of it real, the movement of his lips against hers, his hand cupping her cheek, his tongue tracing the contours of her mouth. If it wasn't real, she didn't have to make him stop.

Heaven only knew, she didn't want it to stop. The paste pot clattered to the ground. As of their own volition, her arms twisted around his neck, drawing him closer, and the kiss changed. She could feel his response in the way his arms tightened around her—not the comfort of a comrade but the passion of a lover, pulling her closer, matching her body to his, his tongue slipping between her lips, kissing openmouthed, exchanging breath for breath, both clinging, fevered, wanting.

It was as it had been at the inn, but better. At the inn, they had been performing to an audience, but now . . .

Now.

Reality slammed in on Laura and she yanked back, her back hitting the wall, hard enough to make her see stars.

"What—," she said hoarsely. What were they doing?

André Jaouen seemed as kerflummoxed as she was. He was breathing hard, his chest rising and falling erratically beneath his coat.

"Laura, I—"

Laura sidled sideways, away from André. Her ears were ringing as if someone had been singing a very high note very loudly just next to her.

She groped after logic. "We have to get back to the inn. We'll be missed."

André followed after her. "None of them are there. They're all putting up playbills. Laura—"

She didn't want to hear what he had to say. "What if they've returned already?" She was already backing out of the alleyway. "I wouldn't want to add tardiness to my other shortcomings."

André stopped short in the middle of the alley. He looked at her quizzically. "Are you running away?"

Who was he to talk about running away? And what was he thinking, going about kissing her like that? Did he think she wouldn't care?

"I'm not your wife," Laura announced. Her voice was pitched too high. It made her wince to hear it. That wasn't her talking. It was someone else, someone briefly inhabiting her body, someone who had been kissing André Jaouen as though she meant it.

Her breasts still ached with it. What was her body thinking? That was the bother. It didn't think; it felt. It was her job to do the thinking, no matter what her body wanted or thought she wanted.

"What are you saying?"

Laura held up the paste pot to ward André off. "No matter what we've been pretending"—her voice sounded unnaturally loud in the small alleyway—"I am not really your wife."

"I was aware of that," he said.

He seemed to be missing the point. "This past week—sharing as we have—" Laura's voice had gone raspy. She coughed to clear her throat. The paste pot hung heavy from her hand. "Perhaps this wasn't the best idea after all. I hadn't thought . . ."

"Hadn't thought what?" he pressed.

There was still a lump at the back of her throat, as though a whole pool of toads had bred and spawned in there. Her lips felt sore and swollen from his kiss, both her brain and lips slower and clumsier than usual.

"I hadn't thought that I would grow so accustomed to you. That's all. Here. You can put up the rest of the playbills."

Pushing the paste pot at him, she set off at a pace that was practically a jog. He didn't try to follow. Or, if he did, she didn't see it.

Only Pantaloon and Leandro were in the common room of the inn, sharing a carafe of the house wine, when Laura came in.

"The children are already in bed," Pantaloon informed her kindly. "Jeannette put them up an hour ago. You might want to do the same. A good night's sleep, always a good thing before a performance. That's what I told the others as well."

"Mmmph," said Leandro, into his wine.

"Well, good night, then," said Laura vaguely as she took up a candle from the table and scurried up the stairs.

It was a good-size inn for a good-size town, although all but empty in the off-season. The troupe had almost entirely taken it over. There were eight doors on the hall, three opening off on either side. The inhabitants of the first room on the left had made the mistake of leaving the door slightly ajar.

Through it, Laura could hear the crinkle of a straw mattress and a voice whispering breathily. "I shouldn't. . . ."

"But you want to," said de Berry confidently.

There was the rustle of clothing being either removed or displaced.

Rose let out a squeal. "Throw myself away on a penniless actor?" she demanded coquettishly.

More rustling. "You'd be surprised at what I have to offer."

"But I imagine"—*rustle, rustle*—"you're going to offer to show me."

Oh, for heaven's sake. Laura knew it was nearly spring, but did that mean everyone had to mate?

She made to hurry past, but was slowed as she spotted Harlequin, standing in the open door of the opposite room.

Catching her eye, Harlequin made a wry face. "Leandro will be sobbing over his wine again tonight."

That was a safe enough prediction. "He already is. I don't see what he sees in her," Laura added waspishly.

"Don't you?" Something in the way Harlequin said it made Laura wonder if it was entirely on Leandro's account that Harlequin was concerned.

"I don't," said Laura firmly. "He's worth ten of her, and you can tell him I said so. Besides, Gabrielle will be devastated if he doesn't wait for her."

Gabrielle would be nothing of the kind. For all that Leandro was a decade her senior, she treated him with the sort of patient condescension usually reserved by empresses for their underlings. But it seemed the right sort of thing to say.

Harlequin smiled faintly. "I'll let him know."

Laura continued on down the hall, to the room she was to share with André. Would he come to bed at all? Or would he emulate Leandro and spend his night on a settle by the hearth, regretting the impulse that had led him to offer consolation in the form of a kiss? Laura tried to imagine the paths of thought that might have led to it. *The governess is whining, must shut her up. Oh, well, best stop her mouth.* Or perhaps it had been some lingering memory of Suzette, the girl men couldn't forget, before he remembered that in real life the beguiling Suzette was nothing more than plain Laura Griscogne, who balked desire simply by being herself.

That hadn't been the case once upon a time.

She might not have been the prettiest girl in the group—and even then she had shown a dampening inclination to actually think things through, an attribute not considered an asset among her parents' set—but she had been young and nubile and curious. Antonio had been a sculptor, come to study with her father. They had conducted several intriguing anatomy lessons down by the pier, with the stars glittering on the water. Laura had never been quite sure whether her parents knew or not.

There had never been any talk of love, although, like any fifteen-year-old, she had imagined herself in love, just a little bit.

But then the commission had come from England, and they had left Lake Como for Cornwall, where the stars were dimmer and the waters colder and the sea leapt up and swallowed up all there was of youth and joy and desire.

She had been a very different girl, that Laura, the one who had dallied with Antonio in Como.

She had thought she was done with that, that she had frozen it out of her blood. That was what was so terrifying—not the memory of desire, but the reawakening of it, like fire in the blood.

When André had kissed her, up against the wall, she had wanted to take him by the ears and yank his head back down to hers.

Laura let herself into her room. It was a simple enough accommodation, but it had amenities she had all but forgotten, like a proper bed with proper sheets and a fireplace with real logs in it. There was even a mirror on one wall, dirty and tarnished, but still a mirror. Laura grimaced at the sight of herself. There were sweat stains under the arms of her blouse and mud on her skirt. Her hair had been washed—water was one thing they hadn't lacked along the way—but the damp air had turned it into a frizzy tangle. She looked like a gypsy. Not just a gypsy, but a gypsy who had fallen on hard times.

Someone had brought up her meager bag and placed it on a chair. After six days of wearing the same clothes, Laura ferreted through, marveling over the items she had so naively packed before leaving the Hôtel de Bac. There were three dresses—gray—and chemises and stockings. There were two nightgowns and, beneath those, a slim, paper-bound volume of poetry.

Ronsard. He who believed in gathering one's flowers while one may.

Well, one could seize the day in multiple ways. Laura untied the strings at the neck of her blouse. It felt like heaven, peeling off the stiff, dirty fabric. There was a basin on the nightstand, with a cloth beside it, and Laura gratefully sponged off some of the dirt of travel. The tapes on her skirt followed. Should she be worried that the skirt could practically stand by itself by now?

It felt almost decadent to let the nightdress slide down over naked flesh, even though, like all her clothes, the nightdress was heavy and serviceable, made of thick, opaque cloth. There wasn't anything the least bit suggestive about it.

It was ridiculous that she wished there was.

It might be rather nice to be Suzette for a bit, rather than Laura, to seize her pleasure where she could find it and think nothing of the morning. What did she have to lose, after all? She had no family, no obligations. There were no chaperones to wag their fingers or employers to threaten her with dismissal. She was utterly afloat in the world, and that circumstance might be as freeing as it had formerly seemed constraining.

Laura made a face at herself in the mirror. Yes, that was all very well, but with whom? She doubted André would be coming to bed. Not tonight.

And even if he did . . . well, he was coming to bed, not coming to bed.

This was what came of associating with actors.

On an impulse, Laura took up the book of poetry as she clambered into the high, tester bed. She could always read about it if she couldn't live it.

> *Ah, time is flying, lady, time is flying / Nay, tis not the time that flies but we . . . Be therefore kind, my love, whilst thou art fair.*

So much time already gone. So many dull and dry and barren years. Ronsard, dust now these two-hundred-odd years, had known that.

> *Shall I not see myself clasped in her arms / Breathless and exhausted by love's charms. . . .*

Laura plumped up the pillows behind her, finding them less comfortable than she had before. The fire was burning down again. It seemed symbolic. That was the problem with poetry. It made everything seem symbolic.

Why hadn't she just grabbed him and kept kissing him while she had the chance?

Laura grimly turned her eyes again to her book. Sermons, that was what she should have brought with her. Or political economy. Not this, not flowers and kisses and breathless embrace.

She skimmed the next few lines. *Kissed by desire . . . breast to breast . . . quenching fire . . .* Goodness, it was warm, wasn't it?

A squeaking noise sent her bolting upright against the pillows, the book clamped shut over one finger.

The door eased open.

Chapter 28

My mouth fell open.

Colin looked as though someone had just socked him in the stomach. Around us, the other party guests obediently lifted their glasses in a toast to Selwick Hall and then drifted on, returning to their drinking, their gossiping, their posturing, entirely unaware that a grenade had just been lobbed into their midst.

"Selwick where?" I heard one woman murmur to another.

The other shrugged, showing off her narrow shoulder bones to good advantage. "Jeremy's family place, I think."

Jeremy's family place? Admittedly, he was a Selwick too, if only on his mother's side, but it sure as hell wasn't his. He didn't live there. And he didn't have the right to promise it to some film company.

At least, I didn't think he did. Did he?

Colin stepped up to Jeremy, taking care, even in the midst of chaos, not to make a scene. "You can't do that. You have no authority to contract for the use of Selwick Hall."

Jeremy took a cool sip of his champagne. "I might not. But your mother does."

And where was Colin's mother? Didn't she realize how this decision would have gutted her oldest offspring? Selwick Hall was his home—more than his home. I peered around for her. She was still there—she hadn't slunk off to wash the blood from her hands or go hide behind an arras or whatever it was that disloyal Shakespearean queens were meant to do—happily chattering away at the center of a circle of adoring friends.

". . . lovely this time of year," I could hear her saying. I didn't think she was talking about Selwick Hall. The tan she was sporting didn't come from spring in Sussex.

"My mother only has a third share."

"Legally," said Jeremy, "that's irrelevant. Any one tenant has full rights to the whole." His teeth were too white. They sat too straight in his smiling mouth. "But let's not talk of the legalities. Legalities have no place among family."

"Did you tell your solicitor that before or after you phoned him?" said Colin curtly.

Jeremy's smile didn't falter. "I'd be a fool not to dot the *I*'s and cross the *T*'s on a deal like this."

"There is no deal," said Colin. "I may not have consulted my solicitor, but I feel fairly safe in guessing that letting out the house to a film crew doesn't constitute normal enjoyment of the property."

Not knowing much about English law post-1815, I couldn't have said whether he was right or not, but it certainly sounded good.

"As I was saying," said Jeremy, with the sort of chiding tone more appropriate from governess to pupil than from lying snake to stepson, "even assuming your mother doesn't have the right, on her share alone, to promise Selwick Hall, wouldn't you agree that majority vote rules?"

"Since when is one-third a majority?" I blurted out.

"One-third may not be a majority," said Jeremy, never taking his eyes off Colin. "But two-thirds is. You can't argue with that."

If Colin had one-third and Colin's mother had one-third . . . It was like a *Sesame Street* math problem, only one in which the Muppets had gone rogue, quibbling over the ownership of the letter *S*.

I didn't need a map to point the way to the owner of the deciding one-third interest. It would have been obvious, even if Serena hadn't looked as though she were trying to disappear into her own shawl. Guilt was written all over her face.

"Serena?" Colin turned to his sister. "You don't know anything about this. Do you?"

It was clear that he expected the answer to be in the negative, despite all indications. My heart ached for him. Don't tell me organs don't work that way; I could feel it as a physical squeeze in my chest. I wanted to wrap Colin up in my pashmina and whisk him away from the whole gruesome scene, transport him safe and whole to Selwick Hall.

Which wasn't, it seemed, entirely his, or entirely safe.

Did this also mean the others could sell it if they took the notion? It was a truly alarming thought. For them it was all a lark—a source of status and prestige or, in this case, spare cash. For Colin, it was home.

After his father's death, Colin had given up a successful career in the City, given up his flat and his job and a regular salary to try to make something out of the old family home. While Colin's university friends were out at wine bars, playing with their Black-Berrys, he was calculating crop yields. Admittedly, no one had held a gun to his head; it had all been his own choice, but from what I gathered, without that choice there wouldn't have been much of a Selwick Hall for Jeremy to rent out.

Serena, for all her other neuroses, had her work at the gallery, a small but expensive flat in Notting Hill, and a fairly active social life in London.

What did Colin have?

"It's for the best; you'll see," Serena was saying, speaking too fast, her lashes blinking rapidly. "We'll all share the money equally. You can use yours on the Hall."

Colin was still a step behind. I was reminded of people stumbling out of the doctor's office after those drops that dilate your eyes, squinting at everyday objects in an attempt to reconcile the distorted images to their regular forms.

"Then . . . you did know?" He sounded incredulous, as though he still didn't entirely believe it.

I thought of all the times Colin had looked out for her, all the times he'd cut short our dates, all the times he'd seen her home, and I wanted to slap her. All she'd had to do was say no. That was all. Was that really so hard?

Serena's thin hands twisted together. "It's only for a month, they say. They'll pay well."

Colin said, very slowly, "That promotion. This is why you didn't tell me about it. It was a quid pro quo, wasn't it?" Colin turned to his stepfather. "You fixed it with Paul. Serena's agreement in exchange for a new title and a thicker pay packet."

I could feel the satisfaction coming off Jeremy in waves, like cheap cologne.

"It wasn't quite like that," Jeremy said smugly, and I understood, for the first time, that it wasn't just that Jeremy was uncomfortable with Colin; Jeremy actively disliked Colin. He wanted to hurt him. And he had. He had hit him in the two places he was most vulnerable: his sister and Selwick Hall.

"It really wasn't," Serena chimed in, inadvertently making matters worse. Just what Colin needed. For her to side with Jeremy. Again. "With the money the film company is paying, Paul is letting me buy into the gallery. He's making me a partner. A junior partner."

And whose idea did she think that was? I'd met her boss. He wasn't much of a wheeler-dealer. Paul had gotten into art in the seventies because he'd been hanging out with the artists in pot-infused lofts, experiencing the colors in a psychedelic haze. Now that they were older, their work practically sold itself, leaving very little for Paul to do other than reminisce fulsomely about the old days before calling in Serena to do the paperwork and close the sale.

To be fair, Paul did scout out new artists, and according to Serena, he had a genuine eye for what would sell and what wouldn't, but he certainly wasn't the sort to take any proactive business decisions without a Lady Macbeth giving him a shove between the shoulder blades. Or, in this case, a Mr. Macbeth.

Colin turned to his sister, struggling to understand. "If you needed the money, why didn't you come to me? I'd have found it for you somehow."

Beneath their layers of carefully applied makeup, Serena's eyes were haunted with ghosts I couldn't even begin to comprehend. Nor, I suspected, could Colin. For all his reticence, Colin's world was a pretty straightforward one. He did what he said and said what he meant, end of story.

"I couldn't," Serena whispered. "It wouldn't have been my own."

"As opposed to doing it this way." Colin sounded like he was still trying to understand, taking in the betrayal piece by piece.

Serena nodded. "Yes."

Colin's face settled along bitter lines. "Behind my back. You might at least have told me."

Serena had all but shredded the end of her shawl. She twisted to look at her stepfather. "I didn't know," she said desperately. "I didn't realize Jeremy planned to announce it like this. I had thought—"

"That you could spring it on me privately?"

Serena nodded miserably.

"And that would make it better?" Colin's voice rose on the last word. It was as close as I had ever seen him come to losing his temper.

Across the room, Caroline Selwick-Selwick blithely downed another glass of champagne. I was beginning to understand why Mrs. Selwick-Alderly, Colin's great-aunt and Jeremy's grandmother, didn't like her.

What was the woman, a gerbil? It wasn't exactly like she was eating her young, but this was cannibalism by proxy.

"Children," said Jeremy, in what I could only generously assume was an attempt to lighten the mood. "Your mother won't like it if you quarrel."

Colin said something entirely unprintable.

Serena flinched. I stared. I had never heard Colin use language like that. Hell, I didn't know he knew language like that. It was rather impressive, even if I understood only about half of it.

I put a hand on Colin's arm, a little in restraint, but mostly in support. Whatever Colin had called Jeremy, Jeremy more than deserved it.

Colin stared at my hand, using it as a focal point as he drew in a ragged breath, pulling himself together. Fixing Jeremy with a level stare, he said in a cold, hard voice, "You can keep your suggestions to yourself. You've done enough already."

Jeremy didn't like that. I'm not sure what he had anticipated, but this wasn't how he had wanted things to play out. What had he expected? That Colin would beg?

Jeremy forgot himself enough that he lapsed back into Queen's English, rather than his carefully cultivated transatlantic mishmash. "At least I'm not making a shrine out of a second-rate plot of land."

Colin's voice was clipped. "If it's so second-rate, why do you keep trying to buy it?"

There was a loaded silence, the sort where no one seems to be capable of drawing breath.

Jeremy's cheeks darkened beneath his tan. "I only asked as a favor for your mother."

"Right," said Colin shortly. "Come on, Eloise. Let's go."

"Wait!" Serena's fingers brushed Colin's sleeve, her nails making an ugly noise as they scraped fabric. "Don't go. We need to—"

"No," said Colin.

And that was all. No. He kept on going. He didn't look back. The door of the gallery swung open in one smooth motion, wide enough for both of us to pass. I could hear it banging into its frame behind us.

"Shouldn't you—," I began.

Oh, the irony. For months, I had been trying to think of ways to get him to say no to his sister, just once. But not like this.

"Um, talk to her?" I finished lamely.

"What for?" Colin was covering the terrain in long, ground-devouring strides. We were already well on our way out of the square, the lights of the gallery barely a smudge on the pavement behind us. If Serena wanted to run after us, she'd have to scurry.

I risked a glance over my shoulder, despite the danger of tripping and/or whiplash at the pace we were traveling. She didn't seem to be trying. The door of the gallery was closed, the brilliantly clad people still partying behind the glass, Serena somewhere among them. Was Jeremy toasting her? Congratulating her on her fortitude in protecting her interests against big brother? The thought made me vaguely sick.

Even so, I had to try. "She is still your sister."

"Is she?" I had to yank on Colin's arm to keep him from stepping off the pavement right in front of a blunt-nosed car. He didn't seem to notice. The driver shouted something out the window. Colin kept going. "Why couldn't she at least have told me first?"

"Maybe she was hoping it would all just go away?" I'd tried that technique a time or two myself. It never works, but that doesn't stop me from trying.

Colin was still fuming. "That bastard. That bloody bastard."

I didn't say anything. What could I say, other than to agree? Jeremy was a bloody bastard.

We were back on the Seine, back on the bridge that had been so charming hours before, in the rose-and-purple glow of sunset. Now it was a dark place, and the damp of the night air enhanced the slight smell of old urine.

Colin kicked a cobble. "My mother hates Selwick Hall. She's always hated it. She wouldn't care less if it burned into the ground. He didn't do it for her; he did it for him. He's been trying to get his hands on the Hall for years, and if he can't, then he'll do his best to ruin it for me."

"It's only a month," I pointed out.

"Only a month," Colin echoed bitterly. "Ha. If he can do this once, why not again?"

I thought of Serena's stricken face, the expression on it as she had watched her brother walk away.

"I don't think he'll find Serena's agreement so easy to secure next time," I said thoughtfully. "I'm pretty sure this was it."

"Oh? What happens when Paul changes his mind about the partnership? What happens when he ups the price? What happens when someone wants to make a fucking music video?"

"She loves you," I said. "She wouldn't deliberately hurt you."

"What was this, then?"

"Business?" I ventured.

Colin slammed the flat of his hand against the stone parapet. It must have hurt him far more than it did the bridge. "Brilliant," he said bitterly. "Sold for thirty pieces of silver."

Okay. I understood he was hurting, but this wasn't precisely the fall of man, here. It seemed like a good idea to shift the blame back onto the real culprit. "Why does Jeremy want Selwick Hall so badly?"

"Because he couldn't have it. Why does anyone want anything?" There was so much acid in Colin's voice I was surprised it didn't corrode the stone. "It came as a shock to him when he discovered my mother didn't inherit it outright."

"You don't think . . ."

"That he married her for Selwick Hall?" Colin's hands tightened on the edge of the parapet. The light of the iron lamp picked out the smattering of gold hairs on the back of his hand, the white of his knuckles. "Jeremy wanted whatever my father had. Selwick Hall. My mother. He got one of the two."

"Ouch," I said, for lack of anything better.

My lips tingled with questions I knew I couldn't ask. *Why did Jeremy hate your father so much? Do you think he loves your mother? Does your mother know? Does she care?*

And the biggie: *How in the hell have you managed to stay on good terms with them for so long? Why didn't you say anything sooner?*

Somehow, I didn't think Colin would appreciate the inquisition.

There were also more pressing issues at the moment. No matter how Colin felt now, he had only one sibling.

"About Serena . . . ," I began.

"Not now." Colin turned to me, his face bleached pale by the streetlamp. I could feel the clutch of his fingers through the wool of my pashmina, pressing into my upper arms. "I don't want to talk about this now. Please."

I nodded, swallowing half a dozen potential comments before saying simply, "Okay. Whatever you want."

He didn't answer in words. Instead, he hugged me tightly—a prolonged squeeze that forced the breath out of my lungs and made me fear for the fate of those gougeres I'd eaten over drinks.

I lifted my head to say something, but he kissed me before I could muster the words.

Normally I would have minded that we were in public and this was behavior better reserved for drawn shades and closed doors. But not now.

I could feel the urgency in his kiss, the desperate push to use the body to forget the things the mind would rather not remember. Not exactly the most reliable method of therapy, but it does sometimes work in the short term. I kissed him back, using the press of my body and my lips to blot out the past hour, Jeremy, Serena, Melinda, Colin's mother.

Colin released me, leaving me wobbly against the parapet. I vaguely registered that I was still holding my purse. I was amazed it hadn't gone over into the Seine.

"Whatever, you said?" Colin's eyes glittered in the lamplight. I was pleased to hear that he sounded as breathless as I felt.

"Well . . ." I'm not a lawyer's daughter for nothing. "Within reason."

"Reason is overrated," said Colin, and pulled me to him again.

Chapter 29

$\mathcal{L}$ aura was already in bed by the time André ventured into their room.

Aside from their difficulties onstage, this past week had been surprisingly peaceful. They had fallen into a pattern as if they were the married couple they had claimed to be, and if he had woken up a morning or two—all right, every morning—feeling uncomfortably, er, wooden, that was something he had been prepared to ignore. Or douse with cold water.

But then, today . . .

André felt strangely off balance, as confused and callow as an adolescent confronted with the first stirrings of desire. All of a sudden he didn't know what to say to her, or how to behave. He had almost elected to stay downstairs in the coffee room with Pantaloon and Leandro, drinking cheap house wine and bemoaning the high cost of lodgings (Pantaloon) and the vagaries of women (Leandro).

Just the fact of their being in a proper room made it strange. In the makeshift confines of the wagon, with theatrical props stacked all around them, it was easier to play make-believe. The pallet on the ground did feel a bit like a soldier's billet, rendering the whole comrade-in-arms argument somewhat more plausible.

Laura had changed out of the clothes she had been wearing for the past few days, exchanging the voluminous blouse and skirt for a white nightdress.

The nightdress wasn't the least bit revealing, but just its being one was enough to make André sweat.

He seized on the book Laura was holding as a suitably neutral topic. "What are you reading?"

She looked down at her hand as though surprised to find a book attached to it. "Oh. This? Just some poetry. Ronsard."

André cleared his throat. "He's a good poet. Ronsard." Ronsard might be old-fashioned, but he never went out of vogue. He had captured certain universal truths about life, love, and the fleeting nature of time.

Laura's head bobbed up and down. "Yes. Quite good."

That exhausted the extent of their literary analysis. André leaned with his back against the door and wondered whether he ought to have stayed downstairs after all. Laura stared down at the book in her hands as though waiting for the paisley pattern on the cover to rearrange itself to her satisfaction.

Hitching herself higher against the pillows, she twisted her braid over one shoulder. "It's quite warm in here, isn't it? I'd almost forgotten what it's like to have a proper fire."

"Not to mention walls," André agreed.

Laura folded her hands primly on top of the coverlet. "It does have a salutary effect on the temperature."

"I guess that means you don't need me tonight," André said, only half jokingly.

Laura thought about that comment for an alarmingly long period of time. "I don't need you," she said at last.

André felt the words like the first stages of a wound—not quite fully comprehended yet, but with the awareness that it was going to hurt like hell in a few minutes when the reality of it registered. What sort of idiot was he? He had handed that one to her. He should have just behaved as though nothing had changed, splashed his face in the water from the basin, pulled back the covers, and climbed into bed next to her as he had these past five nights in their pallet in the wagon. The pallet was considerably smaller than the bed.

But something had changed that afternoon. It wasn't just that this was a proper bed in a proper room with a proper fire. After that kiss, there was no way of pretending they were just colleagues of sorts, maintaining a deception for safety's sake. He wasn't that good a dissembler.

Laura ran her thumb abstractedly along the leaves of the book, making the pages rustle. "I don't need you. But that doesn't mean I don't want you here."

Her face was turned away from him, leaving him only with her profile, the strong angles of cheek and chin, the slender line of her neck, the dark hair curling against the nape of her neck where it had escaped from her braid. She looked like the lady on an antique cameo, and just as unreadable.

André heard the words as though from very far away, through the roaring in his blood.

"What are you saying?" André asked hoarsely.

Laura's eyes shifted warily away. "What do you think I'm saying?" she hedged.

André knew what he'd like her to be saying. On the other hand, they had shared a bed for the better part of a week now. She could be offering him nothing more than a pillow for the night.

He tried to find a euphemistic way to signal what he meant. "Don't ask me to stay unless you mean it."

Laura hoisted herself up against the pillows. "Do you not *want* to stay? I should have thought a bed would have been preferable to a bench."

An act of mercy, then, designed to keep him off the common-room floor? He didn't want her charity. He didn't think he could survive her charity.

"There's one thing we should clear up first," he said harshly. "About this afternoon—"

"The part of the day that comes after noon but before evening?"

"Yes, that one." How to say this? For once in his life, André was entirely at a loss. All his skill at rhetoric had deserted him.

He took a deep breath. "If I were a gentleman," he said, "I would say I was sorry for what happened today. But I'm not."

"A gentleman?"

"Sorry."

"Oh."

André spoke in a rush, knowing that if he didn't speak now, he would never have the nerve to do it. That bench in the coffee room was looking damned attractive just then. "I know our marriage isn't a real marriage. I know I have no claim on you. And I know I have no right to say what I'm saying."

"And that might be . . . ?" Her eyes were as hard and bright as stars. Not the pretty sort that poets mooned about, but the kind that made men's destinies.

"If all you're offering me is a bed," he said bluntly, "I'll take the bench."

On the plus side, she didn't run screaming from the bed. On the other hand, she didn't jump up and down and fling her arms around his neck, either.

Instead, she took up the book of poetry and looked at it thoughtfully, saying, in a conversational voice, as if they were discussing the likelihood of rain and whether the wagon might need an extra coat of paint, "Ronsard has several useful things to say on this issue."

When had they gone back to Ronsard? André felt that he had missed something somewhere along the line. Probably his wits. He had left them back there in that alleyway, along with one large playbill and the remains of his dignity.

"Ronsard?" he ventured. One thing was for sure, Ronsard would have managed this far better, at least if his poetry was any indication. Ronsard wouldn't be sleeping on the bench in the coffee room.

André was beginning to feel pretty bloody unkindly towards Ronsard.

"Ronsard had a great many interesting reflections on the topic. This, for example." Opening the book of poetry, Laura thumbed through until she found what she had been looking for. "'What comes to-morrow who can say? Live, pluck the roses of the world to-day.'"

"Very . . . poetic," André agreed.

"And then there's this." She checked to make sure he was listening, and declaimed, "'Gather, gather the flower of your youth, / Take your pleasure at the best; / Be merry ere your beauty flies, / For length of days will blight it / Like roses that were loveliest.'"

She looked up at him from under her lashes. He had never noticed before just how long those lashes were. "I don't want to wither on the vine," she said quietly. "Even if I have little beauty to blight. Ronsard had a point, don't you think?" She took a deep breath. "Shall we take our pleasure at the best?"

André made a concerted effort to control his breathing. "Are you sure?"

"Do you really want to sleep on the bench?"

André emitted a strangled laugh. "If you put it that way . . ."

He closed the space between the door and the bed, taking her face in his hands. She was so familiar to him by now, the slope of her nose, the slight dent above her upper lip, the one beauty mark above her right eyebrow. How had he ever thought her plain? It was as if she were an entirely different woman from the one he had interviewed on a rainy day in January.

André dropped a kiss on her shoulder, where the nightdress listed to one side. "Between you and the bench, it isn't much of a contest."

Laura rolled her eyes. "The lengths to which I had to go to seduce you."

André found himself grinning like a schoolboy. "I like you," he said, in between kissing her and kissing her again. "I like you so damn much."

"I don't entirely dislike you, either," Laura conceded, although the words were rather impeded by his mouth being in the way.

André reached up to yank off his cravat. "No second thoughts?"

Laura spread his collar open, pushing the edges of the shirt aside to kiss his throat. "None. Nor third nor fourth. When I make a decision," she said firmly, "it stays made."

She looked so adorably smug that André had to kiss her again, just because.

Propping himself up on one elbow, he traced the lines at the side of her eyes. "You really are rather terrifying, you know. But in a good way."

The lines crinkled beneath his finger. "You certainly do know how to flatter a woman."

André dipped in for a kiss. "I'm not so inept as all that." He tugged at the tie holding the neck of her nightdress together. "If I were flattering you, I would have told you that your skin is like honey."

He ran a finger down the side of her breast and felt her shiver in response.

"Or I might have said that there's witchcraft in the curve of your neck." He suited action to words, tracing the area in question with his lips. He tugged with his teeth at her earlobe. "Your ears are rather nice too."

She laughed, but shakily, since by that point he had moved from the lobe to exploring the inside of her ear with his tongue.

"And then there's your hair," he said. He didn't bother with anything so complex as untying; he simply eased the tie off the bottom of her braid, his fingers moving to separate the interwoven strands, fanning it out around her. "You have beautiful hair." He ran his fingers through it, tracing the wild curls and waves. "Like Eve's wild, wanton locks."

"I thought Eve was blond," said Laura breathlessly.

"Not in this version," said André firmly, following the contours of a curl down to her breast. He brushed the nipple with her hair, watching it pucker in response. "In this version, the temptress was quite definitely brunette."

"Are you mocking me?" There was something uncertain in her voice, uncertain and heart-wrenchingly vulnerable.

"Do you really think I'm mocking you?" He'd never been less inclined to mock anything in his life. "Here." He grabbed her hand and lowered it to the placket of his breeches. "Feel. This is how much I'm mocking you."

They stared at each other, frozen, each sizing up the other. Her lips were already red and swollen with kisses, her cheeks flushed. The feel of her hand against him was a Mephistophelean sort of torment.

"Do you think I'm a cad?" André asked.

"No." Her hand tightened. André couldn't tell if it was meant consciously or not. He gritted his teeth against a groan. "Just that you're honest."

André gave a rough laugh. "That's a strange word to apply, given what you know of me."

She rose on one elbow, he hair falling about his face. "There's honesty and there's honesty," she said. "If nothing else, this is honest, what we have together right now. Just us. No dissembling. No pretense."

"Just us," he agreed. "Right now."

ᦞᶂ

Sometime later, they lay together in the sweaty sheets by the dying light of the fire, André playing idly with Laura's hair while she curled up against his chest. They had lain this way a dozen times over the past week, but never like this. Being naked did make rather a difference.

André yawned and pillowed his cheek against Laura's hair. At this moment, he was a very happy man.

"I don't think we should tell anyone," Laura said abruptly.

"Hmm?" Sated and sleepy, André was only half paying attention.

"That we're—well . . ."

"Lovers?" he contributed. "That would be rather odd if we weren't, considering that we're supposed to be married."

Laura propped herself up, her hair falling across his chest. André reached out to toy with the ends of it. "That's not who I meant. I meant our lot."

"Daubier?" André curled a lock of dark hair behind her ear. "I doubt he'll act the outraged father about this."

"It's not Daubier I'm worried about." Laura absently untucked the hair he had just tucked. "It's Jeannette and your children."

"Pierre-André is a little young yet for the birds and the bees," said André mildly. "As for Gabrielle—" That didn't even bear thinking about.

Laura went doggedly back to her theme. "Children pick up on things, even if they don't entirely understand them. Gabrielle and I have only just made our peace. I don't need her coming after me with a dagger."

"The daggers are pasteboard."

"Paper cuts hurt."

There was honesty and there was honesty, she had said. Odd that after playing a part for so long, this subterfuge should seem more repugnant to him than others.

"All right." André smoothed back her hair. "If that's what you want."

With a contented sigh, Laura eased down against him. "Mmm-hmm," she said, rubbing her cheek against his chest. "It shouldn't be too hard. We're already sharing a room and have been from the beginning. As long as we're discreet outside of bed, no one need be any the wiser."

"Let me get this straight," said André. "We're pretending to be lovers pretending not to be lovers."

"Is that right? Or have you got it upside down?" Laura frowned into his chest. "I'm too tired to work it out."

"Do you think we'll be able to keep it under wraps?" he said meditatively.

"I don't see why not." Laura pressed the back of her hand against her mouth to suppress a yawn. "You've led a double life before. How hard can it be?"

"I wasn't sleeping with Fouché."

"I should hope not. His wife wouldn't have been amused."

André tilted his chin down to look at her. All he could see was the tangled mass of her hair. "You have a surprisingly bawdy sense of humor."

Laura snuggled more firmly into his chest. "I had a surprisingly unconventional upbringing."

"I did rather get that." He thought of her as he had first seen her, the very definition of the word "spinster." The image was un-reconcilable with the woman in his arms, all lush curves and sur-prising talents. "How did you manage all these years?"

"What do you mean?"

"Being prim." He tightened his arms around her, enjoying the squish of her breasts against his chest. "You do a very good job of acting prim, you know."

"Years and years of practice." Her hair tickled his chest as she turned her head, searching for a more comfortable spot. "It was sheer self-defense at first. After a time it became habit."

"Hmm," said André, dropping a kiss on the top of her head. "I like your new habits better."

Laura's blurred voice emerged from the vicinity of his chest. "What makes you think you're going to become a habit?"

"I'll just have to make sure of it, won't I? But not right now," he added with a yawn. "I'm not as young as I used to be. Remind me in the morning."

"Maybe," she murmured. "If you're very, very lucky."

André rested his cheek against her head. He couldn't remember the last time he had felt so peaceful or so comfortable. "I'm already very, very lucky."

He was three-quarters asleep when Laura's voice, so low as to be almost inaudible, drifted up to him.

"It's nice not to have to," she said, almost as if to herself.

"What?" André asked sleepily.

"Pretend," she said.

André hugged her tighter, putting into touch what he couldn't into words.

"Mmm-hmm," he agreed, and together, they drifted into sleep.

Chapter 30

"Only a few hours left to go," said Laura, fastening the tie of her ruff behind her neck. Her fingers fumbled on the familiar strings.

Turning her around, André took over the task for her. "Nervous?" he asked.

Laura tried to shoot him a sarcastic look but was stymied by several layers of starched fabric. "I can't imagine why I would be," she said acerbically.

After a month and half on the road, they were backstage in the theater at Dieppe, preparing to go on for what would be, with any luck, their final performance with the Commedia dell'Aruzzio.

Laura would never be an inspired actress, but she had, over the past month, become a reasonably competent one. The stage no longer held the same terror for her. Their flight from France, however, was a different matter entirely. True, they had made it this far, but there was still the boat to England to be dealt with.

Of what would happen when they arrived in England, Laura tried not to think.

So far, their haphazard escape had gone almost unnervingly well. After Beauvais, they had taken again to the back roads for a week (Laura could only assume Cécile had seen the same notices she and André had seen) before venturing again into towns large and small for a performance here and a performance there, seldom staying in any place longer than two nights at a time. They had fallen into a pattern of sorts. In the mornings, she gave lessons to Gabrielle and Pierre-André. In the evenings, they rehearsed or performed, depending on their situation. And at night, she and André retired to the privacy of their wagon.

March dripped away into April. The grass began to look more green than gray, and the first of the wildflowers took advantage of the thaw to stake their claims on the fields and roadsides. There were no more notices on the town hall wall, no signs of pursuit. Laura wasn't naïve enough to hope that the First Consul's agents had given up the chase, but if they were chasing, they were being remarkably laggardly about it.

Apparently, they had bigger fish to fry. In April, word reached them from Paris that Cadoudal had been caught in the second week of March. He had fought to the last, battling his way through the streets until he was overcome and taken into custody. Rivaling the news of Cadoudal's arrest was that of the arrest and trial of General Moreau, accused of conspiring with Artois to turn coat and place a Bourbon on the throne. André had gone grim when he heard the news about Cadoudal and Moreau, but Laura had been quietly thankful. Compared to Artois's chief lieutenant and a general turned traitor, the escaped former assistant to the Prefect of Police and a maimed painter were distinctly unexciting.

André squeezed her shoulders. "All set?"

He was already in his Il Capitano costume, sporting a doublet padded out in front and at the shoulders to provide a comical aspect, with a half cape slung from one shoulder in the style of a century before. On his head he wore an extravagantly curled black wig, crowned by a broad-brimmed feathered hat of the style commonly associated with Louis XIII's musketeers.

A bushy black mustache adorned his upper lip. It wiggled as he spoke. Laura hoped they had remembered to put on enough glue.

Laura squinted at André's upper lip. "Does your mustache feel loose to you? It looks loose."

She touched two fingers to it, pressing it into place.

André caught her hand by the wrist, pressing a kiss against the palm before letting go. He had removed his spectacles for the performance—the blustering braggart of a Captain would never allow himself to be seen in spectacles—but even without them, he saw far too much.

"It will all be all right," he said, knowing, without having to be told, that it wasn't really his mustache that was worrying her. "Don't fret. We're too close to fail now."

Laura cast a glance over her shoulder. She didn't hold with superstition, but if there were such things as premonitions, she was having one. She could feel it trickling like cold water down her spine.

"Don't tempt Fate," she warned. "It wouldn't do to get cocky."

André grinned, making the mustache slant dangerously to one side. "That's not what you said last night."

"See! I told you it was loose." Laura pushed down hard on his mustache.

André seized the opportunity to slide an arm around her waist and press a kiss against her neck—or what he could reach of it, since the high ruff of her costume made most of her unreachable. The padded belly of his doublet bumped against her stomacher.

Laura squirmed. The mustache tickled.

"Not exactly conducive to romance, is it?" André said ruefully.

Laura quickly scanned the wings. For now, they were alone in the hallway. Rose would be finishing her makeup (or de Berry), Harlequin would be joking with Leandro, Pantaloon would be nervously counting the number of people in the audience, Daubier would be supervising the scenery, Gabrielle would be taking tickets, Jeannette and Pierre-André would be sorting props, and Cécile would be wherever the troupe most needed her to be.

They had kept to their resolution to keep their liaison quiet, to pretend to be lovers pretending not to be lovers, which meant that they had plenty of opportunity for consummation—pretending to be married did have its benefits—but a constant struggle to remember to refrain from being too affectionate in front of the three people who might find it suspect: Jeannette, Daubier, and Gabrielle.

It was the little, everyday moments that nearly gave them away. It was next to impossible to remember not to touch each other. There would be times when André would be looking down at her, his lips going on about something perfectly mundane, his eyes saying something else entirely, and she would almost lean up and kiss him, without thinking, just because. Or, at the fireside, when he would forget himself and kiss the top of her head or play with her hands or any of a number of touches that would be too innocuous to notice if only they were what they claimed to be.

Laura had seen Jeannette looking at them suspiciously a time or two and hoped the old nursemaid would ascribe their intimacy to dedicated acting.

Laura patted André's padded stomach. "No wonder Il Capitano has had so little luck with Inamorata."

André's fingers found the gap beneath her bodice and her stomacher. "It's not Inamorata the Captain is interested in."

"Don't say that too loudly. It would ruin the plot if Il Capitano ran off with Ruffiana."

"I don't see why." The ends of his mustache tickled her ear. "It might do them good to get a bit of a happy ending for a change."

Laura turned to press a kiss to the corner of André's mouth, navigating around the mustache. "They're not the sort of characters who get happy endings."

André raised the Captain's bushy brows. Under the stage paint, he looked surprisingly young and boyish. "That doesn't seem quite fair."

Laura felt something squeeze in her chest, something that wasn't supposed to be there. This wasn't part of their arrangement, this fondness.

Why not call a spade a spade? Not fondness; love. That ridiculous, inconvenient emotion her father had immortalized in marble and her mother in print. She had told herself she was proof against it, bolstered by example. But she wasn't.

She looked at André's face, so familiar under even the horsehair and greasepaint, and felt a surge of tenderness for this clever, naïve man, who still, for all his reversals, thought in terms of fairness and the basic equality of man. Didn't he know that life wasn't fair? There was something incredibly endearing about it and, at the same time, terrifying. She wanted to lock him in a box and protect him from the world.

Protect him from the world? Laura shook herself back to reality. This was the former assistant to the Prefect of Police she was talking about. He was perfectly capable of taking care of himself.

After tonight, he would have to. There had been no discussion of what would happen when they arrived in England. She could only assume that they would go, as originally planned, their separate ways.

There were times when she had teased herself with the possibility that it might be otherwise. But it had been easier to push thoughts of the future aside and enjoy the moment, pretending they were the married couple they claimed. It had been all too easy to forget that it was a pretense, and that it must, like all pretenses, come to an end.

Now with the moment upon them, Laura found it impossible to make herself broach any of this. It went against the unspoken code of their arrangement.

Instead, she said mildly, "Pantaloon would have heart failure if you changed the script on him."

"Pantaloon has heart failure every time we go on the stage." Releasing her, André stepped back and pressed a quick kiss to her brow. "All right, I'll behave. When are we to be at the ship?"

"Ten o'clock," said Laura.

André grinned at her, in high spirits. He seemed, perversely, younger the longer they were on the road, more relaxed than he had been in Paris. Laura thought, from time to time, she caught glimpses of the young man who had sat beneath the tree in Julie Beniet's garden.

Julie Beniet's garden, not hers.

"Not midnight?" André said. "I thought it was always midnight."

"Not when the performance begins at six."

They would be done with the play by nine or a little bit after. The sooner they left the theater for the boat, the better. Laura had given instructions to Jeannette to pack the children's things and Daubier's. By mutual consent, neither of them had alerted Daubier or de Berry. Daubier was learning to use his left hand where he had once relied on his right, but his temper was still uncertain. It wasn't that he would betray them, but Laura worried that he might, if given notice, absent himself from the group, choosing to stay in France and court discovery rather than seek a new life in England. He would, she knew, be lionized by those who cared for the arts if only she could get him to England.

As for de Berry, despite his protests that his sense of self-preservation outweighed his libido, they didn't trust him not to let the plan slip to his current inamorata. Whatever else Rose might be, she was still the sometime mistress of Joachim Murat, brother-in-law to the First Consul.

Besides, Laura thought callously, de Berry didn't need to pack. He would have clothing enough waiting for him in England. His costumes would have been discarded anyway, unless he meant to keep them as souvenirs of a coup that had failed.

Everything was in readiness. The *Bien-Aimée* would be waiting for them at ten. Jeannette might be grumpy, but she was efficient and unquestionably loyal. So why did she feel so twitchy?

Laura surveyed the audience, thinner now than it had been on the first three nights, but still reasonably full. In a month, the Commedia dell'Aruzzio would have competition from other traveling troupes, but for now, they were the only new game in town.

There was a man moving down the aisle, clad entirely in rusty black. There was something about him that looked very familiar, and not in a good way.

Laura squinted, leaning perilously close to the edge of the curtain. "Isn't that—"

"What?" André asked, hauling her back by the stiffened peplum of her dress.

Laura shook her head. "Nothing. I'm seeing shadows, that's all." Settling her very unattractive cap more firmly on her head, she made a face. "For a moment, I thought I saw Monsieur Delaroche."

Il Capitano's eyebrows engaged in gymnastics that challenged the strength of their glue. "Delaroche? Here?"

"He was—" Laura started to point and stopped. Where the Delaroche doppelganger had been a moment before she could see only a group of rowdy apprentices, tossing roasted nuts at one another. "I really am losing my mind."

André took her face between his hands and pressed a quick, hard kiss to her lips. "You just need to hold on to it for a few hours more and then we'll be safely on that boat to England."

"England," echoed Laura. "We should be there by tomorrow, weather willing."

Off the boat tomorrow and then what? Back to Selwick Hall for her, she supposed, to see if the Pink Carnation had any further assignments for her now that she was effectively banned from Paris.

She did speak fluent Italian. Perhaps, Laura thought, with an effort at enthusiasm, the Carnation might send her to Italy next time. She hadn't been to Italy since that last trip to Como.

Or she could tell André the truth.

And then what? she asked herself. She couldn't make him love her just by wishing it so.

André touched his fingers to her wrist. "About England . . . ," he began.

Laura felt a tightness in her chest that had nothing to do with the lacing of her stomacher. "A small island off the coast of France?"

"Yes, that one." André's fingers absently traced the pattern of her laces.

She would miss this, Laura thought with sudden clarity. She would miss this ease of touch, this lease they had on each other's bodies. It was like a gleaner's easement, free rein to roam within the prescribed areas during the course of the arrangement.

André plucked at a string. "We haven't really discussed . . ."

"Beginners, on!" shouted Cécile from somewhere in the wings.

André grimaced. "That would be me." He looked at her, hesitated, then shook his head. "We'll talk after."

After? After they would be managing de Berry, shepherding the children, running for the boat. Their chances of privacy were nil.

"What is it? Just spit it out. Quickly," Laura added. "Before Cécile gets agitated."

Cécile never got agitated, but the words seemed to have the correct effect.

André scratched his head, making his wig list to one side. "Once we get to England . . . I'll be starting over. I won't have much to offer. There'll be no Hôtel de Bac. It will likely be hired lodgings at first, while I try to find work of some sort."

Laura's fingers itched to re-center his wig, but at the moment that was rather beside the point. Those little domestic gestures would soon be a thing of the past. If he was trying to say what she thought he was trying to say.

He was giving her the sack, wasn't he? Both as governess and as lover.

"What are you trying to tell me?" she asked flatly. "If this is your way of telling me that we'll be going our separate ways . . ."

Then what? She found she couldn't herself finish the sentence. The flippant words jammed together at the back of her throat.

"No!" André said hastily. The wig wobbled. André made a wry face. "Forgive me. I'm out of practice at this whole wooing thing."

Wooing. Wooing?

"I feel like a besotted fool," he muttered. "Hell, I am a besotted fool."

André grasped her hands in his. "I'd get down on one knee, but it seems redundant at this point—and this blasted belly would get in the way."

"Beginners!" called Cécile.

André didn't turn around. Holding fast to Laura's hands, he said urgently, "We've done everything all upside down. All I'm trying to say is . . . I don't want to lose you when we get to England."

In his brightly colored doublet, the extravagant black wig perched askew on his head, and his mustache wiggling with every word, he had never looked more ridiculous. There were bright spots of rouge on his cheeks and fake hair on his eyebrows and his boots had bells on them.

"What we have," he said. "It means too much. I never thought— but now that we are— Oh, hell. I'm making a mess of it."

"Emotions are messy," she agreed. Her hands tightened convulsively on his. From a long way away, she heard her own voice saying, in a tone like gravel, "You won't lose me unless you want to."

Heedless of the rouge on his cheeks, she reached up both hands to cup his cheeks and pulled his mouth down to hers. André didn't need to be asked twice. His arms clasped around her with a force that knocked the breath right out of her—although that was partly the doing of Il Capitano's fake stomach, which whacked into her stomacher with enough force to leave a permanent dent.

Laura didn't care. Breathing was highly overrated. Her ruff was squished, her greasepaint was smeared, her cap was askew, and she couldn't have cared less.

All her carefully constructed armor seemed to have deserted her. Laura knew it was folly—not the grand, magnificent folly of her parents' affairs, but folly all the same—but she couldn't seem to help herself.

As André had said, why shouldn't Ruffiana have a bit of a happy ending too?

If Cécile was still calling for beginners, Laura didn't hear her. But she did notice when André abruptly let go.

"Wha—," Laura started to say, but broke off when she saw what had arrested André's attention.

"Gabrielle . . . ," he began.

Gabrielle's eyes were round as saucers. Very, very unhappy saucers. She was staring at her father and her former governess with the sort of expression usually reserved for mass executions and invading Viking hordes.

"Cécile sent me to fetch you," she said in a very small voice. There was a distinctly accusing tone to the words.

Laura took a hasty step back, straightening her stomacher. "Gabrielle," she said. "It's not what you—"

She broke off. If there was one thing she demanded of her charges, it was honesty. And what could she say? It was exactly what Gabrielle thought. And probably worse.

Gabrielle backed away, as one might from a house marked

with the plague. She cast Laura an accusing look. "Don't talk to me. I don't want to talk to you again. Ever."

André recovered his voice first. "Sweetheart—"

Gabrielle didn't wait to hear what he had to say. Turning on her heel, she blundered away, knocking into a bit of scaffolding before recovering herself and disappearing in the direction of the front of the house, moving awkwardly, as though she were still reeling from a blow.

"Gabrielle!" Laura started after her.

André caught at her arm. "Gabrielle was going to have to know sooner or later," he said in a low voice. "I'll talk to her after the performance. I'll explain . . . something."

"*Beginners!* Capitano, that means you! Not next week. *Now.*" Cécile might not be agitated, but she certainly sounded miffed.

"She'll come to terms with it," André said. He pressed a quick kiss to her head. "We'll all make it work. You'll see."

Laura watched as André hurried off onto the stage, the feather on his hat wagging.

The audience greeted Il Capitano's appearance with an anticipatory roar of laughter and a smattering of rude comments, which Il Capitano, in character, returned with interest, in the heavy, pseudo-Spanish accent required by the role.

Gabrielle had run off towards the front of the house, where the holders of the lower-priced tickets milled together in the pit. Laura positioned herself on the side of the stage, looking for the little girl in her plain brown dress. There were no women allowed in the parterre—at least, not officially—so that meant that if Gabrielle were there, she would stand out.

There was no sign of her in the pit. Blast.

Laura devoutly hoped that Gabrielle had chosen to nurse her wounded feelings somewhere within the theater. Dieppe was a port town, with all the dangers that implied. A young girl alone on the streets might encounter any number of perils, the likes of which Gabrielle had no inkling. God willing, she never would.

Thank goodness. There she was, taking her appointed place at the ticket table at the front of the theater.

That's my girl, thought Laura with a surge of approval and relief.

They might not adore each other, but Laura felt an odd sense of kinship. She understood what it was to be prickly and stubborn. Good girl, not running off and hiding. There was nothing like going on just as usual to kick your adversaries in the teeth. It might be Laura's teeth being kicked, but she was proud of Gabrielle just the same.

The play was well under way now, Il Capitano making his play for the fair Inamorata while Leandro conspired with the maid, Columbine, to press his own suit for the young lady's hand. The audience seemed to be enjoying it well enough, laughing in all the right places. They were laughing and shouting, calling back quips to the actors on the stage, tossing the odd apple. One man wasn't doing anything of the kind. He was staring at the stage, his gaze fixed on one actor alone: André.

There was no mistaking him this time. That was Gaston Delaroche. In their audience. In Dieppe.

It was too much to hope that he was there on holiday.

"Ruffiana!" Cécile was calling her.

Laura hurried onstage, trusting to the familiarity of thirty-odd days' worth of performance to see her through.

"What ho, lackey!" she called out. The Commedia dell'Aruzzio didn't demand veracity of dialogue from its practitioners. They spoke a sort of theatrical pidgin, designed to sound vaguely archaic, with modern colloquialisms for humor. "You, over there!"

Harlequin struck an exaggerated pose of surprise. "Me, mistress?"

He sidled sideways, mugging for the audience, sending them into anticipatory waves of laughter.

"Yes, you," said Laura. She could see Delaroche's tall-crowned hat making its way through the crowd, heading towards the exit. Where was he going? For the gendarmes? If they all fled now . . . "I have a commission for you, saucy youth."

"A commission? For me?" Harlequin's flexible face betrayed suitable shades of anticipatory horror. "What sort of commission?"

He made a bawdy joke out of it. The audience loved it. Laura felt her skin go clammy beneath the heavy fabric of her costume. Delaroche wasn't heading for the exit.

He was heading for Gabrielle.

Chapter 31

"I have a message for you." Laura's lips were moving and sound was coming out, but she hardly registered her own voice. All her attention was fixed on the scene playing itself out by the ticket table. "A message for you to deliver."

Delaroche had stopped beside Gabrielle and was saying something to her. His head was tilted down, the angle and the hat brim making it impossible for Laura to see his face. Not that she would be able to read his lips at this distance anyway, but it would have been nice to have some inkling of what he was saying.

Damn. Laura looked frantically at the wings. She didn't see André. Where was he?

"Indeed, mistress?" Harlequin all but snapped his fingers in front of her face. He spoke very, very loudly. "What sort of message?"

"An extremely important one."

Whatever it was that Delaroche had said to Gabrielle, he had said his piece. He wasn't there anymore.

Neither was Gabrielle.

This was not happening. This was not allowed to happen. They had made it all the way to Dieppe. The boat was here, for goodness' sake.

"They all claim it's important," riposted Harlequin, winking at the audience.

Laura rounded on him, her skirts swishing in a broad arc. They were very broad skirts, bolstered with a number of extremely stiff petticoats. Harlequin jumped out of the way, making a joke out of it, but he cast her a look that said quite clearly, *What in the blazes do you think you're doing?*

"Hold a moment, trusty lackey," Laura improvised hastily. "I have a message for you, but I seem to have left it in my boudoir, which is not but a moment's walk away."

This was not in the scenario.

"There's many a fine thing lost in a lady's boudoir," quipped Harlequin gamely. "If my lady will deliver the letter with her lips, that too would serve?"

The audience loved it.

"Kiss her!" someone shouted.

"That old sow?" protested another.

Fruit flew, mercifully not at the stage.

"Entertain yourself awhile, resourceful Harlequin, with a song," shouted Laura, "while I fetch the letter from the casket in my boudoir and send my maid, Columbine, to deliver it to you."

"Columbine? I believe I know the wench—," began Harlequin, but Laura was already gone.

On the stage, she could hear him gamely going into a popular song, something about the fickle nature of women.

"What's going on?" Cécile caught her by the arm.

"An agent of the Ministry of Police is here," said Laura, in a low voice. "Gaston Delaroche. He has Gabrielle."

"What did you just say?"

It was André, standing just behind Cécile. Despite his costume, there was nothing comical about him now.

"I saw Monsieur Delaroche in the audience," Laura said rapidly. "I'm quite sure it was he. He spoke to Gabrielle. Now I can't find either of them."

André stared past her, like someone trying to scry the future in a murky pool. "He would have had to buy a ticket from Gabrielle to get in."

"He knows who she is," Laura said reluctantly. "He's tried to use her to get to you before."

André looked past her, his eyes focusing with sudden, terrifying intensity. "That bastard has my daughter."

Something about the very flatness of his voice made Laura shiver.

"We'll find her," said Laura. "We'll get her back."

"We'll hear from him," said André, with terrible certainty. There was something about the cool logic of his voice that was more dreadful than any amount of raving. "He won't have taken her for her own sake. She has nothing to tell him. There'll be a ransom demand; you'll see."

"You for her?" asked Laura, watching him closely.

"Me, de Berry, something," André said, shrugging the question aside as immaterial. "He'll want revenge. For extracting Daubier. That would have embarrassed him."

Laura's eyes flew to his. "You don't think—"

An exchange was one thing. Revenge another. Surely, even Gaston Delaroche . . . But there was no "surely" when it came to Delaroche. She could read the certainty of it in André's eyes.

"He reduces her value as a bargaining chip if he hurts her," Laura argued, as much for herself as André. "He won't endanger his main objective for a little . . . immediate gratification."

"I wouldn't bank on that." André's voice grated like sandpaper. "He can't have gone far. I—"

He stopped as Laura's fingers closed convulsively around his arm, her fingers digging into his sleeve. Her lips moved, but no sound came out.

"Thank God," she breathed. "Thank God."

Dropping his arm, she darted past him, straight at a small figure in a brown dress who was hovering at the end of the corridor, scuffing her boots and looking sullen.

Laura had never seen anything so sulky look so good. She didn't care if Gabrielle glowered at her for the rest of her natural life, just as long as she was there to glower, all in one piece, with all of her fingers and other appendages intact.

"Gabrielle!" Laura swooped down and hugged the little girl so tightly that she nearly knocked the air out of her. "Thank goodness."

Gabrielle wiggled her way free, looking distinctly uncomfortable.

André was making choking noises. He couldn't seem to breathe properly. "Thank God," he finally managed—he, who hadn't worshipped the deity since the churches were closed back in 1792.

He held out his arms to his daughter. With a last glare at Laura, she went into them.

"We thought Monsieur Delaroche had gotten you," he said into his daughter's hair.

"Monsieur who?"

"The slightly crazy-looking one in a black hat." Laura hunkered down next to her. "What did he say to you?"

Gabrielle ignored Laura and addressed herself to André. "He gave me a note for you."

"He knew who you were," André said grimly.

He and Laura exchanged a look over Gabrielle's head.

"What do you think he wanted?" Laura asked quietly. "We know he must have wanted something."

Even in his panic, André felt gratitude for her presence. He had been alone so long that he had nearly forgotten the luxury of having another adult with whom to share his burdens, someone whose judgment he trusted. Someone he could count on to be on his side, with no ambiguities, no crosses or double crosses. Her presence in his life, at this juncture, was nothing short of a sort of miracle. Heaven only knew, they needed all the miracles they could get.

"I have a feeling we're going to find out," he said just as quietly.

Gabrielle tugged at André's sleeve in a bid to retrieve his attention. "Monsieur Delaroche called me by name. I told him he was mistaken, that my name was Arielle Malcontre. He didn't say anything. He just smiled and left. It was," she added reflectively, "a very nasty smile."

"He is a very nasty man," said André. He gave his daughter an extra squeeze, just because. Just because she was alive and whole and not at Delaroche's dubious mercy. He looked over Gabrielle's head to Laura. "We're going to need to move quickly. We need to get out of here before he comes back."

Laura didn't miss a beat. She yanked off her cap and pulled loose the tie on her ruff, moving as she spoke. "I'll collect Daubier and de Berry if you fetch Jeannette and Pierre-André. The baggage is already in a hired hack waiting for us outside the theater."

Gabrielle squirmed against her father's arm. "You haven't read the note," she reminded him, giving Laura a hard look.

"Right. Thank you." André took the folded piece of paper from her, breaking the seal. It was black, of course. Delaroche didn't go in for anything so mundane as red sealing wax.

The note was short and to the point.

I have your son and his nurse. I am willing to make an exchange. I will release the boy and the maid in exchange for your surrender and that of the Bourbon traitor you have been harboring. I expect you both at the

Cauchemar by midnight. You will find the boat in the fifth dock from the left.

After midnight, such lenient terms will no longer apply.

Gaston Delaroche, Assistant to the Minister of Police

Laura found her voice first. "Do you think he really has them? He might be bluffing."

André wished he could share her optimism. Gaston Delaroche might be many things, but unprepared wasn't one of them. "He has them."

"He's mad," said Laura.

"I know he's mad," said André. "Fetch de Berry."

"You're not giving yourself up!"

"What else do you expect me to do?" Yanking off his false eyebrows with little concern for the real ones beneath, André relented. "I'm not going to give up without a fight. But if it comes down to it, yes, I'll surrender myself for Pierre-André."

"I have an idea." Laura's hands were balled into fists, the knuckles white. Her entire body vibrated with tension. "We take de Berry and Daubier to the *Bien-Aimée* as planned. We'll be able to get help there."

"From the sailors?" The crews of smuggling ships generally pursued a policy of not getting involved. Not unless it involved profit.

For a moment, Laura looked as though she intended to say something, but whatever it was, she thought better of it. "Yes," she said circumspectly. "From the ship's crew. I know at least one of them has a personal grudge against Monsieur Delaroche. They will help us."

There was something she wasn't telling him, but André didn't have the time to suss it out. "And what if Delaroche retaliates against Pierre-André?"

"Do you really think, if you followed his instructions, that he would keep his word?"

It didn't help, hearing his own fears put into words. He knew she was right. But he still didn't want to hear it.

André dropped his wig on the floor. His head felt oddly naked without it. "Once again, it seems I have little choice but to trust you."

Laura bit her lip. It wasn't the first time. The bright red paint that coated her mouth was half-eaten off already. "I haven't led you astray so far, have I?"

"No." The one word took more of an effort than it should have. "Let's go deposit de Berry at your ship. And then I'm going to carve Gaston Delaroche into kindling."

"Gaston Delaroche?" Daubier was holding a rolled-up scroll under one arm, a piece of scenery waiting to be deployed. "What about him?"

Laura looked to André before answering. "He has Pierre-André. And Jeannette."

Antoine Daubier, the urbane man who never got involved, lifted his deformed right hand. "Then what are we waiting for? Monsieur Delaroche and I have a score to settle."

At that moment, André wouldn't have been in Delaroche's shoes for all the world.

It took little more than a moment to drag de Berry from his comfortable perch on the other side of the wings. Cécile had taken the precaution of keeping de Berry's role small. So small, in fact, that it was practically nonexistent. He walked on and walked off again at some point during the third act. That point varied based on whether he remembered or not.

They were aided in their efforts by the fact that Rose was on-stage.

"Come along," said Daubier, moving with more energy than André had seen in months. "We're going."

"I have plans for the evening," de Berry protested. "Very pleasant ones too."

"We have a ship waiting to take you to England," André said tersely.

De Berry threw Rose to the wind without a second thought. "Why didn't you say so? Where is it?"

It wasn't actually as stupid a question as it might have seemed. It was more than conceivable that their conveyance might have been hidden in an inlet, somewhere away from the main waterways.

"In the harbor," said Laura. "With the other ships. Please, Your Highness, do hurry. We have a bit of a situation. . . ."

The hack was waiting, as Laura had promised. The five of them squeezed into the interior, Gabrielle on André's lap.

André checked his pocket watch. He had discarded his padding along the way, and his doublet hung in loose folds. "Half an hour since Delaroche gave Gabrielle the note. How long do you think it's been since he took them?"

Unsurprisingly, it was Laura who answered. "They were both still there until just before the curtain went up. Delaroche must have smuggled them out, left them in a carriage, come back, and given Gabrielle the note."

"You mean they were right outside while we were wasting time debating?"

"We don't know that," she countered. "It's only a guess. And knowing Monsieur Delaroche, I imagine he came well armed and well guarded. We'll do better to surprise him with reinforcements. He should," she added thoughtfully, "be very, very surprised."

"Who are these reinforcements of yours?" André asked suspiciously.

"She means me, of course," said de Berry, stretching. "I'll be glad to do what I can for the little lad. Within reason, of course."

It wasn't personal, his tone implied. It was just that royal skin was worth more.

"You will get him back, won't you?" said Gabrielle to her father. Her brows drew together just the way his did when he was worried. From the way she was squinting, he suspected she would soon need spectacles.

"Yes," he said, with more assurance than he felt.

"I didn't really want him gone," Gabrielle said in a small voice. "Not really."

"No one thought you did," said Laura bracingly. "It's just the sort of thing one says. Little brothers can be very trying. I know. I've taught many of them."

"I just hope he's trying Delaroche," André murmured.

"We're almost there," said Laura. "Look. The *Bien-Aimée*."

She pointed to a ship, which to André looked entirely indistinguishable from the ones on either side of it. He had put his spectacles back on, but it was too far and too dark to properly read the lettering.

"Have you been on it before?" he asked.

Laura's lips pressed together in a way he hadn't seen for a very long time. It was her governess look, all prunes and prisms and unsweetened lemons.

"Yes," she said.

Her references had claimed she had been with a family in the interior. What had she to do with a yacht sailing the Channel ports?

"When?"

Like a barometer, sensing tension in the atmosphere, Gabrielle looked from one to the other.

Laura didn't look at him. "We seem to be stopping," she said. "Gabrielle, mind your footing getting out. It's a long way down."

Why in the hell wouldn't she meet his eye? Who were these people who were to help them? It shouldn't matter, André told himself. As long as they got Pierre-André back.

But it did matter.

"Who are these people?" he asked in an undertone as he lifted his daughter to the ground and joined Laura on the pier. "Why won't you look at me?"

"They're English," she said brusquely, in the tone of one making the best of a bad situation. "Cécile made the arrangements, not I."

"But you made the arrangements with Cécile."

Laura made a wafting motion with her hand. She still wouldn't meet his eye. "They'll help you rescue Pierre-André. Isn't that the important thing?"

"We don't know that yet."

She looked at him then. Her lips twisted in another expression he hadn't seen for quite some time. The bitter smile of someone who knows the joke is on her. "Trust me. They will."

Quickening her pace, she stepped ahead of him. A man had jumped down to greet them. She said a few words to him in rapid English. She spoke softly, but André could hear enough to tell that her English was swift and fluent and entirely unaccented.

She had said she was fluent in English. In English and Italian and German and Latin and the devil only remembered what else.

So why did he feel so sick to his stomach all of a sudden, with fears he couldn't name?

Whatever she had said did the trick. She beckoned to them to follow her onto the ship. A gangplank was lowered for them. André hung back, taking Gabrielle's hand to help her up the steep slope. That was what he told himself, in any event. Some other force was at play. Something felt off about the situation.

A trap? But why? He had long ago discarded any apprehension of Laura's being in league with Delaroche. The guard had spoken English; she had spoken English to him. It would be deceit of elaborate proportions for Delaroche to have arranged a kidnapping only to have his own lover bring him aboard by false pretenses.

True it might be that women had given their bodies before and lied all the same, but he couldn't believe it of her, not of Laura.

But, something—something was off. His instincts didn't lie.

Holding Gabrielle's hand, he stepped onto the deck just in time to hear the end of an introduction taking place.

"—who will be conducting you safely back to England," Laura was saying, gesturing from de Berry to a man who stood just beyond, his back to André.

"Delighted," said de Berry. "Charmed to make your acquaintance. I've heard a great deal of you."

"I am equally charmed to have you on board, Your Highness."

The second man's voice sounded familiar, although André couldn't quite place it. He had a faint memory of that same voice, but speaking in French.

They were all speaking English. André's English was rusty, but it was good enough to get the gist.

"We're quite relieved to see you safely off French soil, Your Highness," the unknown man was saying. Turning to Laura, he gave her a brief salute. "Well-done, Miss Grey! An excellent first mission."

André stopped trying to place the voice. There were other, more pressing matters.

"Miss Grey?" he demanded. *"Mission?"*

"I can explain," said Laura.

As soon as she said it, she wished she hadn't. When one had to promise that one could explain, it generally meant one couldn't.

"Later," she added.

After all, there was the pressing matter of rescuing Pierre-André. It wasn't that she was trying to wiggle out of making explanations she didn't have.

"I look forward to it. Miss Grey." The look André gave Laura cut right through her. His eyes narrowed on the man behind her. "*Selwick?*"

They knew each other?

Lord Richard Selwick held out his hand with an expression of genuine pleasure. "Jaouen! I heard you were involved in this business."

As Laura watched, completely speechless with shock, the two men wrung each other's hands. "I haven't seen you since 'aught-two," said André. "I'd heard you retired."

"I've been on honeymoon," said the Purple Gentian blandly, dodging the question. "You switched sides."

André didn't look at Laura. "Say more that I was forced to play a hand I had hoped to keep secret."

"In other words," said Daubier, stepping forward, "our conspiracy was discovered. It was," he added, "through my carelessness."

Laura looked at Daubier with surprise. It was the first time she had heard him say such a thing. Recovering herself, she gestured from Daubier to Lord Richard. "Lord Richard, this is Monsieur Antoine Daubier, the painter. And that young lady over there is Mademoiselle Gabrielle Jaouen."

"Mademoiselle." Lord Richard bowed with debonair flair.

Laura automatically turned towards André to share a smile and encountered nothing but stone. That was right. They weren't on smiling terms anymore.

"We are forced to throw ourselves on your mercy," said Jaouen to Lord Richard. "In fact—"

"Fair enough," said Lord Richard convivially. "I'm glad to have you on board. In both senses. And you, Miss Grey. Well-done!"

Laura brushed aside the praise. "We have a problem," she said brusquely. "Monsieur Delaroche has Monsieur Jaouen's son." It felt strange referring to André by his last name, but stranger to call him by his first. She was Miss Grey again—English operative, governess, spinster. The woman who had curled up naked next to André Jaouen didn't exist anymore. The woman he had thought he loved was a lie. "He wants the duke in exchange."

"And your blood, no doubt," Lord Richard said soberly, turning to André. "How long ago did he take him?"

"Roughly an hour ago. His nursemaid is with him. Will you help us?" asked Laura.

"It will be my pleasure," said Lord Richard, without mockery. "No man should make war on children."

A powerful emotion passed across André's face. "I'm in your debt, Selwick."

The former Purple Gentian was instantly all action. "Don't start tallying the IOU until we get him out. Where is he being held?"

"Delaroche has him on a boat called the *Cauchemar*," Laura jumped in. "Here in the harbor."

There was a glint in the former Purple Gentian's eye that boded ill for Gaston Delaroche. "What do you say we give Monsieur Delaroche a little surprise?"

Chapter 32

Gaston Delaroche never did anything by halves.

André identified the *Cauchemar* long before they reached
it. It wasn't just the tricolore flying from the mast or the uniformed
guards standing sentinel on the pier or even the large, curling
black script proclaiming the boat's name. It was the size of the
ship—double the size of the *Bien-Aimée*—and the fact that it was
hung with lanterns, every single one ablaze.

The crews of the boats docked to either side must have just
loved that.

Sarcasm kept André's palms from sweating; sarcasm kept him
from imagining what horrors Delaroche had in store for Pierre-
André; sarcasm gave him the presence of mind to pretend to stay
reasonably calm and nod in the right places when Lord Richard
Selwick spoke to him.

He had never thought he would one day make common cause
with the Purple Gentian. They had been adversaries not so very
long ago. Courteous adversaries. If anything, André had owed the
man a debt of gratitude—not just for the amusement value of

some of his exploits, but for distracting Delaroche. Whether the
Purple Gentian knew it or not, he had unintentionally facilitated
more than one objective for the Comte d'Artois, simply by keeping
Delaroche occupied elsewhere. False information had been passed,
networks of informers assembled, plots plotted, all while Delaroche was busy chasing the shadow of a cheeky purple flower.

What was it they said? The enemy of my enemy is my friend.
André had cause tonight to be grateful for that old adage. If the
Purple Gentian helped him retrieve his son, he wouldn't have another thing to say about gentleman adventurers and unpronounce-
able essays in botany.

There were five of them in the dinghy.

His Royal Highness, Charles Ferdinand d'Artois, Duc de
Berry, was not one of the party. De Berry had offered to come, but
without marked enthusiasm. He had been more than happy to be
persuaded to stay behind to guard the women and children.

De Berry might not have been so sanguine had he known André's real reasoning. De Berry was their bargaining chip, the only
genuine leverage André possessed. Delaroche might want to wreak
his revenge on André, but when it came down to it, a prince of the
blood was a prize not to be missed—at least, not if one didn't want
to risk Fouché's extreme disapprobation. No one wanted to risk the
disapprobation of Fouché.

When it came down to it, if he had to, André would trade the
prince for his son.

He hadn't told de Berry that, of course. It was a last resort.

Daubier, unlike de Berry, had flatly refused to be left behind. "I
have a grudge to settle," he had said, displaying his hand to Lord
Richard.

No one had argued with him.

André, Daubier, and Lord Richard had been joined in the dinghy by two of Lord Richard's crew—one of whom appeared to be
somewhat inexplicably dressed as a pirate, complete with a stuffed

parrot on one shoulder. The parrot was held in place by an ingenious mechanism of straps, although it did list a bit to one side as
the man rowed. It made André feel a great deal less conspicuous
in the sagging remains of his Il Capitano costume.

There had been room for one more in the boat, a place that
Laura had tried to claim as her own. She had desisted when Lord
Richard had pointed out, apologetically, that her combat training
was fairly rudimentary.

Combat training?

Who in the hell was this Laura? Not Laura, André reminded
himself. Miss Grey. Miss Grey, who somehow knew the Purple
Gentian—not only knew him, but was on terms of some intimacy.

She still looked the same, still dressed in her Ruffiana costume,
the skirts kilted up so they wouldn't trail, her hair scraped back so
tightly that it made her eyes slant up at the corners. She had the
same little curls at the nape of her neck, the same beauty mark at
the corner of one eyebrow, the same eyes, the same nose, the same
hands, the same lips that he had kissed again and again, and which,
it seemed, had returned to him not just kisses, but kisses and lies.

André wondered just how much had been a lie.

Not that it mattered, André reminded himself, as the dinghy
drew towards the brightly lit *Cauchemar*. It couldn't be allowed to
matter, not even if his guts felt like they had been wrenched out
and used for garters. All that mattered was that they save Pierre-
André.

"Right-ho," Lord Richard said, speaking in a voice just barely
audible above the sound of the boats rocking in the water. The
wind had risen, and waves were slapping against the keels of the
boats moored in the harbor. "Here's the plan. I've sent two men
along the pier. In precisely ten minutes"—Lord Richard consulted
his pocket watch—"they will cut the ropes mooring the *Cauchemar*."

Thus making it impossible for the guards on the pier to intervene. Unless, of course, they felt like a swim. André somehow doubted that they did. Delaroche seldom paid well.

"Then what?" André asked.

"As soon as the *Cauchemar* is floating free, we're going to make a bit of a fire on the deck to draw off the guards."

André saw one rather large problem with that. "What if the fire spreads?"

Lord Richard produced a wide and shallow bowl, in which someone appeared to have dumped a pile of greasy rags. "It won't, unless some idiot is fool enough to overturn the bowl. If we do this correctly, it should produce a great deal of thick, black smoke but very little fire. It ought, however, take them some time to realize that. Nothing spooks a sailor like fire on board ship. Stiles?"

"Arrrrr?" said the pirate interrogatively.

Lord Richard rolled his eyes slightly, but forbore to comment. "I'll expect you and Pete to be standing by. When the guards show any sign of returning to their posts, tackle them. Make sure they don't make it below deck."

"Aye, aye, Cap'n!" The parrot wobbled as the pirate saluted.

Lord Richard looked pained. "Oh, and, Stiles?"

"Cap'n?"

"You might want to leave the parrot in the dinghy. Just a thought." Turning to André, he said, "We three will seek out Delaroche and free the captives."

"Your experience with boats is greater than mine," said André. It would be impossible for it not to be; to his knowledge, he had never been on one. All his travel had been accomplished on land. "Where will he have them? And how do we get to them without being seen?"

Lord Richard nodded. "Despite its size, the *Cauchemar* seems to be a fairly simple model. There are two possible places that Delaroche might be holding your son. He could be in the main cabin, to the rear, here." Lord Richard sketched a diagram on the planks of the dinghy with a finger dipped in water. "Or here, in the hold." He sketched a second rectangle below the first. "If I know my Delaroche, he'll have them in the hold. It's the closest he can get to a dungeon."

It sounded like a logical enough conclusion, but for one thing. "Delaroche doesn't follow any known rules of logic these days," André warned. "Your escape sent him around the bend. That, and being separated from his interrogation chamber. They made him pack up his Iron Maiden. It has rendered him . . . unpredictable."

"You can certainly say that," said Lord Richard slowly, squinting at the ship. They were drawing steadily closer, the muffled oars making little noise in the water. He pointed towards the deck. "Look at that."

At first, all André saw were the guards—at least a dozen of them. There were four directly in his line of vision, playing a game that seemed to involve round discs and a mop. As one hit the disc in a broad sweep, the others followed, leaving André a clear view of the mast. The sails were furled, but that wasn't what created the strange bulk at the bottom.

"What in the devil . . . ?"

Two people had been tied to the mast, by the simple expedient of looping a rope around them again and again and again. One woman and one small boy.

"The devil, indeed," Lord Richard agreed. "But a very obliging one. There's no need to search for what's been placed in plain sight."

Daubier appropriated Stiles's spyglass, shaking it open with his good hand. "Where is that Delaroche?"

"Somewhere nearby, unless I miss my guess," responded Lord Richard. "Lurking. He'll be waiting for you to make your appearance."

"There's an hour to midnight yet," said André shortly, appropriating the glass from Daubier.

Even at this range, there was no mistaking the fury in Jeannette's face. Someone had stuffed a gag in her mouth. Jeannette's eyes bulged out angrily over the wide strip of striped cloth. It was the largest gag André had ever seen, and during his time at the Prefecture, he had seen quite a few. Someone was taking no chances. Having been on the wrong side of a few of Jeannette's tongue-lashings, André could well imagine why.

Pierre-André, on the other hand, was fettered but unmuzzled. He appeared to be carrying on a spirited conversation with a sailor who had hunkered down next to him. From the way the man was pointing at various bits of rope, he was either threatening Pierre-André with hanging from the yardarm or explaining the intricacies of rigging. From the man's relaxed posture, it looked like the latter.

No torture, then. At least, not yet.

André didn't want to think about what Delaroche had planned for midnight.

"He's made it harder for us," André said abruptly. "By placing them in plain sight, he makes it impossible for us to creep up unseen."

"There are twelve of them and five of us," said Lord Richard. "I'd say good odds, wouldn't you?"

There were times when that aristocratic, sporting attitude could be a damned nuisance. André would have preferred a bit of bourgeois common sense.

"Thirteen, if we count Delaroche," André reminded him. "And we don't know how many more men Delaroche has belowdecks."

"Sure, an' it be an ill omen, Cap'n," contributed Stiles, tugging at his earring. "For thirteen ha' e'er been a number that brings men to their doom."

"Your accent is slipping," said Lord Richard calmly. "Slight change of plan. Pete, set the fire right in front of the opening to the hold. It will draw the men away from the mast and delay anyone trying to come up from below. Stiles, I need you to open the hold. As the men come running, you might want to, er, help them along. We'll soon thin their numbers."

"What about me?" asked Daubier.

Lord Richard refrained from looking at Daubier's malformed hand. "I need you to free the boy and his nurse. They know you, so they won't kick up a fuss. Get them into the dinghy. Jaouen and I will cover your retreat."

For a moment, Daubier looked like he might argue, then he caught André's eye and subsided. He nodded at Lord Richard's sword. "Give Monsieur Delaroche a good scratch for me, will you? Make it a painful one."

"My pleasure," said Lord Richard. "I still owe him for a memorable evening in his extra-special interrogation chamber." He checked his pocket watch, then looked to the pier. "Ah, there go the ropes. Good lads!"

As the *Cauchemar* began to gently drift, Pete fastened the dinghy to the side of the ship. Lord Richard picked his men well. He scaled the wall silently, the large bowl of greasy rags clamped beneath one arm. Stiles followed, parrot bobbing.

A rope ladder flopped down in Stiles's wake. A nice touch. It would be easier for Jeannette and Pierre-André than jumping. For that matter, it made it easier for the rest of them to climb up. André's had been a desk job. Gymnastic feats weren't in his line.

"Wait for it," Lord Richard murmured. "One, two . . ."

"Fire!" shouted someone. There was the sound of pounding feet on deck.

Lord Richard swung onto the rope ladder. He was up and over the side in an instant. André followed suit, somewhat more clumsily but no less speedily, hoisting himself over the edge to find the deck engulfed in black smoke. From the thuds and yelps, Stiles was doing his job when it came to helping the crew into the hold.

Holding a fold of his too-large doublet over his mouth, André elbowed his way through to the mast.

"Hang on!" he ordered Jeannette.

She narrowed her eyes in a way that would have been a sarcastic comment if she were able to make one.

The ropes holding them had been tied with a particularly complex nautical knot. It would probably be easy enough to disassemble if one had the training on a ship. André didn't. Drawing his knife from his belt, André began slashing at the rope. If he could get one strand free, he could release the whole.

Pierre-André began to wiggle, making the task even harder. Someone grabbed André's shoulder, hard. Without thinking, acting on pure reflex, André rammed his elbow sideways, harder. He heard a choking noise as his assailant doubled over, coughing.

He could hear the whisk of steel as Lord Richard drew his sword from its sheath, driving the remainder of the crew back with the point of the sword. There was a splash as Pete helped a sailor off the edge of the boat, then the vague sound of groaning from the hold.

Two strands snapped, then a third.

"Here!" Daubier came up on André's other side, dodging just in time to avoid being kicked. "Let me see that knot."

"I've got it," said André, and the last bit of hemp came loose.

With his good hand, Daubier grasped the rope, unlooping it as quickly as it would go.

"Mmmph!" said Jeannette.

André plucked at the knot at the back of her gag. He was going to regret this, he knew. As Daubier freed Pierre-André and Jeannette, André yanked the cloth free. Jeannette drew in a deep breath, choking on the smoky air.

"Took you long enough," she gasped. "My tongue was going numb."

"Papa!" With less of him to free, Pierre-André shrugged out of the remains of the rope and flung his arms around André's waist.

André gave his son a quick hug. "There's a rope ladder just there, leading to a boat. Do you think you can climb down it?"

Pierre-André nodded, coughing. His eyes were red and watering from the smoke.

There was one last loud splash and Lord Richard appeared beside them. "That's the last of them. No sign of Delaroche."

"None?" André's hand tightened on Pierre-André's shoulder.

Someone, most likely Pete, tossed a blanket over the fire, abruptly curtailing the smoke.

"Not a whiff of him. And those were sailors, not soldiers," said Lord Richard grimly. "Something smells wrong."

"It was too easy," André agreed.

Delaroche wouldn't have left his hostages virtually unguarded. Unless, that was, he had another goal.

André turned rapidly towards Jeannette. "Where did he go? The man who brought you here?"

"You mean after he tied us to that thing?" Jeannette was not in a good humor. "And a fine lot of good you were, leaving us here for hours on end, and the little one like to take a chill."

"Delaroche?" André prompted her.

"Him." Jeannette's lips pursed as though she tasted something nasty. "He strapped us up here and then went off to visit his beloved. Courting, I ask you! On a night like this!"

Lord Richard's "His what?" clashed with André's "Beloved?"

"That's what he said," said Jeannette stridently. "That's where he went. To visit his *bien aimée*."

Chapter 33

*A*ll was quiet on the *Bien-Aimée*.

Too quiet. There was nothing but the gentle slap of waves against the keel of the boat as the *Bien-Aimée* rocked in her berth, the soft susurration of pages as Gabrielle thumbed through her book, the creak of fabric on wood as de Berry settled more comfortably into his chair. If she tried very hard, Laura could make out the sound of conversation on deck, but it was only a muted burr. The cabin of the *Bien-Aimée* might as well have been wrapped up in cotton wool, well buffered against the world.

There were only the three of them left on Lord Richard's boat—Laura, Gabrielle, de Berry—and four of the crew, all posted on deck, keeping watch and doing whatever it was that crews were meant to do. Swabbing? Laura had no idea and even less interest.

Gabrielle turned another page of her book, paper whispering against paper. The sound made Laura twitchy, like the trail of phantom fingers down her arms. Her costume, gritty with dirt and dried sweat after multiple performances, itched and chafed at her.

She wanted to shout, to stomp, to fling something just to hear it break.

If she made enough noise, she might be able to drown out the sound of André's voice, saying over and over, *"Miss Grey?"* and *"Mission?"*

Laura paced towards the bookcase, pretending an interest in titles in which she had no interest at all. Even pacing provided little solace. Lord Richard's cabin on the *Bien-Aimée* was sumptuously decorated with heavy, dark furniture and rich fabrics. The Axminster carpet on the floor—entirely impractical for a seagoing vessel—blunted the slap of Laura's footfalls, muting her movements into nothing more than a prolonged murmur, like someone whispering *hush*.

Laura didn't want to hush. She wanted to stamp her feet and hear the echo of it. She wanted to argue with someone, anyone. It was infuriating to be left alone with nothing but the tribunal of one's own thoughts and a host of inchoate fears, some practical, some absurd.

Her brain was crawling with might-have-beens, as irritating as lice in one's scalp—crawling, biting, itching, impossible to claw out. If only she had kept closer watch on Pierre-André; if only she had jumped off the stage and tackled Delaroche when first she spotted him; if only she had told André who and what she was rather than waiting to let him find it out at the worst possible time from the worst possible person.

It wasn't my secret to tell, she defended herself to an invisible André. *It wasn't anything to do with you.*

That was another thing. It wasn't as though André had confided in her out of choice. It was circumstance on his side, not moral high ground. If Daubier hadn't been discovered, they would have gone on just as they were, she playing the governess, André playing his double game, neither the wiser.

Of course, then, they hadn't been sharing a bed.

Laura stared at her own reflection in the glass of the bookshelves and wondered, resentfully, why that was meant to change anything. Whores gave their bodies to multiple men multiple times a day—or so she had been told. Did that mean they were meant to give their trust where they gave their bodies? Did giving one's body necessarily mean giving of oneself?

Everything for love, that had been her mother's motto. Nothing held back, nothing denied. All body, all soul, all mind, all heart.

That wasn't love; it was willful self-destruction.

That, her mother would have claimed, *was* love. To fling oneself on the pyre of passion, rising phoenixlike from the ashes—scoured, purified, reborn.

But what if one doesn't rise again? Laura had argued, sixteen years old and stubborn. What if one simply burns?

Her mother had no answer for her. Neither did her shadow image in the bookshelf.

Laura turned away from the glass. It was terrifying, this notion of tearing chunks off one's soul and handing them over to another for safekeeping. It had been easier not to tell André the truth, to keep her own counsel the way one might keep a packed portmanteau, always ready to pick up and move on at a moment's notice, settling nowhere, trusting no one.

If one never got attached, one never got hurt.

Next to her, Gabrielle sat curled up in a wide-armed chair, reading. As Laura paced past, Gabrielle glanced up from her book.

"What time is it?"

Laura consulted the watch pinned to her breast. "Five past eleven."

Gabrielle nodded and went back to her book—Laura peeked sideways at the lettering on the spine—Voltaire's *Candide*. All for the best in the best of all possible worlds.

It was twenty minutes now since André had left with Lord Richard and Daubier. Only twenty minutes. It felt like months.

Laura's skirt dragged against her legs as she paced. She kicked it out of the way. She was still dressed as Ruffiana, although bits of her costume had gone missing along the way. Her cap was somewhere backstage, her petticoats discarded. Without them, her skirts hung too long, despite her attempts to kirtle them up. The stomacher pressed uncomfortably against her ribs, heavy with embroidery, thick enough to repel a bullet.

Perhaps she ought to have offered the stomacher to André, presented it to him as armor. The doublet he wore as Il Capitano was a flimsy thing, the shoddiest of secondhand silks.

Laura wished Lord Richard had let her go with them. She might not have extensive combat training, but she could point a pistol and pull the trigger, or use the proper end of a pointy bit of steel if it came down to it. Yes, yes, she knew there were refinements to such things, but she doubted Delaroche's men were going to be judging her on the niceties of her fencing, and when it came down to it, an extra pair of arms was an extra pair of arms.

Five against however many Delaroche might have mustered wasn't exactly good odds, especially when it was such a five. For all his determination, André's chosen weapon was the pen rather than the sword. He was a petit bourgeois, not a gentleman born. Fencing and marksmanship were a gentleman's occupations, not the province of a provincial lawyer. Then there was Daubier, who couldn't even wield his brush anymore, much less a sword. They were five, against goodness only knew how many, with only one real swordsman in the lot of them.

"You'll wear a hole in the carpet," de Berry said lazily, nearly tripping her as he kicked out his heels in front of her. "Do sit down, Miss Grey." And then, with what Laura recognized as royal condescension, "Care for a hand of cards?"

"No," said Laura shortly. "Thank you. Your Highness."

Gabrielle looked up from her book. "What time is it?"

"Must you keep asking?" Laura snapped, and instantly regretted it. "I'm sorry. I'm just a bit . . . on edge. They'll get Pierre-André back, you know. Lord Richard is an expert at this sort of thing."

Lord Richard *had* been an expert at this sort of thing. He had been retired for more than a year now, running a training camp in Sussex. To teach and to do were two different things. No one knew that better than Laura. What if his skills had grown rusty with disuse? What if he had miscalculated?

"They'll be back before we know it," said Laura, too loudly.

Gabrielle closed her book over one finger, the instinctive gesture of the perpetual reader. Her brows came down over her nose, making her look very like her father. Her eyes were that same peculiar shade of bright blue.

"What happens if they don't come back?" Gabrielle did her best to keep her voice nonchalant, but there was a bit of a wobble in it.

Laura looked at Gabrielle, really looked at her for the first time in days. From the paintings, she had been a pretty baby and would likely be an attractive woman someday, but she wasn't a prepossessing child. Her face was too round and her brows were too thick and her hair had frizzed in the rain. Her shoulders were hunched, her expression guarded.

It wasn't just her father Gabrielle had to worry about; it was her whole world, the only people left to her. Her father, her brother, Jeannette, even Daubier—all of them were in Delaroche's power.

"If they don't come back, you'll have to come to England with me," Laura said levelly. "I know I'm not your first choice, but we'll muddle along somehow. You won't be left to fend for yourself."

Nine was too young for that. Sixteen had been too young for that.

Before either could say anything else, there was the sound of heavy footfalls on deck.

Gabrielle dropped her book and scrambled out of her chair. "They're back!"

"It's too soon—," Laura began, but Gabrielle was already at the door, wrenching it open.

There was a man in the doorway, but it wasn't the right one. He wore a rusty black coat and a hat too high to fit through the doorframe.

He doffed it at the sight of Gabrielle. "Mademoiselle Jaouen. We meet again."

Gabrielle instinctively tried to close the door, but she was too slow. Delaroche caught it on the point of what Laura very strongly suspected was a sword cane. "I wouldn't do that if I were you, Mademoiselle Jaouen," he said, sounding as though he rather hoped she might try. "Terrible things happen to those who attempt to thwart the will of Gaston Delaroche."

The deck of the *Bien-Aimée* was deserted as the overburdened dinghy drew up alongside. There was no sign of the men Lord Richard had left on board. The lanterns that had been burning on deck before had been either shuttered or extinguished.

There was, however, a boat attached to the stern that hadn't been there before.

"This is not good," murmured Lord Richard.

André didn't need to voice the words. He felt them in his bones. He looked at Pierre-André curled up on Jeannette's lap, and felt a surge of terror for Gabrielle.

At least she had Laura with her. Laura was resourceful. Laura would—

Laura wasn't Laura.

André nodded to Lord Richard. "Look. Over there. In the cabin."

The rest of the boat was dark, but the cabin was still brightly lit. Through the window, André could see a man in a dark coat elbowing his way into the room, closely followed by several others. It was hard from that angle to see how many there were. The general impression was that there were a lot. Delaroche was taking no chances.

"He has all his men in there," said Lord Richard with professional disapproval. "That's just poor tactics."

"Or good sense," countered André. "He can pick us off one by one as we try to get through the door. We have to find another way."

Or not. The boat rocked as André leaned instinctively forward. Delaroche's henchmen had their guns pointed on his daughter. Oh, to be able to fly. He was too far away to get to her in time, too far away to do anything.

As he watched, useless, Laura grabbed Gabrielle, using her own body as a shield between his daughter and Delaroche.

Lord Richard looked thoughtful. "Unless we go through the window . . ."

They'd wasted enough time. "Good enough," said André, grabbing the rope on the side of the ship. "Jeannette and Pierre-André, you stay in the dinghy until we give the all clear. Daubier and I will take the door; you, Stiles and Pete take the window. We'll catch them in a pincer."

"Jaouen?" André looked back down. His old adversary, the Purple Gentian, raised a hand to him in salute. "Good luck."

Delaroche hadn't come alone.

There were men behind him, four of them, all of the large and hulking variety. All were holding pistols. And they were trained on the little girl in the doorway.

"Where are they?" Gabrielle demanded, her voice high-pitched with anger and fear. "What did you do to them?"

Laura yanked Gabrielle aside, pushing the girl behind her. "Aren't you on the wrong boat, Monsieur? I thought your taste tended more towards nightmares."

The men Lord Richard had left on deck must have been dispatched by Delaroche's guards. It wouldn't have been much of a contest, four against two, with the two taken by surprise.

Delaroche permitted himself a satisfied chuckle. "No, Mademoiselle. This nightmare is all Jaouen's. He allowed his concern for the boy to blind him to the too obvious ramifications of his actions. It is," Delaroche said contemptuously, "the sort of mistake one would expect of a man who allows himself to be ruled by his emotions."

"Or," countered Laura, "the obligation of a father."

She maintained her stance in front of Delaroche, blocking his path to Gabrielle and de Berry. Weapons . . . weapons. . . . What did they have by way of weapons? De Berry, still in his theatrical garb, was unarmed save for a paper sword. One of the disadvantages of being on a ship was the lack of a fireplace. There was no convenient poker with which to bash away. The furniture was either too heavy to throw, bolted to the floor, or both.

Could they swim for it? If she opened the window, could de Berry and Gabrielle jump through?

Delaroche shrugged aside the bonds of paternal affection. "A weakness by any other word is still a weakness. As much as I have enjoyed this conversation, Mademoiselle, I would be much obliged if you would remove yourself from my path."

Laura stayed just where she was. "Do you have a purpose for your presence, or is this a social call?"

"Yes," chimed in the Duc de Berry. No, no, no, thought Laura, but it was already too late; de Berry was levering himself out of his chair, striding over to look down his Bourbon nose at Gaston Delaroche. "Who in the devil might you be, and what are you doing here?"

Delaroche shoved Laura unceremoniously aside. She staggered a bit, catching at the wall as Delaroche strutted into the room, the guards crowding in after him.

Delaroche snapped his fingers. "Hold them," he said in bored tones.

Someone grabbed Laura's arms, pulling them behind her. Laura instinctively tensed to struggle but thought better of it, forcing her body to relax. The grip on her arms was a surprisingly perfunctory one, as if her assailant couldn't be bothered to put much effort into it. She might need to use that later.

"Gabrielle!" she said sharply, and the little girl stopped twisting and pulling. Laura shook her head. "Not now."

Ignoring them, Delaroche strolled up to de Berry, secure in the knowledge that, while two of his guards might be occupied, there were still two pistols behind him. "Your Royal Highness, I presume?"

De Berry looked Delaroche up and down, tall and proud, every inch a prince. Good heavens, thought Laura, why didn't he just hang a sign around his neck saying *Guillotine me now*?

"Who might you be?" asked de Berry curtly.

"I," said Delaroche, "am your destiny. I suggest you come quietly, Your Highness, or you will find yourself coming . . . very . . . quietly." He gestured with his cane. "Do I make myself clear?"

Delaroche didn't wait for de Berry to respond. He snapped his fingers at his two remaining henchmen. "Bind the Bourbon traitor," he ordered. "And if he resists . . ." Delaroche's lips curled. As Gabrielle had noted before, it was a singularly nasty smile. "Kill the girl."

"Er, which one?" asked one of the thugs, looking from Gabrielle to Laura.

Delaroche clicked his tongue with annoyance. "Must I tell you everything? The small one, you cretin. No one would miss the other."

"I say," said de Berry, his nose going red with annoyance. "This is uncivilized."

"Uncivilized?" Delaroche tilted his head, rolling the word on his tongue. "Or effective? Jean-Marc!"

One of the thugs snapped to.

Delaroche pointed a bony finger at Gabrielle. "Show these people that I mean business."

Gabrielle began struggling in earnest, twisting and wriggling to free herself, as agile as desperation could make her. Her captor grappled to keep his hold on her, cursing in a thick Norman accent as Gabrielle turned into a frantic, biting, clawing thing.

It was now or never. Laura stamped down hard on her captor's foot and wrenched out of his grasp.

They could try to fight their way out or . . .

"Stop!" Laura shouted.

Two guns swung in her direction. Her former captor was too busy hopping up and down on one foot, while Gabrielle's had finally succeeded in wrestling her into a standstill, breathing heavily, a long rip in one sleeve. Blood oozed from a bite on his wrist.

Well-done, Gabrielle, thought Laura.

"Stop?" Delaroche repeated in tones of disdain. "You dare to order my men to stop?"

Laura planted both hands on her hips as though she were still playing the shrewish Ruffiana.

"Yes," she said. "I do. I order you to stop in the name of the Ministry of Police."

"I *am* the Ministry of Police," said Delaroche.

"No," said Laura confidently. She had to sound confident. If she didn't, they didn't have a chance. She narrowed her eyes as far as they would go, giving Delaroche a look of scathing contempt. "You work for the Ministry of Police. And a fine mess you're making of it, I might add. Fouché isn't going to like this. At all."

Delaroche's henchmen looked confused. So did de Berry, who

looked from Delaroche to Laura and back again as though trying to figure out which was most likely to turn into a bat and flap off through the window.

Delaroche clicked a button, causing the casing on the top of his cane to pop. A thin, shiny sliver of steel showed between the panels of polished wood.

"Who are you to lecture me on the likes and dislikes of the Minister of Police, Mademoiselle?"

Laura laughed a low, rough laugh. "Did you really think you were the only one Fouché had entrusted with this business?"

André bumped into Daubier's back as the other man came to an abrupt halt.

Through the open door of the cabin, he could see Laura, but a Laura such as he hadn't seen before. Gone was the self-controlled Mlle. Griscogne or even the practical day-to-day companion of the last few months. This was a shrew of the ranting, carping variety— eyes narrowed, hands on her hips, exuding contempt with every movement.

"I had this well in hand until you came along," Laura spat out, advancing on Delaroche with a swaggering walk that was nothing like her own. "*Well* in hand. And then you come along with your cryptic pronouncements and your evil laughter, making a muck out of the whole operation. Months! Months of planning *wasted*."

Daubier turned to André with an alarmed look, confusion written all over his face. "*Laura?*" he mouthed.

André gave a brisk shake of his head, motioning Daubier to silence.

"Fouché wouldn't have—," Delaroche began, but he didn't sound entirely certain. They all knew that Fouché would.

Laura threw back her head, cutting him off with a very effective snort. "Given the stakes as they are? Your record isn't exactly consistent, you know."

André felt a surge of pride. The devil, but she was good. It didn't matter whether she was Miss Grey or Mlle. Griscogne, she was his Laura and he was bloody grateful that she was on their side.

Delaroche took a step back. "Fouché would have told me."

"Of course he would. Because Fouché always tells you everything," Laura taunted. "You've made a proper mess of things tonight. I could have delivered them to you in one fell swoop: de Berry, Jaouen, the Purple Gentian. Now look what you've gone and done!"

"You lie," said Delaroche, but he didn't sound quite sure.

Laura, on the other hand, sounded quite sure. Heedless of the sword cane Delaroche held in one hand, she marched right up to him. She had, André noticed, cleverly shepherded him away from Gabrielle. Behind her, through the glass of the window, André could see Lord Richard, a shadowy figure in his dark coat.

If he came through now, he would land on Laura. André held up a hand, waiting to see where she would go.

Through the window, Lord Richard nodded.

"Do I lie?" Laura was backing Delaroche up towards the window. "Or can you just not bear the fact that Fouché might have replaced you?"

Delaroche held up his sword cane to ward her off, staring at her as one might at a horrid apparition of the otherworldly variety— too terrifying to credit, but too credible to deny.

"Who are you?" he demanded.

"Don't you remember?" Laura smiled at him, a slow, dangerous smile. "I am the governess."

André brought down his hand. Lord Richard burst through the window in a cascade of glass. Gabrielle screamed, from fear or excitement or both—a high-pitched sound that brought Delaroche whirling one way, then another, as though unsure which way to flee.

Lord Richard landed in the approved heroic pose, both knees bent and sword at the ready.

"Never anger the governess," he said, and sent Delaroche's sword cane flying with one well-placed smack of his own sword.

André and Daubier charged. Gabrielle sank her teeth into her captor's arm just as André dealt him an unscientific but effective blow to the nose. He reeled back, clutching the appendage, blood oozing through his fingers as he landed heavily against the wall, then down into a sitting position and started mumbling.

Laura grabbed Delaroche's sword cane, holding Jean-Marc at bay.

"Drop it!" she said in her best governess voice, and followed it up with a feint to the chest.

Jean-Marc dropped his gun.

Daubier scooped it up in his left hand and pointed it at Delaroche. "Call them off," he growled, in a voice André had never heard him use before. "Call off your men."

Delaroche was known for many things, but common sense wasn't one of them. He backed away, glass crunching under his boots. "You can't shoot that," he sneered. "Not with one hand."

"Can't I?" said Daubier, and pulled the trigger.

Chapter 34

Daubier missed.

The bullet went wild, hitting the glass front of Lord Richard's bookshelf instead, sending bits of glass and chips of cherrywood flying. Delaroche dropped to the ground, shielding his face with his hands.

Laura lunged forward, grazing Delaroche's wrist. More alarmed than hurt, he toppled back, landing flat on his derriere, his legs splayed out in front of him. Laura seized the advantage of his momentary confusion to level the point of the sword at his throat, just at the vulnerable spot between his cravat and his chin.

"My point," she said levelly. "Call off your guards."

Delaroche's guards were milling confusedly, except, of course, for the one crouched against the wall, bleeding from his nose.

"Hold!" André's voice rang out—the sort of voice one could imagine commanding the attention of an entire assembly—perfectly pitched, resonant with authority. Laura risked a peek. He was standing with one arm around Gabrielle's shoulder, the other holding the bleeding guard's pistol. "You're outnumbered. Drop your weapons."

"Don't!" squeaked Delaroche, and scooted back on his behind as the sword grazed his neck.

André looked around at the assembled guards. "Has Monsieur Delaroche paid you? Anything?"

They dropped their weapons.

"I thought so," said André.

Laura held the sword cane steady at Delaroche's throat. "Have no illusions," she said. "I have no qualms about using this."

"I do," said Lord Richard, coming up behind her, "but only because there are some chaps in London who have a number of questions they would be delighted to put to Monsieur Delaroche."

"You are too generous, Monsieur," said Daubier.

"Oh no," replied the Purple Gentian with a smile that wasn't quite a smile at all. "I don't think so. Monsieur Delaroche, of all people, should know what it is to be put to the question."

Delaroche went very, very still.

Lord Richard nodded at Delaroche. "Tie him. As for you lot," he said to the guards as Laura got busy with the curtain cords. "I offer you safe conduct back to shore. You will forget you were here tonight."

"To help you forget," added André, "how about a few carafes of wine?"

Delaroche's henchmen seemed to feel that this was, indeed, a fair deal, although they seemed inclined to haggle over the exact number of carafes involved.

"Ouch!" One suddenly leaped aside, both hands clasped to his posterior.

"Hmph," said Jeannette, sheathing her knitting needle in a skein of wool. "If you had simply moved when I had asked, I wouldn't have had to do that."

"Safe conduct, you said?" said Jean-Marc—at least, Laura thought it was Jean-Marc. She had a great deal of trouble telling them apart. He backed away from Jeannette. "We'll take that safe conduct now if it isn't too much trouble, sir."

Amazing what the application of a knitting needle could do for one's manners. Laura would have to remember that for the next time she taught deportment.

Only—she caught herself up short—she wasn't teaching deportment. She wasn't a governess anymore. She wasn't sure what she was, or even who she was.

"An excellent mission, Miss Grey," the Purple Gentian told her, clapping her on the shoulder in passing. "Well-done, nabbing Delaroche! The powers that be will be pleased."

Laura couldn't help it. She looked at André and saw his head jerk at that *Miss Grey*. Their eyes met for a moment. He had lost his spectacles somewhere on the other boat, and his eyes looked naked and lost without them. She'd always had the uncanny sense that he was looking through her, seeing through to the things she most wanted to keep hidden. Why, then, now that it mattered, did it feel like he wasn't seeing anything at all?

Don't hate me, she wanted to say, but she couldn't, somehow.

Pierre-André made a run around Jeannette, shouting, "Papa!"

André's attention abruptly shifted. He leaned down to hug his son, who flung himself, in his signature fashion, at André's waist.

Laura stepped back, knowing herself to be irrelevant. This past month, after all, had been nothing more than fantasy, a play they played offstage as well as on. She had no place in the family circle.

"Pierre-André!" Gabrielle, for one, was delighted to see her little brother. Abandoning her father, she hugged him until he squirmed.

"Can I have a parrot?" asked Pierre-André.

They sent Delaroche's guards back to shore with cards affixed to their necks bearing the image of a small, purple flower. For old times' sake, the Purple Gentian had said, and since it was his ship, it seemed ungrateful not to let him have his way.

Delaroche they kept on board, well trussed. Jeannette had insisted on retying him, deeming Laura's ad hoc measures insufficiently thorough. All those years of knitting had given her a masterful way with knots. For once, she and Daubier had been in perfect accord.

Gabrielle and Pierre-André had been happily reunited with each other and their father. There was much hugging and exclaiming and general rejoicing while the stuffed parrot looked benevolently on. Pierre-André was much taken with the stuffed parrot. He was already practicing his "Avast, me hearty," slightly hindered by his inability to pronounce aspirates.

André apologized to the Purple Gentian for the ruin of his cabin and the Purple Gentian blandly assured him that it had been due for redecoration anyway.

In short, an excellent time was being had by all.

Among all the merriment, one former-governess-turned-spy wasn't likely to be very much missed. Laura made her way to the back of the ship—she was sure there was a name for it, but things nautical had never been much to her taste, for obvious reasons—and watched France recede in the wake of the boat until the lights of the harbor were little more than an echo on the water, and then nothing at all.

An excellent mission, the Purple Gentian had told her. She had rescued the Duc de Berry and captured a high-ranking, if slightly insane, French operative. She ought to be basking in her triumph.

Instead, she just felt tired. Tired and oddly let down. The thought of going back to England, to the boxes in the basement of Selwick Hall, to her old life as Laura Grey, or even her new life as the Silver Orchid, depressed her.

She found herself wishing, insanely, that she could turn back the clock by a week. She wanted to be back in the Commedia dell'Aruzzio.

Absurd. She'd hated the Commedia dell'Aruzzio. She'd hated acting; she hadn't much liked the other actors; and she certainly hadn't been a fan of sleeping in fields and washing in lakes—washing, that was, when one had the chance to wash at all. She hadn't liked the rowdy audiences or, even worse, the sulky and silent ones. She hadn't liked the mules that had pulled the wagon or the ruts that seemed to be a perpetual feature of French country roads in early spring.

But there it was. She wanted to be back in that dreadful, drafty, creaky wagon where the roof leaked when it rained and the bed wasn't quite large enough for two. She wanted to be on the damp ground by a smoky campfire with burnt stew if it meant that there would be an arm around her shoulders and a familiar voice murmuring things not meant for the rest of the company into her ear. She wanted to go back to being not Miss Grey or Mlle. Griscogne, but Laura of no surname at all.

She wanted to be with André.

Her mother had been wrong. Love wasn't a grand explosion. It didn't blaze onto the scene like a comet; it crept in like a spy in the night, muffled and disguised, worming its way in, not revealing itself until it was too late to do anything about it. Love didn't attack; it infiltrated. The poets had gotten it wrong. Laura held them all personally accountable.

There were quiet footfalls on the deck behind her. Laura didn't need to turn around to know who it was. She knew his tread by now, the same way she knew the way his hair smelled after three days on the road, the different tones of his voice, his trick of pulling off his spectacles with one hand.

"You ran off," he said.

Laura didn't turn. She didn't want to look at him. She'd prefer to remember him as they had been before, not as he had looked when Lord Richard had uttered that first *Miss Grey*. Shouldn't she be allowed to keep just one little memory intact, like a pressed flower in a book?

Pressed flowers were, by their nature, dead. Laura grimaced at the thought. So much for sentimentality.

Without looking at André, Laura said, "I lied to you."

She could feel the weight of him settling on the rail beside her. "I know," he said equably. "I lied to you too."

Laura kept her eyes on her hands, determined to make a clean breast of it. "My real name is Laura Griscogne. For the past sixteen years I've been Laura Grey. The Pink Carnation recruited me last summer."

She had thought he would ask about the Pink Carnation, about her work. He didn't. "Your parents?"

"They died in Cornwall, not in Lake Como. Otherwise, the rest is the same."

"I see," he said. She felt the wood of the railing give a bit as he shifted his weight, turning towards her. "Sixteen years of governessing?"

She was reminded, suddenly, of their first interview, André in his cloak and boots in the grand salon of the Hôtel de Bac, with rain silvering his hair and sparkling on his glasses. She swallowed hard, not liking the way memory made her heart twist. They had been different people then, and they would go off and be different people again—that was all there was to it.

"I wouldn't lie about my credentials," she said stiffly.

"No," said André dryly, but there was something else below it. "I don't imagine you would. Not about something important like that."

If she didn't know better, she would have thought he was joking.

"You were my first mission," she blurted out. It seemed important to remind him of why they were there, of how she had betrayed him. It was too quiet, too calm.

André raised both brows. "I am honored."

Laura turned so that her position mirrored his, each with one elbow on the rail, face-to-face. He looked tired, she thought. She hadn't heard it in his voice, but it was there in his face, even in the shadows. It was there in the lines on either side of his mouth and the bags beneath his eyes.

Laura knew that if she touched his face, there would be the shadow of stubble on his chin. She could practically feel it prickling against the pads of her fingers, more real to her than the damp wood of the railing. She scrubbed her hand against the side of her skirt.

"You shouldn't be," she said tartly. "If they'd thought you more important, they would have given you a more experienced operative. Instead, you were saddled with me."

"To my great good fortune," said André.

"Don't mock," said Laura, and her voice broke on the sharp end of the word.

To her surprise, André's hand covered hers, warm against the damp, cold air. "I'm not. Do you really think I'm not grateful?"

Gratitude. The poor cousin of love. "You don't have to be." Laura tried to tug her hand away, but it was caught between his hand and the rail. "I would have done what I did no matter what."

"Would you?"

Laura yanked free, scraping her palm on the rough wood. "Why must everything be a question?" she demanded in frustration.

"Why are you so afraid of the answers?"

"I'm not a—"

His mouth covered hers, cutting her off before she could finish the word. His lips were warm on hers. Despite herself, Laura leaned into him, luxuriating, for one last time, in the familiar taste and feel of him, in the comfort of his fingers in her hair and his other hand solid and steady on the small of her back.

Gently breaking the kiss, he framed her face in his hands, caging her. "Why did you come with us from Paris?"

Laura had been dreading this one. "Because the Pink Carnation asked me to," she said honestly. "She wanted me to see the Duc de Berry safely to England."

"And why did you sleep with me?" His voice was neutral, but his eyes were intent on her face, belying the casual tone. "Was that for the Pink Carnation too?"

Laura's pride piped up, reminding her that it wasn't too late to save face. She could lie, say it was for the mission, nothing more— just a ruse to convince people they really were man and wife. They would wander off their separate ways, each to their separate lives.

Laura bit her lip. "No," she admitted. "If ever I was honest, it was in that."

André's arms eased around her, drawing her gently to him.

"There's honesty and there's honesty," he said into her hair.

Abandoning common sense and pride, Laura squeezed him back. They clung to each other like shipwrecked souls hanging on to the last spars of the ship.

"What are we going to do?" she asked, her voice slightly muffled.

Loosening his grip, André rested his cheek against the top of her head. "I don't know," he admitted. "I wish I did. What I do know is that whatever I do, I want to do it with you."

Since that was rather the way she felt, it was hard to quibble with that. She had been on her own for too long to mesh her life with someone else's gracefully. She knew herself for what she was: opinionated, stubborn, set in her ways. She knew there would be days when an arm around her might feel more confining than comforting, occasions when they would strike the wrong sorts of sparks off each other rather than the right kind, and nights when she would deeply regret the loss of her own bed and the undisputed rights to the covers.

But when it came down to it, she'd rather fight for the covers with André than be queen of her own bed without him. It might occasionally be difficult, but it would never be boring.

There was just one thing. Laura drew a deep breath. "I'm not Julie."

André looked at her in confusion. "Pardon?"

"Julie," Laura repeated. It came out somewhat more acidly than she had intended. "The love of your life. I can't simply step into her place and fill her spot in your life. I'm not Julie. I couldn't be if I tried."

André let out his breath in a tired sigh. "I wouldn't want you to be. Julie was the love of my youth. We were both very young. We hadn't become the people we are yet." He paused, frowning, as though trying to decide how much to say. "It was . . . different. But you . . ."

"Yes?" Laura prompted.

André shook his head, acknowledging defeat. "It's different. You're different."

For an articulate man, he wasn't doing particularly well. "I did rather get that," said Laura. "It's different. But is it love?"

André rested his hands on her shoulders, giving the question earnest thought. "I want to go to bed with you every night and wake up with you every morning," he said. "I rely on your advice, even when I don't always agree with it. I wonder what you'll say about things, how you'll react to people, what your opinion will be. You've become part of my landscape. A large and important part," he clarified. "Not just a tuft of grass or the odd tree stump. You're more like a river."

"A river," repeated Laura.

"Necessary for life to exist. How's that for declarations for you?" André grinned suddenly. "And then there are all the other bits."

"The other bits?"

"The curve of your hip, the line of your jaw, the way your hair curls on the nape of your neck." His finger traced the fall of her hair down her neck, making her shiver. He drew back, raising a brow. "And I will admit, I am rather partial to your bosom."

"Just rather partial?"

"Extremely infatuated?" Sobering, André looked down at her, his eyes intent on hers. "So there you are. Take it as you will. Is that love?"

"It will do," said Laura, and found she was smiling at him despite herself, smiling so hard she was dizzy with it. "It will do very well."

When they could speak again, André looked quizzically at her. "Simply for the sake of equity . . . do you love me?"

"Well enough to spare you flowery speeches." Laura smiled at him—a slow, seductive smile with more than a little bit of Suzette in it. "Shall I show you instead?"

"By all means." André's eyes were very, very bright as he leaned toward her.

"André, my boy!" boomed a baritone voice.

André cursed. Laura bumped her head on his chin. Clumsily disentangling themselves, they turned to face Daubier, who was regarding them with arms folded and both eyebrows raised.

"And Laura! What would your parents say?"

Now, that was an inapposite question if ever she had heard one. Knowing her parents . . .

"'What took you so long?'" she suggested.

André chuckled. She could feel the gust of his laughter against her hair. She leaned against him, contemplating how nice it was not to have to pretend. They weren't pretending anymore, were they? It was odd and rather wonderful.

Daubier was never one to allow a grand scene to be spoiled by reality. It was seldom he got to play the angry parent.

"André, my boy, am I going to have to force Laura to make an honest man of you?" Daubier considered for a moment. "I've got that wrong way around, haven't I?"

"No," said André dryly. "I'd say that's just about right." He looked down at Laura. "Will you?"

"Only if the children agree," said Laura, only half jokingly. "I refuse to be a wicked stepmother. It's such a cliché."

"Pierre-André won't be a problem. He's been calling you *Maman* for a month," André pointed out, sliding an arm around her waist. "As long as you don't interfere with his ambition to own a parrot, he'll give you no trouble at all."

"What about Gabrielle?"

He didn't brush her off with platitudes. Laura loved him for that. Well, she loved him anyway, but that was one of the reasons why. He thought about it before answering, giving the problem the same consideration he would any other.

"You're good for her," André said eventually. "Jeannette has always preferred Pierre-André. I love her, but I don't know what to do with her."

Laura thought about her own parents, ridiculous and flamboyant as they were. But she had loved them. She had loved them simply for being there. There were certainly things she would have changed about her upbringing, but in the end it had been enough to know that they were there and she was loved.

"I don't think you need to do anything in particular," said Laura. "Just so long as you're there."

André looked at her as though he understood. "It isn't particularly pleasant to be alone, is it?" he said. He twined his fingers through hers, swinging their joined hands. "We'll muddle through. Together."

Laura squeezed his hand in response. "Yes," she agreed. "Together."

Chapter 35

The Prefecture of Police was just as intimidating as Colin had claimed.

When I'd made my plans to visit the Musée de la Préfecture de Police, I had pictured one of those narrow townhouse museums—three stories of exhibits with handwritten cards, flanked by a few mannequins in moth-eaten uniforms. Instead, 1 Rue des Carmes turned out to be a rambling modern structure sunk well below street level and surrounded by police cars and lots of scaffolding.

Feeling furtive, I slunk through the glass doors, into the beige-walled lobby, which seemed to double as a booking station. There were notices in French all over the walls and some dubious-looking characters waiting on benches.

I sidled over to the front desk. *"Où puis-je trouver le musée, s'il vous plaît?"* I asked timidly, wishing I had taken something other than eighteenth-century drama and Renaissance lyric poetry for my college French credits. Ronsard was lovely, but he wasn't much help for coming up with useful phrases like "Hi. I'm not a criminal. I just want to see the archives."

The man at the desk took the crimes I was perpetrating on his language in the kindest possible spirit. He smiled tiredly and pointed me towards a sign that said MUSEUM, 3RD FLOOR.

Oops.

Eschewing the pint-size elevator, I marched determinedly up the stairs. I had left Colin back in the hotel room, by his choice this time.

I had woken up feeling strangely hungover. My head ached, my mouth was gummy, and I had that vague sense of foreboding that generally comes of making a fool of oneself in public. Then I had looked next to me, at Colin, sprawled out with one arm under his head, mouth slightly open, eyes scrunched up in sleep, and remembered. The party. Colin's mother. Selwick Hall. The bridge on the Seine.

It wasn't just that we hadn't discussed it. He hadn't given me time to discuss it. I would have called it passion if it hadn't felt so much like postponement.

But that had been nighttime, with the house lights from the apartments on the Île Saint-Louis twinkling on the Seine, and then, later, in our jewel box of a room, with the birds flying low across the painted mural on the ceiling. It was easier to hide at night, between the shadows and the stars. In the gray, uncaffeinated light of morning, treacherous siblings, overreaching film stars, and vindictive stepfathers/cousins were harder to avoid.

I bagged the first shower, leaving Colin sleeping. When I came out, wrapped in a towel much smaller than the towels to which I was usually accustomed, he propped himself up on one elbow.

"Did you want to go to the prefecture today? Since you didn't yesterday."

Ouch. I made a face at him. "It wasn't entirely a wasted afternoon. One of the artists, Julie Beniet, was the wife of one of the people I was researching. The first wife," I corrected myself, and then wondered if I shouldn't have. Second spouses were a touchy topic at the moment. "She even painted a portrait of him."

"Planning to put it in the dissertation?"

That was a low blow. I lobbed one of the sofa pillows at him before retreating into the bathroom to use the exceedingly rickety French blow dryer on my chin-length hair.

"Why are you suddenly so concerned about my work habits?" I called back over my shoulder, in between the blow dryer breaking down and starting up again. It clearly hadn't had its caffeine either.

"I just don't want you to get angsty about it and blame me," he said speciously.

I rooted around in my overnight bag for jeans and a sweater. No need to dress up today, not until tonight—and then only if Colin reconciled with his family. I wiggled into my jeans. "I have most of the information I needed already, via the Silver Orchid's report to the Pink Carnation." I'd found that in his collection. "I just need confirmation of it from the French side. The Prefecture archives have the old ledgers from the Ministry of Police and the Paris Prefecture."

"You should go, then," he said. "You'll be happier if you do."

I'd originally planned to spend the day researching, and Colin knew it. But that had been when he'd been scheduled for a cozy lunch with his mother and sister. Somehow, I didn't think that was going to be happening.

On the night table, Colin's cell phone buzzed. We both ignored it.

I sat down on the bed next to him. "I'm beginning to feel like you're trying to get rid of me." He didn't rise to the bait. "Are you sure? We could do something fun today. Like, um . . . go see where the Bastille used to be?"

What did one do in France if one wasn't looking at historic

sites? I was at a loss. My idea of fun was tracing the route the tumbril that carried Marie Antoinette had taken from prison to guillotine. I mean, I knew that people did come to Paris to do other things; I just wasn't quite sure what they were. Shopping? Art galleries? Eating lots of pastries?

That last did have its appeal. I did like those marzipan pigs.

Colin levered himself up to press a quick kiss to my lips. "You go research. I'll find you at the Prefecture in a few hours. We can have dinner together, just us."

Funny, just the day before I had been yearning for some just-us time. Now it made me obscurely sad.

"Okay," I said. "I'll give you a call if I finish at the Prefecture early?"

"Or if they book you," he said, "I'll come bail you out."

"Don't laugh," I warned. "I'm terrified of setting off an alarm or touching the wrong thing."

"Just don't walk off with any of their records."

I thought of that as I made my way past the information desk on the third floor—their third floor, our fourth. I'd learned that one the hard way. No, the nice police officers had not been amused when I had almost barged into the administrative offices on what really ought to have been the third floor if they had been counting properly.

This floor, however, was quite definitely the museum. Yellowing, typed card? Check. Wax mannequin in musty uniform? Check. It was spread out across one broad floor rather than upstairs and downstairs on narrower ones, but otherwise it was just what I had expected. There were panoramic maps of Paris, old city ordinances, a smattering of weaponry. I strolled through the exhibits, past the seventeenth-century and the Affair of the Poisons towards the Revolution and my people.

Tucked away in a corner, I found Georges Cadoudal. There was a print of him, a round-faced man with an open shirt collar.

He looked like what my brother would have called "jolly." He didn't seem like the sort to keep the entire Ministry of Police hopping. Which just went to show you couldn't judge anyone by his cover. Notices calling for the arrest of the various conspirators had been framed and posted on the walls. I saw one for André Jaouen, describing him as of medium height, with brown hair and glasses.

There were ledgers too, immured under glass in the display cases that ran at waist height along the walls, one open to the page where Cadoudal's description had been entered upon his arrest. Cadoudal had been arrested in March, after a rather spectacular chase scene, detailed in the typewritten card next to his photo. There was no corresponding entry for Jaouen.

This was all very interesting, but I needed the documents that weren't kept under glass, the other ledgers, warrants, and reports. I made my way back to the front of the museum, where the man at the information desk obligingly led me back into the archives, gestured me to a chair, and, after nobly not snickering at my awful French—well, not too loudly—brought me a large box with the items I had requested.

It was all there. The official bulletins sent by the Prefecture of Police to the First Consul, André's private reports to Fouché, Gaston Delaroche's half-mad mutterings. The man was exceptionally fond of memos. Some of them looked as though they had been crumpled and flung against a wall upon receipt. But Fouché wouldn't do a thing like that, would he?

I found the transcript of the questioning of Querelle, the crucial pages blurred by a spill of ink. Jaouen's report on the matter followed, written in a crisp, clean hand.

I was amused to note that there was mention of a governess in the official papers following Jaouen's disappearance, but only as a potential witness to be brought in for questioning. They had never figured it out, not any of them. Ten points to the Pink Carnation.

I worked my way through the disordered pile of material,

taking notes in pencil in the notebook I keep for the days I'm too lazy to carry a laptop, or archives that won't allow electronics. It was fascinating to see the false trails Jaouen had planted, the misleading reports he had written up for his supposed superiors and, later, the elements of the search for him, set out in painstaking detail, reported by Delaroche to Fouché and Fouché to Bonaparte himself.

Laura was right; the capture of Cadoudal had diverted everyone's attention but that of Delaroche. That man sure knew how to hold a grudge.

The official reaction to Delaroche's capture appeared to be something along the lines of "Good riddance to bad rubbish."

I jerked around as the archivist tapped me on the shoulder. Uh-oh. Had I been drooling on the documents? Talking to myself?

Apparently not. The archivist, looking rather amused, murmured that my boyfriend was waiting for me.

He was? I checked my watch. Wow. Somehow, six hours had passed. I became vaguely aware that my shoulders felt sore and I had the sort of dull headache that's the caffeine addict's warning that too much time has passed between coffees. Mmm, coffee. And maybe some *pain au chocolat*. My stomach reminded me that I hadn't fed it for a while either. Man cannot live on documents alone.

I murmured my thanks to the archivist, gathered up my notebooks, relinquished my ledgers, and wandered, stiff-legged, into the museum to find my boyfriend. I tracked him down in the back room, in front of a collection of miscellaneous implements of destruction, including an early attempt to create a multibarreled gun. He was studying that last with a great deal of interest when I approached.

"Good research session?" he asked.

"Mmm-hmm." I yawned, rubbing my eyes. "I feel like I've been sleeping for two hundred years."

Colin assessed me with an experienced eye. "You need coffee, don't you?"

"Please? I promise I'll be human once you caffeinate me."

He could have made snide comments about not making promises I couldn't keep, but instead he held out a paper bag to me, one of the narrow ones that more resembles an envelope than a shopping bag. "Here. I got this for you. We'll see if this keeps you occupied until I can get some caffeine into you."

I drew out his gift as we walked. Despite being paperbacked, it was pretty heavy, the pages thick and glossy. It was an exhibition catalogue from the special exhibit at the Cognacq-Jay, featuring the paintings of Julie Beniet and Marguerite Gérard. Unlike the exhibit, this version contained full biographical details on both women, with a great deal of text.

I accompanied Colin blindly down the stairs, making my way down by chance and luck and the occasional hand on my elbow. About halfway through, I found the portrait of André Jaouen, with two full pages of text going through his career in the National Assembly and his subsequent employment at the Prefecture. It got more perfunctory as it went on, which made sense; the curator's interest had been in Beniet and the circumstances surrounding this specific painting, not what had happened to Jaouen after her death.

Nonetheless, in the interest of thoroughness, there were a few terse sentences stating that after being implicated in the Cadoudal affair of 1804, Jaouen had relocated to England, where he had remarried, the daughter of the artist Michel de Griscogne and the poetess Chiara de Veneti.

Poor Laura. Even in death she was still Michel and Chiara de Griscogne's little girl. From an art historian's view, however, that was the interesting thing about her. There was even a little round illustration set into the bottom of the page showing one of her father's sculptures, now in the Bode-Museum in Berlin.

Jaouen and his second wife had moved in 1805 to America,

where they remained until Jaouen's death in 1838. Taking advantage of the French-speaking community in New Orleans, Jaouen established a law practice there and eventually became a Louisiana state court judge.

On the facing page, the curator had placed the drawing of a cherubic-looking Gabrielle and the infant Pierre-André. The baby in the picture, Pierre-André Jaouen, the editor pompously informed us, had gone on to become one of the leading naturalists of his day, known for his fine botanical drawings of the foliage of the American South. A colleague of Audubon, they had collaborated on several projects.

Hadn't there been rumors at one point that Audubon was really the lost Dauphin?

I filed that away for later speculation and went on reading. Gabrielle Jaouen had gone on to become a noted diarist, an advocate for the abolition of slavery and, very late in life, a noisy proponent of the rights of women. She had died in her home in New York in 1893 at the age of ninety-five, leaving behind five husbands, twenty-odd great-grandchildren, and a vast pile of tracts and memoirs.

I wondered what Laura had thought of it all and whether she and Jaouen had had any children of their own. There were fairly easy ways to find out—including tracking down the memoirs of Gabrielle Jaouen de Montfort Adams Morris Belmont van Antwerp—but it was well out of the purview of my current research.

I came up for air about a block from the Prefecture, on the doorstep of a small patisserie. "Thanks," I said, rubbing my eyes at the transition from the shiny page to less shiny reality. "This is perfect."

"The book or the café?"

I could smell coffee in the air. There was a long glass case in front of me, displaying an impressive array of pastries, including—yes!—three large marzipan pigs.

"Both," I said, closing the book and stuffing it into my bag, along with my notebooks, my travel umbrella, a bottle of extra-strength Tylenol, and a plastic thing of tissues that had exploded their plastic. "Did you go back to the Cognacq-Jay?"

Colin signaled to the waitress, who detached herself from her conversation at the back of the bar. *"Deux café crèmes,"* he instructed.

"Et deux cochons!" I chimed in. I pointed at the glass. *"Ceux-là? Les cochons de marzipan? Merci."*

Colin gave me a squeeze. "You found your pigs."

"One is for you," I generously informed him. "What did you do today?"

Did you speak to your sister? I wanted to ask, but didn't. *Did you call your solicitor? Did you hire a hit man to take care of your stepfather and/or Mike Rock, aka Micah Stone?*

"This and that," said Colin. We settled ourselves at a rickety table towards the back of the restaurant. "The film crew is scheduled for next month. Fancy coming to stay?"

"As your buffer zone?"

"As my interpreter. Your friend Melinda will be with them."

"Classmate," I corrected. A blackboard behind us advertised a dinner prix fixe. It looked rather good. My stomach rumbled again. I smiled gratefully as the waitress put our coffees and a plate with two marzipan-covered pigs down in front of us. "What about Serena?"

Colin's expression didn't change. "She won't be there."

There was something in the way he said it that effectively cut off future questions. I inched one of the pigs closer to me, idly breaking off its curly marzipan tail, turning it into a little blob of marzipan goo between my fingers.

As much as I hated to admit it, I couldn't entirely blame Serena for what she had done. It wasn't just the lure of a partnership in the gallery—that bit I still found vaguely scuzzy. What I could sympathize with was her need to emancipate herself from the protective affection of her one-and-only sibling. It was sweet, but it was also limiting. The way she had chosen was a crummy way to go about bit, but these things are never pretty. Anyone who has ever faced off against a parent knows that.

Serena wanted to live her own life? She had my blessing. But in doing so, she had hurt Colin. She wasn't my concern; he was. He needed cheering up.

"Look at it this way," I said encouragingly, leaning my elbows on the table. "Having the film crews there could be kind of entertaining."

"Like a pleasant interlude on the rack," said Colin glumly.

"Can I get a side of thumbscrews with that?" Okay, so it wasn't much of a smile, but I still got a smile. I took a big gulp of my coffee. "View it more as your own personal slapstick comedy opportunity. Shakespeare? To rap music? It's bound to be absurd. And you can make them pay through the nose if they damage anything."

Colin perked up at that. "They will, won't they? I'm not letting them into the library, though."

I made a fake laughing noise—part chortle, part evil chuckle. "Don't worry. I'll see to that." Micah Stone and his crew were getting anywhere near those manuscripts over my dead body. They were mine, all mine.

Well, maybe not exactly mine, but I was the one with the use of them at the moment.

Colin lifted his coffee cup to me. "All for one?"

I clinked my cup against his, sloshing foam. "And one for all."

One for both? There were only two of us, after all. Two. As my childhood *Sesame Street* record had informed me, it was a much better number than one.

What would have happened if Colin hadn't had a girlfriend with him this weekend, or any girlfriend at all? I didn't like to think of how alone he would have been. I supposed he did still have his great-aunt, but that wasn't the same. In multiple ways.

"I nearly forgot." Colin drew something out of the pocket of his Barbour jacket. It was one of those incredibly deep pockets, designed to hold ammunition and small animal carcasses. Or, in this case, a slim, red-bound book. "We forgot this at the gallery last night."

The cover looked very red against the green Formica tabletop. So that meant he had spoken to one of them. Who was the most likely to have picked up the book? My money was on Serena.

"That was stupid of me," I said. "I would have hated to have lost it. Did Serena find it?"

I could see Colin trying to think of a way to dodge. Fundamentally, though, Colin is too honest to lie well. He stonewalls, but he has trouble getting around direct questions.

"She recognized it from drinks," he said shortly. Nodding to the book, he said, in a very obvious attempt to change the subject. "Didn't you promise me love poetry?"

Right. There'd be time enough to get the details out of him later. We had—I stopped and thought it out—two whole days left in Paris. Two days just for us. There would be plenty of time for grilling Colin, for love poetry, and for all of those couply things I hadn't thought we would have the chance to do.

Right at that moment, though, I had more important things on my agenda.

"Love poetry later," I said firmly. "In case you hadn't noticed, there's a pig with your name on it. It's oink-oink good!"

Colin regarded me dubiously. "You're not going to start calling it a love pig, are you?"

I had recently made him watch *How to Lose a Guy in 10 Days*. He had been very alarmed by the "love fern."

"That's *cochon d'amour* to you."

"You are coming to Selwick Hall next month, aren't you?"

My free hand covered his. "How could I possibly miss it? All for one, remember? But now . . ." I lifted the pig, adopting a truly obnoxious singsong. "You know you want me. . . ."

The crinkles came out around Colin's eyes. "Bizarrely enough, I do."

Historical Note

On January 26, 1804, after being taken before a military commission and sentenced to death, Jean-Pierre Querelle broke under police questioning at the Abbaye Prison. He confessed that a plot was afoot to kidnap—or assassinate—the First Consul and restore the Bourbon monarchy. The Royalist arch-agitator, Georges Cadoudal, had landed in France months before and was already in place in Paris, ready to set events in motion.

The plot in which André Jaouen is embroiled was lifted from a genuine intrigue, although I simplified some elements and changed others for the purpose of this novel. Uniforms, like those Laura discovered in the Hôtel de Bac, were prepared so that conspirators, disguised as members of the Consular Guard, could nab Napoleon as he traveled to one of his country estates. The conspirators were in negotiation with a high-ranking member of the military, General Moreau, in the hopes that the army could be brought over to their side. A member of the royal family—either the Comte d'Artois, King Louis XVIII's younger brother; or the Duc de Berry, Artois's son—was to be brought to Paris to be placed at the head of the uprising.

In my version, de Berry sneaks into Paris to lead the revolt. In real life, neither de Berry nor Artois ventured across the Channel. In his biography of Joseph Fouché, Hubert Cole opines that "the refusal of either [Artois or de Berry] to venture into France had caused the delay in the scheme and spoiled whatever chance of success it may ever have had." Elizabeth Sparrow, in her *Secret Service: British Agents in France, 1792–1815,* reports that Cadoudal went to the coast to meet the expected prince and, upon finding him lacking, reputedly cried, "We are finished!" Without a proper figurehead, the plot rapidly unraveled. The arrest and interrogation of Querelle and his fellow conspirators, Le Bourgeois and Picot, were as I described. Cadoudal's servant, le petit Picot (not to be confused with the other Picot), was arrested on February 6, when he ventured out to fetch provisions; General Moreau was arrested on February 15; and Cadoudal on March 9, after a dramatic high-speed chase through the streets of Paris. As described, the agitated First Consul took drastic measures. On February 28 (the night of André's make-believe party), the Governor of Paris ordered the gates of the city closed and all vehicles searched. The Senate, in the general spirit of panic, suspended trial by jury. According to Sparrow, 356 people were eventually questioned and arrested in *L'Affaire Georges, Moreau, Pichegru, d'Enghien.*

The investigation of the Cadoudal affair was officially in the hands of Louis-Nicolas Dubois, the Prefect of Police. Fouché, formerly Minister of Police, had fallen out of favor with Napoleon in 1802. The First Consul closed the Ministry of Police, although, as a parting gift, he allowed Fouché to retain the 1.2 million francs from the Ministry's coffers. Fouché used these funds to build an even more elaborate system of informers, setting himself up in direct opposition to the Prefect of Police, André Jaouen's putative boss. Although Fouché was technically out of power and his Ministry of Police closed, he played a large role in the Cadoudal affair, even though the investigation was technically being run by Dubois at the Prefecture.

I tried to capture the flavor of the Fouché-Dubois rivalry by having André serve under Dubois at the behest of Fouché, working at the Prefecture but reporting to Fouché. To minimize confusion and avoid extra explanation, I retained Fouché in his old position as Minister of Police. Fouché was officially reinstated as Minister of Police later that same year—a role in which he continued for the duration of Napoleon's ascendancy. For more about Napoleon's legendary Minister of Police, I recommend Hubert Cole's *Fouché: The Unprincipled Patriot*, as well as the relevant chapters on "Fouché's Police" and "Fouché the Man" in Alan Schom's *Napoleon Bonaparte*. Fouché's contemporaries, such as Josephine's lady-in-waiting, Mme. de Rémusat, and Bonaparte's secretary, M. de Bourrienne, had a great deal to say about the Minister of Police in their memoirs from the period. One can read Fouché's side of the story in his own memoirs, entitled *Memoirs of Joseph Fouché, Duke of Otranto*, although these, published after the Restoration, ought to be taken with several grains of salt.

Unlike the conspirators, who were, with the exception of André and Daubier, taken from the historical record, my artists and actors were all composite characters, based on a combination of contemporary personages. Jaouen's wife, Julie Beniet, was inspired by Élisabeth Vigée-Lebrun and Marguerite Gérard, among others. For a glimpse into the life of a female painter in Paris, I recommend Gita May's *Élisabeth Vigée-Lebrun: The Odyssey of an Artist in an Age of Revolution* and Mary D. Sheriff's *The Exceptional Woman: Élisabeth Vigée-Lebrun and the Cultural Politics of Art*, as well as Vigée-Lebrun's own memoirs. For artists more generally, I relied upon Thomas Crow's *Painters and Public Life in Eighteenth-Century Paris* and Warren Roberts's *Jacques-Louis David, Revolutionary Artist: Art, Politics, and the French Revolution*. Moving from artists to actors, fellow devotees of old swashbucklers will have guessed that the escape via Commedia dell'Arte troupe was inspired by Rafael Sabatini's classic novel of the French Revolution, *Scaramouche*. I tip my hat—and my keyboard—to him.

Many real places were pressed into service for this novel. The Hôtel de Bac was based on the building that now houses the Musée Carnavalet; Daubier's studio was modeled on Victor Hugo's apartments in the Place des Vosges (formerly known as the Place Royale); and the gallery in which Colin's mother's party was held can be found just around the corner from the Musée Victor Hugo. The Musée Cognacq-Jay was taken from life, as was the exhibit *Artiste en 1789*, featuring the work of Marguerite Gérard. I added on an extra "s," stuck in the (pretend) oeuvre of Julie Beniet, and moved the exhibit from 2009, when I was fortunate enough to view it, to 2004. Beniet's portrait of her husband was based very closely on Gérard's *Portrait d'Anne-Louis Girodet-Trioson*, which leapt out at me as the spitting image of André Jaouen. My understanding of André, in the context of his legal profession and political leanings, was deeply influenced by David A. Bell's *Lawyers and Citizens: The Making of a Political Elite in Old Regime France*.

Last but not least, I can attest to the veracity, and the tastiness, of those marzipan pigs. Many were eaten in preparation for this novel.

Acknowledgments

This book was a long time in the writing, which means that I have even more people than usual who deserve a shout-out. The first and biggest thanks goes to my mother, who not only bore and raised me, but also submitted to being dragged through Paris and beyond to every Napoleonic monument/exhibit/tenuously related location, even with a broken wrist. Without you, I would never have found my Hôtel de Bac, tracked down the original location of the Abbaye Prison, or discovered those two-euro bottles of wine (perfect with marzipan pigs). Thanks, Mom!

Thanks are also due to my little sister, for untangling the usual plot snarls; to Claudia, for long walks in cold weather; to Ryan and Lara, for Tuesday Coffee Club; to James, for keeping me saner than usual through Book Deadline Panic Month™; to my usual suspects (Liz, Emily, Alison, Abby, and Weatherly, that means you!) for always being there via cocktail or phone call; to Eve and Sebastian O'Neill, for being even more adorable than Gabrielle and Pierre-André; to Tracy Grant, Tasha Alexander, Michele Jaffe, and Sarah MacLean, for being not just amazing writers but equally amazing friends; to Andrea DaRif, for being the world's best and most patient co-professor; to Lady Jane's Salon and its founders, for providing a forum for romance writers and readers; and to the Badminton Club of NYC, for letting me take out my aggressions on the birdie rather than my characters.

While I was writing this book, I had the great privilege of co-teaching a seminar at my alma mater on the origins and development of the Regency romance novel. To my students in the Yale class, hugs and thanks. Your enthusiasm was a weekly reminder of how much I love this time period and this genre.

Finally, thank you to everyone who came to a reading, popped by my Web site, or visited the fan page on Facebook. Your commentary and feedback are a constant source of inspiration (and procrastination).

The Orchid Affair

Lauren Willig

A CONVERSATION WITH
LAUREN WILLIG

Q. Where did you get the idea for The Orchid Affair?

A. I would love to claim that it came from days of painstaking study in the archives, but the truth of the matter is that this book is the fault of a little bit of recreational channel surfing. It was the spring of 2008. I had left my legal job in January, writing *The Temptation of the Night Jasmine* (Pink V) in a frenzied three-month marathon. I turned in the manuscript and flopped down on the couch, planning an evening of complete and utter nothing. There was a homemade quiche in the oven and ice cream in the freezer and I didn't have another deadline hanging over me for a whole eight months. Heaven.

In between poking at the quiche (Bake for forty-five minutes? Ha! More like an hour and a half), I flipped idly through channels on that big square box in my living room that had been collecting dust throughout my *Night Jasmine* marathon. I hadn't meant to watch anything in particular, but a World War II movie caught my eye, about an American woman gone undercover in Germany as governess to a Nazi official's two small children. The German officer was played by Liam Neeson. Even though I knew the heroine was meant to wind up with Michael

Douglas in the end, I couldn't help but root for Liam Neeson. He was just so . . . Liam Neeson. He might be a double agent. Or something. Something not evil.

No such luck. Liam Neeson stayed evil and the heroine rode off into the sunset with Michael Douglas. Dissatisfied, I began brooding on the possibilities. What if I moved the general idea to an era in which the opposition wasn't necessarily evil? What if I had a governess in the home of a Napoleonic operative? What if that Napoleonic operative looked like Liam Neeson? What if— Oh, crap. My quiche was burning. I filed the idea away in my future plots folder, convinced it would join the graveyard of Lost Plot Premises, and went off to write *The Betrayal of the Blood Lily* (Pink VI). But the idea stayed with me . . . and here you have it!

Q. Why did Mischief of the Mistletoe *and* The Orchid Affair *come out so close together?*

A. Deep dark secret: I began writing *Orchid Affair* before *Mistletoe*. In fact, I started writing it right after *Blood Lily*. About six chapters in, I was asked to speak at a meeting of my local RWA chapter. I can't remember the topic offhand, but I think it was something about crafting a series. As I stood up there, talking about plots and story arcs, I blurted out, "Oh, dear. I've been writing the wrong book."

It wasn't that *Orchid* was a bad book (at least, if you've made it this far with me, I hope you didn't think so!), but it was the wrong book for the series story arc. I'd just written *Blood Lily*, which featured a difficult, deeply disturbed heroine. Laura, the heroine of *Orchid*, couldn't be more different from Penelope, but they had one thing in common: neither was a happy camper. Their books were both darker books. In that moment at the RWA podium, I realized that I needed something light and cheerful to break up the Dark and Serious, something more in the spirit of the original *The Secret History of the Pink Carnation*. And who better than Turnip Fitzhugh? When my publisher asked me, not long after, if I would be interested in writing a Christmas book, I knew it was meant to be. Turnip and Christmas went together like Christmas and pudding—or flowers and espionage.

I put *Orchid* on the back burner and came back to it happy and refreshed after a few months of pudding-related antics and madcap comedy. It is a different and, I hope, better book because of that brief intermission.

Q. Did you go to Paris to research this book?

A. I've spent a great deal of time in Paris over the years, but I put in a special research trip for *The Orchid Affair*. It was a great hardship, but I'm very glad that I made the sacrifice, because a great deal that I would never have been able to discover long distance made it into the book. My favorite instance of life spurring fiction involved the Museum of the Prefecture of Police. Like Eloise, I had imagined it as a town house museum, small and quaint, with mannequins in uniform. Like Eloise, I was rather taken aback at finding myself at a large, modern, and very obviously working police station, with policemen in puffy jackets hanging out by their squad cars smoking Gauloises. It took me several circuits of the building to get up the nerve to go inside, and ask, in my halting schoolgirl French, where the museum might be. It didn't help that there was a guy being hauled into a holding pen behind me. A bored guard pointed at a sign that said MUSEUM, 3RD FLOOR— and I knew that Eloise was going to find herself in just the same predicament. A lot of locations changed because of that trip: Jaouen's house moved from St. Germain to the Marais and Victor Hugo's old apartment was co-opted for Daubier's use.

Q. How did Laura find out about Selwick Spy School?

A. This is the danger of pruning; sometimes crucial information winds up on the cutting room floor. In a deleted scene in *The Orchid Affair*, we learn that Laura met Jane at the wedding of her last pupil in the late spring of 1803. Jane, for all her personal reserve, is very good at encouraging confidences. Hearing that Laura was between positions and impressed by her ability to blend into the shadows, Jane invited Laura to apply for a position with some friends. You can imagine Laura's surprise when she discovered that the "friends," Richard and Amy Selwick, had no offspring to be tutored. What they did have was a spy school in want of pupils. That's how Laura Grey became the first pupil of Selwick Spy School. If you're wondering if you've met her before, you have. Laura Grey was at Selwick Hall for the house party in *The Masque of the Black Tulip*, along with those other early recruits the Tholmondelay twins and Mrs. Cathcart.

Q. Why a Frenchman—and a revolutionary one—for a hero? Isn't that a big departure?

A. It's true. Most of my heroes so far have been dashing English aristocrats engaged in acts of amateur espionage. (I dare you to say that three times fast!) Jaouen is, well, French. Not only is he French, he's not the least bit aristocratic. He's a lawyer from Nantes. To round it off, he's not an amateur. He's employed by the Prefecture, which makes him a card-carrying espionage professional. Oh, yes, and he's a convinced believer in the principles of the original stages of Revolution.

I guess you could call that a departure.

While aristocratic high jinks are entertaining—and Bonaparte endlessly fun to mock—I wanted to do justice to the other side of the equation. I wanted to know what happened to someone who genuinely believed in the original principles of the Revolution, a child of the Enlightenment who fought for *liberté*, *égalité*, and *fraternité*. How would someone who championed the early stages of the Revolution cope with seeing it descend into anarchy, oligarchy, and, eventually, military despotism? Through André, and his memories of Julie, I had the opportunity to explore the psyche of someone who sees a promised utopia go hideously wrong and has to figure out how to go on after.

Q. Will you ever write Gabrielle's book?

A. Several people have asked me about the dramatic life of Gabrielle Jaouen, that cranky adolescent, who, as Eloise discovers, grows up to go through husbands like Kleenex, outlives most of her children, and champions a number of progressive causes. (What else would one expect from a daughter of the Revolution?) One of these days I would love to write about her fiery progress from France to Louisiana to New York—but that's well out of the purview of the Pink series.

Q. What's up next?

A. It became very obvious to me over the course of writing *The Orchid Affair* that Augustus Whittlesby, that ridiculous poet, harbors a *tendre* for our favorite floral spy, Miss Jane Wooliston. And equally obvious to me that Jane does not return those feelings. Apologies to everyone who asked me for an Augustus and Jane match! But don't worry, I have other plans for Jane. . . .

As Napoleon pursues his plans for the invasion of England, Augustus Whittlesby gets wind of a top secret device, to be demonstrated over the course of a house party at Malmaison. The catch? The only way in is to join forces with that annoying American socialite, Emma Morris Delagardie, who has been commissioned to write a masque for the weekend's entertainment. Augustus is willing to take one for the team, especially since it will mean time spent with his goddess, Jane, who has been tapped to play the heroine. But in this complicated masque within a masque, nothing seems to go quite as scripted . . . especially Emma.

For more about Augustus and Emma, please do come visit me at my Web site, where you can find all the latest updates, outtakes, and sample chapters from *The Garden Intrigue*.

QUESTIONS
FOR DISCUSSION

Attention: Some plot spoilers in this guide.

1. Did you know much about the Napoleonic era in France before reading *The Orchid Affair*? Did you learn anything about this period of world history?

2. "I had fallen madly in love with my topic. . . . The Scarlet Pimpernel, the Purple Gentian, the Pink Carnation—what's not to love about dashing rogues in knee breeches racing back and forth across the Channel, outwitting the dastardly schemes of the French?" (page 2) What do you think of Eloise's dissertation subject? Do you share her enthusiasm for it?

3. In considering her larger-than-life parents—and her peripatetic childhood—how did Laura Grey's youth shape her adulthood? What about Laura made her a good spy?

4. Talk about the role of social class in nineteenth-century society as it's depicted in *The Orchid Affair*. How did it dictate Laura's role in the Jaouen household? Did assuming the responsibilities of a governess better allow her to conduct her surveillance of André or would she have had an easier time if she had posed as nobility?

5. What was your initial opinion of André Jaouen? Did it change as you learned more about him? Of the many revelations about André, what surprised you the most?

6. Are there characters in the book's nineteenth-century France setting—Laura, André, Daubier—who resemble any of the modern characters? What are some parallels that might be drawn between the dual narratives that exist in *The Orchid Affair*?

7. Many characters in *The Orchid Affair* engage in forms of acting. What are some examples? Were some figures better actors than others?

8. Unlike the plots of other titles in this series, in *The Orchid Affair* the identity of the villain is established early in the book. Would you have preferred not to know who the "bad guy" was until the end, and that the mystery unfolded throughout the course of the book?

9. Consider how Laura and the Jaouen family join the traveling theater Commedia dell'Aruzzio as a way to escape from Paris undetected. Is it ironic or otherwise funny that even though she's a trained spy, Laura is a terrible stage actress?

10. Continuing the thought above, are there instances in which Laura assumes a character or a role successfully? If so, what were they?

11. In chapter fifteen, André invites Laura to his gathering of artists. Even though doing so went against social norms, why

did he include Laura? Jumping forward to their time with Commedia dell'Aruzzio, did you anticipate that Laura and André would grow as close as they did? Did their coupling come as a surprise?

12. Talk about the genre of historical fiction. What about this style of writing appeals to you? Do you prefer learning about history through fictional characters, or would you rather read a more straightforward nonfiction account?

13. Have you read all the novels in Lauren Willig's Pink Carnation series? Do you have a favorite book?

14. Can you think of any subjects or periods in world history that you'd like to see the author tackle in a subsequent book in this series? Which one would you choose? Why?

15. In chapter thirty-five, Eloise learns that after the Cadoudal affair in 1804, André and Laura marry and move to America. She also learns some details about Gabrielle and Pierre-André's adulthoods; did those revelations surprise you at all? How did you imagine the children growing up?

Read on for an excerpt from

The Garden Intrigue

A brand-new book in Lauren Willig's bestselling
Pink Carnation series.

Available now in bookstores and at www.penguin.com

"Alas!" she cried, "I spy a sail
Hard-by on the wine dark sea.
I know not what it is or bides,
But I fear it comes for me!"
—Augustus Whittlesby

The Perils of the Pulchritudinous Princess of the Azure Toes,
Canto XII, 14–17

"'For, lo!'" proclaimed Augustus Whittlesby from his perch on top of a bench supported by two scowling sphinxes. "'In Cytherea's perfumed sleep / Did she dream of the denizens of the dithery deep. . . .'"

"'Dithery?' How can the deep be dithery?" A female voice, lightly accented, cut into Augustus's stirring rendition of Canto XII of *The Perils of the Pulchritudinous Princess of the Azure Toes*.

Among the smattering of people who had left the dancing in the ballroom to admire, mock, gossip, or, in the case of an elderly dowager snoring in a chair by the far wall, nap, stood two young women.

One was tall and graceful, garbed simply but elegantly in a

white dress that fell in the required classical lines from a pair of admirably shaped shoulders. Her pale brown hair was gathered in a simple twist, her only jewelry a golden locket strung on a ribbon of sky blue silk.

Jane Wooliston was, thought Augustus, all that was finest in womanly charm. He had said so quite frequently in verse, but it held true in prose as well. Not even his execrable effusions could mask her inestimable worth.

She wasn't the one who had spoken.

It had been the other one. Next to her. Half a head down.

What Emma Delagardie lacked in height, she made up for in the exuberantly curled plumes that rose from her silver-spangled headdress. The tall plumes jutted a good foot into the air, bouncing up and down—like great, annoying bouncing things. In Augustus's annoyance, metaphor failed him. Her dress was white, but it wasn't the white of innocent maidens and virtuous dreams. It was of silk, sinuous and shiny, overlain with some sort of shimmery stuff that sparkled when she moved, creating the sensation of a constant disturbance in the air around her.

Emma Delagardie was slight, fine-boned, and small-featured, the top of her head barely level with Miss Wooliston's elegantly curved shoulder, but she took up far more room than her small stature would warrant.

"You might have the dire deep," Mme. Delagardie suggested, her American accent very much in evidence, "or the dreadful deep, but not dithery. It's not even a proper word."

"Your deep may be dire, but my deep is dithery. There is such a thing as poetic license, Madame Delagardie," said Augustus grandly.

"License or laziness? Surely, another word might serve your purpose better. The deep is a rather stationary thing."

Who had appointed Emma Delagardie the Grand Inquisitor for Poetical Excellence, Greater Paris Branch? It had been a sad,

sad day for France when her uncle had been appointed American envoy to Paris and an even sadder one when she had decided to outlast his tenure and stay.

Perhaps America would like to take her back?

"The waves, Madame Delagardie, maintain a constant flow, back and forth, just so." Augustus used the flowy fabric of his sleeves to illustrate, rocked back and forth on the bench. "And on and on they go."

With a hey nonny nonny and a ho ho ho.

Christ, he made himself sick sometimes. You're doing it for England, old chap, he used to tell himself, but the for-England bit had been rubbed bare over time, torn to shreds on the detritus of rhyme.

Oh, bugger. He was thinking in rhyme again. Was there no way to turn it off? To end the adjectives that infected his consciousness? That bedeviled his brain? That assaulted his . . .

Next time, Augustus promised himself. The next time he was recruited for a life of espionage, he was posing as a philosopher or a student of ancient languages, as someone staid and sober, someone who expressed himself in prose rather than verse, and fourth-rate verse at that.

They had warned him of this, his mentors at the War Office. Choose your persona wisely, they had said. Over time, you might just become what you pretend to be. Augustus had scoffed at it at the time. Nineteen and fearless he had been then, confident of the power of both his sword and his pen. It had seemed like such a lark, a decade ago, to couch his reports to the War Office in poetry so bad that even the Ministry of Police wouldn't want to read it. Even fanatical devotion only went so far. For the French surveillance officers, so far generally ended somewhere around the thirty-ninth canto.

What a stroke of brilliance, a code no one could break— because there was no code. No count-ten-letters-and-subtract-one, no book of code words and phrases, no messy paper trails to trip one up, just the information itself couched in terms of purest absurdity, truth drowned in a sea of verbiage.

Sometimes, it felt like truth wasn't the only one drowning. He had been doing this for too long; he felt the weariness of it to his very bones.

Augustus looked at Jane Wooliston, his buoy, his anchor, his island in a turbulent sea. Until she had arrived in Paris, he had been giving serious thought to throwing it all in.

Clasping his hands to his breast, Augustus looked meaningfully at Miss Wooliston. "What can one say about the sea? Oh, the sea! The inconstant sea! As indeterminate as a lady's affections and as unfathomable as the female heart."

Miss Wooliston hid her smile behind her fan. "Beautifully said, Monsieur Whittlesby, but I would urge you to credit our sex with somewhat more resoluteness of character than that."

She managed to make her voice carry without seeming to try. What a lovely voice it was, too, a fine, clear contralto, neither too high nor too low.

Augustus clapped the back of his hand to his forehead, just managing not to gag on his own sleeve. They had played this game before, he and Miss Wooliston. "Resolute in cruelty! Obdurate in obfuscation!"

"Ornate in ormolu?" It was the American again. Of course.

"Ormolu," Augustus repeated. "Ormolu?"

Emma Delagardie gave a little bounce that made her silver spangles scintillate. "Just helping out. You are doing *O*s, aren't you? "

Augustus would have loved to tell her exactly what she could do with her *A*s, *E*s, and *U*s—in prose—but he had spent years perfecting his pose of poetic otherworldliness. He wasn't about to ruin it for one noisy chit from the colonies. The former colonies, that was. If Emma Delagardie was a representative example, good riddance to them.

"*If* I may continue?" he said.

Emma Delagardie fluttered her fan. Augustus sneezed. The fan was made of feathers. Feathers with silver spangles. They had a long reach.

"Oh, do. Please do," she said, far too enthusiastically for Augustus's peace of mind. No one wanted to hear his poetry that badly. In fact, no one wanted to hear his poetry at all. This boded ill.

Augustus brooded. He did it quite well. He bloody well ought to. He had spent hours practicing. "My soul shies back! To flourish, the delicate blooms of poetry must be gently nurtured and watered from the well of an understanding spirit, not withered in the harsh glare of unfeeling criticism."

"Do go on, Mr. Whittlesby," said Miss Wooliston soothingly. "I assure you, we are all attention to hear how Cytherea comes about."

"All thirty dithery cantos," added her friend cheerfully.

Did she think it was easy to consistently perpetrate works of such poetic awfulness?

He could have told Emma Delagardie a thing or two about that. Years, it had taken, years of grueling practice and downright hard work. It was a hard balance to maintain, writing poetry dreadful enough to be laughable but just credible enough to be believable.

Augustus rustled his roll of papers. "Shall I go on? Or need I fear the slings and arrows of outrageous interruptions?"

"We'll be good," promised Emma Delagardie, in a way that signaled anything but. "Mum as church mice."

The church mice he had known had been rather noisy, actually, in the walls of the vicarage of his youth, but that was beside the point. He wasn't going to let himself be drawn into yet another pointless argument.

"In that case . . ." Augustus made a show of scrolling down his page, searching his place. The gilded doors to the music room racketed open and someone skidded into the room, dressed inappropriately for an evening entertainment, in boots with the mud of travel still on them. He was a young man, cheeks flushed, hair mussed, cravat askew. He was dressed in the glorified riding dress that the upper classes had made their common clothing, a tightly fitted coat over a bright waistcoat, tight pantaloons tucked into Hessian boots. The difference was, these clothes had obviously been used for riding, and recently.

A few of the ladies whispered and giggled behind their fans. The dowager made a snorting noise in her sleep and burrowed deeper into her chair.

What in the hell was Horace de Lilly doing here? As a very junior sort of agent, employed for the sole purpose of his aristocratic connections, de Lilly was meant to be at Saint-Cloud, hanging about the fringes of Bonaparte's semiregal court, not in Paris, attending a ball at the Hotel de Balcourt.

This did not bode well.

With a wary eye on his young associate, Augustus returned to his poetry. " 'For in the lady's youth was told / A tale of prophecies ancient and old—' "

Horace began to bounce on the balls of his feet, striving to be seen over Mme. Delagardie's plumes. He mouthed something.

Augustus frowned in his general direction. Raising his voice, he proclaimed, " 'That once in Triton's court did dwell / And ring a nasty watery knell, / With a clangety clang and an awesome—' "

" 'Yell'?" suggested Emma Delagardie, in something that strove to be, but was not quite, sotto voce. " 'Knell'? 'Mell'?"

If Augustus had been holding a book, he would have slammed it. Instead, he jammed the roll of poetry under his arm. "No more! My sensitive soul can endure no further interruptions! The Muse has fled. The Graces have left the building."

He jumped down off the settee, landing with a thump on the parquet floor, and had the satisfaction of seeing Mme. Delagardie take a step back. He had landed rather close to her feet, inadequately shod in Grecian sandals that showed off the diamond rings on her toes.

Augustus wafted a trembling hand in the air. "I beg you, good people! Do not attempt to follow! I must soothe myself and my muse in the only way available to one of my delicate temperament, with a spell of solitude and solitary reflection, making humble homage to the Muses in the hopes that they will once again heed my call after so brutal and rude a series of interruptions of their delicate endeavors."

The excess fabric in his sleeves made a highly gratifying swishing noise as he swept towards the door.

As he passed de Lilly, he murmured, "In the study. Five minutes."

He didn't wait to see if de Lilly would answer. Casting a lingering backwards glance at Miss Wooliston—exaggerated yearning with just a hint of lustful smolder—he paused only long enough to give the footmen time to open the doors before swanning out into the throng in the next room, where refreshments had been set out among Balcourt's collection of faux Egyptological artifacts. At least, Augustus hoped they were faux. A selection of pastries had been set out on a sarcophagus that served as sideboard, while uniformed footmen scooped champagne punch from bowls constructed of Canopic jars.

Augustus was no antiquarian, but he did recall hearing somewhere that those jars had been used to contain the internal organs of the deceased. He made a mental note to stay away from the punch.

The same couldn't be said for the rest of the company. The punch was flowing freely, the party the sort that would be termed in England "a sad crush," fashionable people jostling one against the other, doing their best to see and be seen. Balcourt might not be admired, but he was known to set a lavish table and he was not without his contacts at court.

It was easy enough to waft his way through the crowd, the eccentric poet in his own private fog, with the occasional murmur of "The Muse! I must set it down!"

No one would think anything of finding him in Balcourt's study. When the Muse demanded . . .

Augustus closed the door of Balcourt's study behind him, shutting out the revelry without. It was quiet here, the drapes closed, the only light the candles that had been left burning, as a matter of course, in the sconces above the hearth. Balcourt was no scholar. The only thing in the room that didn't show a fine film of dust was the decanter.

The man couldn't be more different from his cousin, Miss Jane Wooliston.

The Pink Carnation.

The door racketed open as Horace de Lilly came charging in as though all the hounds of hell were behind him, the nasty, yippy ones with particularly pointy teeth.

Augustus slammed the door behind him, turning the key in the lock. "What in the blazes was that all about? Aren't you supposed to be in Saint-Cloud?"

"It is of the most urgent!" Horace declared importantly.

It had bloody well better be. Junior agents weren't meant to make direct contact with their seniors. Especially not in such an exuberant and noisy fashion. If Horace had something to report to him, there were channels for that. Quiet channels. Discreet channels. Unfortunately, to ignore the other man out now would serve nothing. Whatever damage had been done was done.

"If anyone asks, you're here to commission a poem. You, lover. Me, Cyrano. Understood? You're mad with love for—someone. You can pick the girl; I won't dictate that part—"

For how can one dictate the dictates of the heart? whispered the poet in Augustus's head.

Shut up, Augustus told it.

"—but you'd better make a good show of being lovelorn. That will explain your"—Augustus looked pointedly at Horace's muddy boots, his inappropriate attire—"exuberant arrival. Everyone understands young love."

For a moment, Horace looked as though he might argue. Augustus Whittlesby was universally agreed to be the worst poet in Paris, and, like so many young men, Horace harbored vague poetic aspirations of his own. But sacrifices must be made from time to time.

"So it will be," he said manfully. "I'm here to commission a verse. Now, wait until you hear—"

"Did anyone follow you?" Augustus cut him off.

Horace shook his head. "No one suspects me."

Augustus wished that he could share the younger man's assurance. Ever since a plot to assassinate the First Consul had been uncovered last month, Bonaparte's police force had been working overtime, cracking down on threats anywhere they found them, and sometimes even where they hadn't.

Augustus knew he was lucky to have escaped the net this long. Ironically enough, that very longevity was a large part of his protection. He was like an old oak table or a particularly dingy patch of carpet; the Ministry of Police was so used to him that they scarcely noticed he was there.

Horace, on the other hand, had come over with a wave of émigrés who were being invited, in bits and pieces, back into Paris to lend aristocratic polish to Bonaparte's new court. He was new and therefore automatically suspect. Bonaparte craved the recognition of the old aristocracy, but he also mistrusted them. With reason, in this case.

"Well, they don't!" Horace said indignantly. "I have been of the most subtle."

"Right." Augustus eyed de Lilly's pink and green striped waistcoat. Not exactly what he would call subtle. "What was it that sent you running to Paris?"

Horace flung himself into Balcourt's desk chair, his spurs digging into the imported Persian carpet. "It was like this," he began, clearly determined to milk every moment of glory from the retelling. Augustus remembered when he had been like that. A very long time ago. Horace's beardless face shone with excitement. "I was with the court of the First Consul in Saint-Cloud, when the Consul received a visit from Admiral Decres——"

A sound caught Augustus's attention. A creak, as of a floorboard being depressed slowly and carefully by a person trying very hard not to be heard.

Augustus held up a hand, signaling Horace to silence.

"Edouard?" It was a female voice, raised in a questioning tone. A fingernail scratched against the wood of the door. "Edouaaaard?"

Augustus deliberately rustled the papers on the desk. "Who disturbs me?" he called out, stretching out the vowels in the most annoying way he could. "Who disturbs me in my poetic reverie?"

The scratching stopped. "Pardon?"

"Is it too much to ask for a humble poet to find a bit of peace to court the muse in private?" Augustus inquired mournfully. "Oh, the world is too much with us! Chattering and clattering, we lay waste our talents, consigning our patrimony of poetry to the wasted wind of the idle hour. Oh, woe! Woe it is to be——me."

He broke off as he heard the floorboards creak in rapid retreat.

Horace leaned forward. "Was that——?" he hissed.

"Balcourt's mistress."

"Oh." Horace shrugged off the intrusion. Mistresses were an inconsequential part of urban existence, like tavern owners or those annoying little people who collected bills. "As I was saying, I was at Saint-Cloud, when——"

Augustus cut him off. "Balcourt's mistress is an informer of the Ministry of Police."

It took Horace a moment for the words to register. "Is she?" He seemed more intrigued than alarmed.

De Lilly's insouciance set Augustus's teeth on edge. "Madame Perdite is just one of thousands, but any one of those, no matter how insignificant they may seem, can be your downfall. A land-lady, a chambermaid, the boy who holds your horse. Fouché has half of Paris in his pay." An exaggeration, but not by much. "Say nothing in front of anyone, not even the servants. Particularly not the servants. Do you understand?"

Horace nodded, but Augustus could see he didn't understand, not viscerally, not in that place in one's gut that shouted danger long before the conscious senses perceived a threat. Horace had been a boy during the Terror, an adolescent in the safety of Lon-don. He had no memory of the stench of blood and sweat, the buzzing of the blood-gorged flies in the Place de la Concorde; he had never spent a night in the damp-walled hospitality of the Con-ciergerie, never heard the screams of a man being put to the ques-tion as he moved from begging for life to praying for death. The prisons of Paris were just names to him, names and blank facades; he had no real understanding of the true nature of the terrors within.

This was what happened of hiring boys who were still wet be-hind the ears and sending them out into the field with nothing more than a few vague instructions and a slightly outdated map of central Paris.

Augustus preferred not to address the fact that he had been equally amateur when William Wickham had first recruited him for covert operations, fresh out of Cambridge. At the time, he had been an aspiring poet by vocation, a fledgling clergyman by neces-sity, resigned to the prospect of taking a parish and sandwiching verse between his sermons. His encounter with Wickham had changed all that.

Twelve years later, Augustus could hardly imagine having been that young or that naïve. That young, that naïve, and that eager.

Augustus cocked his head, listening. After this many years in the field, he could discern the subtleties of a silence, the way a painter could distinguish between the various forms of black. There was no listening presence from behind the door; he would have known her from the breathing.

Augustus turned back to Horace. "She's gone," he said. "What do you know?"

Leaning forward, Horace braced his palms on the knees of his breeches. His hands were too large for his frame, as if he hadn't quite yet grown into his height. "The First Consul summoned Admiral Decres to Saint-Cloud. It was a warm day, so he left the window ajar. I," he added modestly, "was beneath it."

"What did you hear?"

"The fleet. They're readying it."

"Which fleet?" There was more than one.

"All of them!" Horace said excitedly. "The plan—it has been approved at last. I heard it direct from the First Consul's lips. Save just one thing, all is readiness."

Augustus didn't need to ask, but he did. "For?"

"The First Consul, he is giving the orders for the invasion of England!"

The author of seven previous Pink Carnation novels, **Lauren Willig** received a graduate degree in English history from Harvard University and a J.D. from Harvard Law School, though she now writes full-time. Willig lives in New York City.